FRIENDLY FYRE

A Cozy Queer Kingdom Builder

Kia Leep

PULSAR PUBLISHING

CHAPTER ONE

PHOENIX

So this is what dying feels like, I think.

There's no fear. No sadness. Just clinical observation as the pain fades from my chest, and the surrounding cubicle walls are consumed by the darkness of my tunneling vision.

Died at my desk, was it? They always said I would. Ah, well. It was a good run. Over fifty years. Not as long as I would have liked, but longer than some. My life doesn't flash before my eyes as my consciousness fades, but I do think about the big moments. Marriage. Divorce. The nurse placing my daughter in my arms.

It's only then that sorrow crashes through me. Becoming a father was my greatest joy, and my greatest failure. I would have liked to have seen her one last time.

As sight, sound, and sensation leave me, all I can do is heave a mental sigh of regret. I suppose now comes The Great Mystery. Afterlife or oblivion? Reincarnation, or something inconceivable? It will be interesting to finally know, if nothing else.

Abruptly, malice closes around me. It licks at my essence like acid, faintly eating away at my mind. I try to flinch away from this new, horrific sensation, but it seems to be everywhere, and the more I struggle, the more I can't make sense of where I am, or what I'm experiencing. I spiral with disorientation, all comprehension of time and space slipping away from me. All I understand is that this is bad—existentially bad—and I need to escape.

As the biting void whirls around me, I encounter a tiny, fragile grain of kindness suspended in the enmity, like the faint glow of a candle in the dark. I try to move toward it, and surprisingly find I'm able to. I huddle close and begin to notice other small flickering lights nearby as well. I can't see them, exactly, but I can feel them there. Other... *presences.*

I'm sorry. The words come from the small spark of warmth. *I didn't mean for this to happen. I'm sorry.*

Hello? I try to reply. The other lights—people?—are also emitting confusion, fear, curiosity. *What's wrong?* I ask. *Where are we? What can we do?*

If the light hears me, it doesn't respond. I'm not sure how I can tell, but I can sense it struggling to not go out. Struggling to not be swallowed by the hunger. Its attention is elsewhere—external? I try to cast my mind outward and am rewarded with a chaotic tangle of sensations. A blur of colors, the stinging smell of the sea, a distant roar like a waterfall, and feelings of hatred and famine that aren't mine, pounding at me from every angle. I—my mind—my soul?—begins to ache.

"...hoping you'd forgotten about me..."

With a surge of anger, an impression of movement passes through me. Time and space feel more concrete again. I'm being lurched around even as the darkness continues to eat at me, like I'm slowly being digested in the belly of a giant beast.

Something is happening outside. A struggle. The hungry dark is exuding a sense of triumph—which suddenly shifts to hesitation, then alarm—as everything is illuminated with a burst of light.

The world careens around me once more, and now the maelstrom of emotions are injured, upset, desperate. I can almost feel myself slipping from the grasp of the dark cloud of hunger. I can feel its viscosity thinning. Then—

Pain slams through me. For a moment, the acidic corrosion magnifies a thousand-fold, stripping my essence away.

It's going to eat me, I realize. And there's nothing I can do to stop it.

Then, just as abruptly, it evaporates. The other minds are gone. That single spark of warmth has vanished. I'm left alone with the lingering pain of an intangible wound as I fade into the world.

I take in a shuddering breath, the cold of my surroundings immediately digging its claws into my skin. I blink my eyes rapidly, but can see nothing. This isn't the same nothing I'd previously experienced, however—that was a true absence of sight. This is just dark. Pitch black. Like I'm in the bowels of a cave.

What even *was* that? Was it real? A strange dream? I thought I had died. I touch a hand to my chest, recalling the moment I felt my heart stop. My fingers run over something soft, like a downy blanket, but beneath it I can feel the steady beat of my pulse. Well. I seem to be alive now. But where am I?

I groan, rolling onto my side as the cold, hard ground grinds against my hip bone. Maybe I *am* in a cave. There's freezing stone beneath my hands, and I still can't see anything. My body feels strange and clunky, as if each movement is not exactly what I intend it to be. A shiver runs through me, cold prickling all over my body. Am I going numb? I might be experiencing early stages of hypothermia. If I don't do something to warm up soon, I'll be in trouble.

[New user established. Populating stats.]

I tip my head at the feminine voice. Not a human voice, though. Vaguely mechanical, like something out of an arcade.

"Hello?" I call. I clear my throat. My voice doesn't sound right. "Is someone there?"

Definitely not right. My voice has always been quiet and slightly croaky—like I had a cold I couldn't quite get rid of. The words coming out of my mouth presently are the same low alto they've always been, but now they're warm and smooth, like all the roughness has been sanded away.

Also, they're distinctly feminine.

"What..." I trail off, touching my throat. Something soft and skin-tight is wrapped around my neck. The covering ruffles as I run my fingers over it, but doesn't come away. What's happening? Where am I? There are too many questions to process at once.

[Compilation complete. Role assigned. Displaying stats.]

[Name: Faber]

[Species: Harpy]

[Subspecies: Phoenix]

[Class: Psion]

[Level: 20]

[HP: 100/100]

[Mana: 200/200]

[Role: The Dark Lord]

My mind spins as words abruptly appear in the dark. I reach a blind hand out, but no light reflects onto my skin. Somehow, I instinctively recognize that the words, like the voice, are not physical, but inside my own head.

I'd think this were a dream if it didn't all feel so real. The stone is hard and cold beneath me, and my breathing echoes in the cave around me. I shudder against the freezing air, and I suspect if I could see, my breath would be fogging. Whatever strange thing is happening, whomever this voice is and however I got here, one thing is clear enough: I'm in danger of perishing if I don't find shelter soon.

I push myself up onto my hands and knees, the feeling of acute physical strangeness persisting with the motion. It's not numbness, I can tell that now. Something is different. My limbs keep getting in the way of each other, bending oddly, my feet scraping strangely across the floor. I reach a hand back to try to feel what's going on, and I bump into my arm. But it's not my arm. What's this?

I stretch my limbs out, then flinch, hissing in a startled breath as *six* limbs respond to the instinct.

"What's happening?" I wonder in that warm, unfamiliar voice.

Tentatively, I reach back again, touching the extra set of limbs that shouldn't be there. My fingers encounter soft resistance, skimming across a series of velvety... well, I know what they are just from touch, but it's difficult to bring myself to believe it.

Feathers?

I trace the wing down to my back, where the limb appears to be fixed along my lower spine, just above the hips.

Harpy. The word comes to me unbidden as my attention flickers back to those strange words fixed in the corner of my vision. *Phoenix.*

I huff out a disbelieving laugh. This might not be a dream, but it certainly can't be coherent, sane thought. A hallucination? Drugs, or a concussion, or...

I shiver. Death?

The heart attack was so vivid. I was so sure I had died, and maybe I had.

A faint pressure of anxiety squeezes around my heart. I take in a shuddering breath, and let it out slowly. No, I can't let myself panic. Fear impedes reason. I have to keep myself together. Think through all this rationally. There's a logical explanation for everything—even if that explanation is one I won't like.

Like being dead.

But even if that's true, it doesn't make what I'm experiencing any more sensible. "I'm not *really* a harpy, am I?"

[Affirmative.]

I freeze. Did the voice just respond to me?

[Affirmative.]

In my mind, too! Unless it was only a coincidence. I decide to test that hypothesis. *Can you really hear me?* I think.

[Affirmative,] the voice repeats.

I shake my head at the absurdity of it all. But at least I have someone to speak to—someone who might be able to give me answers.

What are you? I think, deciding that's less unsettling than hearing my new voice. *Are you a person? A program?*

[This unit is a clone of the unit designated Echo,] Echo says. [This audiovisual display acts as the interface between your neuromagical pathways and the extraplanar arcane network which governs select users' metaphysical evolution within the System.]

That's a lot of interesting words. *There are other users in this... System?*

[Affirmative.]

How many? I ask. *Are there any nearby?*

[This unit does not have access to that data,] Echo says.

Can you ping anyone? I wonder. *Escalate a service request?*

[Command not recognized.]

I smile to myself. Well, it was worth a shot.

Alright, then, Echo. How else can you help me? I shift into a more comfortable sitting position, blinking against the black. Still in awe, I run my hands across the feathers that cover my arms and legs. *Don't suppose you can summon a blanket to warm me up?*

[Negative,] Echo says, which pulls a small, unsurprised chuckle from me. But then she says something that *is* surprising. [However, the user may create a source of warmth via spell activation.]

I blink. "Spell?"

[List of user's known spells,] Echo recites.

[Spark: Summon a small flame maintained above the caster's hand. Mana cost: 1 per minute. Required affinity: Fire.]

[Blaze: Summon a flame of variable size and shape capable of moving with the caster's intent. Mana cost: 10 per cubic meter per second. Required affinity: Fire.]

[Psionic Touch: Communicate telepathically with any thinking entity while maintaining physical contact with the target. Required Class: Psion. Mana cost: 1 mana per 5 seconds.]

I reel with this new information. She can't mean *magic?* I can't do magic. I'm an engineer!

Or, I was.

I struggle to wrap my mind around what Echo is saying. Magic flies against everything I've ever known. Everything I've ever studied, and every assumption I've ever made in my career.

Then again, magic is just a word. Perhaps there is a rational system here, merely hiding beneath the veneer of mysticism. I suppose whichever way the coin falls, there's only one way to find out. Even if my well-being didn't hinge on the immediate need to find a source of warmth, my curiosity wouldn't allow me to dismiss all this out of hand.

Alright, Echo, I think, trying to suppress my skepticism. *How do I go about casting Spark?*

[The user may activate the relevant arcanum simply by envisioning the spell, though audio cues typically assist in concentration.]

Sounds a bit wishy-washy to me. But I won't knock it until I try it. I hold my hand out in front of me, still invisible in the complete darkness. I imagine a fire there, hovering in my palm, warming my shivering body, and I say, "Spark."

Light flares into existence. I jerk my head away and squeeze my eyes shut as the light stabs into my skull and a white sphere is burned into my vision. But the warmth that kisses my face, hand, and arms is unmistakable.

Cautiously, I peek an eye back open. There, nestled in the palm of my hand, the size of a peach, is a flickering orange flame. I stare at it in awe. I made this? This came from me?

It's too close to my hand, I realize. Practically resting on my skin. Yet, it only feels pleasantly warm. A wonderful, soothing warmth that's already spreading down my arm and driving the fangs of cold away. I bring it closer to my chest to try to warm the rest of my body as well. *Why isn't it burning me?* I ask Echo.

[In addition to providing the Fire Affinity, harpies with the subspecies of "phoenix" are allotted Fire Damage and Burn Effect resistance,] Echo says.

I snort at that. Clearly. Of course.

But I'm only fire resistant, I note. Not fireproof. Good to remember as I use this ability to stave off hypothermia.

I gingerly bring my other hand close to warm over the fire, then pause as light spills over my arm. It's covered in a layer of delicate feathers, and my fingers are sharpened into claws. It's such a bizarre sight. I can't *really* be a harpy now, can I? How does that even happen? What's caused all this?

Questions neither I nor Echo, it seems, have an answer to. Instead, I move my cupped hand of fire up and down my limbs in fascination, warming myself as I get my first look at this strange new body.

The feathers are all the colors of a sunrise. Purple, red, orange, pink, yellow. A burst of warm colors to rival the flames in my fingers. The feathers are shorter on my arms and longer on my main body. And longest, of course, on my wings. I timidly stretch one out: The tip vanishes into the darkness, but even then I can tell it's around six feet long. I frown. A wingspan of twelve feet? That shouldn't be nearly enough to produce sufficient lift for flight. How much do I weigh, at any rate? I don't *feel* like I have the hollow bones of a bird.

[Weight: 45 kg,] Echo reports.

Hm. Handy. *Are there other numbers you can display?*

[Most physical or quantifiable attributes can be displayed.]

Interesting. But there you have it: I might have lost a little weight, but I'm still much too heavy for flight with wings this size. At least, according to conventional aerodynamics.

Carefully and awkwardly folding the wing back in, I catch a glimpse of my fire reflecting off something near my feet. Upon closer inspection, I find the light is reflecting off my feet themselves. If they can be called feet.

Each of my legs end in an eagle-like talon—three clawed toes in the front, one thumb-like claw in the rear. I flex the digits, and am rather disturbed by their immediate response, as if I'd somehow been expecting them to be false boots concealing my *actual* toes. But they're real. As real as the wings.

I take a steadying breath in, and slowly let it out. A breathing exercise I'd been doing as long as I could remember. This is all very strange, but it's manageable. I can work with these new... *accessories*, at least as long as I need to in order to find out what's going on and how I ended up in this state.

It's even a bit fitting—or perhaps ironic is the better term. I spent my whole life obsessed with planes, learning aeronautics, dreaming about flight as birds passed overhead. And now I am one, of a sort.

As I finish examining my feet, the firelight illuminates yet another change in my body parts—or rather, the lack of one.

My eyebrows shoot up as I double check my body. That can't be right. I run a hand down my chest, which feels rather flat, I think—though I suppose that wouldn't be surprising for a bird, as avians don't have mammaries. Coupled with my voice, and a specific lack of equipment...

Echo, I ask. *Am I a woman?*

[Sex: Female]

[Gender: Undetermined]

I stare at the word Female printed over the top of my vision. Harpies were always women in mythology, weren't they? It shouldn't be surprising. It makes sense. I suppose I should have put it all together right away.

I lean back, trying to process this newest bit of information. My mind chews on it, forces it down the gullet, and reluctantly starts to digest.

I died. I was reborn. I'm in the body of a harpy. I can do fire magic. And I'm a woman.

I try to find the words to sum up my feelings on the subject. "Well this is all just... rather unexpected, isn't it?"

CHAPTER TWO

RATHER UNEXPECTED

Perhaps "unexpected" is a bit of an understatement. I am certainly surprised. More than a little disbelieving. Yet the proof is in the pudding, as they say, and I cannot deny the reality of this new body simply by deciding it is not so.

"Alright then," I say, allowing myself to listen to my new, unfamiliar voice. I suppose I should try to get used to it. "Where do we go from here?"

As much as I desire answers about this body and how I got here, my immediate needs are clear: food, water, shelter.

I cup my flame between both hands, bringing it closer to my chest as I revel in its warmth and marvel at its existence. I suppose shelter is partially covered. At least I'm no longer at risk of freezing to death in this place. But what *is* this place?

Cautiously, I gather my taloned feet beneath me and stand. I immediately stumble backward and threaten to fall over, overbalancing from the unexpected weight of my wings. I flap them instinctively, like pinwheeling arms on a tightrope, the gusts of which threaten to snuff out my wildly flickering flame. Hunching forward, wings spread to either side, I recover.

"This will certainly be an experience," I mutter.

Glancing to my left, I watch and feel my wing flex with no small amount of awe. The feathers are a fiery display of colors, starting with the deepest maroon at the base and brightening to an intense yellow at the tips. I splay the wings wide, arcing them up above me as high as I can reach. These things really are a part of me. I'm controlling them.

The feathers at my wingtips brush against something in the dark. I lift my fire above my head, but its small shell of illumination isn't enough to expose the ceiling overhead. I suppose I'll need a bigger flame for that.

Hadn't Echo mentioned something along those lines?

"Echo," I say, folding my wings back in to tuck the long leading-edge feathers behind my back (and away from my flames). "I had another fire spell I could use, didn't I?"

[Affirmative,] Echo says. [Blaze: Summon a flame of variable size and shape capable of moving with the caster's intent. Mana cost: 10 per cubic meter per second.]

"And how much mana do I have to work with?"

[Check,] Echo says, my stats reappearing from where they'd slowly faded from my vision and mind. [Mana: 199/200]

That missing point must be from the Spark spell I currently have going.

Ten mana per second is a lot if I only have two-hundred altogether. A resource I'm hesitant to burn through if it's the only thing keeping me from descending into hypothermia.

"Is there a way to recover mana?" I ask.

[Affirmative. Various spells and items may replenish a target's mana pool. Additionally, this user passively recovers mana at a rate of 1 per minute.]

That's convenient.

"If memory serves, doesn't the Spark spell deplete mana at a rate of one per minute?"

[Affirmative.]

Then I can effectively keep it going forever. That's one small comfort. In that case, one large burst of flame to get an idea of where I am won't hurt anything.

"Let's try one of those Blaze spells then," I say, focusing on the fire in my hands. If this works how the previous one did, all I have to do is envision it, right? I mentally push on the fire, imagining it growing larger, brighter.

[Blaze spell activated,] Echo says.

The flame swells to the size of a watermelon. Alarmed, I hold my hands out at arm's length, but the flame doesn't engulf them as I'd feared. Instead it seems to be moving exactly as I intend it to, staying carefully away from my fingers.

In the corner of my vision, my mana starts to tick away.

Right. No time to marvel now.

I pull my hands back, and the fire continues to hover before me. I shape it larger, pushing it higher in the air as the heat begins to sting my face. Larger. Larger. In just a few seconds it's the size of a kitchen table. My mana plummets, so I mentally throw the ball of fire as high into the air as I can manage, then disperse it in the shape of an expanding ring, the fire racing away from me like a pulse of radar. I quickly spin around, taking in my surroundings. The room momentarily bursts with color, as bright as sunlight. Then my fire collides with the far walls, extinguishing itself, and I'm wisped back into darkness.

[Blaze spell ended.]

[Mana cost: 53]

For a brief moment, however, I caught a glimpse of my surroundings, and my heart squeezes in fear. I'm certainly in a cave, that much is clear. The cavern extends radially around me by about sixty feet, and is peppered with stalactites and stalagmites. More importantly, however, are the objects which litter the floor.

I breathe into the silence, ears ringing. The vision of the room lingers, burned into my retinas, like hundreds of grinning ghosts. Finally, I raise a hand.

"Spark."

The small flame reappears above my fingers. I crouch down to the smooth stone, running my free hand over the surface. Perfectly smooth. Spotless, too, like I'm at the epicenter of... *something* which blew everything else away.

Balancing like this in a crouch, my wings naturally unfold to either side, countering the slight tilts and shifts of my body. One of my wingtips, extended into the dark, brushes against something on the ground there, and I hear the wooden clatter of small objects falling over one another. Like a cascade of pebbles. Only, from the glimpse I caught earlier, I know they're not pebbles.

I cautiously step toward the edge of the clearing I now know surrounds me. Beyond this flat bed of rock is rough slate, stalagmites, and...

I hold my light over the ground, the spots of white almost seeming to glow against the contrast of their dark surroundings.

...Bones.

Hundreds of bones. Maybe thousands. The skulls are easiest to pick out, round like stones. But they don't all appear human. Some have horns, while others are much too large or small, and squashed or stretched. I pick my way carefully around my small death-free island. Now that I'm really looking at the skeletons, only some of them seem to be human. A few have wing structures—possibly harpies, like me. Others seem to be made of some material that's not quite bone and have... far, *far* too many legs. I suppress a shudder at these remains.

After making it all the way around the circle, it's clear I'll have to pick my way out. There's no clear path through the chilling graveyard I find myself in, and even if there was, I need to explore this cavern. Without water, I'll only be able to survive here a few days at most. Another bright light would help me explore the area, but—I Check my mana, and find the Blaze spell reduced it to 146. No, this little Spark will have to do for now.

"Sorry, friend," I murmur as I step carefully around the remains of the nearest skeleton. My talons slide and clatter noisily over the loose rock. My wings open once more to help balance me, and I try not to marvel at them, how instinctive they're becoming, as I focus on where to place my steps next.

Glints of metal occasionally shine among the stones and bones. Perhaps this was a battlefield from long, long before. The cave smells of must and earth rather than decay. That gives me hope that there must be some open-air passage out of here—and also fills me with concern that these remains have been left to be lost to time. Whoever fought here—would their people not have tried to reclaim their remains? If they made no attempt to lay them to rest, then why? Was this location too remote or inhospitable? If so, that doesn't bode well for me.

I make it to a wall without stepping on too many bones, cringing each time I feel them break beneath my talons, and then begin to trace it around the room. The quiet has become eerie, or perhaps that's just my imagination now that I know what surrounds me. I'm quite certain I'm alone, but even so it's hard to shake the unsettling feeling of being watched while lost in some ancient necropolis.

I trace the wall for what I estimate to be two-thirds of the way around the room before coming upon something unusual. The wall here is crumbly and loose instead of the smooth limestone I'd become accustomed to, and as I move my light over its surface, it's clear this space has been filled in, naturally or otherwise. Giant rocks and slabs of stone block what might have been a tunnel out of the cavern. Perhaps there's still a way around this rockslide. Searching the sealed exit, I'm not paying near enough attention to my feet, and trip over something on the floor. Alarm flashes through my mind. My wings shoot out to catch me. One of them immediately strikes the wall, which only serves to leverage me over and expedite the fall.

I collapse to the ground in an unruly heap, wincing as I check to make sure nothing's broken. The bones in my wings seem hardier than those of a bird, however, and in the end the only thing injured is my pride. I move my Spark over the ground, searching for what I'd tripped over.

Another skeleton is buried in the rubble. The lower half of their torso has been swallowed by the boulders, but their upper half is uncovered and largely preserved. Something glints in their hand.

A large blood-red gem rests atop the bones. Perhaps a garnet. But *rests* isn't entirely accurate. The jewel seems to have... seeped around the bones. Melted somewhat back into the rocks. Dozens of veins zigzag away from the gem, embedding themselves in the limestone floor like lines on a circuit board. How strange.

My fire flickers on the surface of the precious jewel as if a second fire burns within its depths. Staring into that light, I'm overcome with a strong sense of familiarity. Like I've seen this exact stone somewhere before. Like I *know* it.

The feeling is troubling. "What *are* you?" I ask the ruby. What made it so special that this person died clutching it?

[Check,] Echo says, as if I'd been asking her. [Dormant Dungeon Core. Psionic Touch available.]

"What?" I say.

[Dormant Dungeon Core,] Echo repeats. Apparently she isn't well versed in rhetorical questions. [Psionic Touch available.]

"That means it can think?" I ask. "You said Psionic Touch only worked with creatures that could think."

[Affirmative.]

A thinking rock. Of course. Why not?

What could a rock have to think about? And I suppose more to the point, would it know anything that could help me get out of here?

It's the first potentially useful thing I've come across so far. I suppose it can't hurt to try to speak with it. Perhaps it will know something about my circumstances. Still holding the fire in my right hand, I reach out my left to touch the stone. The surface is cold and hard, just like any other rock.

Psionic Touch, I think, willing myself to cast the spell. Triggering this one doesn't seem as intuitive as wishing a fire into existence, but mentally saying the name seems to do the trick.

[Psionic Touch activated.]

[Cost: 1 mana per 5 seconds.]

Oh right, I forgot about that part. I'll need to keep a closer eye on the costs of these spells. At this rate, it will eat up my remaining mana in roughly ten minutes. Which means I'll need to switch off my Spark if I want to stretch that number at all. Not a problem, just... an uncomfortable thought to be alone in a dark room full of bones while speaking to a strange entity in my mind. But I'll cross that bridge when I get to it. For now, I'll play this by ear.

At first, nothing happens. I'm just touching a rock, trying to mentally speak with it. The thought makes me laugh. How absurd this all is! But I give it a mental nudge anyway. *Hey there. Are you, um, alive?*

And then I feel it. Something *stirs* in my mind. A presence slowly unfolding. Sensations roll into me in abstract waves. It's tired. Confused, but curious. It's wondering what roused it from its slumber.

"That would be me," I say, amazed that I'm actually speaking with a gemstone. It really can think! Fascinating.

The Dungeon Core's mind shifts, noticing me. It's becoming more solid in my mind now, more alert, as if it's shaking off the vestiges of sleep.

Mana, I can feel it realize as it focuses on me. All at once, its budding consciousness swells into a storm of thoughts and emotions that crash into me. There's mana! Oh, it needs mana so bad. It's desperate. Disoriented. Eager. Ravenous—

I gasp, snapping my hand away, and the mental presence vanishes. [Spell ended.]

My mind spins as it tries to process the stone's words. It's nothing like speech with a person; my mind can only try to interpret it that way. But at its core, it's such a chaotic thing, a swirl of emotions and impulses, no clear structure to its turbulent thoughts. And for one fearful, irrational moment, I felt I was about to be swept up in them.

"Echo?" I ask, hesitant to touch the stone again. "You said this thing is a Dungeon Core. What precisely does that mean?"

[A Dungeon Core is an entity capable of infusing essence of itself into its surroundings, thereby gaining the ability to manipulate and transform the affected landscape into a sentient dungeon.]

I raise both eyebrows. I suppose I should be beyond feeling surprised by anything I learn at this stage. Nothing should be stranger than waking up in a new body, with feathers and wings and the ability to summon fireballs.

Although a stone which can create a living dungeon *does* stretch one's suspension of disbelief.

Curiosity draws my hand back to the stone, but practicality has me pulling it away once more. "It can't hurt me, can it? It's just thoughts." Then something else occurs to me. "Am I inside a living dungeon right now?"

[Negative. The Dungeon Core has expired its mana supply, and is therefore incapable of enacting its will on its surroundings.]

That's a relief. "So alive, but dormant," I surmise.

[Negative,] Echo says. [The targeted object does not meet minimum requirements to qualify as 'alive.']

"Rather, it's sentient," I correct myself.

[Affirmative.]

"And sapient?"

[The degree to which the Dungeon Core is capable of logic and reason could be debated.]

I chuckle at that. It did seem quite driven by its instincts. Pity. I thought maybe I could ask it to open a door or turn on a light or some such. I give the rock a sympathetic look. "Looks like you and I are stuck in here together."

Not in any hurry to experience the unsettling swirl of emotions that come from touching the Dungeon Core again, I decide to leave it be for now and continue to map my surroundings. My mana hasn't recovered from the earlier Blaze, as the Spark spell consumes mana at the same rate I recover it, but all it will take is enduring an hour or two in the darkness to restore that amount. For now, I rely on my Spark to finish my lap around the cave, careful to avoid tripping over any other sentient jewelry.

There's not much more to uncover, however. The room is roughly circular, littered with bones, and, as far as I can tell, only has the one blocked exit I found. I briefly entertain the idea of trying to fly and see if there are any exits higher up along the walls. Feeling rather self-conscious, I flap both of my wings, stirring up a wind and scattering some of the smaller bone fragments. I push harder, flapping them with all my strength, but my feet don't even begin to lift from the floor. I quickly stop the absurd endeavor, chastising my own foolishness; I knew that wouldn't work.

I'd rightfully identified the wings as too small to provide sufficient lift the moment I'd first laid eyes on them. Are they merely ornamental, then? A vestige of evolution in the process of generationally dwindling?

These are not useful things to be wondering about while stuck in a cave and at risk of gradually succumbing to dehydration.

[Spell Level Up,] Echo abruptly speaks, causing me to jump. [Spark: Level 2. Mana consumption reduced to 1 mana every 2 minutes.]

Well that's nice, if not a bit strange. Levels? I recall seeing something like that on the Stats Echo provided, now that I'm thinking about it. But in all my years of reading, I've never encountered a magic system that seems so quantifiable.

I think I like it.

Eventually, I make my way back over to the blocked exit, hoping to find a way to loosen the stones and clear a path through. I step carefully around the Dungeon Core as I search, tugging on rocks and shining my Spark through every crack and crevice. No luck. The collapse of this tunnel clearly happened a long time ago—judging by the skeleton half buried in the rubble, as well as all of these fallen warriors. The stones might as well be cemented in place. I look back toward the ceiling. If I can't fly up there, perhaps I could climb?

No, not up these smooth walls. I'm more likely to get myself hurt, and if I end up with a broken leg, then I really will be done for. So what's the answer?

My gaze falls back to the Dungeon Core.

"Echo. You said that stone is dormant because it doesn't have any mana, correct?"

[Affirmative.]

"And gaining mana would reactivate it?"

[Affirmative.]

"And if it's activated, you said it can manipulate its environment?" I press further. "As in, shift the earth itself?"

[Among other influences, affirmative.]

I chew my bottom lip, having serious doubts about the soundness of this plan. I know nothing about this thinking rock. It could as easily be friend or foe. But given everything else at my disposal—which is to say, nothing—and the time ticking down until my inevitable demise, I'm not left with many alternatives.

I crouch beside the stone, hesitating before I touch it. I know it poses no physical threat, though a mental one remains yet to be determined. But if nothing else, I can always pull my hand away—and if for some reason I can't do that, the Psionic Touch spell will eventually end on its own once my mana is extinguished. It should be safe to touch the thinking rock.

The thought makes me lean back, and I huff out a laugh. How peculiar it is that I'm already growing used to all this strangeness. Yet, how intriguing! The mystery of all these new things sends a thrill through me. When was the last time I felt so excited to explore, to learn something new, to solve a problem?

If only my life didn't hang in the balance!

Even so, I can't help but grin as I reach for the Core, my fingers buzzing in anticipation.

[Psionic Touch activated.]

Once more, some *thing* springs into my mind, whirling with a dozen thoughts and instincts at once. Elation, suspicion, hunger, urgency—I push back, imagining a wall between us, and surprisingly, this works. The Core's mind suddenly feels distant and muted. Cautiously, I shift the form of my imaginary wall into that of a screen: a filter through which its mind can pass. This time, instead of the foreign thoughts blinking through my mind in a turbulent mess, the flow becomes more laminar.

Can you hear me? I think toward the Core. *Can you understand?*

There's a spark of recognition. Yes, it understands me. Its mind eagerly presses toward me, and I can sense it sensing my own mana. Starved. It is starving!

I know, I tell it. *I can help with that.* I pause. *At least, I think I can.*

The Core swells with elation. Yay! It needs mana. Any mana. Now, give it now!

"Bit demanding, aren't we?" I chuckle.

I will, I tell it. *But I need your help. If I give you mana, would you be able to open a way out of here for me?*

The Core hungrily accepts. Easy! Trivial. Effortless. It can shape mountains, with enough mana to power it. It will show me! I will be so impressed.

I smile at its enthusiasm. At least it's cooperative. And it doesn't seem to have any ill intent. More like a starved animal than a calculating predator. But I haven't actually established that I can hold up my end of the bargain.

"Echo?" I prompt. "Can I lend mana to this Dungeon Core?"

[Negative,] Echo says, and I grimace in disappointment. I should have thought to ask this sooner. [You do not have the correct class or skills to disseminate mana to other targets, living or otherwise. However,] she adds, [this entity is capable of forming a Pact with another creature.]

"Pact?" I ask.

[A Pact involves sharing resources between two targets,] Echo explains. [In this instance, the Dungeon Core would gain access to the user's mana reserves, while the user would gain access to several of the Dungeon Core's skills and abilities.]

Seems like a fair trade, not that I'm in any position to bargain. I can mentally feel the Dungeon Core's presence pacing at the edge of my mind, like a dog impatiently waiting for its bowl to be set down.

Well, why not? There's no other way out of here that I can see. And I'm sure this sentient rock is just as eager to leave this place as I am.

"Alright, then," I tell the stone, mentally echoing the thought. "Let's form a Pact."

The Core perks up at those words, practically vibrating with anticipation. I can feel it extend a portion of itself toward me, and I bridge the gap, completing the mental handshake. The moment our minds touch, an electric thrill passes through me, and my perception of the Core abruptly shifts.

For a moment—just a fraction of a second—a pane of reality seems to slip. Like a mask falling away. Like briefly conceiving a three-dimensional cube for the four-dimensional tesseract it truly is. The Dungeon Core is a small, tiny jewel—and then it's a vast canyon of unfathomable depth. A black hole of bottomless hunger. Fractaling shards of existence threatening to pull me into its infinite potential.

And then it's merely a gem once more.

My mind reels with shock. But before I have a moment to process all this—or voice any newly raised concerns—Echo speaks up.

[Pact initiated.]

Chapter Three

PACT

"Is it too late to, ah, *un*initiate a Pact?" I ask.

[Dungeon Core abilities interfaced,] Echo says. [Pact formation complete.]

I take that as a no.

Even now, that sense of vastness I'd felt is rapidly fading. The Dungeon Core just appears to be a stone. Granted, a very excitable stone that seems eager to get to work, but certainly not some other-dimensional bottomless well of darkness. I almost believe it was just my imagination, though the strangeness of this world has shown me that anything seems possible.

I suppose it's too late regardless.

The Dungeon Core nudges my mind, silently begging for its promised mana.

"Alright, alright," I say. "Now, I don't have much. And if I want to keep speaking with you, I'll need to hold onto a bit. So we need to nail down the parameters of my request now, before we lose the ability to communicate. Understand?"

The stone practically vibrates with excitement beneath my hand. Yes. It understands. It will rip this cave apart.

"No!" I object. "Uh, no, not like that. Here, let me think."

Instead of trying to describe with words, I focus on an image of what I want: the fallen stones in the passage being pushed out of the way. Being able to walk out of the *still intact* cave. Minimal disruption.

The Core considers this. Yes, it supposes it could do that. Not nearly as fun, though.

I snort. "Well so long as you're having fun, that's all that matters, isn't it?" I shake my head. "Alright. Now how do I give you access to my mana?"

Instead of an explanation, I feel a mental ping. A request, almost like a tug of a current, ushering me forward. Hesitantly, I allow myself to be pulled along.

[Mana transfer initiated,] Echo reports.

It takes all my willpower to not stop the transfer. I can feel the energy flowing away from me, and while I don't notice that I'm particularly weaker or more tired as a result, the sensation is still distinctly unsettling. But if I want out of this cave, I need to follow through on our agreement.

I wait until my mana reserves dip below 10%, then I mentally pull away from the Dungeon Core.

[Mana transfer complete,] Echo says.

[Mana: 7/200]

[Psionic Touch Level up! At Level 2, Psionic Touch mana cost is reduced to 1 mana per 10 seconds. Spell evolution available! Psionic Link: form a permanent connection between two minds, allowing the individuals to communicate at will. Mana cost: 150]

That's interesting. A one-time cost to prevent future mana drain would be much more efficient. But I don't have enough magic to use Psionic Link even if I wanted to. And frankly, I'm not sure I want to. That previous peek behind the Dungeon Core's curtain was unsettling, and it would be rash of me to permanently fix such an unknown entity to my mind.

Of course, I'd just formed a Pact with the thing, so who am I to talk?

It will take me hours to recover my mana anyway. Plenty of time to decide how I want this relationship to develop in the long term. For now, I only have another minute left to continue talking with the Dungeon Core before Psionic Touch expires. And speaking of which...

Yes! The Dungeon Core rejoices. Energy. Finally! Now it will—No, wait... Not enough! Not nearly enough. Pathetic amount of mana. So pitiful. Shameful. Well, it must work with what it has.

I breathe out a laugh. "Rude."

The Core ignores me, too focused on what it wants to do next. First, extraction. It can't stay here. It needs a new lair. A better lair. It needs to tap into a larger energy source. Where? Searching. Deep.... Deeper...

Every thought is accompanied with the flash of an image or abstract impression: stones buildings, glowing veins in the rocks, a network of caves and passages.

The Core is disappointed. No, it can't reach. Ah, why doesn't it have more mana to work with? Such a sorry excuse for a Pact... Okay, mobility first—

[Mana Expired,] Echo says. [Psionic Touch ended. Spark ended.]

And just like that, I'm plunged into darkness as the Core's presence vanishes from my mind. It certainly wasn't impressed with my mana reserves, that much is clear. And what was all that about lairs and veins of energy? It's getting off track. But without any mana to communicate, I can't redirect it now. Hesitantly, I remove my hand from the stone. I'll just have to hope the Core will do as I intended even without my mental direction.

A sound in the dark scratches at my ears, driving a shiver down my back. It's coming from the ground in front of me—a shifting of pebbles and stone, I think. Very likely the Dungeon Core moving the earth around it, but being unable to witness what's happening is more than a little unsettling. I Check my mana: still at 0/200. It should only take another 30 seconds or so to gain 1 point back, at which point I'll be able to light a new Spark. In the meantime, there's nothing but blackness and the faint scratching of stone on stone.

While I wait, my mind wanders back to my Stats. It's so strange to have everything about me labeled like some plane model in a textbook. A phoenix harpy? It sounds absurd. And yet, there's something else in that stat block that catches my eye—something I haven't had much of a chance to process before now.

"Echo," I say. "What does this Role stat mean?"

[Every user is assigned a Role,] Echo replies. [The user must fulfill the role requirements.]

Well that tells me very little.

"And my role is... The Dark Lord?" I ask, skeptical.

[Affirmative.]

"What are the requirements for that role?"

[The Dark Lord must defend her kingdom.]

Vague. And vaguely ominous. No one called The Dark Lord has ever ended up being one of the good guys.

"I don't suppose there's room to negotiate a new role?" I ask.

[Negative.]

Of course not. Yet another aspect of my predicament it seems I have no control over. Well, I'll just have to roll with it for now. And I don't even have a kingdom. It probably doesn't mean anything... right?

I wait a few more minutes, as long as my patience can handle in the ringing dark, then I cast Spark once more.

The earth around the Dungeon Core has come alive. What once was solid stone has now become sand and loose pebbles, all strangely cubic as if diced by a laser cutter. The ground is shifting, pushing upward, forcing the Core and all the jewel's circuit-like tendrils from the earth. Seeing what it's trying to do, I decide to help out. I dig my hands into the now-loose rubble and pull upwards. The bits of stone cascade away between my fingers, leaving just the Dungeon Core dangling dozens of ruby-red stone roots, like fossilized veins leading away from a heart.

I reactivate Psionic Touch, and the mental deluge of its thoughts starts once more.

From the flurry of excitement, recognition, and eagerness that floods through me, it seems happy to realize I'm back. I saved it some mana by assisting in prying it from the ground. Now it can focus on finding a suitable new lair—

"No," I hurriedly interrupt, watching my mana start ticking back toward zero far too quickly. "The passage. Clear the passage." My impression of the Dungeon Core is gradually shifting to something like a toddler hyped up on sugar. Working with this entity is going to be like herding cats.

Disappointed, the Core relents, and I can feel its attention shift. It plunges into its own memories, and like getting caught in a pocket of differential pressure, I'm briefly dragged in with it. It's been in this chamber a long time. Once great, its area of influence shrunk to just this cavern, then its immediate surroundings, then nothing. After its mana was depleted, cut off from its source, it became stuck. It spent decades—centuries—trying to grow, reach out, find a new vein of magical ore it could tap into for power. But it only managed these meager few inches of geological growth. Now, though. Now…

Sand hisses away from the collapsed passage. I hastily step back, fire in one hand, gem in the other. Bits and pieces of the rock slide down the face of the collapsed wall, all shaped in perfect cubes of various sizes. The rubble spills into the room around my feet and I retreat even further in alarm. How much did the Core need to clear out? What if it ends up filling the cavern with sand before I can find a way out?

My alarm seems to make it through to the Core, as it flickers with a new idea.

Don't worry. It will make a hole! Then the room won't fill with sand.

Its thoughts are accompanied by images of giant crevices splitting open the floor flitting through my mind. This does little to ease my alarm.

Wait, I think. *I don't think that's a good—*

Something *cracks* behind me like a gunshot. My ears are suddenly muted and ringing. I'm hardly able to make out the hiss of sand still falling from the collapsed passage. But now there's a giant crack bisecting the room, and it's zig-zagging right toward me.

The Dungeon Core sends me a mental impression of something along the line of *oops.*

[Mana depleted. Psionic Touch expired.]

I leap off to the side, scattering bones and flapping my wings to keep upright as the ground gives way. The sand—and skeletons—pour through the gaping hole in the floor, quickly vanishing out of sight. The crack reaches the collapsed passageway and then stops.

For a moment.

The boulders groan. A puff of dust escapes the passage as the stones shift, jolting downward. Then, all at once, they vanish through the floor in a rockslide. The chamber shakes with the cascade of crashing boulders, first grating against each other and the floor, then more distantly shattering like bombshells somewhere far beneath us.

"Stop!" I shout over the calamity, even though I'm no longer using Psionic Touch. "That's enough!"

But the Dungeon Core had already stopped. The receding echo of cascading stones rumbles through the cavern for a minute more, gradually growing fainter and fainter until finally all hint of the rockslide fades away.

I wait until my pounding heart has stopped threatening to burst out of my chest, which also gives me some time to recover a few points of mana. Once I've sufficiently recovered from nearly experiencing my second heart attack of the day, I reestablish a Psionic Touch.

The Core happily greets me. Sadly, it's used up all the mana I gave it. But! Didn't it do so well at clearing out the tunnel?

I glance toward said tunnel. A cloud of dirt obscures the entrance. The fissure that's running through the room leads straight up toward the tunnel, so I pick myself up and carefully make my way over, gauging the slope and sturdiness of the ground with every step. I stop a few feet away.

The dust clears to reveal a dark tunnel. Sure enough, it's empty, just as the Dungeon Core insists. But there's also a giant shaft running through the passage floor, effectively halving the width of the tunnel and creating a cliff on one side. The remaining ledge is only a few feet wide.

"Yes," I say with a grimace. "You did great."

I hold my Spark over the crevasse, but the light is quickly swallowed by the dark. I don't even have enough mana to drop a Blaze down there and see how far it might fall. I guess I'll just have to try not to slip—or I'll get to find out how effective these wings really are.

Unfortunately, the ledge in the tunnel is on the opposite side of the fissure as me. At its narrowest point, the crack is a little over three feet wide. Physically, an easy space to jump. I could practically step over it if I stretch far enough. But it's something rather different mentally when you know one misstep or crumbling block of stone will lead to your untimely demise.

Well, maybe not untimely. I've already died once today.

"Okay," I say, glancing down at the Dungeon Core. "If I'm going to do this, it would sure help to have my hands free." Unfortunately, I have a lack of pockets—or any sort of clothes for that matter.

But the Core seems to understand. It can take many useful forms.

Images flit through my mind of the Dungeon Core's rocky veins reshaping into an intricate stone lattice to form a crown, with the jewel at its center.

"Useful," I acknowledge. "But a crown might fall off. How about..."

I picture a bracelet instead, woven about my forearm like a bracer, skin tight so it can't accidentally slip off.

The Dungeon Core examines the design and happily agrees. It likes trying new shapes. It's been a long time since it's gotten to change its form. It can only reform once per Pact, and it's been a long time since it's had a Pact. A very long time.

"Wait," I say. The tendrils of stone twitch, then come alive, snapping around my wrist. I can't help but flinch as it does so, jerking my arm away as if to dislodge it. The veins of stone lace around my arm, settling the stone on the back of my wrist, then just as quickly become inert once more. "What do you mean you can only reform once per Pact?"

[Form Change complete,] Echo says.

"Er, can it change forms again?" I ask Echo, since the Dungeon Core doesn't seem capable of—or interested in—explaining. "Can I get it off?"

[Negative,] Echo says. [Until a new Pact is formed, this form of the Core will remain unchanged.]

I grimace. I should have seen that one coming. Well, I guess I *really* don't have to worry about losing it now. Next time, I'll ask more clarifying questions in advance.

Seeing my mana hit 1/200, I deactivate Psionic Touch once more, so I can keep my Spark going. This really is getting inconvenient. Perhaps I'll commit to that Psionic Link after all. In the meantime, however, I'll just have to flick the spell on and off as needed, and as my mana allows.

I look back at the crevasse with a sigh. The stone stuck to my arm is the least of my worries right now. At least with Psionic Touch off, it can't say anything to distract me.

"I suppose there's nothing for it." I back up a few steps, then take a running jump, giving my wings a good—pointless—flap as I do, and soar over the crack. I effortlessly land on the other side, scattering a half-disintegrated skeleton.

Oh. Well that was far easier than I'd made it out to be in my head.

I watch my feet—claws?—as I slowly pick my way along the tunnel's ledge. I'd never been the spelunking type. Air was more my domain. Caves are just so claustrophobic. Cold and dark and damp. I pause, brushing my hand against the wall. It's rough and dry here, likely from the rocks that have been shaved away. But if I can find a damp area of the cave, that might be my salvation. Now that I found a way out of that first cavern, finding water will be my next priority.

The tunnel goes on for a minute more, longer than I had expected. The end is marked by a wall of black that my Spark can't penetrate.

Cautiously, I step out the end. The Core's fissure has tapered off into a gap only a handspan wide, but it continues on into the darkness ahead of me. I lift my light to try to survey my surroundings. I'm in another cavern, I think. But judging by the echoes of my footsteps, this one is much more massive.

"This may be a problem," I mumble to myself. I can't wander aimlessly about this cave system. Aside from getting lost, it's simply an inefficiency I can't afford. If I end up heading down tunnels that loop back on themselves, would I even know? I need to explore as much of this place as possible in the hopes of finding a way out, or at least some water. But without a map or way to track my pathing, there's no way to be systematic about it.

[Map available,] Echo suddenly speaks up.

I pause. "I'm sorry, what?"

[Map available,] she repeats.

I frown. "You've had a map available all this time and I'm just learning about it now?"

[Negative,] Echo says. [Map Interface unlocked upon Pact formation.]

"Oh," I say, mollified. "I see. Sorry I doubted you, Echo."

This must be one of the Dungeon Core "tools" she said I would gain access to. "Alright. Let's see it then."

Like Echo's Stats, an image appears superimposed over my vision. At first it appears like a ball with a tail sticking off of it. It takes a moment to realize I can mentally zoom in on the image and rotate it at will. It takes that reorientation to realize what I'm looking at: a three-dimensional visualization of the places I've been so far. The ball—or hemisphere, now that I can rotate it—is the cavern I started in, while the wavy tail is the tunnel I took out. Now I'm standing in a new area. Experimentally, I walk a couple paces to my right. The map similarly illuminates, tracing my new path. I see. It's a map that's only revealed to me as I explore it. Not the most efficient way to travel, but at least it gives me reference points, and I'll know if I ever end up retracing my steps. In that case...

I turn Psionic Touch back on, just for the company. "Now, we walk."

The Dungeon Core doesn't know what that means. It is just a rock.

Guided only by my Spark of light and the Map Interface of a sentient bracelet, I strike out into the caverns.

"Do you know if there's water anywhere in here?" I ask as I walk. "An underground river or pool?"

Water? Its thoughts spiral around that concept for a second. It doesn't remember water. It was a long time ago that it knew water. Now it knows only stone. Earth. Rocks. Pebbles. Dust. Boulders—

"Alright, alright," I say, cutting it off. "I get the picture."

Looks like I'll be on my own as far as trying to find water and food goes. Perhaps it would be capable of searching for such things if I could provide it with more mana. I Check my mana at the thought: [2/200]. At this rate, it will take another six hours to fully regenerate. Then again, I have nothing but time.

I walk for hours. Sometimes the way slopes down, and sometimes up. Sometimes the cave narrows to a small passageway, and sometimes it widens into large caverns. The ways split, and they converge. They occasionally twist into passages too tight to continue. Sometimes there's giant holes and chasms that my light can't reach into, or passages halfway blocked with loose, dusty stone I expect came from the Core's earlier rockslide. The walls have become moist, which I count as a good sign, but there's not enough accumulated to quench my growing thirst. I know I should be able to go for days without water, but the exertion of my exploration isn't helping. Each step I take carves out more of the Map on the Dungeon Core's display, but without having any real destination, it's just a tangled yarn of paths. I try to ignore my mounting concern. It's early, yet.

A faint sound makes me come to an abrupt halt. This whole time, the only noises I've encountered are the echoes of my own footsteps and Echo's occasional status update.

But this is something physical, some source of sound that's not coming from me. I tip my head, straining my ears, as I try to make it out.

Silence rings through the dark. Had I imagined it? A pebble I'd kicked just to hear it clattering down some crack in the stone? No—I'm sure it was something organic. A sigh, or whisper, or...

A grunt breaks through the silence. Excited, I hurry ahead, pausing before the passage I swear I can hear the sound coming from. Now, don't get *too* overeager, I have to remind myself. It could be a wild animal. Something dangerous. And I'm just as likely to provide a food source to it as it is to me. But this is my first indication of any signs of life, and that's an opportunity I can't pass up.

I wait at the passage, weighing my options. My mana has finished recovering, Between turning my Psionic Touch on and off, which tells me I've already been aimlessly wandering these caverns for far too long. But that also means I have Blaze at my disposal. And if it's a creature that can be reasoned with, I might be able to try Psionic Touch. Apart from those two things, I don't seem to have many other tools at my disposal. The passage is dark and long enough to swallow the light of my Spark. It would be wiser to snuff it out so as not to alert the creature of my approach, but then I'd be walking blind, and given the uneven floor and countless holes, that would be unlikely to play in my favor. Perhaps I could—

A single word, quiet and strained, interrupts my thoughts as it echoes down the passage.

"Fuck."

It's a person! I'm not alone in here. Granted, a slightly foul-language and perhaps unfriendly person, but someone I can talk to, nevertheless. Hopefully they can help navigate me out of this maze. I press ahead, my Spark raised before me. As I approach, I can make out the scuffing sound of something hard against stone and more heavy breathing and muttered swears.

"Hello?" I call.

The sounds stop. Slightly more cautiously, I continue on in the same direction. As I turn a corner in the cave, my light spills over a small cavern. It takes me several moments to parse what I'm looking at.

The space is small, only a dozen feet across. The opposite wall is not a wall at all, in fact, and actually appears to be a carved, artificial tunnel, though it's half caved-in with boulders. And between that tunnel and me, pressed against the fallen rocks, is a person.

Or... a spider?

A black, seven-foot-tall spider, with the torso of a human extending from where its head should be. Metal armor decorates its—her?—arms, legs, and chest, while long dark braids cascade around her shoulders. Her face almost appears human: she has two ears, a nose, a mouth, and eyes.

That is, eight eyes.

"Um, hello," I say after a moment, trying not to let any preconceived biases toward eight-limbed arachnids color my impression. "I don't suppose you have a map?"

CHAPTER FOUR

SPIDER

The spider woman hisses at my light and raises a hand to shield all eight of her blinking, black eyes.

"Ah, sorry," I say, lowering my light and turning to place myself between the spider person and my flame. "Didn't mean to bother—"

She doesn't give me a chance to continue. Even as I'm speaking she snatches something from behind her and swings it around toward me. I hastily stumble backward, letting out a cry that bears an embarrassing resemblance to a squawk. The woman swipes at me with her spear, but I'm out of her range, and she doesn't pursue.

"Intruder!" she hisses, jabbing her spear in my direction for good measure. "Are you the cause of this, then? Are you Jorrian? It is a siege!"

"I… what?" I say, completely baffled

The woman makes another swipe at me, this time stretching her long, spindly limbs as far as they'll take her—then collapses with a cry of pain. One of her legs is pinned between the boulder and the tunnel, and while I might not know much—okay, anything—about spider biology, the angle her leg appears to be twisted at can't be normal, and the sight sends an unpleasant flutter through my gut.

Echo, have any insight on this situation? I ask. *What did I just walk into?*

[Check,] Echo says, and more stats appear in my mind.

[Name: Mirzayael]
[Species: Arachnoid]
[Class: Silk Warrior]
[Level: 29]
[HP: 198/240]
[Mana: 110/110]

Oh, wow. I can get stats for other people, too? This is incredibly useful. I wonder how much more I could learn about her this way? At the thought, several other fields immediately populate: weight, height, even her pronouns. But there are some interesting discrepancies between her and my stats as well—discrepancies I'll have to sort through later, given the arachnoid's health.

"You're hurt," I say. "Please, I mean no harm, and if I'm an intruder, I promise it's entirely by accident. Will you let me come close?"

Mirzayael pushes herself off the ground, though she doesn't attempt to stand, instead keeping her spider torso—and trapped leg—carefully still. She glowers at me, hand still curled around her weapon.

"Who are you, then?" she demands. Her voice is velvety and warm, though it's a bit hard to appreciate beneath the way she bites off her words, as if each syllable is a nuisance to spit out. "How did you get here?"

"Those are... extremely fair questions that are actually quite difficult to answer." I hold up my hands, one empty, one still with my Spark hovering above the palm. "I can try to explain. Will you let me look at your leg?"

"No," Mirzayael snaps. "Not until I know your intentions. How did you find this place? Did the Jorrians send you here?"

"No one sent me," I say. "At least, not that I'm aware of. I've been lost in these caverns and stumbled down here after hearing your voice."

I settle back on my haunches, deciding the most tactful move would be to sit at eye level with her. My wings awkwardly open and splay to either side as I do so, too long to tuck nicely behind my back while seated. Mirzayael's gaze jerks in their direction, squinting against the light. Then her eyes widen.

"You're a harpy," she says, surprised.

"It certainly seems I am," I agree.

"Lift up the light," she demands. "Let me get a better look at you."

I comply with her request, cupping my other hand around the fire so the flame is less blinding. Then I move it slowly before my face, wings, arms, and talons, letting her take it all in.

"A phoenix harpy," she says, a tinge of awe in her voice. Then, after a moment of silence, she adds, "Why are you naked?"

"Uh." My mind short circuits. I mean, I knew I wasn't wearing any clothes. But being covered in feathers, it kind of *feels* like I'm covered up. And frankly, I don't have the same equipment that requires covering as I'm used to. I guess I had just assumed harpies didn't *need* clothes.

Warmth rises up my neck and settles in my cheeks. I tuck my legs up close beneath me, and my wings wrap around my shoulders like a shawl. "I, ah, suppose I didn't come with any clothes," I stammer. "Sorry about that. Ah, I don't suppose you have anything to spare?"

Mirzayael frowns at me for a moment longer, then barks out a single syllabled laugh. "Well, you're definitely not an enemy scout, that's for sure. How did you end up at the bottom of a cave with no clothes, Outsider?"

I try to rub the flush out of my cheeks to no avail. "I can tell you the complete and honest truth, though I suspect you will find it unbelievable. Even so, please try to understand I have no motive to create such an outlandish story."

"Try me," she says.

So, I do. I tell her about dying, about waking up here, about this body decisively *not* being the body I died in, about Echo, and the Dungeon Core, and then finding her here now.

I shrug helplessly. "That's the long and short of it."

Mirzayael regards me with a strange, thoughtful look. "Well, you're right," she says. "That is an outlandish story that's entirely unbeliev-able."

I laugh. Fair enough. "I guess I should have expected that. Will you allow me to provide some supporting evidence?"

She eyes me suspiciously. "What do you have in mind?"

"Well," I say, "Echo tells me your name is Mirzayael."

The woman stiffens. "You're a mind reader."

"No!" I object. Then I remember Psionic Touch. "Oh, well, I sup-pose yes, actually. But I'm only able to do that with physical contact."

Shockingly, this appears to do little to unseat her suspicion of me. "What do you really want?" she demands. "Why did you come here?"

I sigh. "I don't think you'll find anything I say to be satisfying. But it's all true. I'm lost and just as stuck as you are." I tip my head at the boulder behind her. "If you don't mind my asking, how did you end up in this position?"

Mirzayael glowers at me. "Cave in. Some several hours ago. An earthquake, perhaps. I don't suppose you were *in this world* when that happened?"

Her last words are spoken with clear skepticism and mockery, but I'm shaken nonetheless. I *was* in this world. In fact, I was probably the cause. Very likely, the rockslide that ended up here originated in my chamber when the Dungeon Core was breaking me out. She's injured and trapped because of me.

I swallow down my guilt. "I was here, yes. And I'm sorry you were caught in all of this. If you aren't willing to believe me when I say I have good intentions, would you let me show you instead? I believe I can free your leg from that rock."

Mirzayael glares at me for a moment longer. Then she gathers all of her legs beneath her and staggers to her feet. She hisses in pain, leaning on her spear as she straightens. After taking a moment to recover, she looks down her nose at me and sizes me up.

With me on the floor, and her standing at her full height, she towers over me. Even without her armor and weapon, she'd be a terrifying foe. After regarding me for a moment longer, she finally lets out a grunt.

"Fine," she snaps, scuttling the rest of her legs to the side to expose her pinned limb. "While I have my doubts about your claims—how you ended up here *and* that you have some way to free me—you seem to pose little threat without any weapons... or clothes to conceal them beneath."

Thanks for the reminder. But she's offering an olive branch, and I'll certainly take it.

"Thank you." I push myself to my feet. "This should only take a moment."

Cautiously, I step forward, keenly aware I'm now entering Mirzayael's spear range. She watches me, all eight eyes unblinking, hand tight around her weapon, but she doesn't move as I offer a tight-lipped smile and step around her. I kneel by the boulder to inspect the pinch point.

"If you try anything," she says, voice unsettlingly quiet, "I will part your head from your torso before you're able to blink."

"I believe you will," I say. "And I'd much prefer you wouldn't, for both our sakes."

I move slowly, so Mirzayael can track my every move, and lay a hand on the boulder. Then I activate Psionic Touch, focusing on the Core.

It bursts happily into my mind. Mana? Is it time for more mana? It's starving!

Yes, I think, pressuring it to focus. *I've got some more mana for you. I also have another job. Think you can dissolve some of this stone for me?*

What stone? It can't see anything. It needs more mana! It's blind! And so, so hungry. Why aren't I feeding it? Please, it will *die.*

I raise a skeptical eyebrow. *You seem to have hibernated in here for quite some time before I came along. I don't think a few hours without mana is killing you.*

The Core grumbles at this. What job? What does it need to do for me?

Let's see if you can sense a bit of our surroundings with some mana, I think, offering up access to my stores.

[Mana transfer initiated,] Echo reports.

The Core excitedly takes it in, and as it does so, I notice a change taking place on my map overlay. I mentally zoom in on the map, blowing up the image of this room.

While the map might be three dimensional within my mind, it is, at the end of the day, still a map. The diagram shows the room we're in, and even the boulder blocking the passage, but there's no marking or representation of Mirzayael or I. Just the stone. As I watch, the revealed radius of the room expands, seeping over the boulder in the passage, and even a few feet down the hall beyond.

Only the rock, I urge the Core, keenly aware of its destructive interpretation of the last request I gave it. *Perhaps could you just dissolve the boulder in this passage?*

The Core feels a little put out. Oh, alright. That's not very fun. Really, though, when can it get more mana? This is nothing! It needs a bigger source. Much bigger. Much, much, much, much, much—

The boulder, please.

Heaving what appears to be a gemstone's equivalent of a mental sigh, the Dungeon Core gets to work. In the Map Interface, I can see bits and pieces of the stone light up, like individual cubes of rock have been selected and highlighted in an 8-bit computer interface. Then the graphics break apart and fall away. Beneath my hand, the stone turns into perfect cubes of sand, hissing between my fingers.

Not all of it, though. Some grains don't cascade to the floor, but appear to vanish into thin air. I raise my eyebrows.

Is that you? I ask the Core. *Are you doing that?*

The Dungeon Core mentally skitters away, like a dog caught with a bone it knows it shouldn't have. It only ate a little bit of it! It's so hungry. A little stone won't hurt anything!

*You can **eat** the rocks?* I ask, baffled.

Of course! Rocks are its favorite thing.

I shake my head. *Next time, ask me first,* I tell it. But it appears consuming the rocks—whatever that truly means—didn't cost any more mana than breaking them up, so at least there's no downside to it sneaking in its geological snack. And this revelation does unlock new possibilities. It appears the Dungeon Core can do more than just deconstruct its surroundings. What else might it be capable of?

As Mirzayael's leg comes free, I pull my hand away and take a cautious step back.

She gasps with pain as her leg shifts from the relieved pressure. The revealed limb is crushed almost entirely flat, and immediately begins to ooze a thick, black paste. Mirzayael stumbles away from the passage with an anguished cry, leaning against a nearby wall as she steadies her breath.

The Core, meanwhile, is still dissolving the rest of the boulder, happily chewing away at the stone. My mana is rapidly plummeting, however, and soon I'll be left without a way to speak with it—not to mention, without a light—so I cut off my flow of mana.

That's enough, I tell the Core. The boulder is mostly gone by now anyway, reduced to a pile of sand of a noticeably smaller mass.

The Core tries to object, but without my mana flowing into it, it doesn't have a choice. It pouts, clinging to its last little reserve of unspent mana. This isn't much at all. What is it supposed to do with this? I still am holding onto so much more mana I could give! Why not just a little bit—

I end Psionic Touch, turning my attention to Mirzayael instead.

The injured leg looks bad. Mirzayael has let it droop limply on the ground behind her, and I'm unsure if that's because she doesn't want to move it, or can't. Just below the joint—ah, knee?—the leg is entirely collapsed, crushed flat and shattered into several jagged fragments that leak a viscous blood. I worry the entire leg will come off if too much more force is applied. As I speculate on the extent of the damage, I apparently trigger another one of Echo's Checks.

[HP: 181/240]

I'm pretty sure that's lower than it was before.

"We need to get you to a doctor," I say. "That injury seems grave."

"I will be fine," Mirzayael hisses through clenched teeth. "I am Captain of the Guard. I've trained for worse."

"You won't be able to do much guarding if you bleed out," I say. "Come, we need to get you to someone who can help, as quickly as we're able." I step toward the passage, now largely clear from rubble. "Is your city in this direction?"

Her spear whistles through the air, snapping to a stop inches from my face and barring my way. "I cannot allow outsiders access to our town. It is my duty."

"You won't be able to stop me if you're unconscious from blood loss," I point out. "And given you're the first sign of life I've found in these tunnels, I'm not going anywhere either. You can let me help you make it back to your town, and I can finally get some food and water, whatever the consequences of my arrival may be, or we can both sit here until you kill me, or you pass out. Now choose quickly." I grimace. "Although I'd rather prefer if you chose the option where you don't kill me."

To my surprise, Mirzayael's grimace shifts into a pained grin. She coughs out a strained laugh. "You are a strange phoenix." The spear tip lowers, and then she turns it around to use as a walking stick. Mirzayael jerks her head toward me. "Alright. Help me get through the passage."

Relieved, I clamber out of her way, scattering a portion of the sand in my haste. Mirzayael limps toward the tunnel, leaning on her spear as she carefully steps over the remains of the boulder. Her injured leg drags behind her, scraping over the stone and sand until she needs to hoist it over the pile of sand.

"Here," I offer, coming up behind her. "I can help lift it. It's going to hurt, however."

"I can handle pain," she growls.

No one should have to handle this kind of pain. And there's only so much anyone can really tolerate, no matter what they claim. I doubt voicing any of this would improve Mirzayael's mood, however, so instead I just say, "Alright."

Picking up her leg will require me to extinguish my Spark. I'll have to rely on the Map Interface to track my surroundings, then. But when I snuff out my light, I find there's a distant glimmer of blue at the far end of the tunnel. Not much, but enough to travel by.

I bend down to lift the end of her leg. The feet end in a bristle of tiny claws, so I grab halfway down her leg, away from the injury, but enough to give leverage. The chitinous material is smooth and cold, as firm as a rock beneath my grasp. It truly must have taken tremendous force to cause such damage.

"Here I go," I warn her, lifting the limb slowly upward.

Mirzayael screams through pressed lips, stumbling forward and over the remains of the boulder as I hurry to keep pace. On the other side I don't lower the leg back down. It would be worse to drag it, I think—though I am certainly no doctor. At least, not of the medical variety.

"Keep going," I urge. "I'll carry it like this for as long as you need."

"Keep it still," she snaps through clenched teeth. "Stay steady."

"I'll do my best."

Each of us step cautiously, trying to match the other's speed, as we make our way down the tunnel. As much as I can, I try to snatch glimpses of our surroundings. Not only is the tunnel man-made—(ah, I suppose that term might not apply here. Sentient-creature made? Artificial, let's say.) Not only is the tunnel artificial, it's carved with old, weathered patterns and images. I can't make out the subject of the murals in the dim light—only the occasional vague suggestion of a wing or claw. But I feel there are ancient stories here, carved into the walls. At some point, I'd desperately love to come back.

The faint blue light grows closer, and as we approach the end of the tunnel, a strange feeling of anticipation stirs in me. I don't know where we're going. I haven't been here before. Yet, that same sense of familiarity when I'd found the Dungeon Core flutters through me now. I grasp at it, trying to pinpoint its source, but it slips through my fingers, evasive as a breeze, and then is gone once more. Even so, I keep glancing toward that growing blue light, wondering what it could mean.

We step out into a giant chamber. At least I think it's giant—the way sound reverberates around the cave tells me this is the biggest space I've set foot in, yet. The source of the blue glow is a spot on the wall near the tunnel entrance. I do a double take when I realize it's some sort of circular design like an alchemic circle.

What is that? I ask Echo. *Ah. Check?*

[Check: Spell circle for a simple Glow spell. Mana remaining: 15. Time remaining: 3 hours.]

I tip my head. A design that can be used to cast a spell. *Can it be recharged?*

[Affirmative. The quantity of mana imbued in the circle determines the duration of the spell.]

Amazing! Like a battery. That's incredibly useful. *Would I be able to imbue it with mana, too?*

[As the requirement for this spell does not have any particular affinity requirements, affirmative, anyone may be able to activate the spell circle.]

My mind swirls with the possibilities. That means I'm not limited to just the three spells I innately know. I should be able to do other spells as well, as long as I can find or replicate these circles. Fascinating! This magic certainly does seem to have some concrete rules to it.

Maybe not so different from laws of physics after all. Just a new logical framework I need to learn.

We keep close to the wall as we traverse the chamber, our way lit with more spell circles carved into the rock. Their glow is dim and they only illuminate our path for a few meters before petering out into the dark. Opposite from the wall, I can almost feel that giant, sprawling cavern like the presence of a beast. From the way our breaths and scraping footsteps echo back down at us in a parade of delayed susurrations, I know it's not empty. There's some structure that's scattering our echoes about. I'm dying to investigate, but *not* dying comes first. I need to make it to Mirzayael's town so I can finally get some water, a bite to eat, and begin to take stock of my situation.

Half bent over as I carry Mirzayael's maimed leg, my back begins to ache in protest. Ah, back pains, how I haven't missed you. In fact, since arriving on this world, in this body, I've felt better all around. No cracking joints or tight muscles. I feel rejuvenated. Fresh. It's nice.

It's just so strange that it comes with a new body and gender. I mean... I suppose I'm not sure about that last part. I lived my whole life as a man. I fathered a child. And mentally, I don't feel any different about who I am now, no matter how different this body is. So that means I am still a man, right?

But this body is female. And strangely, I don't feel any shock or repulsion over that. If anything, the harpy physiology feels much more peculiar to me. So does that mean it's the body or the mind that determines one's gender? Or some amount of both?

I puzzle over this thought that I'd never really had any reason to think about before. There had been a couple of gay kids working at my office. I'm sure they would have had some ideas on the subject. Maybe I should have tried to speak with them more.

Maybe I should have tried to speak with my coworkers in general, more.

Too late for that now. I suppose this is an enigma I will need to solve for myself.

"Here," Mirzayael abruptly says.

I look up and find we're standing before a wall. Nothing of note. Just a blank face of stone.

Yet Mirzayael steps through it anyway. I awkwardly lurch forward in surprise, still trying to keep her leg steady, as the wall rapidly swallows the front half off the arachnoid. I instinctively lean back as her forward progress draws me toward the rock face as well. But my hands vanish into the stone without so much as a whisper. In another step, my arms, feet, and head all pass inside. My vision goes dark for only a moment.

Then warm light bursts into existence all around me, and a notification on my map blinks in the corner of my vision.

For the first time, some textual overlay has appeared.

[Fyreneth's Keep,] it reads. [City of the Forsaken.]

Chapter Five

CITY OF THE FORSAKEN

The first thing I notice, strangely enough, is all the mushrooms. Before now the caves had been barren, empty of any sign of life—save Mirzayael, I suppose. But the humidity is immediately apparent in this new space, and I'm met with a sudden urge to wipe off glasses I no longer have. In fact, the scene before me is crystal clear; it seems glasses are something I no longer require.

Mushrooms blanket the walls and floor, the source of the cavern's light. Thousands, *millions* of them litter every surface, filling the chamber with a turquoise bioluminescent glow. Some are as small as a grain of rice, while others are nearly the size of a watermelon. They even spot the ceiling like distant stars.

We're standing at the rise of a shallow basin, within which is nestled a small town. The houses look carved from stone, like rough cut gems, and the flora grow all over them. At the far end of the village is a waterfall—if you can call it that—trickling down the wall and casting a wavering reflection over the nearby houses. There are maybe a hundred buildings all told, with a couple dark paths cutting through the fluorescent ground. A handful of figures mill about, though they're too distant for me to make out any details.

"Mir!" A voice cuts through the quiet murmur of the cave.

I glance around for the source of the voice and find a figure hurrying over from a field of strange plants. Ferns maybe? Although I've never seen ferns turn yellow and light up before.

The appearance of the individual rushing our way takes me a moment to comprehend. At first glance he appears to be wearing the furs of a spotted snow leopard over his large, muscular frame. When he reaches us, however, it's clear the white and black fur is very much a part of him. I skim his stats with an abbreviated Check.

[Nek: Level 28 Felis Arctic Warrior.]

The man's ears—*cat ears*—flatten as he catches sight of me. "Who is this?" he asks, his fur puffing up. I'm beginning to wonder if my initial impression of muscle was just due to an obscene amount of long cat hair. His eyes shift to Mirzayael's leg. "You're hurt!"

"Astutely observed," Mirzayael grunts. "And she's an outsider. She helped me escape a rockslide and get back here. Now are you going to stand there posturing all day, or will you go fetch Lord Beryl?"

She. It's such a foreign experience to be referred to as a woman. I instinctively open my mouth to correct her, but the protest dies on my tongue. Strangely, it doesn't feel wrong to be called *she*. Instead, it sends an unfamiliar, warm flutter through my stomach. I frown, unsure what to make of that.

Nek looks me over once more, his ears twitching curiously. "A harpy?" he asks, looking between me and Mirzayael. "Where did she—"

"My leg, Nek!" Mirzayael snaps.

Nek's ears flip back and he bobs his head in apology. "I'll be quick." He lopes down the trail toward the town, a fluffy white tail snapping in his wake.

With a hissed sigh, Mirzayael sinks to the ground. If she can't even make it the rest of the way to the village, she must have been about ready to drop our whole way here. I carefully help lay her injured leg down in a position that I hope puts the least amount of strain on it. Then I awkwardly stand by her side, wings wrapped around my torso, wondering what will come next.

"It's Mirzayael," she says abruptly. "Not Mir. Don't call me that."

"Oh," I say, realizing she'd never actually introduced herself. I'd forgotten I'd sniped that info from Echo. "Sure. Of course."

A moment passes in silence.

"Well?" she speaks up again. "What am I supposed to call you? Besides Outsider."

"It's..." My response withers away.

Faber, of course, is my name. But I've never liked it. My parents, who read too much sci-fi, named me after the Fahrenheit 451 character, and when I was old enough to read it, I didn't entirely find the parallels flattering.

I suppose if I were to choose a new name for myself, now would be the time to do it, and no one would be the wiser. But which name? I spent years as a young boy daydreaming about changing it to something else, but nothing ever felt quite right. So Faber it remained.

"It's... a work in progress," I eventually say.

Mirzayael snorts. "Who says their name is a work in progress?"

"I suppose I do." I give a pained smile. "You may call me what you like."

"Alright, Outsider." Mirzayael shakes her head. "If you say so."

Nek comes hurrying back a few minutes later, trailed by a much slower figure. Much stouter, too.

[Beryl: Level 46 Dwarf Alchemic Healer.]

If I had to estimate, the woman appears roughly three hundred years old. Her skin is so dark and wrinkled it might have been tree bark, and her hair and beard—braided and wrapped around her waist like a belt—is as white as ice. Her eyes are sunken into her face so deeply, I'm not even sure if they're open.

I step out of the way as she approaches Mirzayael. The dwarf passes a hand over the wound and tuts to herself.

"This injury will not heal itself," she says, her voice surprisingly strong in spite of her prehistoric appearance. She *tsks* again. "I will stop the bleeding here. The rest must be addressed in my hut."

"Do it," Mirzayael said. "Whatever needs to be done."

The dwarf crouches down—though, really, she doesn't need to crouch far to reach Mirzayael's leg—and green light blooms from her hand. I watch with interest as a few points of Mirzayael's HP are restored. *Only* a few.

"Nek," Beryl says, beckoning him over. "Help her to my house." She looks at me next as Nek begins to pull Mirzayael to her feet. The woman shoos him off, using the butt of her spear to stand. Nek then wraps an arm around the arachnoid's torso and lifts, pulling pressure off her bad side, and together they begin to limp slowly down the slope.

"So you're the outsider," Beryl says.

I bow my head respectfully, suspecting the old dwarf is likely to be in some position of power within this community. "I apologize for intruding on your town uninvited. I wish to seek shelter here."

Beryl snorts. "Mirzayael brought you here. Seem plenty invited to me. What are you seeking shelter from, fledgling?"

"From, ah, the cave," I say, feeling a little embarrassed with that answer. Not exactly the most threatening antagonist to be fleeing.

Beryl *hmphs*. "Got lost in the caverns, did you?"

"Yes."

"And before that?"

I grimace, knowing Beryl's as likely to be as skeptical as Mirzayael had been. "There is no before that."

The dwarf grunts, stroking her beard. Then she turns away, gesturing for me to follow. "Come, harpy. We will sort through your appearance later. I have a patient to prepare for. You will stay out of the way until then. Understood?"

"Understood," I say, relieved to have passed the initial barrier to being let into this society. I follow after her.

Shelter, water, food, I think, looking around at the fields of mushrooms and glacial waterfall that decorates the chamber. I did it. I'm no longer in immediate mortal peril. Finally, I can allow myself to think about what comes next.

And also, what came before.

I inhale a slow breath of air that smells like earth and ice. I let it out again, warm and level.

I'm in another world. Earth is a relic of the past. The mechanism of how I got here I still don't understand, but it's clear enough that getting back isn't an immediate option. And perhaps it's an option I'd be uninterested in regardless, if not for one specific factor.

My daughter. Little Caroline. God, I wish I'd been there for her more. I wish I'd spent more time with her. One weekend a month was not nearly enough. Even though I felt her growing more distant from me, thinking about her now makes my heart squeeze with an acute pain and summons a prickling to my eyes. I blink rapidly, bottling the tears away, but the heartache remains. The idea of never seeing her again is eviscerating. I wish I'd had one last moment with her. I wish I'd been able to tell her how proud I am of her. How sorry I am that I wasn't a more present father. I wish I'd been able to say goodbye.

I take a shuddering breath in as I wipe my eyes. I let it out, clearing my throat and swallowing down the pit that's become lodged there. She is likely better off without me. If I could do it all over again, I'd spend more time being married to her mother and less time being married to my job. But time only moves in one direction. Caroline can just focus on her studies now. No more barely tolerated weekends spent at her estranged father's place. God, I hope she moves on. I hope she doesn't mourn me for long. I hope she lives a full, happy life.

And now, I have this life to think about. This new, very different life. Will I be able to find the happiness here that seemed to elude me in the last? The self-doubt in me says *no*. Despite the new body, I am still the same mind, and that was ultimately the source of all my problems before.

But the hope in me says *yes*. You are not the person you were yesterday. You are the culmination of all your experiences. You can grow. You can become someone new.

"Outsider."

My head jerks up, pulled from my thoughts, and I come to an abrupt stop before running into Beryl. The dwarf woman, who's stopped in the middle of the path, is looking up at me with a frown. I think I can make out the reflection of two critical eyes buried within the folds of skin, but they vanish as quickly as they're revealed.

"Sorry," I say. "Is there something you need?"

"This is my house," Beryl says. We're standing before an opening in the stone, built into the wall of the cave itself. It appears chiseled out of the rock, but the mushrooms growing over its surface indicate it's been here long before Beryl. As I'm examining the structure, Nek steps out the open doorframe, pushing a tattered curtain aside.

"I will go help Mirzayael now," she says to both of us. "Outsider, go with Nek. He will give you clothes."

"Oh," I say faintly, my wings curling around me at the reminder. I can feel another blush burning its way into my cheeks.

If Nek is flustered by my nakedness, he doesn't show it. He looks me up and down with a frown. "I'm not sure she can be trusted. We don't know anything about her."

Beryl waves him off, hobbling into her house. "She won't be any less trustworthy with clothes on."

"But..." Nek starts. But the curtain swings back down into place, and Beryl has left us both outside, clearly putting an end to the conversation.

Nek grumbles out a sigh. "Alright then. Hurry up. And don't try anything funny, now."

I can only bob my head in acknowledgement as I try to keep up, the felis beating a rapid pace through town.

Down here in the valley, the air is chilly. I restart my Spark as we hurry through the streets, keeping the comforting light just before my chest to help warm my arms and face as we walk. Other figures stop as we pass and begin to poke their heads out of doorways. It seems there are not nearly enough people for the houses we pass, but word of an outsider must be spreading fast, because more and more faces appear in windows, and whispers chase us through the street.

Echo identifies a few other dwarves like Beryl and felis like Nek, but there are other species here, too. More arachnoids, which I am still making my best effort not to be creeped out by, and briefly, I catch a glimpse of one lizard-like face peering out a window, belonging to something called a dracid, but they don't seem as common as the others. Such a strange, diverse mix of creatures! And not a one of them human.

Nek stops outside a building, larger than most, and pulls the curtain in the doorframe aside. He tosses a frown back toward me, then does a double-take when he notices my fire.

"What is that?" he demands. I'm not sure if his tone is angry, awed, or somehow both. "Fire magic?"

"Ah, yes, I suppose so," I say. "Sorry. I'll put it out. I don't intend to catch the drapes on fire." I snuff out my Spark.

"Not wind magic?" he asks, eyebrows still raised.

"Sorry?" I say, unsure what he's getting at.

He just shakes his head. "Follow me. Quickly now." He beckons me inside.

The building is dark, humid and very faintly warmer than the air outside. A spread of glowing mushrooms on the ceiling provides the majority of the light, though there's also a smoldering fireplace toward the back. In the middle of the room is a giant pile of cloth and blankets, at least twenty feet across, which is where Nek takes me. He prods around for a moment, then pulls a cloak free to hand off to me. I take the clothes, awkwardly shrugging it around my back; this attire was clearly not designed for someone with wings. As I'm struggling to make the thing comfortable, the pile of blankets moves.

I take a startled step back as I hear a snuffling and catch a glimpse of scales. I call on Echo for a Check.

[Yana, level 16 dracid,] she reports. But she doesn't stop there. [Linimus, level 14 dracid. Jotal, level 19 dracid.] And the list keeps going. Dozens of dracid, all piled into one giant heap, buried beneath scraps of fabric.

"Are they okay?" I ask, tugging on my cloak as it snags on my wing.

"They're in brumation," Nek says. Grabbing my cloak from me, he pokes a claw through the fabric, then rips two long slits through the back of my attire. I stand still as he helps pull it around my wings. "The cold is hard on them, so they are only active about half the year. They take turns on who rests when. The best us non-dracid can do is try to keep them warm with the heat from those stones." He nods to the back of the room where'd I'd noticed the smoldering fire burning. Upon closer inspection, rocks are clustered around the edge of the pit, likely warming up, while more lay scattered across the ground around the pile of dracid.

"That doesn't sound very efficient," I note.

Nek only grunts noncommittally, finishing with the makeshift bathrobe he's made for me. I pull the front of the cloak around my waist, fixing it in place with a frayed strip of the cloth.

"Would a better fire help?" I ask. "I could build it up with my magic."

"No," Nek says. "We could build it higher, but it would burn through all our fuel. This is as much as we can spare at any time."

"I don't require fuel," I say. "What about heating the rocks directly with my flame? That shouldn't cut into your supply."

Even in the dim lighting, I can tell Nek is looking at me strangely. He's silent for a long moment before he answers.

"You are an outsider. Why would you do that for us?"

"They need help," I say. "It's just the right thing to do. May I?"

Slowly, he nods.

I crouch down near the edge of the pile of dracid, picking up one of the flat stones that lay scattered about. It's long since grown cold, and my heart pangs in sympathy. I can't imagine this pile of people, sleeping on rocks, huddled together to save every calorie of warmth, is content to live like this. What horrid circumstances must have driven them to live this way—if you can call it living at all?

I coax my Spark back to life. The little fire blooms a halo of warmth around me, casting faint, flickering shadows along the wall. Some of the slumbering dracid stir at the glow. I hold the stone to my flame, starting the long slow process of warming the rock.

After a few minutes of waiting, I realize I'm going about this all wrong. I pull more rocks over and stack them close together, then plunge my Spark into the midst of them. This way I'll be able to do several at once. Blaze might be faster, but it's also not sustainable. I wait, my flame flickering inside the stone pyramid, as the rocks begin to heat.

More dracid stir as time passes, my fire's heat radiating outside its circle of rocks, even if only barely. One wiggling pile of cloth squirms away from the rest, and when a blue-scaled snout pokes itself from the blanket's folds, I'm met with the small, curious gaze of a child. I offer them a smile, but they just watch me with round, blinking eyes, reflecting my flickering flame. After a few minutes, I take one of the smallest stones from the pile and roll it around my hand. It's warm, but not hot: or maybe that's just my fire resistance talking. Still, it seems safe to the touch. I hold it out to the child.

"Here. Try this," I say.

The dracid wriggles forward, snatching the stone from my grasp. They clutch it tightly between their claws, then vanish back into the dogpile. I replace the rock I'd given them with another, and keep the fire going.

Eventually, another dracid takes note of what I'm doing. I pass them a warm stone as well. Gradually, more curious heads poke out from beneath the cloths. The pile is shifting as more come awake.

A faint murmuring of hushed conversations slowly begins to hum through the room.

"Praise Fyreneth," one dracid says when I give them a stone.

Fyreneth. I think I saw that name before. I check my map to be certain: sure enough, the town is labeled Fyreneth's Keep, City of the Forsaken. I wonder who Fyreneth was that they got a city named after them, are still considered with positive regard, and yet also managed to become Forsaken.

"Praise Fyreneth," the next dracid repeats when I give them a stone. And the next dracid as well. Whispers of the name begin to permeate the cavern. By now, most of the lizard-like people have woken up and are murmuring to one another. Of all the words spoken, Fyreneth is the most common, like bubbles rising to the top of a stew. But there are other words that are occasionally repeated, too. Returned. Awakened.

Reborn.

A shiver runs down my back, and I try to rid myself of it with a shoulder roll, already stiff from sitting in one place for so long.

"Nek?" I ask. "Who's Fyreneth?"

The felis is quiet. When I look at him, the uncertainty and hostility I'd felt from him before is gone. Instead, he's watching me with an awed look.

"I think," he says slowly, "you might be."

Chapter Six

THE FORSAKEN

"What are you talking about?" I ask. "I'm not Fyreneth. I don't even know who that is."

Nek still watches me with a reverent look. "Her return has been prophesied for generations. She swore her death was not final. That she would return again."

I shake my head. "You're not making any sense. I don't know what you're talking about."

"She was a phoenix harpy, just like you," Nek insists. "Her affinity was fire instead of air. And she wielded an artifact so powerful, it drew the wrath of the gods themselves. An artifact which could shape the nature of the world."

I glance at the Dungeon Core skeptically. It's broken some rocks apart, but it can't really shape the nature of the world, can it?

[Affirmative,] Echo says, answering my thoughts. [One of the Dungeon Core's many features allows for the shaping and restructuring of material.]

I blink, then surreptitiously tuck the Dungeon Core beneath a sleeve of my cloak. Alright, maybe the Dungeon Core is some powerful artifact. But prophecies? Gods? It all sounds like myth to me.

Then again, I hadn't believed in magic or reincarnation either, and look where that's gotten me. Perhaps I should try to keep an open mind to their beliefs. Though, the idea that I am some reborn legend of old is still too much for me to swallow.

"I can't be the only phoenix harpy in the world," I say instead, turning my focus back on the rocks I'm still warming for the dracid. "Surely you don't go around calling every one you meet Fyreneth."

"No," Nek agrees. "But you're the only one I've ever seen."

I frown, staring into my flames. "Are there no other harpies here?"

"No," Nek says. "The caves were too much for them. They left generations ago, and haven't been seen since."

"Seems like they should have taken the dracid with them," I note as another shuffles forward, holding his hand out for a warmed stone. I pass one over, and he nods his head respectfully before submerging back into the pile of blankets and dozing dracid.

"They tried," Nek says. "Many have tried. But the trek is inhospitable, beasts prevalent, and the Jorrians still see us as a threat. At least the harpies were able to escape due to their flight, but the rest of us have been forced to remain. The last attempted expedition across the ice was when Mir and I were only children."

"Ice?" Jorrians? Escape? There's clearly much to learn. "I don't suppose you have a history textbook I could borrow?"

Nek shakes his head. "Lord Beryl might have a few scrolls, however texts have become very rare. I'm told there's a library in the Catacombs, though I've never seen it myself. I don't think much would have survived all this time."

This explanation only has my head spinning with even more questions. "Nek, I'm afraid I'll be asking a lot of very basic questions of you, if you'd humor me," I say. "You see, I don't even know where I am. This city—this *world*—is all new to me. About the only thing

I have been able to figure out is that we're somewhere underground, and certainly not on the planet I came from."

"Quite an interesting claim," Beryl says.

I twist around to find the dwarf woman standing in the doorway.

"Mirzayael told a similar tale," she says. "I'll decide what to make of that myself."

Beryl looks me up and down—or at least, I assume she does, given the tip of her head—and grunts in satisfaction. "See you've got a scrap of clothes now. Good. We'll make you something more fitting later. Come with me."

"Oh," I say, looking between Beryl and the dracid. "But I was helping to warm rocks..."

"The rocks aren't going anywhere," Beryl says. "Now come on."

I hurriedly push the remaining half-warmed rocks toward the nearest dracid, who murmur their thanks. Then I scramble to catch up and follow Beryl out of the room. Nek is already ahead, speaking in quiet tones to the dwarf.

"Fyreneth?" Beryl repeats loudly, causing Nek's ears to go flat. "Poppycock. You better not go stirring any rumors up, now. I know how you like to gossip."

Nek glances back at me as I hurry to get within earshot. "But she bears the signs—"

"Bah!" Beryl waves him off. "Make yourself useful with those claws of yours, not your tongue. The Glowcap family is low on meat. Go hunt some skitters for them."

Shoulders hunched, Nek slinks off without another word. I watch him go, curious, but more interested in what Beryl has to say.

"Is Mirzayael doing alright?" I ask.

"She'll be fine," Beryl says. "Such a fuss over one broken leg. I've healed it up as best I could and sent her off to rest. All she needs now is time."

"Oh, good," I say, relieved.

"Of course, she lost the leg, so it'll take some getting used to walking without," Beryl adds.

"What?" I cry. "It doesn't sound like she's fine!"

Beryl grunts. "She's got seven more to spare."

I must look horrified, because the dwarf cracks a smile.

"Mirzayael is tough, and she doesn't like being coddled. I doubt one missing leg will hold her back. Don't worry about her; she wouldn't want you to, anyway."

The dwarf turns and keeps walking, and after a moment's hesitation, I follow after. I'm still not quite sure what to make of Beryl. Or anyone here, for that matter. But there's only one way to learn more.

Beryl's house is much smaller than the dracid chamber, but better lit. The fluorescent mushrooms that act as natural lights are also accompanied by a small fire, which is sitting beneath a stovetop covered in all sorts of jars and simmering pans and herbs. A few bloodied rags are piled in the corner. Thankfully, I don't see Mirzayael's leg anywhere.

Beryl gestures for me to take a seat on a cushion across from a raised stone which I now recognize as a table. The dwarf mixes some of the herbs and spices, tossing them in a pot of boiling water, then portions the resulting concoction out into two clay mugs. She sets one before me as she takes a seat opposite with a long, pained grunt. She lifts her own cup after she sits. I give mine a cautious sniff. A sharp earthy sting fills my nose.

[Check,] Echo says, answering my guilty conscience. [Mugroot brew. Affect: minor calming of nerves.]

Just a kind of tea, then. Not trying to drug me. That's nice to know.

"You're causing quite the stir in town," Beryl says, taking a drink from her mug. I also try a sip, and find the drink has a delightful toasted flavor. "Nek is just the start of it."

"He thinks I'm Fyreneth reborn," I say. "Or that's what he told me. But I assure you, I have no idea who this person even is, or even where—"

"Yes, yes." Beryl waves off my words. "I know all this. Mirzayael filled me in on what you told her. Quite the claim."

"It's entirely understandable if you don't believe me," I say.

"Belief," Beryl repeats, thoughtful. "Irrelevant. My belief won't change your reality. You are here now. You are an outsider. You know little of our world. Correct?"

"Right," I agree. "And I'd very much like to—"

"I will explain things," Beryl says, interrupting me so abruptly I'm not even sure if she heard me start speaking in the first place. "And you will listen quietly."

I open my mouth to say 'okay,' then close it again and simply nod. I clutch the mug between my hands, taking another sip.

"This world is Lusio," Beryl begins. "And this region is the Polar South. We are on the outskirts of the Jorrian Kingdom. Once, this community was a kingdom of our own.

"Long ago, we were a small yet flourishing nation. It's unclear where many of our ancestors came from, however what drew them together is certain enough. A charismatic and powerful sorcerer, Fyreneth, promised a land where every creature had a voice, no matter their heritage or abilities. It is said she raised her castle from the tundra between two moons, growing from the earth itself like a tree blooming from a seed. At first, Jorria was wary of this new kingdom. However, Fyreneth brokered an accord, offering many precious stones and metals for trade with anyone who would treat with her. The amity she fostered with Jorria brought incredible wealth to the country. For close to a century, she ruled in peace, and the kingdoms flourished."

Beryl pauses to take a long drink from her mug, frowning at a spot on the table.

"However, it did not last. It is uncertain if she was betrayed, or if it merely took so long for the gods to notice. But the gods did, eventually, notice. Overnight, their champions appeared on our doorstep. They claimed our kingdom was founded on heresy; our wealth and prosperity bought through the abilities of a cursed relic. They decided our civilization was to be destroyed. Every evidence of the relic and its stamp on the world erased from existence.

"Fyreneth fought them all on her own, for no other mortals could stand against the gods' chosen few. But even she could not possibly hope to win against such odds. The fight was merely to buy time. While she battled, her people slipped from the kingdom to take refuge in Jorria. Our allies, she thought. But at their gates, we were turned away. They declared us Forsaken by the gods and threw us back out onto the ice.

"Left no other choice, Fyreneth protected her people in the only way she knew how. In one last, desperate move, the kingdom was swallowed by the ice, entombed back into the earth from whence it had risen.

"As for the gods' champions... they were never seen again. Nor was Fyreneth. She gave her life to protect her people. Unfortunately, it was her magic and leadership that had kept her kingdom thriving. Without both, we began to wither."

Beryl sweeps a hand around the room. "Until we became what we are today. Some still venture out onto the ice, seeking to map a path that might lead to a more hospitable home. However, the Kingdom of

Jorria keeps a watchful eye out for any of our explorers—the Forsaken, they call us—preventing us from traveling far. Occasionally, they even come looking for us, hoping to root the last of us out once and for all. But our city remains hidden well enough that they've never been able to find a way down. Sometimes a select few make it into the caves, but they've always perished within the labyrinth before they had a chance to find our settlement. And so, caught between certain death and a slow one, we remain, and we wane."

Beryl takes another sip of her brew. "Which raises the question: How did *you* find your way to us? Especially, as it seems, you did not even know we were here."

I set my cup down, letting out a long breath. "This is all quite a lot to process at once. I am sincerely sorry for the hardships your people have faced. I never meant to intrude on your society or cause a disturbance. It's clear any outsiders at all are a deserved cause for caution and alarm."

I hesitate, then hold out my wrist, offering the Dungeon Core for Beryl to examine.

"To answer your question, this is how I found my way here. I discovered it when I woke up in this place. The stone—this Dungeon Core—provided a way for me to map out the tunnels and prevent myself from wandering in endless circles. Do you know what this is?"

The woman lightly touches the stone. She tips her head as if listening.

"There is a... presence here," she says. "I cannot understand it. But I feel it is trying to speak to me."

"I can speak with it," I say. "It also seems I've formed some sort of... *Pact* with the entity in there." I shift uncomfortably. "Is this why people thought I was Fyreneth reborn? This strange artifact, like the one in your legends?"

The Dungeon Core hasn't done anything near the scale of raising or sinking entire castles from the ground. Then again, it's only had the pittance of my mana to work with, and it *does* seem eager—and capable—of moving more earth than I've let it.

"I can see how that would fan the flames for someone like Nek," Beryl says, withdrawing her hand from the Core. "Although your species also is likely feeding the rumors."

I can feel a headache coming on. "Yes, Nek mentioned she was a harpy."

"A phoenix harpy, specifically," Beryl says. "Do you know what that means?"

I shake my head.

"Phoenix harpies cannot perform wind magic like the rest of the species," Beryl explains. "Instead, their affinity is fire. Phoenix harpies are rare; perhaps one in a hundred born with an affinity for fire instead of wind. Some consider this a handicap, as wind magic is needed for a harpy to achieve flight."

Aha! Now it all comes together. No wonder I found the wings insufficient for lift on their own. Of course magic is involved. If you could summon a wind, smooth the flow, alter the surrounding air pressures, who needs control surfaces? Receiving the answer to a question that had been nibbling at my engineering brain fills me with satisfaction. At the same time, I'm struck with disappointment; I'll never be able to fly, then.

"There is another thing about phoenix harpies," Beryl continues. "A belief which is largely considered superstition, but a belief that persists nevertheless. It is said that phoenix harpies have the ability to reincarnate. That some, with enough magic and willpower, may become reborn."

I shake my head. "Well that settles it. We can prove to everyone I am not Fyreneth, because I have none of her memories. My memories are from…" I trail off with a grimace.

"…From another life?" Beryl supplies. "That's what Mirzayael told me."

"Ah." I wrinkle my nose. "Yes, well, I do see how this looks."

The dwarf chuckles. "It is almost as though you are *trying* to impersonate our lost hero."

"No!" I object. "I swear, that was never my intention. This is all merely a series of extremely unfortunate coincidences."

Beryl regards me with a faint smile. "Perhaps."

I rub my face, trying to massage out the headache I can already feel forming. "Please believe me when I say I desperately do not wish to be mistaken for your founder."

Beryl cackles. "That much I do believe. If you'd been trying to impersonate her, you wouldn't be so insistent to the contrary. So now we arrive at the question: Where do we go from here?"

An excellent and fair question to ask. "I'm not sure," I admit. "I would love to stay in your village for now, if you'd allow it."

Beryl snorts derisively. "Of course. We are not Jorrians who would cast you back out into the desolate cold. If you have nowhere else to return to, then you are welcome here."

"Thank you," I say, bowing my head for emphasis. "I'm not sure how I can repay your hospitality, but I will try to be of use wherever I can. Offer my warmth, if you think it would help."

"Like you did with the dracid?" Beryl asks.

I shift, embarrassed. "I am now seeing how that entire encounter did not help disperse any rumors of me being Fyreneth. But yes, I believe my fire can be used for good here."

Beryl sets her empty mug down with a decisive clank. "Good then. More hands are always needed. You may continue to provide heating for the dracid chamber until we can find a more permanent place for you."

"Actually, I've been having some thoughts about that," I say, glancing at the Dungeon Core. It almost seems to shimmer excitedly in the flickering light. "I think I might have a way to make the heating in that chamber more efficient."

Echo said the Dungeon Core could not only alter the shape of rocks, but their structure. And if that implies the possibility of chemical alteration, then it opens the door for thermodynamic applications as well.

But if I'm right, making these changes will do nothing to convince the people here I'm not some ancient savior reborn. In fact, quite the opposite.

Chapter Seven

THERMODYNAMICS 101

Despite my eagerness to revisit the dracid chamber and investigate how I could improve the insulation, Beryl orders me to eat, drink, and rest first. I suppose that's fair. Weariness hangs heavy in my bones, and without a source of natural light, I've lost all sense of time. The water they offer me has a sharp mineral taste, and the food is some chopped form of mushrooms and other vegetables I'd seen growing throughout the town. It's bitter and far from filling, but I'm too hungry and tired to care. After I finish my meal, Nek finds me a repurposed storage shed to stay in—like the other houses, it's a small, roughly cut cave with only a few furs for decoration—and I almost immediately fall asleep.

Waking back up is disorienting. For a moment I don't understand where I am or what I'm looking at. Stone and glowing mushrooms overhead? Then I shift, and feel my wings beneath me, and it all comes flooding back.

Grief, wonder, disbelief, and fascination assail me all at once. How is this real? How has this become my body? Will I never see Caroline again? Magic. I can do magic. Was any of Fyreneth's myth true? And if so, do I now wield the same cursed artifact? This 'Dark Lord' role attached to my name has suddenly taken on a more sinister implication. But even if the Dungeon Core is cursed, can I still find a way to use it for good? It might be able to help the people here. The dracid—they should come first.

I disrupt my jumble of thoughts as I climb out from under a pile of furs to where a small basin of water has been left for me. I cup some into my hands—my strange, taloned hands—and quench my thirst, then splash a bit over my face to freshen up. The chill brings me fully awake. My reflection swims into view as the water stills once more, and it's only then I get my first good look at myself.

A young woman's face stares back at me. Well, young is relative, I suppose, but she certainly doesn't reflect the fifty years I lived as a human. Delicate feathers frame my face, and my eyes are yellow and intense, like a hawk's. I pinch my cheeks and stretch my skin: that's definitely me.

As I stand, the rest of the blankets fall away, and I immediately find myself shivering from the cold. Almost by instinct I call a Spark to my fingers, curling around the small flame as I warm myself. A minute later, the curtain that serves as the door to this tiny hut is pulled aside.

"Ah, you're awake," Nek says. "I thought I saw a light. How are you feeling?"

"Well, thank you." I stretch out my stiff wings as much as the cramped quarters will allow and crack my neck. "What time is it?"

"Late morning," Nek says.

"Really?" It feels early to me. My circadian rhythm must be really messed up. "How do you tell the time down here?"

"It's relative," Nek explains. "I couldn't even tell you where the sun is. We use rune circles to track time, all spelled to synchronize with each other; you'll see them on walls and in buildings. Are you hungry?"

I think about the bitter mushroom and lichen salad and decide hunger might be somewhat relative. "I can wait a bit. I'd like to return to the dracid chamber, if you'd allow me."

"Of course, Fyreneth," he says, holding the curtain open for me.

The name twists my stomach. "I don't think you should call me that," I say, ducking out the door. "It feels... fraudulent."

Nek frowns. "Do you have a different name you would prefer?"

I grimace. 'Faber' feels like it died with my body back on Earth. But I still haven't had time to think through what feels more right. What feels more like *me*.

"I'm not sure," I admit. "I suppose you can call me whatever you like—so long as it's not Fyreneth. I have no claim to that name."

He gestures to the spark of flame I'm still clutching to my chest. "Fire, then? You've come to us offering its warmth. It seems fitting to identify you that way."

I roll the name around in my mind, getting a taste for it. Feels a bit on the nose. But it's not an association I would be opposed to. If nothing else, it's acceptable as a stop-gap.

"Alright," I agree. "That will work for now."

[Name change accepted,] Echo pipes up. [Stat sheet updated.]

Nek grins, showing off an impressive array of feline teeth, then beckons for me to follow.

The dracid chamber is a little more active than I'd found it yesterday. Some of the people are sitting up, moth eaten rags wrapped around their shoulders. There are more stones on the firepit, around which a few dracid are huddled. Some are being passed back and forth between the flames and the dogpile of still sleeping dracid. A few look up at my approach.

"Fyreneth! You've returned."

I wince.

"She would prefer *Fire*," Nek emphasizes.

I give him a thankful smile. "I'm back," I tell the dracid. "And I'm here to help."

Several of the dracid mumble their thanks and begin to shuffle apart to clear a spot for me at the fire. I raise a hand to stay them.

"Not quite like that," I say. "I can help warm some more rocks for you, too. But I think there's a better long-term solution. May I?" I hold a hand out for one of the stones.

Several clawed hands shoot up, all offering me various rocks. I awkwardly choose the closest one. Then I activate my Psionic Touch.

Words burst into my mind with a dramatic cacophony of emotion. Ahhhhhhhh it's been so long! It thought I had died! It was left to wither, alone and without any mana to feed it or anyone to keep it company for seconds upon seconds upon seconds upon seconds upon seconds upon seconds—

Hush, I tell it. *I just had a nap. I'm back now.*

The Dungeon Core grumbles at this and radiates clear confusion over what a nap actually is or why that should explain anything.

Doesn't matter, I think. *Here's something you will understand.* I lightly tap the stone to the Dungeon Core. *What all can you tell me about this?*

A tasty rock! Can it eat it?

Not really what I'm going for, I think.

The Dungeon Core is disappointed. Can it at least taste it?

I pause at that. There's something deeper behind the meaning of 'taste' just like there had been something deeper behind the meaning of 'eat.' I could tell the latter was similar to what the Dungeon Core had done when it freed Mirzayael's leg. The stones vanished, like they were being digested. *Taste,* however...

Some sort of mental switch flips in my mind. Like when I first summoned the Map Interface from my Pact with the Core, I can feel there are other features available.

Alright, I tell the Core. *Go ahead and give it a taste.*

Abstract concepts flood my mind. At first, they're colored by the Dungeon Core's thoughts: Sour. Cold. Soft and crunchy. It's tasted a lot like it before.

But when I dig deeper, when I try to pry the information that's hidden beneath the descriptions, the analysis resolves into something more coherent.

[Substance: Limestone. Type: Quartzite.]

[Mass: 4.13 kilograms]

[Density: 2.65 grams per cubic centimeters]

[Thermal Conductivity: 3.2 watts per meter per degree Kelvin]

Ahhh, there we are. Now, I'm no geologist, but I do know the lower the thermal conductivity, the harder it is to get something to change temperature. Normally this wouldn't help me much, but I suspect my rock-eating friend might be able to fill in some gaps for me.

Core, I say, prodding its mind. *Have you tasted other rocks that are... warmer?* It takes me a moment to figure out how the Dungeon Core interprets thermal conductivity, but I try to steer its attention toward the metric I'm getting at.

Yes! It has tasted many, many types of rocks. Some warm, some cold, some that change slow or fast—

Great, I say, cutting off its rambling. *Then let's go through the ones you know.*

More information begins to flood through my mind, and the hints of a headache are beginning to pinch my skull. Trying to mitigate the flow of data, I filter for only the thermal conductivity of the different types of stone the Dungeon Core has categorized. After a moment, I find a number I'm looking for.

[Thermal Conductivity: 5.6 watts per meter per degree Kelvin]

[Substance: Dolomite.]

Not as high as I'd prefer, but it should result in the rocks heating up in half the time. That means they will also impart their energy twice as quickly, but it's the faster turn-over rate that I'm concerned with, since that appeared to be the bottleneck I witnessed the day before.

This one, I say to the Core. *Dolomite. Can you change this rock from quartzite into dolomite?*

The Dungeon Core gets very excited by this proposal. Oh yes! It loves playing with all the tiny dots. Pull them out, put them in other places. Breaking the little vibrating clusters is very satisfying. Sometimes there's bits and pieces left over and it likes to eat those.

I blink. *Ah, are you talking about chemical bonds? Molecules?*

The Dungeon Core has literally no idea what I'm talking about.

But you can do it? I ask. *You can change this rock's structure?*

I receive an emphatic yes. It just needs some of my mana. Or maybe more than some. It would only take some for such a little stone, but more is better. More is always better!

I guess there's nothing to it but try, then. I allow the Core access to my mana, and I can feel the energy start to flow into the Core.

[Mana: 181/200,] Echo reports as the magic wicks away.

Meanwhile, the Core excitedly prods at the rock like a kid squishing their fingers through Playdoh.

[Target selected,] Echo says. [Transform targeted quantity of quartzite into dolomite?]

Execute, I say, smiling to myself and feeling like quite the nerd.

The Dungeon Core gets to work.

It's such a strange sensation to behold. Instead of breaking down the stone, like it had done before, now it feels like the rock is being pulled apart and stuffed back together again. But it's merely a mental sensation. Physically, visually, the stone glows for just a moment. Then, it stops.

[Transformation complete,] Echo says.

It doesn't look noticeably different. In fact, the shape and weight doesn't seem to have changed either. Conservation of mass, I expect. The two types of rock must have a similar density, then. Even so, I give the rock a Check.

[Check,] Echo reports. [A piece of dolomite.]

It worked! *Nice job*, I tell the Core.

The Dungeon Core beams, and then asks for more mana.

I chuckle. *In just a moment. In fact, here in a minute, I'll have a lot more for you to work on.*

The Core vibrates with anticipation.

I look up to find all the nearby dracid staring at me.

"Here," I say, offering the stone back to the dracid I'd taken it from. It reverently takes the rock from my hand. "This should heat up faster now. I'm also going to work on increasing the insulation of this room." I glance around at the few windows and the vent in the ceiling above the firepit. "We'll need to be careful about maintaining sufficient airflow, however..."

I shake my head. One thing at a time. "Let's see about those other rocks, first. Can you help me gather up all the ones you've been using for warmth?"

Nek jumps into action. "Of course, Fire!" The dracid follow significantly more sluggishly after him, but I suspect that's as fast as they can move, given the circumstances. As the others get to work, I crouch down by the firepit and touch the stones resting there, transforming the rocks one by one. I only change half of them, leaving the others in their original form; I figure they can use the faster heating or slower heating rocks on a case-by-case basis.

Insulating the rest of the room requires the opposite treatment. Whereas I want the warming stones to be able to transfer heat very easily, I want the stone that comprises the room to have a low thermal conductivity.

At first, this stumps me a little. It seems the limestone that this room is carved out of already has the lowest thermal conductivity of all the stones in the Dungeon Core's catalog. But then it hits me: air is an excellent insulator. If I can make the stone more porous, it would reduce the strength of the stone overall, but also decrease the average thermal conductivity.

This takes quite a bit of explaining to get my idea across to the Dungeon Core. I don't want to destroy the room, and I don't want to change the material: I just want to introduce enough air bubbles to increase the insulation. But not *so* many air bubbles that it can't support its own weight. The Dungeon Core finds this idea exciting and suggests we experiment with how many air bubbles to add until the room *does* collapse, but I veto this idea, much to its disappointment.

As the dracid continue to pile stones up near the fire, I work on my porosity idea, taking the Dungeon Core's suggestion to experiment on a simple rock, first. Which is a good thing, too, because as soon as I have the Dungeon Core add tons of microscopic air pockets to the rock, it nearly doubles in size. A quick Check from Echo tells me it's the same mass, just lower density. I suppose that makes sense, but it poses a problem if I want to alter the stone of this room. I can't do that without also affecting the shape of the room, it seems. Darn conservation of mass.

Not so! The Dungeon Core happily informs me it could eat the extra mass instead.

I shake my head. *I'd rather not deal with an avalanche of sand like before.* Although now that I'm thinking about it, sand might be a good insulator, too.

No, no, not like that. It can eat the stone. Store it inside itself. It doesn't have to just break it down; it can take it away, too!

Wait, that's right. I'd witnessed it eating some of the sand yesterday when it was freeing Mirzayael's leg. Perhaps it could eat away the bits of stone while introducing the air pockets.

Are you sure you can do both those things simultaneously? I ask.

Yes! Of course. It can do anything!

I chuckle at its confidence. *Let's try it, then.*

The Dungeon Core obliges. The stone I'm holding glows for a moment, then grows noticeably lighter as the Core makes many tasty mind noises.

But where has the stone *gone* exactly?

It's like Echo was waiting for me to ask.

[0.42 kg of limestone stored in the Dungeon Core's Inventory.]

"Oh?" I say aloud. That's new. Focusing on 'Dungeon Core's Inventory,' a new mental display pops up. There are tons—literally—of stone already in there. Presumably, rocks the Core had 'eaten' at some point in the past. I find this vaguely disturbing.

Do I have an Inventory of my own? I ask Echo.

[Affirmative,] Echo says. [Inventory space: 0/1]

I snort at that. One Inventory space? The Dungeon Core has literally hundreds of thousands of spaces. Ah, well. Even just one space presents interesting possibilities...

I vanish the stone into my personal Inventory, then pop it back into existence a moment later.

I smile. "Interesting, indeed."

Yet another tool to experiment with. Later, however. Now that I know the Dungeon Core can help vanish away tiny pockets of limestone into its Inventory without compromising the structure of the room, I've bigger fish to fry.

Alright, Core, I think, splaying my hands over the ground. *Let's get to work.*

A patch of ground lights up and the Core eagerly starts chewing away at it, providing me a moment-by-moment description of how the stone tastes. (Sour and crunchy, apparently. Said taste does not ever actually change, yet it apparently feels compelled to remind me after each bite.) However, after only a few minutes of this, Echo cuts in.

[Mana extinguished: 0/200]

[Psionic Touch expired.]

Darn. I hadn't been paying attention to my mana levels. I made it through about half the floor, but it looks like I'll need to wait to finish it later. It's also inconvenient that running out of mana prevents me from speaking with the Core. I think I'll do that Psionic Link with it after all. The Dungeon Core seems far too transparent to have ulterior motives, even if it is a supposedly cursed relic. Being able to speak to it without burning through my mana is simply the most practical thing to do. Once my stores have recovered, I'll initiate a Psionic Link.

"Nek!"

The call makes me jump. I straighten up, rubbing my neck and back as I look toward the door. Mirzayael is standing in the frame, glaring at me.

"What is she doing?" she snaps. "I told you to watch her!"

"I have been!" Nek objects, hurrying over. "She's been with me the whole time."

I stand up, stretching my wings with a groan. "Sorry," I say, hoping to diffuse the situation. "I was just trying to help insulate the—"

"You were supposed to be keeping her under house arrest," Mirzayael tells Nek. "Not letting her throw fireballs around the city."

That seems like a bit of an exaggeration.

"You don't understand," Nek says, shooting me nervous looks. "She's not what you think. The things she can do—it's just like the legends."

I grimace at that. "It's not me, it's the Dungeon Core," I say, holding up my wrist. "I was only trying to help."

"I'll be the judge of that, Outsider," Mirzayael says cooly. She turns to look down at Nek. "I'll take custody of her from here. You may return to your previous duties."

"But Mir," he starts.

She silences him with a glare, and his tail and ears droop. He quietly slinks away.

Mirzayael turns her glower back on me. "I've had plenty of time to hear the rumors," she says. "You fancy yourself some kind of savior, do you?"

I wince. "I assure you, I do not."

"Good." She jerks her head toward the door. "Then come with me. I have more important work I need you for."

Hesitantly, I follow her out of the dracid chamber. "How can I help?"

"You will show me where you came from," she says. "How you managed to navigate our tunnels." She stops, seizing me up with an unimpressed look. "If I like your answer, I'll let you come back to our village."

"And if you don't like my answer?" I ask.

She smiles, revealing a row of needle-thin teeth. "Then you won't be coming back."

Chapter Eight

THE EYE OF LORATA

The tip of Mirzayael's spear glows blue, providing a small bubble of light not much brighter than my spark. Occasionally, she uses it as a walking stick when the terrain gets tough, favoring her injured side. It apparently had not been some form of incredibly dark humor when Beryl had said she'd removed Mirzayael's injured leg. The limb is severed just above the joint, seemingly scarred over already; though I expect magic may have something to do with the rapid recovery. The missing limb doesn't appear to slow the woman down, as I struggle to keep up with her rapid pace, though as the caverns grow steep and rough, she occasionally slips, threatening to fall on her injured side. Each time she falters, I say nothing.

I tap back into a Psionic Touch, hoping for an unbiased assessment of my situation.

Do you think, when she said I wouldn't be returning if she didn't like my answer, she meant she'd just leave me in the caverns? I muse to Echo and the Dungeon Core. *Or do you think she intends to kill me?*

[Query not recognized,] Echo says.

The Dungeon Core also has no idea what I'm talking about. Who wants to kill me? Why? I should not let that happen. Then the Core would have no source of mana!

Your concern is appreciated, I think. Excellent insight from the both of them. I flip Psionic Touch back off to conserve my mana.

Lifting up my Spark, I gesture to the left. "This way next."

"How are you doing that?" Mirzayael asks.

It's the first question she's asked since she ordered me to take her to where I first entered the cave system.

"What do you mean?" I ask.

"Harpies don't have low light vision like arachnoids," she says. "Yet you keep noticing these small side passages before I do. How are you seeing them?"

"Oh," I say, squinting into the dark. Actually, I've just been focusing on the small illuminated patch of ground before my feet. "I'm not. I'm navigating by a map the Dungeon Core has given me access to. It's rather incomplete, but it at least allows me to retrace my steps."

"A map?" Mirzayael asks. "Show me."

I shake my head apologetically. "I don't think I can. The map is in my mind." But just saying that aloud gives me pause. "Actually. I might be able to show you after all. I have a spell, Psionic Touch, that allows me to speak mind-to-mind."

Mirzayael narrows her eyes at me. "This is the mind magic you mentioned before?"

"Yes." I guess Echo and the Dungeon Core also probably count as mind-magic of a sort. Is it strange I'm growing used to their presences already? "It might be able to give you a peek into what I'm experiencing," I say. "Potentially. I'm not sure if it would work as intended, but—"

"That won't be necessary," Mirzayael interrupts. "I have no intention of ever giving you access to my mind. If you lead us true, that will be proof of your claim."

"Fair enough." If someone asked to perform mind-magic on *me*, I'd be equally skeptical. "In that case, best save our breath. We've another few hours' climb to go."

We progress largely in silence, which I pretend to interpret as comradery, pointedly ignoring the spear in Mirzayael's hand. I know the chamber I'm taking her to will not provide the answer she's looking for, especially as she's expecting me to take her to some cave exit leading up to the surface. Which means I have the next few hours to try to predict how she'll respond—and prepare to defend myself if necessary.

I refresh my memory on her stats with a covert Check.

[Name: Mirzayael]

[Species: Arachnoid]

[Class: Silk Warrior]

[Level: 29]

[HP: 235/235]

[Mana: 110/110]

She's got a leg up on me—no pun intended—in just about every regard except for Mana. Her Level and HP are formidable, not to mention I can see how she moves: she's faster, stronger, and has armor and weapons, while I'm all bird-bones and rags. If she decides to kill me, she has a clear advantage.

Which means I'll need to be clever. I've only four spells at my disposal; Spark, Blaze, Psionic Link, and Psionic Touch. Spark isn't good for anything other than a small light. Psionic Touch and Link are both unlikely to help in a combat situation. Blaze could certainly be effective, though it has the potential to eat up all my mana in a matter of seconds. But I've got the Dungeon Core at my disposal, too. That might be my saving grace. If I could open a hole beneath her feet, or summon a wall between us, the element of surprise might be enough to land a decisive blow.

Though I'd prefer to avoid that scenario, if at all possible, considering my continued survival depends on access to her city.

I run other scenarios through my mind while we walk, occasionally re-establishing a Psionic Touch with the Core to ask it questions (which by and large provides entirely unhelpful answers).

Surprising her with Psionic Touch to get across the honesty of my intentions: likely to get me stabbed in the stomach.

Using Blaze as a flashbang: might be good to buy me a few extra seconds, but would only be effective if she's not expecting me to go on the offensive.

Spark: mostly useless in this scenario as far as I can tell.

Dungeon Core: altering the terrain is a solid option. (Again, no pun intended.)

Summoning items from the Dungeon Core's Inventory: potentially the winning strategy, depending on how quickly and efficiently it can be done.

Adding items to *my* single-space inventory: could be good if I can get a hand on her spear without getting stabbed by it first.

Echo, is there a limit to what sort of things can be added to my Inventory? I ask.

[Apart from the limited storage space, living creatures are not compatible with Inventory space.]

No adding people, then, got it. I chew on this for a moment more. *You said the Dungeon Core didn't qualify as life. Does that mean it could be added to my Inventory?*

[Affirmative,] Echo says.

The Dungeon Core, itself listening to this conversation, doesn't understand exactly what I'm talking about, but decides to be alarmed anyway.

That was pure scientific curiosity, I let it know. *I don't have any intention of adding you to my Inventory… whatever that truly means.*

The Core remains rightfully nervous, and I decide it's probably prudent to let the line of questioning drop for now. I turn off Psionic Touch so I can begin to recover my mana more quickly.

I'm at 148/200 right now, as Spark is effectively free at this point. It'll only take another two minutes to get up to the 150 mana that Psionic Link requires, but if I activate it then, I'll have completely emptied my mana stores, leaving me helpless. I decide to wait until my mana has fully recovered first; then I'll have an extra 50 just in case I'll need it.

I hope I won't.

The minutes seem to crawl by as I watch my stats creep back up. The adage that a watched clock seems to run slower certainly feels true in this case. But inevitably, finally, I get confirmation from Echo.

[Mana: 200/200]

My stomach flutters nervously. Here we go. For better or worse, no turning back now. *Activate Psionic Link*, I tell Echo. *With the Dungeon Core.*

[Spell activated.]

Like I'm activating a Psionic Touch, I can feel the Core's presence resurface in my mind. It happily greets me, as usual. Also as usual, it asks if I have any mana to spare.

Not this moment, I say. *But I have something that will give both of us access to more mana going forward.*

Yay! The Dungeon Core hopes it's much, much, much more.

Er. Not really. But every little bit counts, right?

More is better.

I extend my offer to it anyway. The Psionic Link stretches between our minds like a bridge. It takes both parties to establish the link, it seems. I've anchored my side. But will the Core take hold of the other?

Okay!

Oh. That was easy.

[Psionic Link established,] Echo says. [Mana expended.]

I wait a beat. I don't feel any different. Did the spell even work? I mentally reach for the Dungeon Core.

Oh! The Core happily bounces around my mind. We can still talk! Does this mean we can always talk now? Without stopping? Do I have any more mana I can give it?

I'm beginning to wonder exactly what I've gotten myself into.

By the time we reach our destination, I'm trying not to pant from the exertion of the climb. My legs feel like they're made of lead. My feet sting from all the walking. It seems even in this body I could stand to work out more.

"Here we are," I finally say, pausing to take a breath. "Please watch your step. There's a large hole along one side of the passage."

"Are you sure?" Mirzayael asks, looking around. "We're not at the surface, yet."

"Well, this is where I came from," I say. "Do you want me to lead, or you?"

She waves me ahead. I shrug, acting far more fearless than I feel, and hold my Spark before me as I carefully pick my way into the tunnel. I try to ignore Mirzayael's spear leveled at my back.

The room is just as I'd left it. The giant crack the Dungeon Core had made still runs through the floor, through which several of the skeletons have fallen, but the rest of the room is untouched. Bones, stones, and hints of ancient weaponry litter the floor. I carefully pick my way around them, trying to be as respectful to the remains as possible.

"The room was sealed when I woke up here," I tell Mirzayael as she steps into the room, looking around. The only hint of surprise in her expression is slightly raised eyebrows. "The Dungeon Core is what got me out. It turned the stones blocking the exit into sand, like it did to the stone that had trapped your leg."

Mirzayael moves slowly through the room, glancing around at the floor and nudging some of the bones with the butt of her spear. My firelight doesn't reach far, but I'm still able to catch flickers of reflected light from her polished, shell-like body as she moves about the near-darkness.

I follow her to the center of the room, the one space of empty, flat stone.

"It was here," I say, crouching down to touch the rock. Still so cold to the touch. But I guess it's no wonder if I'm really in the arctic. Ah, how I would love to see the sun again. Feel the warmth against my skin.

Mirzayael doesn't respond as she slowly walks the perimeter. She holds her glowing spear tip to the ground, clearly illuminating whatever she points it at. After a minute of exploration, she pauses, bending down to pick something out of the pebbles and bones.

"What is it?" I ask, not particularly expecting to get an answer.

She stares at it a moment, then finally angles her hand to show me. It appears to be a small bronze badge of some sort. There's a symbol carved into the surface, something like a stylized eye, though it means nothing to me.

[Check,] Echo says. [The sigil of Lorata, marking the bearer as her champion.]

"Who's Lorata?" I ask.

Mirzayael stares at me for a long moment. Finally, she tucks the badge away in a breast pocket and returns to our surroundings, keeping her gaze carefully on the floor as she picks her way across.

"Lorata," Mirzayael finally says, "is the god of light, wisdom, foresight, and is the head of the pantheon. It is also said she was the one who declared our people forsaken."

It takes me a moment to digest all this. "Then, that skeleton…" I raise my eyebrows. "All these skeletons…?"

"At least the one, so far as I can tell," Mirzayael says. "But yes; that one appears to be the remains of a champion. This very well may be the chamber where Fyreneth made her last stand."

"Oh," I say, faintly. The implication of Fyreneth dying here—of my being reborn in the exact spot—does not escape me. Yet, I can't quite process how I feel about that. Disbelief, certainly. I know who I am, and it is not the ancient leader of these people. But if this is the place of her fall, if the skeletons of others have been preserved here for hundreds of years, where are Fyreneth's remains?

I certainly hope the reason I was given a phoenix harpy's body is a mere coincidence. But given all the other circumstantial evidence, I find that statistically unlikely.

"Perhaps," I say, "we could *not* tell the rest of the town about this room being the location of my reincarnation."

Mirzayael looks at me strangely. "I think that might be wise."

I nod, relieved. Any way we could prevent the rumor mill from being stoked is preferable to me. Not to mention, I need time to process these new revelations myself.

"Do you believe me, then?" I ask her. "That I am not from this world? That I have no idea how I ended up here or came to inhabit this body?"

"Well, it is at least certain that you came through this room," she says. She points her spear to marks on the ground. "Recent footprints I picked out before you had a chance to disrupt the terrain. That, coupled with your ability to lead me here, and with what you've demonstrated with the Dungeon Core... Yes, I believe you appeared here, even if I still find the story unbelievable." She turns to me. "I also do not believe you are Fyreneth."

"Good," I say, relieved. "Please, I have no desire to inherit that burden of responsibilities. That is, if you intend to let me return to your village."

Mirzayael tips her head at me. "You are a strange person, Outsider."

"I suppose that fits," I say. "Everything about this is strange to me."

"Hm." She smiles faintly. "Alright. I'll give you a chance to prove your trustworthiness. You may return with me to the Keep."

"Thank you," I say, my shoulders sagging. Oh, thank god. I never would have won a fight against her.

The Dungeon Core, meanwhile, seems a little put out about not getting to summon a bunch of rocks or cause another fissure.

"Come," Mirzayael says, gesturing to the exit. "We should begin to make our way back. It will still be some hours before we return to town, and by then we will both be hungry."

I'm rather hungry now, actually, given my unwise decision to skip breakfast, but I doubt complaining will earn me any points with her.

"Excellent," I say, despite my aching legs. At least this trek will be downhill. "Then, if I am officially accepted as one of your own—"

"—Contingent upon proving your trustworthiness," she cuts in.

"Right, that," I say. "Assuming I can demonstrate my authenticity, I believe it would be to my benefit to learn as much about this city, the history, this *world*, as possible. Nek mentioned there might be books in the Catacombs. Do you think I would be able to get my hands on those, in whatever state they might be in?"

Mirzayael leads us back out of the room, snorting at my remark. "Nek is a fool. Nothing save for its stone has survived the Catacomb's decay."

"Ah," I say, deflating. "That's unfortunate. It would have been terribly convenient. What are the Catacombs, anyway?"

"The remnants of the lost kingdom," Mirzayael says. Happily, she seems to be more responsive to my questions now, though I'd perhaps stop shy of calling her friendly. "When the city was returned to the earth, at first people stayed within the castle walls, determined to continue living their lives as they had before. But without Fyreneth's magic to power it, the castle slowly died. The lights flickered out. The water dried up. All the warmth leeched away. Eventually the inhabitants were forced to leave and seek more fertile caverns. That is why we dwindle in the cavern we currently live in today. We suspect there is a thermal spring which passes beneath us, allowing such flora to thrive in our section of the cave system, but we've been unable to tap into it. So we live in our makeshift home as best we can. Having seen what remains of Fyreneth's Fortress, our ancestors must have lived in such prosperity, in comparison."

A thermal spring? Interesting. I wonder if that's something the Dungeon Core would be able to sniff out.

But the Catacombs intrigue me just as much. If the city was powered by magic, does that mean it's just waiting to be turned back on, given the right parameters are met? They had lighting, plumbing, heating—all things the people of Mirzayael's city are in desperate need of. Could the answer be buried there, somewhere in the ruins?

"I would very much like to visit the Catacombs," I say.

Mirzayael shrugs. "You are more than welcome to. A few have wandered into the Catacombs only to become lost and perish there: I would warn you to be wary of meeting a similar fate, except it seems your Core would help you in this respect."

I nod excitedly. "Can we go tomorrow?"

"We?" she repeats skeptically.

"Correct me if I'm wrong, but I suspect you're unlikely to let me go anywhere alone until I've earned your trust," I say. "Unless you'd rather it be Nek who accompanies me?"

Mirzayael laughs.

She actually *laughs.*

"Alright, Outsider," she agrees. "I will take you to the Catacombs."

Chapter Nine

THE CATACOMBS

After Mirzayael and I return to the city, I'm ready to collapse back into bed. But all I've had to eat all day were a handful of tough, smoked mushrooms Mirzayael had brought with us for the trek, so when Nek invites me to dinner, I wearily and graciously accept.

A group of townsfolk have gathered in a communal area similar to the dracid chamber. It's a large, artificial cavern carved from the rocks, with several entrances and windows, and four rings of sunken stone divoting the floor. People are sitting within these rings, arrayed around spreads of food laid at the center.

"Come, sit with my family," Nek says, inviting me over to one of the meal circles. A few people are already seated there, including several dwarves and a dracid, bundled in many layers of blankets.

Nek hops down next to the dracid, snuggling up close to her and nuzzling her nose.

"This is Sora, my wife," Nek says, wrapping an arm around the dracid. She shuffles the blankets around, and suddenly two children clamber out of the folds. One is a little felis girl, and the other is a dracid boy. The kids pounce onto Nek, who falls back with an exaggerated cry.

I stare at the children for a moment, pondering the nature of their conception. Probably not something that would be polite to ask about.

Nek's wife, Sora, looks up at me with a friendly smile as I step down into the meal circle with them. She snakes a hand out of her blankets, and I accept it.

"We've already met," she says, "though I understand if you don't remember. You gave me one of the stones you were warming. I owe you my thanks."

"Oh," I say, sitting down cross-legged beside them. "Yes. I'm glad to see it's helped. Is that why you're up and about now?"

Sora chuckles. "No, today was my shift to work the waters. While we may spend much of our time conserving our strength, we are not *entirely* helpless without your aid."

My neck grows heated with a blush. "Sorry. I didn't mean to imply you were."

Nek rumbles with laughter as well, sitting back up as he sweeps each giggling child under his arms. "Bah, don't believe her teasing. In truth, your work has already nearly doubled our efficiency."

"With working the waters?" I ask, looking to Sora. "What does that mean?"

Nek passes the dracid child back over to Sora, who wraps him in her blankets. "Due to our water affinities, we dracid spend much of our waking time filtering the drinking water," she says. "During these winter months, we must take careful shifts, as we each can only be active for about half the week. We're much more energetic in the summer."

I'd been wondering how their population was sustained, given their apparent lethargy.

"Enough work talk," Nek says, reaching out to grab a clay bowl. His other child has climbed up his side and embedded herself in the fur around her father's neck. "Food now. Here, I'll show you all the best toadstools."

Not terribly thrilled with another meal of uncooked fungus, I nevertheless find the glowing variety fascinating, and follow Nek's lead as I fill my plate.

A shadow falls over our meal circle.

"Outsider. I see you've found some food," Mirzayael says.

"Ah, yes, I have." I nod to Nek. "Thanks to him. Is there anything I can help you with?"

Mirzayael's gaze sweeps over our circle, then she shakes her head. "I merely intended to confirm you received proper sustenance. You will need the energy for tomorrow."

"Of course," I say.

The arachnoid taps a few of her feet against the ground, and an awkward silence settles over our meal circle.

"Would you like to join us?" I offer.

"No," she quickly replies. "I will be taking my leave. Nek, continue to ensure the Outsider is seen to."

"Yes, Captain," Nek says. But Mirzayael has already glided away, her dark form vanishing into the cavern's dim.

Sora turns to me. "Well she certainly seems to like you."

I laugh at the joke, but no one else joins in. "Wait, you're serious?"

"She has a... subtle way of showing it," Nek agrees. "But she came to check on you, which is something."

"I figured she was just double checking that I still had my security detail," I say.

Sora chuckles. "Possibly that, too. But what was this about needing energy for tomorrow?"

"I asked to visit the Catacombs," I say. "I'd like to learn as much about this place as I can. With the Dungeon Core to help, I might be able to unearth some of the lost magics which made the city habitable."

Nek and Sora stare at me in wonder.

"You really think such a thing is possible?" Nek asks.

I hesitate, wondering how much I should say, and how that would play into their already biased perception of me. Though I suppose it might be too late for that. Nek has already seen and heard plenty. No reason not to be honest.

I hold up my wrist, gesturing to the Core. "It's eager to excavate, that much is clear. And I'm not sure what I'll discover, exactly. But it seems as good a place as any to uncover more information about this place's history."

Sora raises a reverent hand, but doesn't touch it. "Fyreneth's artifact."

I grimace. "I wouldn't assume that."

"No?" she asks. "It can alter the structure of the Keep, just as the legends say. It brings gifts to our people. It is even carried by a phoenix harpy—"

"Please," I say. "I am not her."

"Maybe," Sora says, but her tone is doubtful. "Even so, that artifact can only be one thing."

I frown at the jewel. I would be foolish not to have drawn these parallels myself already. But there's a part of me that still isn't quite willing to accept all these prophetic signs.

This is a world full of magic. It's full of rules and laws of nature I can't even begin to conceive. Things that were impossible on Earth are clearly not so here. I am not blind to the assortment of data that has been laid before me. By Occam's razor...

No. I won't yet form a belief without first obtaining all available evidence. Evidence which might lie within the Catacombs. To do otherwise would be premature.

This is what I tell myself to deflect from the true root of my reluctance: these prophecies of rebirth and fate. If all of it were true, what would that mean for me?

This body. My mind. My identity. Would any of it truly be my own?

As Nek and Sora return to their meals, coaxing their children into eating their portion of glowing, earthy mushrooms, I brush my mind against the Dungeon Core.

Do you remember Fyreneth? I ask. *Do you have memories of who you worked with before we forged our Pact?*

The Dungeon Core doesn't understand. Memories? Fyreneth? Before? All very strange concepts. It is. It always has been. It always will be! But sometimes, it sleeps. Not right now, though, right now it's very much awake! And hungry. It would love to eat some more rocks. When will I give it more food? It's had so much more food in the past. The magical ore had given it so much power!

I massage a temple. *So you* do *remember something. You do have some concept of the past.*

Past? It doesn't understand. When can it get more magical ore?

I sigh out my irritation. *Tell me about the magical ore*, I say instead. *What does it let you do? Do you remember where it might be?*

The Dungeon Core doesn't know. Somewhen, it had a lair of its own, which allowed it to tap into a vast network of stone. Its veins went everywhere, through the whole mountain, deep into the earth. Some of these veins were burrowed into a magic source that that brought it life and sustained its immense, growing body.

The Dungeon Core's thoughts are accompanied with images which flash through my mind, impressions of an enormous artificial structure—artificial, yet alive. It was connected to every stone, conscious of every pebble. It sculpted each arch and doorway, placed all the cobblestones, one by one. Complex patterns of tiles tessellated across ceilings, and basins filled themselves from the thermal springs deep, deep beneath the surface.

I blink my eyes rapidly, dispelling the visions.

"Why didn't you mention that sooner?" I demand.

Sora looks up at me. "Sorry?"

I shake my head. "Hot springs."

Sora and Nek exchange a concerned look.

"There's hot springs," I insist. "Somewhere buried beneath us."

And if I could harness its warmth and divert it here, it would be the first step toward providing these people a real home. Somewhere they could not just survive, but thrive.

Despite Mirzayael agreeing to accompany me to the Catacombs, we don't actually leave the next day. I wake up sore and stiff from the previous day's walk, and though Mirzayael doesn't show it, I suspect she feels similar. When she instead suggests I take a day or two to rest, I accept. While I am still eager to visit the Catacombs, Mirzayael also needs time to recover. It's only been two days since she lost her leg, after all. The injury stings me with guilt every time I see it.

Instead, I spend my time working on the Dracid chamber, building up the structure's insulation and providing more stones with higher thermal conductivitites. Perhaps if we could find a better source of fuel, such measures would not be necessary, and we'd instead be able to sustain more and larger fires.

I also investigate the waterfall. Mirzayael had said the reason the cave of Fyreneth's Keep was able to remain warm enough to sustain flora and liquid water might be due to an underground thermal spring. I'd wondered if the waterfall might help me locate it, but it appears from a crack in the ceiling, and likewise disappears into cracks of the rocky floor. Not easy to trace from here. But I hadn't expected it to be that easy: there is still much to uncover.

Several more days pass this way. My Spark has leveled all the way up to 5, which means it only consumes 1 point of mana every five minutes, and its range and brightness has marginally increased. Blaze still has hovered at level 1, as I've been too busy, and in too bright a place, to need it for anything. Psionic Touch also has stagnated at Level 2, since I exclusively use Psionic Link with the Dungeon Core. But my frequent use of Psionic Link has resulted in an increase to level 4: this has reduced the mana cost to establish a new link to 100, and has increased the number of people I can form a link with to three. Not that I expect I'll have many opportunities to form new links. Two other voices in my head is already plenty.

Speaking of voices, Echo and I have also been talking quite a bit.

This Role, I ask her one evening. *The Dark Lord. You said it means I must defend my kingdom.*

[Affirmative,] Echo says.

But what does that mean? I wonder.

[To defend: to refrain from leaving something unprotected.]

Yes, thank you for the vocab lesson. *I don't have a kingdom. And I doubt this little community could count as one.*

Echo remains silent.

I suppose that wasn't technically a question. But the implications of such a Role do not escape me. I've just not wanted to believe it. *This role,* I venture. *Are you saying I'm... I'm meant to be the bad guy?*

[Query not recognized.]

I sigh. *Why do I have a Role?* I ask, switching tactics.

[Any individual who gains System Access is required to have a Role.]

System? I ask. *What System?*

[The adapted iteration of the neuralarcane network which governs the progression of System users.]

Are you also a System user, Echo?

[Negative. This cloned interface provides audiovisual access to System functions.]

You're a component of the System, I surmise.

[Affirmative.]

My GUI, I suppose. But I'm getting off track.

You said someone in the System must have a Role, I think. *Is the inverse true? If one does not have a role, they are not in the System?*

[Affirmative.]

That explains why no one has any idea what I'm talking about when I've tried to explain Echo or Stats to them. No one else that I've seen has a Role listed at the bottom of their statistics. Only me.

How can other people have stats if they're not in the System? I ask. *For that matter, why don't they have access?*

[Populated stats for non-system users are an estimated representation of evaluated qualities,] Echo says. [Non-system users have not met minimum requirements to access the System.]

And the minimum requirements are...?

[<ACCESS DENIED>]

I jump when Echo comes back with this rather loud and firm response. *Who has access?*

[<ACCESS DENIED>]

That's troubling. There are different levels to this System then, and someone, or someones, have elevated privileges. This only summons dozens of more questions from me, but I appear to be digging too deep and only run into more permission issues from Echo.

It's certainly a strange mystery. A mystery I intend to unravel, one way or another. I can feel there's answers here, just out of my reach. All I need to do is puzzle out the right questions. Poke around for a back door.

Finally, nearly a week after our last excursion, Mirzayael announces it's time to visit the Catacombs.

"I don't see why you are so excited." She roughly tightens a strap around my waist, and I wince. "Even if you find the source of these thermal springs, how can that be of any use?"

I hold my arms up as Mirzayael adjusts my tunic, then spins me around, pulling the fabric around my wings. I stand there awkwardly as she adjusts the clothes to her standards. Apparently it's been so long since they've had a harpy in their midst that the townsfolk had to tailor-make something suitable for me. The tunic is designed much like any other, except the lower back of the shirt parts into three separate strips to drape around and be tied beneath the wings.

"The Dungeon Core should be able to help with that," I say. "If the Catacombs really do have a plumbing system, the Core should be able to trace the pipes to their source. From there, we might be able to find a way down to the springs. Or a way to bring them up to us. Can you imagine what it would do for the dracid? For this whole community?"

"Hmph." At first I think Mirzayael is scoffing, but as she turns me back around, I can make out a faint smile on her lips. "You are certainly a dreamer, Outsider."

She steps back to appraise me and gives a curt nod. "That will do for now. Here." She hands me a pack next. "Make sure this fits. Tighten the straps under the arms—I'm sure you can figure that much out yourself. You'll be carrying all your own supplies, so make sure the bag doesn't chafe."

I take the pack, which is heavier than I suspected, and sling it over my shoulders. It stops just short of where my wings protrude from my lower back, which is appreciated. I tighten the straps as instructed. "Is all this food necessary? It will only be a day trip, won't it?"

"Ideally." Mirzayael straps a pack of her own onto her back. That is, her spider back, not her human back. She twists around to secure the supplies in place. "But I don't plan on ideals. There's three days' worth of food and water in here just in case. The Catacombs are not to be trifled with."

"Fair enough," I say, recalling a couple Boy Scout backpacking trips I attended as a kid. Better to be over prepared than under. "Anything else I should know before we set off?"

"Yes. Plenty." Mirzayael begins ticking advice off on her fingers. "Speak softly. Use little light. Pay attention to any noise you hear: clicks could be rock bats, chirps could be poison-skinned salamanders, and grunts mean you run. Don't open anything that is already closed. Always watch your footing; holes and weak flooring are common. Keep an eye out for patches of ceiling which might appear unstable. Move carefully around corners. Watch for signs of stinger nests—loose masonry and grooves carved in nearby surfaces are the biggest tells." She pauses. "Those are the most important things."

I chuckle. "Watch the floor, ceiling, and passage all at once? I think I'll be needing more than two eyes."

"It helps to have eight," Mirzayael says flatly.

I laugh.

She stares at me.

I turn the laugh into a cough. "Should we be off, then?"

Mirzayael cracks a smile. "Yes, Outsider. We can depart." She ducks out of the house, not waiting for me to follow.

Nek and a handful of dracid wish us luck as we leave the city; seeing the draconic people awake and moving about fills me with warm satisfaction. I'm being helpful here. I'm doing good.

Maybe more than I ever did back home.

Not that I didn't try. I loved my work. Airplanes have always fascinated me. And the ability to fly—who wouldn't want that? In an indirect way, I could give something to people that would bring them happiness. Allow them to take trips. Visit family. Explore the world! Airplanes brought people closer.

Though it had the opposite effect on my family.

My heart sinks at the thought, and I extract myself from those memories, trying to focus on the here and now.

Unsurprisingly, Mirzayael keeps chit-chat to a minimum as we travel. She strikes me as the type who enjoys silence—or, perhaps, loathes the sound of people's voices. So why was she stationed in a leadership position if she didn't like interacting with people?

"If I may, what exactly is there to guard against down here?" I ask as we leave the Keep. "The entrance to this place seems well disguised."

"To your eyes, maybe," Mirzayael says. "To a keen enough ear or nose; perhaps not. While it's true I've never had Jorrian Scouts make it this deep in the caves, wild animals sometimes find their way in. Not to mention the cave-dwelling varieties which already live here."

"Yes, you mentioned some of those," I say. "Rock bats and, ah, stabbers?"

"Stingers," she corrects me.

"Anything I should be worried about?" I ask.

"Not if you stay close," she says. "Creatures native to these caverns are all rather small, and harmless when alone. In groups, and if agitated, they might defend their territory. But that's why you have me." She drums her fingers along the shaft of her spear. "So long as we tread carefully, there's nothing in these halls I can't handle."

We enter the large, dark cavern outside of Fyreneth's Keep, our footsteps echoing ahead of us into the large chamber. Instead of following the path we took before, however, tracing the lit runes along the walls, Mirzayael turns away from the illuminated path, leading us into the dark. She mumbles a few quiet words as we do so, and the head of her spear illuminates in a soft, blue light. She carries the spear before us, like a torch, and I similarly summon a Spark to my fingertips. My orange light joins her blue, blending on the floor before us.

As we walk, I bring up the Map Interface in the corner of my vision. I can feel the Dungeon Core curiously watching the map as well; this is the first time since our original exploration that we're filling out new portions of the map, even if it appears to just be a large, flat, open space of rock. The Core doesn't discriminate, however. All rocks are delicious, apparently.

"Here we are," Mirzayael says after a moment, raising her spear

"Really?" I ask, surprised. "We're here already? I didn't realize it was so close to the Keep."

"This is merely the entrance," Mirzayael says, gesturing above us.

The light falls over a great arch, and finally I see where we are. A gateway stretches a dozen feet above us, and castle walls reach three times as high above those. Beyond that is darkness, but the echoing vastness of this chamber suddenly makes sense.

"Can I summon a bigger light?" I ask Mirzayael. "That wouldn't harm anything while we're still out here?"

She gestures for me to go ahead.

I take a few steps back. "Blaze," I say, forming the fireball in my hands. It rapidly grows to the size of a cantaloupe, and Echo begins counting down my mana. I toss the fireball into the air, willing it to rise higher and higher yet. It flies ten, twenty, thirty, forty feet, and it's still going. I imagine it could go twice as high if I willed it, but with my rapidly depleting mana, that will have to be enough. I will the fireball to break apart, and it explodes outward in a flare of light, turning into a sort of firecracker as the embers scatter through the air. In that burst of light, I get a single still-shot of the Catacombs, stretching hundreds of feet above us.

It's a fortress. Entombed in the rocks is a tiered city, growing from the cavern like the stalagmites themselves. It must have once housed thousands of people. Even when the light has died out, an impression of the grand, deceased citadel remains burned in my vision.

"It's beautiful," I say, quietly. But its emptiness feels wrong. The silence an intangible scar. "And terribly sad."

"It's dangerous," Mirzayael says bluntly. "Don't forget what I said. Now come on. Will you stand there gawking all day, or did we come here for a reason?"

"Right," I say, summoning a new Spark to my fingers. "Lead the way."

Mirzayael steps over the threshold and I follow quickly behind. Crumbling buildings rise up around us on either side, cutting off the view of the surrounding city, and a curve in the ancient street rapidly puts the castle's entrance out of sight. Soon, we're swallowed up by the Catacombs.

Chapter Ten

DUNGEON DELVE

Unlike the echoing chamber outside the gates of the Catacombs, within its deserted streets everything is unnervingly still, quiet, and close. It's the kind of place that demands whispers and soft footfalls. I step carefully, keenly aware of every scraped talon and kicked pebble. Something about the place makes me tuck my wings in close.

Speaking to Mirzayael now feels like it would break some tacit law, so instead I turn my dialogue inward.

What can you tell about this place? I ask the Dungeon Core. *Does any of it feel familiar?*

Yes! Rocks. The rocks are very familiar.

I grimace. *Right... anything* about *the rocks? Like, how they were made? Why they were placed this way? Who might have asked you to build such a fortress in the first place?*

The Dungeon Core finds this line of questioning extremely confusing. Who asks why rocks are? They just are!

Ah well. It was worth a shot.

How about the hot springs? I ask instead. *Can you sense pipes, plumbing, anything like that?* I try to visualize what I mean—dark round tunnels cutting through the stone.

The Dungeon Core doesn't know. It can't sense very far. It needs more mana to see further. Lots more mana would be preferable. Or better yet, lots, lots, lots, lots, lots—

I get the idea. And I can give you a little bit for now. Not as much as you want, but until we can find this 'mana ore' you're looking for, you'll have to make do with my scant reserves.

The Dungeon Core finds this entirely unacceptable.

It eagerly holds out its metaphorical hands for whatever mana I can spare.

I shake my head, but allow the Core to tap into my reserves regardless.

Now that I'm getting a feel for how this Pact thing works, it helps for me to visualize the exchange like a faucet. I can fully open the stream and allow all my mana to pour through at once, or I can just barely twist the handle, letting my mana trickle into the Dungeon Core bit by bit. It's clear which version the Core would prefer, but I've got my own wellbeing to consider.

I Check my mana, just to be safe: 139/200. Looks like I spent a lot on that Blaze spell earlier. I'll need to work on refining that magic later. Level it up so it will reduce the cost. For now, I slowly open the valve to my mana, watching the numbers as I trickle a stream into the Dungeon Core.

[Mana Depletion Rate: 2 mana per minute,] Echo reports.

At the same time, I watch the range on our map grow larger. I myself can't actually see more of our surroundings, but the Dungeon Core's awareness expands with the increase in radius on the map. It doesn't *see* exactly, either, but it can sense the surrounding stone, taste the lime deposits in the rock, smell its age and structure.

It's difficult to not become lost within such sensations. Just thinking about what the Dungeon Core is doing pulls my mind in its direction, threatening to spill me over into it. I lightly clap my cheeks, drawing my attention back to my physical surroundings. I need to focus on walking; time to leave the Dungeon Core to do its thing.

With the scant amount of mana I'm feeding it, the Dungeon Core doesn't have much depth to what it can sense, but it already begins feeling out any hints of structure that might be the thermal pipes I'm looking for.

I twist my mana valve open a little bit more.

[Mana Depletion Rate: 5 mana per minute.]

There. That should be enough for now. The Dungeon Core can sense the stones all around us in a twelve-foot radius, or focus all its sensation about forty feet in one direction. At the current rate of depletion, I can have the Dungeon Core searching our surroundings for the next half an hour. After that, I'll need to start recovering my mana.

Watching our snaking path eat into the surrounding dark on the Map display, I can't help but wonder if we have any specific destination in mind. Mirzayael knows why I'm here, but it would be best if we didn't wander aimlessly. If there's a bathhouse of some sort, that would be the best place to begin.

Not to mention, I'm still on the lookout for any form of historical documents I can get my hands on, on the off chance they have survived their time spent down here. Maybe stone carvings or mosaics?

"Mirzayael," I finally whisper. Even that sounds too loud for this place, and echoes of my voice chase after me, reflecting from crumbling, empty doorways we pass like ghosts living in the abandoned halls.

She looks back at me with a sharp gaze.

I grimace apologetically. "Where are we headed?"

She lifts her spear to point into the darkness ahead and above us. The streets are wide, and our lights reflect off the stone of the nearby buildings, but above them everything is black, like a starless night sky.

"The palace," she murmurs. Oh good. At least whispering seems to be allowed. "Most likely place to discover any relics of our past."

Makes sense to me. "How far?"

"Fifteen minutes."

She knew that offhand. "You explore here often?"

She looks back at me again, raising an irritated eyebrow. "Is this an interrogation?"

"Sorry," I say. "Am I being too loud? We could use my Psionic Touch if you want to speak mind to mind."

"No," she quickly says, clearly uncomfortable with the suggestion. "Your volume is acceptable. Complete silence was wishful thinking anyway; your clumsy steps announce our presence louder than your voice." I wince. "Though a little noise will also give notice to any nearby creatures so they will not be startled," she adds.

"Oh. Good," I breathe. I guess she was more irritated that I was asking questions than that I was making noise. "Sorry about the interrogation. My wife always said I was too curious for my own good. Asked too many questions."

Mirzayael's look turns into one of surprise. "You have a wife?"

"Had," I say. "We were no longer together when I... before I came here. I wasn't a very good husband."

"Husband?" Mirzayael repeats, her voice loud with surprise. She lowers it again, giving me a double take. "You are a man?"

"I..." The words knot themselves up on my tongue, just as my feelings on the matter feel all knotted up in my head. "I was, at least."

"I'm sorry," Mirzayael says. "I've been assuming incorrectly this entire time. That was wrong of me."

"No," I object. "You've done nothing wrong. I didn't speak up because I wasn't sure what to say. In all honesty, I'm not sure about all this myself."

Mirzayael tips her head. "Not sure about what?"

I'm thankful for the dark, as I can feel another flush threatening to overtake me. "I don't know. Being a woman. I should be more horrified by all this, shouldn't I? It should feel wrong. But for some reason, in some way I can't explain, this feels more natural than the body I spent my whole life living in. Like I was dreaming all those years, and have only just now woken up. It doesn't make sense."

Mirzayael regards me thoughtfully. "Perhaps," she suggests slowly, "this is who you have always been?"

I shake my head. "No, no. I was a man back on my world."

"You are referring to your birth body," Mirzayael says. She reaches out to tap me once on the chest, and once on the forehead. "I mean in here."

I frown. "I... I don't know. I never thought of it that way. I guess I never really thought about it at all. I mean, what you're saying..."

"This body doesn't define you any more or less than your last," Mirzayael says. "What's inside hasn't changed. Whether you wish for me to identify you as a man or a woman—or anything else—is something that I would expect to remain consistent regardless of which world you are in."

Her words shake me.

It's not that I've never heard of transgender people. They were there, on the periphery of my awareness, in the same way basketball or nail salons were concepts of which I knew but never spent much time thinking about.

I don't object to the idea of being labeled as a woman. In fact, I haven't objected to it since coming here because it felt... natural. Comfortable. Implicit.

But how does that fit with the life I'd led on Earth? I'd been a man. A husband. A father. Or at least, I'd assumed I'd been all those things. I'd never really considered there was an alternative before now. But could there have been?

I take a difficult mental step back. I try to imagine my old self—my human self—as a woman. Would I have felt uncomfortable being called "she" and "her?" Would someone calling me Ma'am instead of Sir make me feel warm, or cold? Was that ever-present sense of wrongness, of my life being off kilter, of always waiting for some intangible change to snap my life into focus like a pair of glasses, rooted in all this?

My stomach churns with uncertainty. I'm not sure I have an answer.

But shouldn't I? Shouldn't the answer to such a simple question be obvious?

"I... I guess I didn't know that was an option," I say, a little dazed.

"Regardless, how should I refer to you now?" Mirzayael asks.

Panic wells up inside me. "Uh, well, that is..." The words tumble out of my mouth without any direction, without me even knowing what I'll say next. "I would prefer..."

What? What would I prefer? I can't expect her to use *no* pronouns with me at all. Just pick something!

I take in a breath.

And it all comes out in a gasp as my foot plunges through the ground and I go careening forward.

Oh, the Dungeon Core notices. By the way, there is a hole there!

My other foot goes through the next instant. I'm falling even before I've begun to process what's happened—by the time my wings strike the ground, I have enough time to throw my arms out to the side, trying to catch myself. But by then my momentum is too much to overcome, and in a dozen flashes of pain that happen in an instant, my arms and wings fold up beneath my weight and the ground swallows me whole. I let out a cry as gravity takes me. Then, impact.

[10 points of Fall damage sustained,] Echo reports.

I'm on the ground, every limb throbbing but nothing screaming. A faint light over my head indicates the hole I fell through is at least two stories above. I wince, gingerly flexing each leg, arm, and wing, but nothing appears broken. Small miracles.

Thanks for the head's up, I grumble at the Dungeon Core.

Mirzayael's face, barely illuminated by her spear, appears at the hole in the ceiling.

"Are you alright?" she calls. Her voice is tense—concerned. I'm flattered.

"I think so." I carefully pick myself up. There's a few cuts and scrapes on my arms where a layer of feathers has been shredded away. Some aches in my wings, knees, and hip where bruises will no doubt form. Will I even be able to see bruises beneath the feathers? A curious phenomenon I'll have to investigate later.

"Can you fly back up?" Mirzayael asks.

I shake out my wings, holding them to either side. "I don't believe they can provide sufficient lift."

"Right," Mirzayael says. "Phoenix harpy. Sorry. Forgot you don't have wind magic."

Lighting a new Spark, as the old one got snuffed out somewhere in the fall, I glance around my surroundings. My Spark doesn't illuminate more than a small radius around me, but from the Dungeon

Core's Map interface I can detect that I'm in a long stone chamber. The floor and ceiling are within the Core's sphere of influence, along with two opposite walls, but the others are outside its range.

"Perhaps I can look around for a way out," I say. "There might be stairs somewhere around here."

"No, hold tight," Mirzayael says. "The gap's too small for me to fit through, but I should be able to spin you a rope. It should only take a moment. *Don't* go wandering off. The ground down there might be compromised as well. And getting separated in here can be a death sentence."

No kidding. But she's right that I should pay more attention to where I'm walking. I give the Dungeon Core a pointed look.

Speaking of the Core, I wonder if I could use it to assemble my own staircase back up.

What do you think? I ask. *Can you do something that refined, without compromising this room or, say, squashing me into the ceiling?* I mentally picture a stone staircase rising from the ground, leading up to the gap in the ceiling for emphasis.

Oh yes! The Dungeon Core excitedly presses forward. Of course! Easily. Not a problem to reshape the stone. It just needs enough mana to do so.

I remain skeptical it understood either of my preventative instructions. Still, it's worth investigating if I even have enough mana to achieve such a feat.

Echo, I start to ask, bringing up a visual of my mana levels: [91/200]. However, something else snags my attention before I can complete the thought.

Several something elses.

A hiss echoes from the dark.

I spin to face the sound, holding my Spark before me as I strain to make anything out in the dark. A large shadow squats on the ground a few feet away, its eyes reflecting my fire in two perfect orange circles.

I call for a Check.

[Check: Level 14 Greater Stinger. These stone-skinned scorpions often dwell in dark, humid, and isolated environments. Although highly venomous, they are generally passive and avoid conflict so long as their nest isn't threatened.]

"Oh, shit," Mirzayael says from above.

I take a cautious step back. "No need to worry about me," I tell the stinger. "I'm not a predator. I don't mean any harm." And as long as I don't disturb its nest, I should be able to walk away without drawing its ire.

Then other shadows shift in the dark. Echo displays a label over each new one that skitters forward.

[Level 9 Stinger. Level 10 Greater Stinger. Level 8 stinger. Level 6 stinger. Level 11 Greater Stinger.]

A dozen more blink into existence like fireflies illuminating a forest.

So much for not threatening their nest.

"Oh shit, indeed," I say.

Chapter Eleven

STINGER NEST

I continue to back away from the stinger nest, mind racing.

Core, keep an eye out on the ground, I tell it. *Watch for any thin spots. Weak points. Make sure I'm not about to step through a hole and fall again. Got that?*

I'm not sure it does, but I don't have time to be more explicit. I snuff out my Spark next, summoning two Blazes in their place. A small fire, only the size of a Spark, appears over each hand. Unlike my Spark spell, however, I can manipulate the size and movement of each Blaze. When I step back again, I leave the two flames where I'd summoned them, hovering next to each other in the air.

[Spell Level Up,] Echo abruptly announces. [Blaze spell now Level 2. Mana cost reduced to 8 per cubic meter per second.]

Ah, yes! About time. I'd neglected the spell before, but this experience is really underscoring how I should be leveling up offensive abilities as well—especially if I continue to explore the Catacombs with Mirzayael. Mana appears to be an invaluable resource in this world, so any way I can help reduce my mana consumption is—

One of the stingers hisses, darting forward and breaking me out of my strategizing. Against all instincts, I force myself to remain still, instead sending my Blaze spells forward to meet the creature.

The stinger falters as my two fires rush toward it. With any luck, I'm pulling off a tried-and-true feature of defensive evolution: tricking a predator into thinking I have much bigger and more intimidating eyes than I do.

I slowly swivel my pair of eye-flames around to the side, and the stinger thankfully turns to face them. So far so good.

I take another step back.

Oh! The Dungeon Core abruptly speaks up. Yes, it would not step right there. That's a bad place to step.

I throw myself forward, even as my foot begins to plunge through a gap in the floor. The stone crumbles away behind me as I land on my knees and scramble forward, away from the widening gap in the floor, until I find myself on solid ground once more.

"You have to tell me *before* I step on a bad spot," I cry, adrenaline shooting through me, my heart thrumming like an engine inside my chest.

Oh. The Dungeon Core didn't know that. Okay!

I let out an irritated breath, but I don't have time to recover; the stinger is no longer facing my flames. It's facing me—and it's not alone.

"Mirzayael!" I call, my voice tight as I try to remain calm. I pull my flames back between me and the stingers again, hoping to deter them. "Any time now!"

The woman swears. "They'll attack you if I try to pull you up. I can't fit through this hole either—here, take this for now. Heads up!"

I glance toward the ceiling in time to see Mirzayael's spear flying down toward me. I scramble away with a surprised squawk.

A squawk? Really?

The spear stabs into the floor next to me, its tip still glowing an ethereal blue. I grab the shaft and yank it from the ground, but the force was unnecessary: it slides smoothly free of the stone. Perhaps that magic is doing more than just making the point glow. I'm glad Mirzayael never had a chance to use it on me.

Hissing and clicks surge in my direction. I slash the spear in a circle around me, buying space as the stingers close in, while I flare my Blaze spells, feeding more mana into them and sending the flames crashing into the nearest creatures who dared venture too close. Several of them screech, darting back into the shadows, but there are more to take their place.

[7 points of Fire damage dealt,] Echo reports.

Now that they're close enough to my firelight to make out, I can't help but shiver. The creatures do look similar to scorpions, though horrifyingly they vary from the size of a small cat to a large dog, each equipped with dual tails curled up over their backs, ending in wickedly sharp points. One of the greater stingers surges forward, crashing through my flames and straight toward me.

I slash at it with Mirzayael's spear, slicing through two of its forelegs. The creature screeches as it crashes to the ground, its other legs still scrabbling to push it forward, its tails slashing wildly at the air. Horrified, I stab the spear into its back, whereupon the creature screams again, flailing wildly.

"The head," Mirzayael calls down. "You have to stab it through the head!"

My stomach turns with horror at the tortured display occurring before me. "Good God." I yank my spear free, flecks of black juice splattering the stone, and then I stab it down once more, straight into the cluster of eyes and clicking jaws. The creature shudders, then goes limp.

I pull the spear away, but I don't get a chance to recover as another stinger races toward me. Steeling myself, I attack once more.

It takes killing another three of the large stingers and burning a dozen more with my flames before the nest begins to back off. I'm constantly spinning, slashing, flaring my fire to keep any of them from getting within tail-stabbing range. It can't have been more than a minute or two, but it feels like hours.

Abruptly, a giant shadow scurries over the wall. I stagger away, spear raised. This is much bigger than anything else. If it's a high-level stinger, then I'm in serious trouble. I squeeze the spear, heart hammering against my chest, as I flare my fires brighter. The form leaps, and I brace myself.

Mirzayael crashes down on top of one of the stingers, her legs stabbing through the creature. She spins toward me, snatching the spear from my grasp before I have a moment to react, then becomes a blur of death as she sweeps through the stingers' ranks. The creatures scatter before her, but Mirzayael is unrelenting.

Finally, the Captain stops, flicking her spear to the side to fling viscera from its point. What stingers still remain alive flee back into the shadows, leaving dozens of their fellows stabbed or charred on the ground before us. I could claim only perhaps six of those.

"Well done," Mirzayael says, turning to me. "You did better than I would have thought."

"You make it sound like you were expecting me to get eaten," I say, finally allowing myself to relax. My wings droop, and my arms ache.

"Don't be ridiculous," she says. "They would have stung you, not eaten you. That only comes after their prey has succumbed to the venom."

"Right," I say flatly. "That's much preferable."

A smile pulls at her lips. "Sorry I couldn't help you sooner. It took a few minutes to find a way down." She points behind us into the black. "There's a staircase back that way which leads to the main floor."

It's the same direction as the unstable ground I'd nearly fallen through. "Might be tricky for me to make it back that way. I lack the ability to walk on walls."

"Pity, that," Mirzayael says. "Such a useful skill. Well, we'll figure something out. First, help me with these." She gestures to the dead stingers.

I raise an eyebrow. "Help how?"

She grabs the nearest one and pulls it over to a pile of others. "Gather them up. We'll take these home for food and materials. Here, you form a pile while I work on securing them." She produces a length of white, shimmering rope I strongly suspect to be spider webbing. I try to keep my staring as subtle as possible while I watch her create more silk. Sure enough, she produces the material from the back of her abdomen, spinning new lines of the material and rapidly weaving them together to form thicker braids.

I don't know what else I had been expecting.

I desperately try not to think about it when she hands me a piece to tie up the stingers.

It's sticky.

I think about it.

We get around twenty of the stingers tied to Mirzayael's rope, attached in a daisy chain. Once secured, Mirzayael drags them over to the wall, then begins to pick her way up. Watching her scale the surface is fascinating. Like a mountain goat finding impossible footholds. At the ceiling she maneuvers her way over to the hole I'd fallen down, then fixes the end of the string to the gap, leaving the string of dead stingers hanging in the air. A minute later she climbs back down.

"There," she says, breathing heavily. I guess even she can get worn out every once in a while. "We will be able to haul them up from the other side on the way back to the Keep. For now, we can carry on."

How she intends to drag all of those creatures back to the city, I have no idea. But I'm beginning to know better than to question Mirzayael.

"Great," I say, looking back into the dark. I snuff out one of my Blazes and push the other forward, floating it across the room. There are cracks in the floor I can make out from here, even without the Core to tell me the stone is unstable.

Core, is there a safe way across this room? I ask it. And since clearly I need to be more specific when I ask it questions, I add, *And by safe, I mean a path I could walk across without the ground crumbling beneath my feet.*

The Core can't tell. It can barely see anything! I stopped giving it mana, and it is soooooo hungry. Why can't I give it more mana? It really could do so much more if I found it mana ore. Then it could see everything! The whole mountain! Its power would be limitle—

Alright, alright, I cut it off. *I'll keep an eye out for this mana ore of yours.* Although I'm not sure I like the idea of giving this creature limitless power. Not that I think it would do anything evil, per se, but I also don't trust it has the self-awareness to not cause harm. Like an excited dog prancing around a litter of puppies.

In the meantime, I check my own mana stores: 23/200. Not looking great, and we've only just barely begun to explore the Catacombs. I'll need to be more judicious with my mana expenditure going forward.

"Looks like we'll just have to carefully pick our way across," I say. "I should be able to use the Dungeon Core to find a safe path, but I won't be able to tell if the ground is stable more than a few steps ahead of me, so it might involve some backtracking. Not the most efficient route, but until these wings decide to start working, it's the best I've got."

Mirzayael nods. "Here, tie this around your waist," she says, offering me more spider silk. "At least next time you fall, I can be prepared and haul you back up."

"*If* there's a next time," I add.

Mirzayael nods. "Yes. Next time."

I sigh, tying the rope around my waist.

Slowly, I begin edging my way across the room. Mirzayael keeps to the side—*literally*—as she half walks along the floor, half on the wall. I try to follow, figuring the edges of the room are more likely to be stable than the middle, but even then the Dungeon Core abruptly and loudly bursts into my mind, suggesting maybe I shouldn't step on the half-decayed tile, or rotted out floor. Its suggestions to avoid death are very much appreciated, even if they all come nearly a moment too late. Finally, we make it to the opposite wall.

"The staircase is just ahead," Mirzayael says. "Then we can get back on track."

As if me nearly perishing was only a detour. "Sounds great to me," I say. As we head in the direction Mirzayael suggested, we pass a crumbling statue built into an alcove of the wall. My firelight falls over it as we pass, moving shadows over the features of the statue almost as if it's come to life. A harpy, I note. She's twenty feet tall, hands raised above her and wings splayed to the side. Bits of her hands and wings have broken off, and a pile of rubble lays at her feet. I turn my attention away, searching for the stairwell, as

WAIT!

I jump as the Dungeon Core practically screams into my mind.

Wait wait wait! Go back. There's stone there—different stone! It must taste it—it's new, different, something it hasn't tasted ever! Or at least, in a long time. But that's basically forever! It needs it, I have to go back, please please please please—

"Shhhh," I hiss, shaking my head. "Calm down."

"What is it?" Mirzayael asks.

"Ah, sorry," I say, pausing to look back at the statue. "The Dungeon Core noticed something in the rocks we passed. It's just being... insistent."

"Noticed what?" Mirzayael asks.

"I'm not sure." Carefully, I backtrack to the statue. *Well?*

The stone. It's so light and fluffy and soft! And infused with mana. It wants to eat it! Can it eat it?

Curious, I bend down and pick up a piece of broken stone. "Ah!" I say, my hand coming up fast. I open my hand, palm up, and it almost feels as though I'm holding nothing at all. "It's so light!"

Mirzayael peers over my shoulder, looking from the stone to the statue. She picks up a piece as well.

"Ah yes, cloudstone," she says, tossing the rock into the air. It floats up, and up and up until it vanishes into the dark. A moment later, it begins drifting back down.

"Amazing," I say, bouncing the rock in my hand. "I've never seen anything like it." I squeeze the stone, expecting it to crumble like dried sand, but it remains firm and solid in my grasp. "How can it have such strength?"

"Air arcana infused in the rock," Mirzayael says. "I'm surprised there's any mana in it after all this time. The statue must have been radiating magic when it was first made."

"Fascinating," I say. "I can't even imagine what kind of aircraft we might have been able to achieve with composites like this." My mind is already spinning with the applications. Lighter than air—or perhaps nearly as light as air—fuselages. But how would that affect its center of gravity? Hmmm...

Please. Please please please it wants to eat some, just a little bit, it's so soft and fluffy and it will feel so good to devour it!

I snort as the Dungeon Core pulls me from my thoughts. It's like a child begging for cotton candy. *Alright,* I think, allowing the Core to consume the piece I'm holding in my hand. At least that will add another type of material to our catalog. And I'm definitely eager to read into its attributes at a later date.

The rock glows, then disintegrates out of existence as the Dungeon Core exudes all sorts of happy food-related sensations. It's almost enough to make rocks sound appetizing.

[Mana Gain: 1]

Ohoho. What's this? We *gained* mana from consuming it, rather than losing any. It must be because of the air arcana Mirzayael mentioned. Which means consuming things infused with magic will help restore my own mana store. This is excellent information to know.

Mirzayael watches curiously as the stone vanishes from my hand. "What do you intend to do with that?"

"I don't know," I admit. "But it stokes the imagination, doesn't it?"

Mirzayael tips her head at me. "You are a strange one, Outsider."

"That's what they tell me," I say with a chuckle. "Now, come on. We've got a whole kingdom to explore, don't we?"

"Indeed we do." Mirzayael leads us away from the statue, and the staircase is only a thirty second walk beyond. She holds her spearhead out into the dark stairwell. "Come, then. We've still much climbing to do. And more danger lies ahead."

Despite the warning, I can't help but smile. What other treasures will I find within these walls? What other mysteries lay in wait to be discovered?

I step onto the stairs, eager to find out.

Chapter Twelve

BENEATH THE PIPES

We spend the day wandering the Catacombs, exploring buildings, temples, and empty fields. It's all fascinating to me. The tall, swooping architecture, the flame motif that decorates the buildings, the statues of Fyreneth—it speaks to a culture wholly unique from anything I'd encountered on Earth. I ask Mirzayael about every crumbling statue and mural we pass, trying to absorb any bits of history I can manage, but she doesn't seem to know any more than Beryl had. Mirzayael also appears to be right about texts. We find a room that was clearly intended to be a library, but all the papers have been eaten away by time and mold and bugs; nothing but dust remains. Disappointing, but I'm not deterred.

"Here we are," Mirzayael says, leading the way into an echoing chamber. A hissing sound and flickering of shadows indicate a flurry of small creatures fleeing before us. Such occurrences are not uncommon, though luckily all have been significantly less violent than the encounter with the stingers.

"Where are we?" I ask. My talons click strangely as I step into the room, and I glance down at my feet even as the Dungeon Core perks up excitedly in my mind. "Tiles?"

Yes. The Core would love to sample some of these! They are different colors, too! It bets they all have different flavors. The yellow one might be sour and the red one might be sweet and the green one—

"The bathhouse," Mirzayael says. "At least, that's what I gather. If you want to search for your connection to the thermal springs, this place is probably your best bet."

The visible path we've blazed through the Dungeon Core's Map display has taken us on a sinuous route deep into the heart of the Catacombs. We're somewhere in the lower levels of Fyreneth's palace, though we've yet to make it higher, where the throne room might be, as a glacier has bisected the route we planned to take. It also appears to be cutting off a portion of the city, but no matter; I'm sure we'll be able to find a way around it eventually. As Mirzayael said, I need to start somewhere.

"Thank you," I say, continuing to ignore the Core's constant pleading to eat the different colored tiles. "Well, then. Let's see what we've got."

I tell the Core to get back on track and make sure I'm not about to step through any more weak spots in the floor. It reluctantly complies once I let it know it can eat some of the tiles on our way out. For now, I venture into the room, sending a small Blaze ahead of me like a floating candle.

The chamber is covered in a mosaic of tiles, swirling like sunbursts across the ground. Large basins pockmark the floor, no doubt different pools that had been filled with steaming water once upon a time. But where did that water come from?

I carefully lower myself into one such cavity, slowly picking my way across the bottom of the pool. I crouch down over a hole in the floor, glancing inside. Unlike the cracks and crevices that run wild in the Catacombs, this one is perfectly round.

I Check my mana: 112/200. I've managed to recover a good amount despite the trickle I'm expending on keeping the undersized Blaze going. I can afford to spend some more on the Dungeon Core here.

The Core vibrates excitedly when it hears this. Yes! A great idea. Give it more!

I will, but you need to keep your range very narrow, I say, mentally picturing what I mean for emphasis. *Follow this tunnel. See how far you can sense it.*

The Core deflates a little. That doesn't sound as fun as eating rocks, but it supposes it can go looking anyway. And maybe just take a tiny nibble on the way.

No nibbles.

Despite being an inanimate stone, the Core seems to sigh. No nibbles.

I close my eyes as I begin funneling mana into the Dungeon Core, and I feel its presence expand into the rocks beneath us. It swirls around the hole carved into the ground, and sure enough, it finds the perfectly round tunnel is made of a different material—metal.

The Core traces the pipe down, then off to the side, zig-zagging as its path twists and bends into the earth. Many other tunnels open into it, or the pipe we're following splits into several different paths. I instruct the Core to follow the largest pipe at any juncture. Hopefully that will eventually send us in the right direction.

I follow its progress, concentrating on all the sensations the Core is picking up—the coolness of the earth, the contrasting texture of the pipe, densities, compositions, temperature, humidity—

I'm so focused on what the Dungeon Core is experiencing, that my mind gets pulled right along with it.

Disorientingly, I no longer feel my body. I no longer experience sight and smell and taste. At least, not the same way. The way the Dungeon Core experiences the world is far more quantifiable. Like I'm peering beneath the veneer of reality itself, exposing matter in its purest, most mathematical form. It's dizzying and exhilarating. I don't want to let these sensations go.

As we bore into the earth, following the pipes toward an ever-widening path, something shudders our surroundings. The Dungeon Core doesn't pay attention at first, brushing it off as some sort of minor earth tremors, but my human senses recognize it for something else.

Wait, I tell the Core. *Stop. What was that?*

The Core affects some sort of shrug—I'm beginning to suspect it's picking up these mental approximations of gestures from me—but stops burrowing. Our consciousness hovers, some hundred feet beneath our bodies, waiting for anything to stir in the dark.

The vibrations come again, knocking dust from the walls as they echo up the pipes. This time, I'm sure of it. That's not an earthquake: that's the roar of an animal. A very big animal.

[Mana Expired.]

The Dungeon Core's range is abruptly yanked back up like a fish on a line, boomeranging both our minds back into our bodies. I gasp, falling back on my butt, blinking rapidly as I readjust to normal human—er, harpy—sensations again. Mirzayael grabs my arm.

"Are you alright?" she asks, suddenly beside me. "You stopped moving. I thought you stopped *breathing*. You wouldn't respond to me."

"I'm fine," I say, panting as if out of breath. *Had* I stopped breathing while following the Core down that rabbit hole? If so, I'll need to be a lot more careful about using its abilities that way. "Sorry to worry you."

Mirzayael's concerned look purses into a frown. "I was not worried. Merely confused. Did you find what you were looking for, then?"

I check the Map Interface: sure enough, a thin thread of "explored" stone burrows through my display. It heads down, but also cuts off to the side, as if diverting into a neighboring cavern.

"We've still a long way to go," I say. "But I think we can start from a different point in the castle, closer to where the pipes are headed, and continue exploring from there once my mana has recovered. However," I add, "there might be a bigger problem. Literally. Do you know of any large beasts dwelling in these tunnels?"

"What do you mean?" she asks.

I explain the roaring sound I'd heard; I wish I had anything more to give her.

She shakes her head. "I know of nothing that lives in these caverns that could produce such a bellow as that. Perhaps out on the ice sheets, there might be frost cats or direwolves, but they would be more likely to wander into the higher caverns above us, near the surface. I can't imagine any large creature would have enough of a food source to survive at this depth."

And yet, there's no denying what the Dungeon Core and I heard. "I guess we'll find out when we track down where those pipes lead," I say. "However, I believe it would be wise to bring backup."

Mirzayael nods. "I am in complete agreement there."

Since I'm out of mana for the time being, there's not much more I can do to investigate. We pause beneath yet another statue of Fyreneth to eat lunch—or perhaps dinner. Without natural light, I've lost all sense of time.

I nod to the statue as we eat a bowl of toasted mushrooms and sweet ferns. "Do you believe all the stories about her?" I ask.

Mirzayael glances up at the figure. "Depends on the stories."

"Do you think she really raised a fortress from the ground in less than a month?"

She shrugs. "Such kinds of magic are not impossible. You yourself wield an artifact that allows you to shape the earth."

She's right about that, although it doesn't seem nearly powerful enough to do what Beryl described. Or is it only the size of my mana pool that is restricting its potential?

"And you really think the city was buried because it was forsaken by the gods?" I ask, a bit skeptical. "Is it possible, say, the castle was instead swallowed by an earthquake? Tectonic shifts?"

It's Mirzayael's turn to look skeptical. "And the structure remains intact?" She sweeps her hand around pointedly. "Why would you suggest that?"

"I suppose I find it difficult to swallow the existence of gods," I admit. "The story is fantastical; I wondered if it could be more myth than history."

"So you find a perfectly sunken city more likely to be the outcome of nature than magic?" she asks.

I chuckle. "It does seem silly when you put it like that. It's hard to square everything I've ever known—or thought I knew—with this new reality. I suppose I could believe it was the cause of something magical." I glance at my wrist, where the Dungeon Core sits glistening.

"As you pointed out, I've plenty of irrefutable evidence for that at my fingertips."

Mirzayael grunts. "The gods are real. Best to start believing in them now." She spits to the side. "But don't believe that they care about us. If they did, they would have answered any one of our prayers and saved our people generations ago. No, they want us buried and forgotten. And the Jorrians ensure their will is carried out by slaughtering any Fyrethians who dare attempt to venture across the ice."

I shake my head. "If true, that seems immeasurably cruel. What's worth condemning thousands of souls over?"

Mirzayael eyes the stone on my wrist. "They deemed Fyreneth's relic a threat. But why they considered it so dangerous is an answer that has always remained obscured."

I look at the Dungeon Core dubiously. "Seems like such a small thing to kill so many people over. No matter their reasons, such an act cannot be just."

"In that we both agree," Mirzayael says stiffly. She shovels the remainder of her food into her mouth, then begins packing the bowls away. "The question is: What will you do if the gods come for you, too?"

That gives me pause. I'm a nobody. A career engineer. A failed father. Someone who clearly ended up in the wrong place—in the wrong body—at the wrong time. It certainly was never my intention to draw anyone's ire.

Yet that Role continues to linger at the bottom of my stat sheet: The Dark Lord.

Looks like I might not be given much of a choice in the matter.

"Well, I suppose I'll have to cross that bridge if I ever come to it," I say. "But if helping the people here is against the will of the gods, then it seems my mission is already doomed to be sacrilegious."

Mirzayael smiles. "Good answer, Outsider."

We pack up our things as Mirzayael decides it's time to return to Fyreneth's Keep. She lets me lead the way back out—testing how accurate my Map Display really is, I suspect. On the way we stop by the hole I'd fallen through and reel up the string of insect bodies, securing the entire, enormous tangle to Mirzayael's back. She stumbles a few times beneath the weight, favoring one side due to her missing leg. I wish she didn't have to suffer because of my actions. Somehow, I'll make it up to her.

"Fire!" Nek calls when we return through the city's hidden entrance. He comes bounding up the path, rather cat-like. "You're alright!"

I smile, happily spreading my arms as he sweeps me up in an enormous, fuzzy hug.

"Glad to see you concerned that the *both* of us have returned," Mirzayael says.

Nek releases me, wrinkling his nose at Mirzayael. "We all knew you'd be fine. It was Fire we weren't sure would make it out alive."

My smile turns into a grimace. "Thanks for the vote of confidence."

"Now what's this?" Nek asks, stepping around Mirzayael's side. "Stingers! A whole pile of them!"

"You can thank the Outsider for that," Mirzayael said. "She fell into a nest and I had to go dig her out."

"I took six down on my own, thank you very much," I object.

Nek's eyes go wide. "You did? Amazing! We will feast tonight. You must tell me all about it. Come! Come now, let's get this back into town."

"So long as we have your permission," Mirzayael grumbles. But she and I follow as Nek races ahead, surely already spinning inaccurate and uninformed tales of our escapades.

"I apologize," Mirzayael says as we walk. "I used 'she' again, but you never said if that was acceptable."

I'd noticed that as well. Yet, it didn't bother me. In fact, the more I hear others refer to me as a woman, the more right it feels. All this is certainly confusing. I don't think I'm educated nearly enough in this subject to understand the implications of my circumstances—socially, psychologically, biologically.

But maybe this puzzle of emotions is something that can't be solved with logic. Maybe this is something I just need to feel.

"I... I think I like it," I say, that nervous, giddy energy fluttering in my stomach once more. Like sharing a secret. Like confessing love. "I think I would like for you to continue to refer to me that way."

"Of course," Mirzayael says.

[Pronouns updated,] Echo reports.

Can it truly be that simple?

More dracid are awake and helping to prepare dinner when Mirzayael and I finally stumble into camp. Beryl welcomes me back with a friendly nod. Sora sits me down and refuses to let my half-hearted attempts to help with food prep come to fruition. Truthfully, I'm exhausted from the journey and happy to let others take care of me for a while.

The stinger stew is delicious. It's the first meat I've eaten in the week I've been here. The broth is warm and fills me with a hearty nourishment I hadn't been able to find in all the cave fungi I'd been given before now. That's another thing I should add to my ever-growing to-do list: establish some sort of corral where livestock like the stingers can be kept. I'll have to ask Mirzayael why that hasn't already been established; she's sure to have some insight.

The hall is warm with laughter and company. Sora asks me about my travels, and her kids chase each other around the meal circle. It's strange to find the conversations with these people coming so naturally. It's foreign to feel welcomed, for my presence to be wanted. Why had it been so hard for me to find such connections on Earth? I always thought I couldn't relate well to other people, but it's been coming easily to me here. Maybe the whole time on Earth it was just me getting in the way of myself. Perhaps I'd allowed that ever present feeling of discontent—that instinct that something wasn't quite right—to cast a shadow over the rest of my life. If I'd been more certain in who I was then, would things have turned out differently? Would I have been happy? Could I have made my family happy?

Hypotheticals I'll never know the answer to. I am here now. I am with these people now. Even if my last life was steeped in regrets, this one doesn't have to be.

I smile as Mirzayael sits down with the rest of us, and I laugh as she wrinkles her nose at the shrieking kids. Yes, I think I can find a new home here.

That night, my sleep is long, deep, and dreamless.

Over the next few days, I help out around town and make several more expeditions to the Catacombs in an effort to continue mapping out the system of pipes. The townspeople have really taken a liking to me, different groups inviting me to eat with them every meal. Between such socialization, I set aside some time each day to practice spells, intent on not being caught off guard and weaponless again. In that time, I manage to get Blaze up to Level 4, nearly cutting its mana expenditure in half.

On our third expedition into the Catacombs, we trace the pipes beneath the glacier that's bisected a corner of the city. Unable to go through, I spend some time with the Core trying to find the most traversable set of caves and tunnels that could take us beneath the wall of ice. On the fourth expedition, we start to map it out.

This time, Nek and three others have accompanied Mirzayael and I: a dwarf named Opal, an arachnoid named Zakaiya, and a felis named Rei. Mirzayael says it's good training for the younger scouts. I suspect she's concerned that knocking down walls and spelunking in unfamiliar caves will stir up more nests of stingers. I certainly don't intend to object to more security.

"Here we are," I say, stopping in front of a wall. Via the Dungeon Core's map, I can tell the stone in front of us is only two feet thick. "Once we break through this wall, we should be at the roof of a cavern. It goes deep enough that it should allow us to bypass the glacier. From there, the city pipes end only another two hundred feet on. That must be where the springs are." At least, I really hope so.

"Will you be able to create an anchor as you do so?" Mirzayael asks. This time, she brought a long coil of pre-spun silk. "That will greatly assist me in securing our rope."

I relay the idea to the Dungeon Core, who is more than happy to make new shapes in the rock. It will be fun! "Shouldn't be a problem. Ready?"

The young scouts lean closer as I raise a hand to the stone. None of them have seen me work with the Dungeon Core before, and I'm sure they've heard all sorts of stories by now (no thanks to Nek).

"Proceed," Mirzayael says.

Alright, I tell the excitedly buzzing Core. *Eat your fill.* Then I hastily add, *Within reason!*

I mentally provide a mental picture of a hole, shaped in a circle with a three-foot radius, cut into the stone before us. The Core happily gets to work. Metrics about the stone it consumes stream through my consciousness like a torrent of water. Witnessed from a distance, it's all sensations filtered through the Core's interpretation, which it likes to describe in ways such as sour, cold, or, most often, crunchy. But if I plunge my mind into that stream of information, the details resolve into data: mass, density, composition. It's tempting to lose myself in the raw numbers, but I focus on the external world instead. Before us, a hole appears in the stone, steadily widening as if eaten away by an invisible horde of gnats. And strangely, a glimmer of light and a burst of strong, stale wind blows through the opening.

Nek bounds up beside me, leaning forward to peer through the hole and into the glistening chamber below.

The glowing, white gemstones are the first thing I notice, covering every inch of the wall—and I taste them, like rock candy, like vanilla ice cream, as the Core consumes some of the crystals and their data is added to our ever-expanding database. Interestingly, the Core also eats a layer of ice that covers some of the luminescent gemstones, almost indistinguishable from the crystals themselves.

Then, the crystals move.

Nek throws himself back as a roar crashes into us, shaking the stones in our tunnel and resonating through the cave's crystals like windchimes.

"Holy shit," Mirzayael mutters, glancing over my shoulder.

As my mind finally catches up with what my eyes are processing, the shifting wall of crystals abruptly comes into focus.

Amidst the crystalline cavern, a giant, white serpent lies coiled around the stalagmites at its base. It spreads its translucent blue wings and cranes its head in our direction.

The dragon's maw parts in a toothy grin.

Chapter Thirteen

THE DRAGON

The dragon's mouth snaps open and another roar tears through us. A white light begins to glow down the back of its gullet. Mirzayael grabs my shoulder and yanks me back. I stumble, my wings flailing wildly, which in turn knock over Nek and Rei. The entire heap falls into a haphazard pile as a concussive blast crashes into the ceiling of the crystal chamber. A cold wind and bright light flashes through the tunnel.

Mirzayael extracts herself from the pile first, picking up each of us one by one and hoisting us to our feet like a bunch of stumbling kittens.

"Good god," I say, staring at the hole. A dragon. A real life dragon! Of course, plenty of things have been fantastical before now, but to see a creature you daydreamed about as a child—it's truly something else! I immediately begin to wonder how the aerodynamics of such a creature would work. Does it need wind arcana to fly, like harpies? Can animals also wield magic? Can a creature have more than one type of magic? Each subsequent question leads to a new one.

Ice partially covers the hole, spearing toward us in long, jagged spikes along the ceiling and walls. Cautiously, yet with equal fascination, I creep back over and run my hand along the ice.

That explains why some of the crystals were covered in a layer of ice, then. "How is it doing that?" I ask Mirzayael. "Ice magic?"

"It seems to be a frost dragon," she says. "And yes, they have ice affinities. Able to summon a hailstorm with their very breath." She frowns. "I thought the Jorrians had hunted them to extinction. How one ended up down here... it doesn't make any sense."

The cavern rocks once more with the beast's roar, sending a scattering of ice shards cracking off the rocks and raining down on us.

"Well," I say, dusting myself off. "This certainly complicates the hot springs endeavor."

"Are you sure it's through here?" Mirzayael asks.

I close my eyes, summoning the Map Interface. Feeding more of my mana into the Core, I ask it to reach down into the chamber, then follow the path we'd already traced from the Catacombs plumbing system. The Core excitedly munches on some bits of ice and crystal as it complies, focusing its awareness down toward the base of the dragon's cavern. The area surrounding the cave is solid stone. We might be able to dig beneath the dragon's chamber, though that would take mana and time—not to mention, running the risk of structural collapse.

"It's not the only way through," I say. "But it's the quickest. Tunneling beneath remains an option, though the dragon's chamber would be much more convenient."

"We should leave it be and return later," Mirzayael suggests. "Either the creature will wander out the same way it came in, or it will starve, and then it will no longer be an issue."

Nek brightens. "What do you suppose dragon meat tastes like? Maybe we *shouldn't* let it wander back out."

Mirzayael gives him a critical look. "And how do you plan to slay it, exactly?"

The felis falters.

Nek's idea might be dangerous, but it's not bad, really. It would be a pity to kill such a magnificent creature, but it would certainly simplify access to the hot springs. Not to mention, the Fyrethians are in desperate need of resources, and the meat and hide of a dragon could do wonders for the community. Survival comes first.

"Slaying it might be possible," I say, considering my options. "Of course, getting the meat out of this chamber won't be trivial."

Mirzayael snorts. "Only an outsider would think slaying a dragon is easier than transporting its meat." Even so, she tips her head at me curiously. "What do you have in mind?"

"The Dungeon Core," I say. "It's very good at eating away stone. With its help, we wouldn't have to fight the creature directly; rather we could let gravity do the work for us."

Nek barks out a laugh, though it seems to be more from nerves than amusement. "A cave in? Can you really do that?"

I think back to the cave-in I'd inadvertently caused the first day I appeared here. "I am fairly sure I could."

Mirzayael considers this. "Can you guarantee it would be safe? We can't risk compromising the caverns around us."

"That is a valid concern," I allow. "And it might disrupt the Catacomb's plumbing system, which would be problematic for tracking the pipes to their source. I suppose I could try to fix them all in the aftermath, but... Hm, yes. Let me think on this, first."

Cautiously, I edge my way back over to the hole I'd carved into the chamber.

"Careful," Mirzayael says.

I slowly peek my head through the hole in the stone and ice.

The dragon is pacing impatiently around the bottom of the chamber. Its tail lashes from side to side, crashing through bits of ice and stone. It spreads its wings and attempts to flap them, but the chamber is too small for it to open fully. It growls, looking left and right, then puffs up its chest, rears back its head, and lets loose another blast of frost, which coats the nearby wall in a layer of white ice several feet thick. The dragon huffs, turning away in what seems to be frustration.

What's it trying to achieve? Maybe Mirzayael is right and it somehow got trapped down here, and now it's trying to find its way back out. But from my vantage point, the cavern seems entirely sealed—apart from the small hole I carved, anyway.

It probably will starve at some point. Who knows how long that would take for a creature of such size. But I can't imagine it would be a pleasant death. My cave-in plan might truly be a mercy.

Now, how much HP are we dealing with? *Check*, I think.

[Name: Ollie]

[Species: Frost Dragon]

[Class: Hunter]

[Level: 43]

[HP: 2432/2500]

[Mana: 231/850]

[Role: The Dragon]

My stomach turns to ice. "God almighty."

"What?" Mirzayael steps up behind me. "What's wrong?"

I turn back to the others, Checking each of them just to be sure: none of them have a Role among their stats. I Check the dragon once again: its Role is as clear as day. And it has a *name*, despite none of the stingers or other creatures I've come across having any personal identifiers. I recall a conversation I'd previously had with Echo on a similar subject. Only System Users have Roles.

A chill runs down my spine.

"It's like me," I say. "It has a Role. I—I think there's a *person* in there."

"What?" Nek asks, skeptical. "What do you mean? It's a beast. They're not intelligent."

"This one might be," I insist. "I think I can talk to it."

"Dragons can't speak," Mirzayael says. "No more than wolves or stingers can."

"But they can hear, can't they?" I ask. One stats even include pronouns; another quality I've noticed attached to sapient individuals, but not wild animals. "He should be able to understand what I say, at least."

"He?" Mirzayael asks, skeptical.

"His name is Ollie," I say.

They all stare at me like I've lost my mind.

"Please trust me," I beg. "Let me at least try to talk to him first!"

Nek and Mirzayael look at each other. Mirzayael shakes her head with a sigh. "Alright. But I'll be standing right behind you, and at the slightest sign it intends to attack, I'll be ripping you away from that opening, and we won't be taking any more chances at exposing ourselves to that creature. If it *does* attack, then we move forward with your plan to collapse the cave on it. Agreed?"

I don't know that I agree with that at all. I'm certain that this dragon is just like me—I can feel it in my core. Another lost soul slotted into an unfamiliar body.

A memory comes to me abruptly. Foggy, more like a dream than reality. After I'd died, I was in a dark place, surrounded by an acrid hate that was eating away at me like acid. But there were other people there too—other minds floating nearby, like bubbles in a sea.

How many of us were there?

Had all of them ended up in similar situations as Ollie and I?

I step forward, leaning into the hole as far as I dare. I spread my wings to either side, still in the passageway, using them as bracers to keep me from falling into the cavern. The dragon roars and thrashes, shooting blasts of ice randomly into the walls. He certainly looks like a wild beast from here.

But looks can be deceiving.

"Hello!" I call down into the cave.

The dragon jumps, whipping his head left and right as my voice bounces around the chamber. An amusingly human reaction.

"Up here!" I call again, waving an arm. "I want to help you!"

The dragon—Ollie, apparently—looks up.

"Hello! I—"

The dragon pounces forward, rearing up on his hind legs and slamming his front claws into the wall. The entire chamber shakes, stalactites of ice and crystal breaking away and crashing to the floor. The shock knocks me from my feet, and Mirzayael grabs my arm, starting to drag me back.

"No!" I cry. "No, not yet! He understands me!"

I shake myself from her grip and crawl back over to the opening.

The dragon's head is right beneath me. My heart flutters as he looks up at me, tongue flicking between his teeth. Each canine is as long and sharp as a sword, and I'm keenly aware of how easily he could snap me up before I'd even have a chance to react. Instead, however, he tips his head to the side, regarding me.

I take a steadying breath and try to force my pulse to slow. "You *can* understand me, right?" I say.

The dragon growls, and his head dips. Was that a nod, or coincidence? I need more data.

"Okay, try this," I say. "If you can understand me, lift your left hand."

The dragon shifts, his claws digging into the ice along the wall and carving deep grooves into the surface. Then, he lifts his left claw.

Relief and joy flood through me, and I let out a nervous, happy laugh.

Nek whistles.

Mirzayael sucks in an awed breath. "It's true, then."

"Good job, Ollie," I say. "Now, I'm going to come down there, okay?"

"What?" Nek cries.

"Absolutely not," Mirzayael snaps.

"It's fine," I assure them. "He understands me."

"That doesn't mean he won't hurt you," Mirzayael says. "Even if just by accident! That beast—person—is huge. One misplaced step or swipe of his tail could be enough to end you."

I know she's right. The dragon is enormous, unthinkably powerful. But if this person is like me, if he's really someone else from Earth, I have to do whatever I can to help him. And for that, I need to be able to speak to him.

"Please lower me down?" I ask Mirzayael. "We can communicate if I can just touch him. But I'll need your help for that." I turn back to Ollie. "And can you reach an arm up here? The closer, the better."

The dragon huffs out a breath of cold air, sparkling with snowflakes. He stretches an arm up and grabs a clawful of ice, digging his talons into the material as easily as taking a handful of sand. It's still at least six feet below me, but Mirzayael should be able to help close that gap. I look back at her.

The arachnoid is glaring at me as if her look could summon daggers. Finally, she grumbles, turning to her pack and withdrawing a coil of silk. (After the stinger fiasco, she sat down to spin a long length of rope to carry on-hand in case of future emergencies.) "Fine. But if anything goes wrong, I'm pulling you back up."

"Works for me," I say. She begins unwinding the rope as I turn back to Ollie. "Just a little bit longer!" I call. The dragon's tail swishes back and forth impatiently.

Once Mirzayael has secured the rope around my torso—and under my arms and around my shoulders in a very thorough harness—I step cautiously to the edge. I wonder if I should have some harpy sense that doesn't make me afraid of heights. I glance down, and my stomach flips, nerves tickling like static in my fingertips. Maybe only the wind-affinity harpies get that.

"Okay," I tell Mirzayael as I sit on the edge, slowly easing my legs over. "My life's in your hands."

She snorts. "It has been since you set foot in my caves, Outsider."

The rope goes taut, and with a flutter of terror, I lower myself over the edge.

I try to hold onto the ledge as my feet scrape down the side of the ice, toward the dragon's massive paw beneath me. My wings flare to either side like a tightrope-walker's balancing pole, and now more than ever I desperately wish they were there for more than just aesthetics. Beneath me, the dragon huffs, and a puff of cold air blasts up toward me. My hand slips from the icy ledge, and I plunge for a terrifying fraction of a second before Mirzayael's silk catches me.

At the same time, Ollie startles, leaping up toward me. His nose bumps against my back and I let out a yelp, scrabbling for purchase. As the dragon drops back down, one of his teeth hooks on my line. The silk goes taut—then it snaps. Then, I'm falling.

I pinwheel head over heels, terror and vertigo clutching my gut. Someone from above shouts after me, their voice saturated with fear, but I don't have any time to register who it was or what they said as I aimlessly flail and make a futile attempt to flap my wings, the ground racing toward me.

Chapter Fourteen

OLLIE

Something hard and dark wraps around me, stopping my fall and obscuring my vision. I tumble over myself like a bean in a shaken can, but at least I'm no longer falling to my death. Given my surroundings are white and scaly, it's clear enough what's caught me—the dragon's claws.

He releases me, and I go spilling out onto the icy floor of the cave. I start to slide down the gentle incline until I dig my talons into the ice, likewise grabbing hold of the ground with the sharpened nails on my hands. I breathe out a shaky sigh of relief, then look up.

The dragon is craning his head down toward me. His lips peel back in what I hope is a smile, revealing dozens of pointed, sword-like teeth.

I have to remind myself that there's a person in there, someone sapient and empathic, just like me.

I hope they're empathic, anyway.

"Uh, hello!" I call. "Thank you for catching me." Assuming he had knocked me down by accident in the first place.

The dragon puffs another breath of frost at me, and I shiver.

"Ollie, right?" I ask.

The dragon nods. He nods!

I tentatively smile. "I take it you can't speak?"

Ollie growls, makes some strange huffing sounds, then roars.

"Right," I say. Carefully, I climb to my feet. "Your mouth isn't really designed for that. Well, I think I have a workaround." I hold up a hand. "I'll need to touch you, if that's okay."

Ollie grumbles, head tilted to the side, then leans his head down toward me. Carefully, gently, his nose bumps into my hand. It's cold and pebbly. It feels like I'm touching a glacier.

Okay, I think to myself. *Let's activate Psionic Touch.*

[Spell activated.]

"*—SO SMALL, LIKE A BIRD!*" The words burst into my mind, painfully loud and clear. "*IT'S A GOOD THING I DIDN'T SQUISH HER IN MY CLAWS! THAT WOULD HAVE BEEN BAD. I WONDER IF SHE HAS FOOD? I BET SHE TASTES LIKE CHICKEN NUGGETS. I WANT CHICKEN NUGGETS! NO, I SHOULDN'T EAT THE BIRD PERSON, THAT WOULD BE MEAN. UGH, I'M SOOOOOOO HUNGRY!*"

I open and close my mouth in surprise. It's a boy's voice—not just male, but young. Just a little kid. *Echo, can you Check his age?* I ask.

[Age: 7]

"Oh my god," I murmur. He *is* just a little kid.

"*Ollie?*" I think, mentally pressing my thoughts toward his mind. "*Can you hear me?*"

"*WHAAAA—*" The voice is cut off as Ollie flinches his head back, blinking in surprise.

I wave my hand. "You have to be touching me, or I can't hear you!"

Narrowing his eyes suspiciously, Ollie leans back in and bumps his nose against my hand.

"*—MY GOSH I HOPE SHE DIDN'T HEAR ME THINKING ABOUT EATING HER EARLIER.*"

"I'd prefer if you didn't," I think.

Ollie's eyes go wide. *"OH NO, SHE HEARD THAT TOO!"*

I chuckle. *"Yes, I can hear anything you think while we're touching. And you can hear me. Nice to meet you, Ollie."*

"NICE TO MEET YOU, TOO!" the boy cries. Even though it's all in my head, his voice is so loud, it's almost painful. *"I'M A DRAGON! ISN'T THAT COOL?"*

"Very cool." I smile. *"So tell me about yourself, Ollie. How did you end up here?"* I glance around the cave. *"I don't see a way out. Or in, more specifically."*

Ollie flares his wings up behind him. *"I HAVE NO IDEA! I WAS PLAYING BASHERS WITH JESSICA AND THEN MOM YELLED SOMETHING AND THEN I WOKE UP HERE AND EVERYTHING WAS COLD, BUT IT DIDN'T BOTHER ME THAT MUCH BECAUSE I'M A DRAGON. **RAWRRRR!** HOW COOL IS THAT!"*

I wince at the mental volume. "Bashers?" I ask.

"IT'S MY FAVORITE GAME," he explains, his tail whipping back and forth excitedly like a puppy. *"JESSICA—THAT'S MY COUSIN, BUT SHE'S BASICALLY LIKE A SISTER—JESSICA AND I GOT THESE REMOTE CONTROL CARS FOR CHRIST-MAS, WHICH WAS FUN FOR A WHILE, BUT THEN IT GOT BORING, AND THEN WE FIGURED WE COULD MAKE LEGO CARS AND TIE THEM ON A STRING TO THE BACK OF THE REMOTE CONTROL CARS, AND THEN WE'D EACH TRY TO RUN OVER EACH OTHER'S LEGO CAR WITH OUR OWN REMOTE CONTROL CAR BUT MAKE SURE OUR OWN LEGO CAR DIDN'T GET HIT AND WE CALLED IT **BASHERS**. BECAUSE OF TRYING TO BASH UP THE LEGO CAR."*

"I gathered," I say, frowning slightly. *"And that was the last thing you remember?"*

Ollie grumbles, heaving an enormous shrug. *"I GUESS SO. JESSICA JUST BASHED MY CAR SO I WAS GOING OUT TO PICK UP THE PIECES."*

A chill goes through me. *"Out where?"*

"IN THE STREET IN FRONT OF MY HOUSE," he says. *"THAT'S THE ONLY PLACE WITH ENOUGH ROOM TO PLAY."*

I decide to stop my current line of questioning. I can infer how this story ends.

"You're from Earth, right Ollie?" I ask, turning to a slightly safer topic.

"OF COURSE!" he cries. He tilts his head. *"ISN'T EVERYONE?"*

"Well, you and me, at least," I say. *"But we're not in Kansas anymore."*

"NO, I WAS IN TEXAS," he tells me.

"Well, welcome to Lusio," I tell him. *"I'm not sure how we got here, exactly..."* Apart from dying being involved. *"...but we're on a very different world, now."*

Ollie rumbles, which briefly alarms me until I realize it's a laugh. *"AND I'M A DRAGON NOW!"*

He tips his head back with a roar, and the chamber shakes from the sound. I clap my hands over my ears until he's done.

"Yes!" I shout up to him. "Yes, I can see that!" But a pang of sympathy hits me. He's just a kid—too young to understand the implications of his situation. But like me, this is probably the body he is stuck with, now. And while my own adaptation has been... confusing to navigate, to say the least, at least it's a body I now feel comfortable with. A body that will allow me to live a normal life—well, normal given the circumstance. But living as a *dragon* is something else entirely. He can't communicate with others. Will he ever find companionship? Fulfillment? What will he eat?

That thought gives me pause. I wave my hand at Ollie, and eventually he calms down enough to nudge up against my hand once more.

"*I CAN SHOOT ICE OUT OF MY MOUTH!*" he excitedly tells me. "*AND I HAVE WINGS! BUT IT'S TOO SMALL TO FLY IN HERE.*"

"*Yes, I was going to ask about that,*" I say. "*Have you been stuck in this room the whole time?*"

"*YES,*" Ollie says, the thought accompanied by the impression of a dramatic sob. "*IT'S SO BORING! THERE'S NOTHING TO PLAY WITH, AND I CAN'T EVEN FLY, AND I'M SOOOOOOO HUNGRY.*"

It's been nearly two weeks since I reincarnated. Days that I've been having warm meals with Mirzayael and the people of Fyreneth's Keep. Days that Ollie has been slowly starving down here—although, given his mass, I suspect starving to death would take some time.

But there's other things to worry about, like water and air.

"We need to find you a way out of here," I say, glancing around the chamber. Honestly, it's a miracle he appeared in a place that had enough room for him. Could he have appeared inside of a wall instead? Could *I* have?

I try to push that disturbing thought out of my mind.

Echo, can you tell me anything about the air composition of this chamber? I ask.

[Negative,] Echo says.

I figured as much, but it was worth a shot.

[However, the chemical composition of the user's surroundings could be accessed through the Dungeon Core.]

Oh? I knew it could do that with earth, but I hadn't realized the same capability applied to the surrounding atmosphere. It makes sense, I suppose; it's just been so obsessed with eating every rock and stone in sight that I hadn't thought its abilities extended to other elements and states of matter.

I turn my attention toward the Dungeon Core. *Have you been holding out on me? Can you analyze the composition of things besides stone?*

The Dungeon Core perks up. I've been ignoring it all day and it's sad. It's also hungry. It hasn't gotten to eat anything in forever!

I shake my head. *You literally just ate some stone and ice a few minutes ago. Which also means I haven't been ignoring you all day.*

It's so hungry. Soooooo hungry!

Good lord. That's two terrifyingly powerful and hungry children I have to take care of now. *Core, focus. Can you analyze the chemical composition of things beside stone?*

The Core pouts. Of course it can. It can analyze whatever it eats.

Finally, progress. *And what can you eat?*

The Dungeon Core smiles in my mind. Everything.

The thought is accompanied by an impression of a bottomless hole: an endless hunger. An event horizon.

I try not to shudder. As disturbing as the implications are, the Dungeon Core's ability is an incredibly useful asset.

Well, then, eat some of the air in this room, I tell it. *But only a little bit! One cubic meter or less.*

The Dungeon Core regards this command unenthusiastically. It doesn't like to eat gas. It's not crunchy like rocks. Gas makes it feel bloated.

I resist the urge to not drag my hand down my face. *Just a little! Please. We need to see how long the air in here will last. Especially with a giant dragon taking up all the oxygen. I'll give you some more mana if you do.*

The Dungeon Core snaps to attention. Mana! It loves mana. Okay, well, maybe just a little bit of air is fine.

I let out a relieved breath, turning back to Ollie. "Okay. I'm working on something. In the meantime, I need to go speak with my friends."

Having to be touching Ollie to speak with him is inconvenient—not to mention it's draining my mana. It occurs to me I could use Psionic Link to form a remote mind-to-mind bridge with Ollie like I did with the Dungeon Core. But do I want to do that? The spell would be permanent, and I've only just met the boy.

And I'm also the only one who can talk to him. Ollie needs me. That outweighs any long-term repercussions.

"Ollie," I say, gesturing him forward so he can touch my hand once more. "I want to try something that should make it easier for us to talk."

He bumps his nose against my hand again. *"OKAY! WHAT IS IT?"*

"I can establish a mental link that will let us speak like this without having to be touching," I say to him. *"However, it would be permanent. Is that okay with you?"*

"UH, SURE, I GUESS." I get the mental impression of a shrug. *"IT'S NICE TO HAVE ANOTHER PERSON TO TALK TO. ECHO CAN BE SO BORING!"*

I tip my head. *"Echo? You also have an Echo?"* Not that I should be surprised, given both of our ties to this System.

"YOU KNOW ECHO, TOO?" he asks. *"COOL!"*

We're getting off track. *"Are you sure you're alright with establishing the mental link?"* I ask him again. I don't think he fully understands the implications of its permanence, but that might be irrelevant any-way, given our need to communicate.

"*YEAH, THAT'S FINE,*" he says. His tail starts to wag again. "*WHAT DO I NEED TO DO?*"

[Psionic Link initiated.]

I can feel the barrier between our minds vanish. I extend my mind toward him. "*Here. Can you feel this?*"

"*OOOOOOH.*" Ollie huffs. "*THAT'S SO WEIRD.*"

"*You'll need to reach out toward me, too,*" I tell him. "*Like a hand-shake.*"

Ollie's mind surges toward me, bowling through my consciousness and scattering my thoughts. I fall back to the floor, dazed.

[Psionic Link established.]

[Mana: 38/200]

"*OOPS! ARE YOU OKAY?*" Ollie asks.

I sit up, dizzy. I guess I should have specified for him to be gen-tle—then again, that might be difficult enough as it is for a child, let alone a child dragon.

"*It's okay, I'm fine,*" I mentally tell him as I stand up and dust myself off.

"*OH!*" he cries. "*I CAN STILL HEAR YOU!*"

"*Great.*" I smile up at him. "*Now we can keep in contact even while I leave the room.*" I gesture up toward the hole I'd carved into the cavern, which now seems so far above me. "*Can you give me a lift?*"

"*OKAY!*" Ollie leans toward me, opening his mouth.

"Ah, wait a second!" I say, alarmed. I'm not sure if he intends to pick me up with his mouth, but I don't exactly trust him to have complete control and awareness of his own strength.

Ollie pauses, tipping his head to the side.

"I'll climb up on your neck if that's alright," I tell him. *"Will that work?"*

"MMMM, OKAY." Ollie leans his head down and turns it to the side.

The Dungeon Core begins pestering me. It ate that little bit of air I asked it to, and now it doesn't feel good, but it did it anyway, so now I have to give it mana. With a mental sigh, I relinquish a few points of mana to the Dungeon Core; the chemical composition of the air it consumed is already in our database, I just need a moment to go through it. In the meantime, I have a dragon to climb.

Exceptionally aware of my talons, I gingerly place my hands on Ollie's neck and push myself up, attempting to throw a leg over the other side and straddle him.

Ollie giggles. *"THAT TICKLES!"*

"Sorry," I say. *"I'll try to be careful."*

I manage to climb up somewhat less fluidly and with significantly more flailing than I would have liked, but I eventually settle behind Ollie's head. There's a row of spines that fan out and frame his head, so I grab two of these for purchase. I also needn't have worried about nicking him with my talons: his glossy white scales are far tougher than I'd have thought.

"READY?" Ollie thinks, already straightening up.

I throw myself forward, tightening my grip around the spines. "I suppose I have to be!"

Ollie rears up on his hind legs and stretches toward the hole in the cavern wall. We still come up short, but now I'm at least close enough I can make out the others clustered in the gap.

Nek is watching me with an awed expression, while Mirzayael's face is creased in a frown.

"Are you alright?" she calls down.

"Yes," I say, clutching Ollie's spines in a death-grip. I try not to think about our height and the fact that there's nothing at my back to prevent me from slipping and falling all the way to the cavern floor. "We've just been getting to know each other. Everyone, meet Ollie. He's seven."

Nek splutters. "Seven centuries?!"

"Seven years," I say. "He's just a kid. So I expect you all to treat him nicely."

Mirzayael eyes the dragon dubiously. "If you say so."

"*OH MY GOSH,*" Ollie says. "*THAT ONE LOOKS LIKE A KIT-TY!*"

"*Yes, his name is Nek,*" I tell Ollie.

"*AND THAT OTHER ONE LOOKS LIKE A SPIDER,*" Ollie says. "*THAT'S CREEPY!*"

"*Don't be rude,*" I tell him. "*Her name's Mirzayael, and she's just a different species, no different from you and me.*"

I can feel his mind wilt. "*OH, SORRY.*"

"*It's okay, Ollie.*"

"We have a bit of an issue," I press on, trying to juggle the two conversations. "Ollie here ended up in this cave the same way I ended up in mine. Which is to say, neither of us are exactly sure how we got in it. One thing is clear however; this little hole I carved is the only way out."

"What are you suggesting?" Nek asks, shaking himself out of his shock. "Dig a way out?"

"The Dungeon Core should be able to help me do something like that, yes." I bring up the Map Interface and try zooming out. The lines of explored cave swirl through the 3D interface like tunnels in an ant farm. There's one windy path that leads up to where I had woken up, and dozens of crisscrossing paths which indicate my exploration of the

Catacombs with Mirzayael. Apart from that, the only area that's really been fully revealed is Fyreneth's Keep. Where we're currently located is partially between the Catacombs and the Keep, but the entire rest of the map is still obscured by darkness.

"Do you know anything about the cave systems above us?" I ask. "I could begin to tunnel a way out for Ollie, but I don't want to compromise stone that might affect the city."

"This area is outside the known cave systems," Mirzayael says. "There could be anything above us. Beryl might have an old map or two, from explorers before my time, but we'd have to return to the Keep to check."

"Let's do that," I say, nodding to the young guards who have hung back, whispering to each other with wide eyes throughout this entire event. "Do you three think you could find your way to the Keep and back?"

Zakaiya, Rei, and Opal exchange a look, then give me a nod. "I can use my silk to create markers," Zakaiya says. "We should be back in a few hours."

"Good," I say. "Thank you. Please go." Then I hesitate, looking to Mirzayael. "If that's okay?"

She snorts. "Yes, it's fine." She flicks a hand to the guards. "Go!"

"*THIS IS BORING*," Ollie says. "*AND MY LEGS ARE GETTING TIRED!*"

"*Sorry,*" I tell him. "*We'll hurry it along.*" I look to the others. "Would you all come down into the chamber? It would make speaking together easier."

The look on Nek's face tells me exactly how little he likes that idea, but Mirzayael nods curtly. "I will work on creating a line for the others to rappel. Unless you're capable of forming a staircase to help."

I take a look at my mana reserves and then dip into the Core's inventory. It's eaten plenty of stone I could now bring back out into the world, placing it anywhere and in any form I like. However, the mana cost makes more than a bit of rearranging prohibitively expensive.

"I can try, but I don't think I'll be able to do very much right now," I say. "I can at least shape an easier platform and hole for you all to use to rappel from. That will have to be sufficient for now."

After some brief back and forth and Nek's clear reluctance to rappel down the sheer cliff of ice, I hand over most of my mana to the Dungeon Core and it excitedly gets to work on widening the hole and forming it into a more stable platform. Under my guidance, the Core reaches into the nearby wall and pulls the crystalline stone outward, shattering the ice. The resulting terrace is blocky, but functional.

"*THAT'S SO COOL!*" Ollie cries, once again practically yelling into my head and causing me to wince. "*LIKE MINECRAFT. CAN I DO THAT?*"

"*Not right now,*" I say, although given Ollie's high mana levels, that does pose a terrifying possibility. "*Right now we need to focus on getting you out of here.*"

As Nek and Mirzayael make their way down and Ollie lands back on the floor, I slip off his neck in relief, and prompt the Core to do another air sample. It's extremely reluctant to get the taste of fresh mana out of its mouth, but eventually gives in. I bring up the two breakdowns of atmospheric compositions and begin to sift through the results.

"What now?" Mirzayael asks as I'm pouring over the numbers. "Can it understand us?"

"He most certainly can," I say, distracted by the chemical combinations. They're not exactly the ratios I'm used to from Earth, but I suppose it makes sense the atmosphere and biology here would be slightly different. I need to focus on any variances in the two samples. "Why don't you go introduce yourself?"

Mirzayael must be able to catch the distant tone in my voice, as she steps away so as not to bother me any further.

Echo, can you calculate the percent CO_2 in these two samples? I ask, desperately missing my graphing calculator. *Rounded to the first significant decimal place that is different between the two numbers.*

[Calculated,] Echo says. [Sample 1: 3.88% CO_2. Sample 2: 3.89%.]

Hardly a difference, it appears. Although that number already feels high for my liking.

Calculate the rate at which CO_2 has increased, I say.

[CO_2 increased at a rate of 0.02% per hour.]

I frown, counting back how many days I've been here. Throwing some basic math into the mix...

"Damn," I say, getting Echo to double check my work. The numbers come out the same. "Damn!"

At the exclamation, Mirzayael wanders back over to me. Nek is monologuing to Ollie, who's tilting his head curiously, his tail whipping back and forth in amusement. I step away from them, lowering my voice.

"We have a problem," I say to her. "Ollie's been stuck down here for as long as I've been in this world. The air in this cave is growing toxic."

Mirzayael wrinkles her nose. "How bad?"

"Unclear," I say, glancing at Ollie. Would CO_2 rates affect a body like that the same way it would affect someone like Mirzayael or I?

"But within a few days, it might be too toxic for us to come back. And that means if we don't find a way out for him soon, this cave will become his tomb."

CHAPTER FIFTEEN

BORING OLD ROCKS

"What do we do?" Mirzayael hisses.

"Ventilation, first off," I say, glancing around the cave. "More holes like the one we carved to get in here should help. But Carbon Dioxide sinks, so the real danger is down here at ground level."

I could maybe get Ollie to stir the air up with his wings. Or perhaps the Dungeon Core could help; if it can change the composition of stone, and it can eat stone and air alike, then it should be able to change the composition of air, too. I mentally prod the Dungeon Core, wondering if it could work as a filter.

I receive dismayed denial. Eat more air? No! It would feel so sick. So, so sick. It only likes tasty rocks. Those make it feel good!

So, you **can** *change the composition of any air you consume, to be clear?* I ask it.

I received a skittish evasiveness which confirms my suspicion. But it doesn't want to! It would hurt its stomach.

You don't' have a stomach, I say, fairly sure it picked that analogy up from me.

The Dungeon Core doesn't know what I'm talking about.

I sigh, resolving to try to convince the Dungeon Core later. Maybe it will be willing to continuing taking small air samples, at least, so I can keep an eye on the CO2 levels. But even if I can convince it to cooperate, cleaning the atmosphere is only a temporary solution. There's still water to worry about—and food. How much does a dragon need to eat, anyway? Would all of Fyreneth's Keep even have enough?

I groan, rubbing my forehead. Too many variables, and the equation keeps getting more complex.

Mirzayael puts a hand on my arm, causing me to startle. Her touch is smooth and cold. "We'll figure it out," she says.

"Yes. You're right." I comb my fingers through the feathers on my scalp, trying to calm myself. "One thing at a time."

"Besides," Mirzayael adds, tapping the floor with one of her feet. "At least you found your hot spring."

"What?" I ask, looking down.

The ground is shimmering beneath us. I'd taken that to be the same stone in the crystal walls that was providing illumination for the whole room, but now that I'm looking closer, the light is wavering and rippling.

It's running water.

"Oh!" I exclaim. "I can't believe I missed it." And surprised the Dungeon Core didn't say anything, given its passive range is six feet in any direction. Suspiciously, I nudge the Core.

What! The Core wrinkles its nonexistent nose at the presence of the underground water. Liquids are gross. Hot springs are especially gross. They taste rotten.

I laugh in spite of myself. This is it! We found the springs. There has to be a way to get the flow reconnected to the Catacombs—or a way

I can reroute the thermal springs to the Keep. Either way, that's heat, water, and energy flowing into the community.

First, however, is the dragon problem.

I check my mana: [2/200]. Between the Psionic Link and widening the entrance to the cavern, I'm practically bone dry. If I want to carve new vents into this room, I'll need more mana, and that will take hours to recover. Even then, I worry it won't be enough.

"If you've got any ideas, I'm open to them," I tell Mirzayael.

She pokes the tip of her spear at the ice, grunting in thought. "Maybe he could shoot more ice at the ground. Raise the level of the floor. That would get him higher up, closer to the hole."

A good stopgap, perhaps. But even if we were able to widen the exit, it would need to be at least ten times the size for a dragon to fit through. Not to mention all the tunnels beyond that would equally need to be widened. And where would we go from there? The passageways throughout the cave system are all far too small for a dragon. He'd be able to fit inside areas of the Catacombs or Fyreneth's Keep, but even then it would be cramped, and we'd just have the same problem all over again. Not enough room, not enough air, not enough food.

"We need to get him to the surface," I say. That's the only viable solution.

"How?" Mirzayael asks. "Can you carve a path with that Core of yours?"

"Given enough time, yes," I say. "However I'm low on mana at this moment, and even if I weren't I don't have nearly enough to carve a dragon-sized hole all the way to the surface. Not to mention, I don't even know how far we are beneath the surface. It's impossible to tell." My Map Interface displays a total depth of 1631 feet between the highest and lowest known locations I've explored—which happen to be the room I spawned in, and here, the room Ollie spawned in. But what if that high point is still far below ground?

Mirzayael shakes her head. "Not impossible. The room you led me to, where you say you came from—that wasn't far from the surface. There are a few known entry points in that area of the cave system. Perhaps another hundred feet above that room."

"So close!" I exclaim. No wonder she suspected I'd come from the surface. "Then in total we may be less than half a mile below ground." Better than I'd feared, but that still doesn't bring us any closer to finding a solution—not unless we can guide Ollie to the best path toward the surface and let him tear and trash his way through the rock. But that might be just as dangerous to him as it could be to the city. What if all this disturbance causes another rock slide, like that one that injured Mirzayael? Or worse, a cave in.

I shake my head. "What I need is mana. Much, much more mana."

"Hmm." Mirzayael taps her feet against the ground in a drumming pattern as she thinks. The rhythmic movement of her seven legs is somewhat unnerving. "Lord Beryl has the type of magic that can be used to pass mana between individuals. It's a type of healing magic, I believe. But I doubt she has enough to support what you need."

"The Dungeon Core can apparently absorb it from eating items imbued with magic," I tell her. "We got a couple points from that cloud stone the Core ate. It also says there's something called mana ore around here, but we've yet to find any in our explorations "

"Oh?" Mirzayael perks up. "We've got some mana ore in town. Not a lot, but we've collected some stones over the years. They're mostly reserved for emergencies."

I think about the brumating dracid, and how desperate they are for any source of heat. "You haven't used it all up by now?"

"They regenerate, as long as you don't suck the pieces dry," Mirza-yael says. "We think they passively absorb and retain mana from their surroundings. But it takes a long time to recharge—decades, depending on the size, so we have to be careful with them."

"How much do you have?" I ask, excited.

She shrugs. "A couple dozen gems. Each is enough to start a bonfire, if we used all the mana they contain at once."

A couple dozen bonfire's worth of mana. Comparing that to my Blaze spell, I estimate it to be maybe a few thousand mana. I can't know for sure without analyzing them directly, however. Damn, maybe we sent the scouts back too early; we could have asked them to bring the stones back with them.

But would two or three thousand mana be enough to burrow through a mile of solid rock? I close my eyes, accessing the Dungeon Core's interface, reaching out through the Core's area of influence to calculate how much mana it would take to eat through a few feet of the surrounding stone. If I can extrapolate that across half a mile of rock, I'll get a good idea of how much total mana I'll need for the entire tunnel. Let's see, if the Core ate straight down, through the ice and water and rock, we'd come out to a loss of...

[Net Mana Gain: 11]

My eyes snap open. "Gain?!"

"What?" Mirzayael asks.

I shake my head, skimming through the results of my analysis.

[Ice Consumption: – 153 mana]

[Spring Water Consumption: + 319 mana]

[Limestone Consumption: – 155 mana]

A net gain for consuming the water? But why? *Echo, what's going on with the springs?* I ask.

[Check: The water in the underground spring has become infused with mana over the centuries due to prolonged exposure to mana ore.]

"That's it," I say, excitedly dropping to my knees, placing a hand over the icy ground. "The spring. It's full of magic." And no *wonder* the pipe system was so prevalent throughout the Catacombs. The water itself was a source of the kingdom's energy.

"Interesting," Mirzayael says. "We've always considered the waters in the caverns to have healing attributes, and the stories say the waters of Fyreneth's Fortress were capable of miracles. I never thought they literally contained mana, however."

Healing properties would make sense if the waters were infused with magic. But more than just healing, they could have acted as a source for any kind of magic. Perhaps even used to power the city back in its heyday. Either way, tracing the spring back to its source should also lead me back to some mana ore.

This also means I effectively have an unlimited source of mana. Well, not *literally*, but at least for digging a tunnel...

"We can do this," I say, my heart lighting with hope once more. "With the water here to draw on as a source, the Dungeon Core should have more than enough power to carve an exit. So long as we're careful to not disrupt the rest of the cave system, there's a way out."

Isn't that right? I excitedly ask the Core.

Surprisingly, however, it doesn't return my enthusiasm. I'm presented with a very potent mental impression of a gag.

Chewing tons of stone sounds delicious, but consuming all that rotten water is terrible! It will get sick!

You can't get sick.

It will feel so sick!

Do you even know what that feels like?

The Core is offended. Okay maybe it does not understand but it really really doesn't like the taste of the rotten-egg water.

Enough that you'll turn your nose up at all this mana? I ask, skeptical. *I thought gaining more mana was your entire personality.*

The Dungeon Core doesn't understand what I mean but decides to feel offended anyway.

I sigh. *If you do this, it will be a brief amount of rotten-egg taste now, but an incredible amount of mana to spend later. I don't suppose you understand the concept of delayed gratification?*

The Dungeon Core responds to this new concept with the mental equivalent of radio static.

"Or maybe not," I mumble, turning to Mirzayael. "Convincing the Dungeon Core is proving harder than I expected."

"Convince it?" she repeats. "It answers to you. Can't you make it?"

I hesitate. "I don't know. I've never tried to force it to do anything. Isn't that a bit... cruel?"

Mirzayael steeples her fingers over the blunt end of her spear and rests her chin on her hands. "It's a tool, isn't it? You can't be cruel to something that isn't alive."

Isn't it alive? I guess not, according to Echo; she'd said as much when I first discovered it. However, even if it doesn't meet the classification of life, it's certainly sapient. Just, not in a way I've ever encountered. But it has a will. Desires. Personality. If nothing else, that should count as artificial life, shouldn't it?

I shake my head. "I don't like that reasoning. I'll find some way to convince it."

Mirzayael shrugs. "Suit yourself. In the meantime, we can try to find some other solution for the dragon situation. But if it comes down to it, making a decision between Ollie's life and that rock's autonomy—well, the choice seems obvious to me."

She steps away to go rescue Nek, who's managed to fend off Ollie's attempts to pet the cat-man with claws as long as Nek's arms.

I frown, looking back down at the running water beneath the ice. *It really would be to your benefit,* I halfheartedly tell the Dungeon Core. But it's too much like a child, too motivated by instant gratification, to understand my point.

I glance over at Ollie. He might look like a murderous beast, but the voice he uses to speak into my mind is just like any seven-year old. It makes me think of Caroline—no longer a child, to be sure, but always my little girl. What is she doing now? Does she mourn me? Does she even know I died?

My heart aches at the thought, and I box the feelings carefully away. I need a clear head right now. This child's life is on the line.

"Is everyone acquainted?" I ask, wandering back over to the others.

"I suppose as much as we can be, considering we can't communicate," Mirzayael says.

"*THE CAT MAN IS SO FURRY!*" Ollie excitedly reports. "*I HAVE A KITTEN BACK HOME. HIS NAME IS PEANUTS. DO YOU THINK I'LL BE ABLE TO GO BACK AND SEE HIM AGAIN? OR MAYBE WE CAN BRING HIM HERE!*"

I wince. He still doesn't understand all this is very likely permanent. "First we need to focus on getting you out of this cave," I say instead. "And then we can worry about getting you some food."

"***FOOD!***" Ollie cries, and I flinch. "*OH YES, I AM SO HUNGRY! I COULD EAT A WHOLE HORSE.*" In my head, his voice giggles. Externally, the dragon huffs out several loud growls. "*DO YOU THINK I COULD **ACTUALLY** EAT A HORSE? GROSS!*"

"We'll... figure that out when we find one," I say, raising my eyebrows at Mirzayael. "Or whatever other animals live around here. Ah... I don't suppose you know what ice dragons eat?"

She gives a helpless shrug. "I'd never met one before today."

Oh boy. Well, another obstacle to deal with later.

"DO THEY HAVE ICE CREAM HERE?" Ollie asks. *"OH! OH! DO YOU THINK I COULD* **MAKE** *ICE CREAM? ECHO SAYS I CAN MAKE ICE! I BET I COULD AT LEAST MAKE SNOW CONES. WHAT DO YOU THINK?"*

"Sounds like a good thing to practice," I say, trailing off with the last word. Kids do like their desserts, don't they? They can be pretty food motivated. What else motivates kids? What motivated Caroline?

Sure I can't convince you with some tasty mana? I ask the Dungeon Core again. *It would be a lot easier if you ate your vegetables first, then had tons and tons of tasty mana at the end.*

The Core is completely confused by the mention of vegetables here, and reiterates its desire for mana, but equal and vehement dislike of the sulfur water.

Ah, well, I say, reluctantly beginning to think that Mirzayael had the right idea all along. *If you won't choose the carrot...*

"Hey, Ollie, can I get your help with something?" I ask.

The dragon hops to his feet, tail swishing and wings fluttering. Mirzayael and Nek scramble back. *"WHAT CAN I DO?"*

"Over here." I lead him to where the running water can be seen through the ice. "Can you break through this for me?"

"OF COURSE I CAN!" Ollie declares. *"BUT THE WATER UNDER THERE SMELLS TERRIBLE AND TASTES EVEN WORSE. BLECH! THAT'S WHY I COVERED IT UP WITH ICE IN THE FIRST PLACE."*

If the Core could hear him, I'm sure it would agree.

"That's alright," I say. "The water might be a bit sulfuric, but it's also a bit magical. I'll need access to it in order to get you out of here."

"*WELL, ALRIGHT THEN*," Ollie says. "*I'M GOING TO SMASH IT!*" He rears back.

"Watch out!" I call to the others, hurrying back myself. "Ollie, hold on until—"

The dragon smashes his claws into the ground. Chips of ice go flying in every direction, and I raise a defensive wing to block stray flecks from stabbing into my face. The whole cavern shakes with the concussive blasts, and several more stalactites break from the ceiling and come crashing down around us.

"Ollie!" I call again. "Hold on, stop!"

Mirzayael and Nek are also yelling at him, but the dragon is so absorbed in his task with scratching and slamming his claws into the ground that he doesn't seem to notice. After a minute of Ollie clawing up the ice and us dodging near-death experiences, he finally stops.

"*I DID IT!*" he happily reports.

My heart is practically beating out of my chest. "Yes, yes it seems you did." I swallow, giving his nose a pat. "Great job."

Ollie smiles, which looks downright terrifying.

"Well, that was... something," Mirzayael says, hesitantly following me over to the hole in the ice. "Now what's your plan?"

A sulfuric smell—much like rotten eggs, as the Dungeon Core so aptly put it—wafts from the opening. The ice goes about a meter down, and the water appears at least twice as deep. Luckily, it doesn't seem to be flowing very fast.

I glance down at my wrist and give the Core a half-hearted tug. Still securely stuck to my wrist and not going anywhere.

Echo, what's the temperature of that water? I ask.

[60 degrees centigrade.]

A touch on the high end. Good thing I have fire and heat resistance. I grab the lip of the hole and dangle my legs over.

"Now..." I say, lowering my feet in. It feels warm, but not hot. Good. "Now, it's bath time."

I jump down into the springs. My hands hit the water.

The Dungeon Core screams.

Chapter Sixteen

BATH TIME

I grind my teeth as the Dungeon Core shrieks into my mind.

It hates it! It hates the water! It's everywhere! It can taste it! It's drowning! Ahhhhhhh!

"You're not drowning!" I wince, sticking a finger in my ear as if that could stop the mental tinnitus. "You are a rock! You can't drown."

"Outsider!" Mirzayael appears above me, her voice tinged with alarm. "Are you alright?"

"It's fine!" I say, treading water. My feet don't reach the bottom, but the water is actually rather pleasant—aside from the noxious smell. "I'm just teaching the Dungeon Core to eat its vegetables."

"You're what?" she asks, baffled.

Nek and Ollie poke their heads curiously over the edge, too.

"WHAT ARE YOU DOING DOWN THERE?" Ollie asks.

"Just give me a minute," I call back up to them. "You'll see."

The Core is busy making an impressive impersonation of retching sounds. *It's going to be sick! The water is terrible. Terrible!*

"Well, there's one way to get rid of it," I say. "You can always absorb it."

The Dungeon Core is appalled. That would mean consuming it! Then it would taste even WORSE!

"Maybe, but it'll only be temporary," I say. "Plus, afterward you'll have all that mana to get the taste out of your mouth. Have to eat your veggies before you can have dessert."

The Dungeon Core is wounded. Tricked. Betrayed! This is betrayal.

Complain all you like. But while I enjoy my first bath I've had in almost two weeks, you have a decision to make.

The Dungeon Core wails. It begs and pleads and throws a tantrum. I float on my back, finding my wings act as excellent flotation devices, and let out a pleasant sigh. This would actually be really nice if I didn't have an infant rock screaming in my head.

Eventually, the Dungeon Core seems to catch a whiff of my resolve. It simmers back down into wounded resignation. Hesitantly, reluctantly, it reaches its will out into the waters.

An ounce of thermal spring water vanishes from my surroundings and appears in the Dungeon Core's catalog. Numbers start populating the field: density, temperature, mass, mineral composition. And of course, 5 mana.

I smile.

The Dungeon Core shudders at the hydrogen sulfide, but perks up a little when it notices the new mana it has access to.

See? I think. *Not so bad, huh? Now, how about we get some real mana in our stores.* I open my eyes and flip back over so I'm facing into the current. Time to get serious.

The Dungeon Core doesn't quite share my enthusiasm, but now that it's gotten a taste of the mana in the water, there's a curiosity rising in it once more. It dissolves a little bit more water into its catalog. Then, some more.

I stretch my hand out before me, and I can feel pockets of the water vanishing and then collapsing back down around my fingers almost as quickly.

[Mana: 42/200]

[Mana: 68/200]

[Mana: 79/200]

The numbers keep ticking up until I hit 200/200. Then, a new stat appears.

[Bonus Mana: 31]

"Fascinating," I say, watching that metric start to rapidly increase as well. I wonder how high we can push it? "Come on, Core, we can do better than that. You've been begging me for absurd amounts of mana. Now's your chance to seize it!"

I'm not sure if my pep talk actually got through, or if my enthusiasm is mentally infectious, but the Core's uncertainty flares into eagerness, and its area of influence blooms around me.

With a loud clap, a cubic meter of water vanishes. I hardly have a moment to register it, surprised, as the water collapses back in to fill the void. But the Core doesn't pause. It continues to suck up all the water in a sphere around me, until abruptly the water beneath me vanishes, and I fall to the smooth, spring-weathered floor. Despite my initial shock, I keep my hand—and the Dungeon Core—raised against the river flooding my way.

The Dungeon Core has dropped all reservations now, and it mindlessly gulps up all the water that enters our range. The river seems to hit an invisible funnel, spiraling down toward my hand and the stone at my wrist, before simply blinking out of existence. Meanwhile, in the Core's inventory, the number next to "Cubic meters of spring water" is skyrocketing. Not to mention, our bonus mana.

"Great job!" I shout over the splashing and churning of the water. However I'm beginning to feel the first hints of trepidation. Glancing up, I'm now very much out of reach of the hole I bored through the ice. If the Core were to stop absorbing the water, the underground river would immediately crash into me, sweep me away from the only known exit, and very likely drown me in the process. I try to keep these worrying thoughts away from the Dungeon Core, in case I cause it to falter. Instead, while it's still doing its thing, I catch Mirzayael's eye.

"So about getting back up…"

She snorts. "I don't think you thought this strategy all the way through."

"I admit I underestimated the Core's capabilities," I say. "So, have you got any ideas?"

Mirzayael tosses down a line of spider silk. There's a small slipknot at the bottom. "Step your foot through, hold on tight, and we'll haul you up."

I beam up at her. "I knew I could count on you."

"Don't get used to it, Outsider," she says. "I won't always be around to save your ass."

Ollie gasps. "*SHE SAID A BAD WORD!*"

"Sorry, Ollie," I reply aloud. "Mirzayael will work on keeping her language appropriate for small children. Won't she?" It takes a lot of willpower to deliver that with a straight face.

"*I'M **NOT** SMALL*," Ollie objects.

Mirzayael wrinkles her nose. "I do not censor myself."

I can't help but chuckle.

"*You're right, Ollie, you're absolutely not small,*" I think to him. "*My apologies.*"

With my free hand I grab the silk and steady the line, slipping my clawed foot through the loop as instructed. "You know, I don't think you're half as callous as you pretend to be."

Mirzayael scowls. "What's that supposed to mean?"

"Careful." Nek laughs. "She has an image to uphold."

I hold the rope tight, focusing on the mana and the Dungeon Core's state of mind as the numbers continue to skyrocket. The smallest hint that it needs a break, that it's grown bored, that it's "full," and I'll shout for the others to pull me up. Not that I think the Core would intentionally kill me—it's an unintentional death I find much more probable.

The Bonus Mana stat hits fifty thousand and keeps rising. Running some quick calculations based on how much stone the Core had been able to bore through before, I estimate a hole big enough for the dragon to be able to fit through, leading all the way to the surface, would need around half a million mana. Dungeon Core willing, I intend to gather twice that much to establish a comfortable factor of safety. I don't know that I'll be able to get the Core to fall for this trick twice.

Miraculously, the Core continues to cooperate. We hit a hundred thousand mana. Then two hundred thousand. Then three. The amount of magic I could do with these numbers is mind boggling. I should figure out if there's a way I can transfer some of it to others—individuals who might have abilities more practical than my fire or telepathy. What's the most efficient way this energy can be distributed to enact the most progress?

The Dungeon Core's attention begins to waver. It's antsy. Like a kid hyped up with sugar.

"Up!" I call, not taking any chances. "Pull me u—"

I lurch and nearly lose my balance as the line goes taut and I'm jerked into the air. As I'm lifted up, the Core curiously wonders what's going on, and its focus on the water shifts. A wave crashes into the stone beneath me, water splashing up to spray my feathers as I'm hastily pulled from the hole.

Nek whistles. "Close one."

"Thank you," I say, shakily falling back onto the floor of the cave.

"Too close," Mirzayael adds, winding up the line of silk.

I undo the loop around my foot as I check my mana: 745,238. "But ultimately a success. It appears I've multiplied my mana stores by a factor of over three thousand, all told."

Nek and Mirzayael stare at me, stunned.

I chuckle. "Quite a bit, isn't it?"

"Stars above," Mirzayael murmurs.

"I'd say 'a bit' is an understatement," Nek agrees.

"Well." I push myself to my feet and shake out my damp wings. Now that I'm no longer in the heated water, the cold of the cave is starting to creep back in. "Time to put some of it to use, don't you think?"

"Right now?" Nek asks.

"Might as well."

Ollie tips his head at me. "*WHAT ARE YOU GUYS TALKING ABOUT?*"

"Making you a way out of here," I say, speaking both mentally and aloud, for the benefit of all parties. "About time you got to stretch your wings on the surface, don't you think?" Not to mention, make sure he has access to fresh air and, hopefully, a food supply.

Ollie rumbles, his tail swishing excitedly from side to side. "*REALLY? YOU MEAN IT? DO YOU THINK I CAN FLY?*"

I glance critically at his wings. They look proportionally bigger than mine, but even then he's incredibly massive. I'm not even sure those wings are behind his center of gravity. From an aerodynamic standpoint, I am skeptical.

Then again, there's always magic.

"Only one way to find out," I say.

"*THEN WHAT ARE WE WAITING FOR?*" Ollie cries. "*LET'S GO!*"

"Alright, alright," I say with a chuckle. "Just keep behind me. I don't want anyone too close in case part of the cave collapses while the excavation is taking place." Times like these, I wish I had more background in civil engineering.

"Hold on," Mirzayael says. "If it collapses, we should be sticking close to you to make sure you don't get squished."

"I'm not sure what you would be able to do against falling boulders," I say. "I'd prefer if everyone stayed back in this cave until I've finished, actually."

"Not a chance," Nek says. "If you're putting yourself in danger, we'll go too."

"Besides, I still don't entirely trust that dragon," Mirzayael says.

"*IS SHE TALKING ABOUT ME?*" Ollie asks. "*THAT'S MEAN!*"

I'm not sure she trusts anyone. But I also see the futility in trying to argue with these two. "*Sorry, Ollie,*" I think. "*She's just saying that because she's worried about me. Sometimes adults say things they don't mean when they're worried.*"

"Alright then," I relent. "Just keep an eye out for any possible cave-ins. Everyone, please be careful."

"Speak for yourself," Mirzayael grumbles.

I'm rather touched.

"Okay." I rub my hands together. "Let's see what we're working with."

I close my eyes as I switch over to the Map Interface, calling on the Dungeon Core for its attention. It can already sense I'm planning to start feeding it some of that bonus mana it's collected, and I can feel it vibrating with excitement.

Ready? I ask the Core. *This first bit is just to expand your range, so we can see what we're dealing with. I'm thinking... a five-meter radius. That should create a passage wide enough for a dragon to squeeze through.*

The Dungeon Core doesn't particularly care about Ollie, but it's very excited for the increased range—and of course, the mana that comes with it.

I let some of the mana begin to trickle through the Pact, like water pouring from cupped hands. The Core happily gobbles it up, and the mental map of our surroundings increases.

Let's focus this way first, I say, walking toward a wall, my eyes still closed. I can sense the ground through the Map Interface so perfectly, I don't even need to see it. I place my hand on the wall, sensing nothing but solid stone ahead of me.

The Dungeon Core surges forward. Can it eat it? Can it start eating all the rocks?

Not yet, I think. *Let's plot a route first. Feel out the surroundings. I don't want to destabilize the cave system. First we need to sense a safe path to the surface.*

The Core pouts. Sounds boring.

We'll be doing that by extending our range for at least half a mile.

Oooh! Yes, it wants to do that right now!

I smile. *You got it.*

I pour the mana across our bridge, more mana than I've ever accessed before, and even then it hardly makes a dent in the pool of Bonus Mana we've accumulated. The Core's range balloons tenfold, encompassing the entire chamber before I direct it to focus in only one direction, crawling into the rock wall like an ever-growing snake. I let the Dungeon Core take the reins as we reach for the surface.

Chapter Seventeen

THE SURFACE

Free from my restraint, the Core happily dives into the stone. Its sense of self plunges ahead, dragging me along like a fish on a line. I hold tight, letting it explore the rock while I mentally catalog the spaces we pass through. As I suspected, it's not merely solid stone. Our sphere of influence moves through dozens of caverns, intersects tunnels, and skirts around giant pits that seem to stretch without end.

The more of the Map Interface that becomes filled out, the more I picture our route to the surface as some kind of labyrinth. Which route could I plot that wouldn't cause us to hollow out a space beneath another cavern, causing a collapse? Which way can we go that doesn't intersect that giant crevice that runs through the stone, which would necessitate a bridge to traverse? Can we go around, over, beneath? It's a puzzle—a puzzle I'm uncertain has one single solution. But I start running through all the scenarios I can think of regardless.

Finally, the Dungeon Core breaks through the surface. It hesitates as cold wind blows through our sphere of influence.

For a moment, it's like I'm there. I can't see anything—everything I can experience is limited to the Dungeon Core's senses of touch and taste. But it's almost like I'm standing there, eyes closed, face turned to the sun. A distant warmth bathes my skin as an arctic wind ruffles my feathers. Snow-flurries blow over my talons, and packed ice is hard and unyielding beneath my feet. I feel a sudden urge to spread my wings, finally free from being caged beneath the ground, and take flight.

Like a worm nervous of birds, the Dungeon Core sinks hesitantly back into the stone. The air—the sky—the open space. It's too much. This is not its element.

Reluctantly, my mind sinks back into the ground with the Core. *That's alright,* I assure it, checking our mana stores. We're still over six hundred thousand. Good. *You don't need to worry about the sky. Let's reduce our range—backtrack through the stone. A different route, though, so we can expand what's revealed on our Map.*

The Core is more than happy to leave the surface behind and keep exploring the cavern system. As much as I don't share the Core's trepidation and am eager to see the sky with my own eyes, we have the mission to focus on; I need to scout a safe path to carve.

And eventually, I find it. It's a bit more meandering than I would have liked, and it's going to cut our mana stores close. We might have to go back to the hot springs for more mana, actually, but I keep this thought from the Core so it doesn't have the chance to do something melodramatic. Finally, I open my eyes. My eyelids crack like I've been asleep, and I take in a deep breath. My body feels warmer than I remember it being.

"She moved," Nek says. "I think she's awake."

"Outsider." Mirzayael puts a hand on my arm. "Are you alright?"

"What?" I ask, taking my hand from the wall. "What do you mean?"

That's when I notice the others. Mirzayael's scouts, Opal, Rei, and Zakaiya, have returned, along with a few new faces whose names I haven't yet committed to memory. The group is sharing a meal around a makeshift fireplace, the source of the warmth that was washing over my back.

Ollie lifts his head, leaning over toward me. I pat his snout as he puffs a breath of cold air over me. "*OH MY GOSH WE THOUGHT YOU WERE DEAD!*"

I flinch at the mental yelling. "Inside voices, please." I turn to Mirzayael. "Are they back already? How did the new ones get here so quickly?"

She looks at me strangely. "It's been nearly four hours," she says. "When you touched that wall, you appeared to enter some kind of trance. We tried calling out to you, but you didn't respond. Nek wanted to try to shake you, but I wasn't sure if that would be wise."

"What?" I cry. "Four hours? That's impossible. It only seemed like a handful of minutes."

But did it? Even now, trying to reflect on the time I'd spent mapping out a path through the stone with the Dungeon Core, the experience feels hazy and abstract. When I fully immerse myself in the Dungeon Core's senses, do I lose perspective on my own? If so, using it too much is potentially dangerous. Losing a few hours is alarming, but what if I'd lost days? Weeks? Would I have awoken when my body needed sustenance, or would I have withered away, entirely unaware?

"Next time something like that happens, please attempt to wake me," I say, a little shaken. "I'm sorry to have made you worry."

"Apologize to the dragon," Mirzayael says, turning away to head back to the fire pit. "He's the one who was worried."

I scratch Ollie's nose, who lets out a grumbling sigh and rests his head back on the ground. "I'll try not to do that again," I promise to him and Nek as the latter wanders over to check on me.

"No apologies necessary," Nek says, watching Mirzayael settle down for some food. "We're just relieved you're alright. Her especially, I think."

"She sure shows her concern in strange ways," I tease.

Nek laughs. "That she does. Now, I'd hazard you're in the mood for some steamed glowcaps."

I can't say I've ever been in the mood for bitter, unseasoned mushrooms, but Nek is right that I'm suddenly starving. As soon as we get the hot springs rerouted to warm the city, cultivating new and more flavorful dishes should be at the top of the priority list.

"Lunch would be lovely," I say as he leads me over to the others. "Or dinner. Or whatever time it is now."

As I sit down to eat, Nek offers Ollie a bowlful of greens. The hungry dragon enthusiastically opens his mouth for the crumbs of food to be tossed in—and spits them out with equal enthusiasm, retching at the "GROSS" and "POOPY" taste. It seems he'll be needing meat after all. The town still has some dried stinger meat they're preserving, but I doubt even their entire store would be more than a single bite for Ollie.

Some of my stamina returns to me over the course of shared food and good company, but throughout the meal my mind is elsewhere, tracing over the route I'd created from the Core's Map Interface. The three young scouts hand over a few of the cave system maps Mirzayael had mentioned. Comparing them to my planned tunnel, I'm happy to find my initial assumption had been correct, and the direction we're tunneling should pose no threat to the Keep or the Catacombs. At least, assuming these maps are right. Eventually, I'll want my own Map Interface fully populated. I need to know everything about this cave network. To take full advantage of the resources available, to help these people to their utmost potential, I'll have to leave no pebble of these caverns uncatalogued. It will take time, but given the thermal springs can be used as a mana source—assuming I can continue to wrangle cooperation out of the Dungeon Core—it should be possible.

As everyone is packing the meal away and dousing the fire, I stand back up. "I'll be carving the tunnel now," I announce. Since I'd already warned them before about keeping too close, I decide to not repeat the warnings again—Mirzayael would take it as an insult, anyway.

"Ready?" I ask the Dungeon Core, raising my hand to the wall. I summon the mental blueprint of the path I'd plotted through the stone and make sure the Core is paying attention. "This'll take a lot of mana. Maybe all of it."

Oh yes! The Dungeon Core cannot wait to do it! Eating through stone is its second favorite thing, and its first favorite thing is eating mana, and now it gets to do both! The Core is practically quivering from excitement on my arm.

Great, I think. *Just stick to the Map.*

It will. It will!

In that case...

I open the floodgates, allowing the mana to rush into the Dungeon Core.

The stone roars to life.

And in contrasting complete silence, a giant block of stone and ice vanish in front of me. There's no warning: it just evaporates. The Dungeon Core powers forward, grabbing the next piece of stone to consume. That block vanishes too. Piece by piece, swaths of rock unnervingly vanish from existence. I step forward into the makeshift cave, following the path on our Map. But as the Core surges ahead, eagerly gobbling up everything in its wake, it feels more like I'm being pulled along; a little girl holding onto a string who's managed to leash a hurricane.

And with the incredible amount of mana that's pouring into the creature, with its presence swelling in my mind, from such a simple, small stone, to some entity far more vast—far more dangerous—I begin to doubt if I should have trusted it with such fearsome power. I consider pulling back, trying to throttle the deluge of mana that's still pouring into the creature, but for Ollie's sake I can't stop carving the tunnel, now. Not to mention, a part of me wonders if I even *could* wrest control from the Core as it is.

If the Dungeon Core hears any of these thoughts, it pays me no mind. It only has one objective. One purpose. And that is to consume all the earth it can. Devour every stone and pebble that enters its range. It truly is like some kind of black hole—maybe even more insidious. At least a black hole betrays its existence with a gravity well. You can see its danger from the glowing accretion disk. But this beast is silent: its force undetectable. The matter it targets, gone in an instant without a trace of it ever having existed a moment before. It's a good thing, I'm now realizing, the only thing it seems to have a taste for is rocks.

It turns out that keeping the Core on track, following the Map, is a constant exercise. It's so single-minded that it forgets where it's supposed to be chewing only a minute after I remind it again. It's like steering a bull by its horns. Exhausting, and at any moment I fear I could accidentally become skewered by the very force of nature I'm attempting to direct.

Yet, we progress. We climb. We carve our way around giant pits, pick carefully around loose rock, cut in and out of caverns. The others follow behind, speaking to each other in hushed, awed tones that I'm too distracted to parse. We travel this way for over a half hour. And then...

The Core cuts another block away, and sunlight crashes over us. I flinch away, squeezing my eyes shut and tucking my head down from the painfully bright light as the Core continues to widen the hole, exposing the surface. A buffeting, freezing wind blows down into the tunnel, and I'm nearly knocked from my feet.

Mirzayael grabs my right arm, and Nek is there at my left. Both their heads are also turned down, eyes squinted painfully. I focus on the Map Interface for a moment, waiting for my eyes to adjust as I watch the exit grow wider and wider.

Ollie roars with glee. "*THE SURFACE! WE MADE IT!*" He leaps over us, crashing out onto the snow and ice.

"Wait," I call. "Be careful!"

"He'll be fine," Nek says.

"He's only a child!"

"A five-thousand-pound child," Mirzayael adds. "There are no predators out here that pose him any threat."

I suppose that's probably true. Even so, it's hard not to worry as he goes frolicking out into the snow drifts. I raise a hand to my eyes, squinting against a white sky and whiter landscape. As my eyes adjust, I realize it's only twilight, but compared to the previous darkness, it seems impossibly bright.

"Come on," I say to Mirzayael and Nek. "Don't you want to see the surface?"

Both of them hesitate as another gust of wind hits us, catching my wings and threatening to pull me away like a kite. I cry out, in giddy alarm as much as from the thrill, returning the grip Mirzayael and Nek have on my arms to anchor me. The second the gust has passed, I take advantage of our entwined grasps to pull them up the final stretch of the slope.

Ollie is bounding around like a puppy, diving into drifts of snow, rolling around on his back, then jumping up and shaking off the ice. I can't help but laugh at the scene, and Nek joins in with a chuckle of his own. I glance at Mirzayael, but she isn't looking at Ollie. Her face is full of awe, her head slowly turning to follow the horizon.

"It's so…" She trails off, leaving her thoughts unspoken.

"Bright?" I offer. "Empty?"

"Far away," she finally says. "I never knew anyone could see this far."

I feel a pang of sympathy for her. I can't imagine what this must be like, having spent her entire life in dark, close spaces. Nek and the other guards, too, lapse into an awed silence, clustered nervously together as they look around the sweeping plains and turn faces to the sky.

All of us jump when Ollie roars, spreading his wings as wide as they'll stretch, the membrane rippling with gusts of freezing wind.

"I'M GOING TO DO IT," he cries, springing forward. *"I'M GOING TO FLY!"*

He takes one, two, three lunging leaps—and on the fourth one, he doesn't come down. We all watch in amazement as the dragon climbs into the sky, spiraling white against white. Such a mix of emotions overcome me then, prickling at my eyes. Pride. An incredible yearning to join him in the air. Sorrow and regret and relief, all at once. I don't understand what all of these feelings are even attached to. My ex-wife, perhaps. My little Caroline. Grief for what I've left behind—hope for this fresh start, in this new body, with this new, growing family. It's such an ugly tangle of memories from my past life and hopeful dreams for this new one. But maybe they can't be untangled. Maybe I am all these things simultaneously.

[Bonus Mana extinguished,] Echo reports.

The Dungeon Core's mind collapses back into me like a dog falling down at my feet, having chased one too many balls. Its presence is now back to its pitifully small size, only able to sense a few feet of our surroundings in any direction. The Core is disappointed all the mana is gone, yet content with what it achieved. It ate a *lot* of rock today.

I chuckle. It certainly did.

[EXP threshold met,] Echo says. [Level up!]

[Name: Fyre]

[Species: Harpy]

[Subspecies: Phoenix]

[Class: Psion]

[Level: 21]

[HP: 100/100]

[Mana: 250/250]

[Role: The Dark Lord]

"Fyre," I say, startled. "My name. Not fire like flames, but Fyre, short for Fyreneth." I look to Nek and Mirzayael. "Is that true?"

Nek at least has the good sense to appear embarrassed. "The dracid were all calling you that anyway. And since you didn't give us a different name to use..."

I look at Mirzayael. "You knew about this."

She nods curtly. "I had assumed you were aware of the association."

"I'm sorry," Nek says. "Should we use something else?"

"I don't feel such a title is deserved," I say. "You know I am not this Lord Fyreneth reincarnated, don't you?"

Nek hesitates, but to my surprise, Mirzayael laughs. "I think after today you will be hard pressed to convince the town otherwise."

"What do you mean?" I ask.

"You held back a river of water with one hand," Mirzayael says. "You discovered an ice dragon, thought to be extinct, then called it your friend. You've given warmth and life to the dracid. You wield the stone-eater. You have brought us to the surface." She gives me a level look. "Whether you are her, or merely her successor, is irrelevant. You have earned the name many times over."

I'd never thought of it that way. I was just doing whatever I could manage to be as helpful as possible. If those with the power to help others don't do so, then what is the purpose of having such power in the first place?

"I don't feel as if I've earned it," I say anyway.

"It doesn't matter if you feel you've earned it," Mirzayael says flippantly. "Do you accept it? Or do you have a better name suggestion in mind?"

I think of my human name. The name that never felt like me. The name that still leaves a sour taste in my mouth. No, that name died with my body.

Alternately, the name Fyre warms me. It feels familiar. Comfortable. And the association is simultaneously humbling, and fills me with pride.

"It's big shoes to fill," I say. "But I want it. Fyre is a good name. I'll just have to hope I can live up to everyone's expectations."

"Yes," Mirzayael says flatly. "Don't let us down."

Nek looks horrified.

I laugh, shielding my eyes as I raise my face to the sky, watching the dragon circle overhead. "I'll do my best."

CHAPTER EIGHTEEN

EXPLORATIONS AND EXPANSIONS

Days trickle into weeks as I continue to help grow Fyreneth's Keep. Per Mirzayael's direction, I build a set of enclosed corrals in the caves just outside the Keep. As her scouts assist with exploring the Catacombs, they capture and bring back small creatures to add to the enclosures and raise as livestock. The next job I focus on is making Ollie's living quarters more comfortable. I smooth out his cavern, adding two staircases down (one person sized and one dragon sized), and widen the exit at the top so he can crawl through into the surrounding area at the base of the Catacombs. He can't make it to Fyreneth's Keep, as the passages there are too narrow, but the abandoned city provides plenty of space for him to explore and stretch his wings.

And of course, he has the skies. The tunnel from his cave to the surface is a large, winding path, but its accessibility makes Mirzayael nervous.

"It provides a direct access point for the Jorrians," she tells me. "We should keep it closed except when Ollie needs access."

"Since he needs to eat, that's every day," I point out. Luckily, Ollie has found animals to hunt out on the ice. Which is an incredible relief, to be honest, or I don't know what I would have done. He doesn't seem to particularly mind eating raw meat—I guess his dragon physiology helps with that. When he's not hunting animals or playing in the sky or snowbanks, he returns to the caves to talk to me, since he can't communicate with anyone else. Another puzzle to solve. The puzzles seem to be stacking up faster than the solutions.

"I would need to accompany him up and down to close or open the way each time," I say. "But are we sure it's even an issue? When was the last time Jorrians have bothered you? They may have been enemies in the past, but what if their modern counterparts have moved on?"

Mirzayael's mouth presses into a displeased line. "There is evidence enough to believe they are still pursuing us. Every few years, we find one of their scouts dead in some remote tunnel near the surface. Scouts who came looking for us, and perished after becoming lost."

"Or they fell through a crevasse in the glacier," I suggest.

"We have also lost scouting parties of our own," Mirzayael says. "The last one to leave Fyreneth's Keep and search for more hospitable lands left forty years ago, and never returned."

"Do you think maybe they *did* find those lands and never came back?" I ask.

"Impossible," she spits, with a vehemence that surprises me. "They would never abandon us. They are dead, or they would have returned."

"That doesn't mean the Jorrians killed them," I say. "What about natural disasters? Blizzards, or treacherous terrain."

Mirzayael's eyes narrow. I've seen her annoyed before, and certainly suspicious, but I've never seen her this angry. "They were far too strong for that. Natural causes never would have been their downfall."

This seems naive to me, but I am socially aware enough to know I'm already pushing buttons I shouldn't push. I suspect biases might be coloring Mirzayael's beliefs here, but I decide not to press the subject any further.

"How about this," I say. "I can ask Ollie to keep an eye out for any signs of people whenever he's out. If he sees anything, he's to come straight back, and I can close the caverns off. I can also close the entrance while we sleep." Though I suspect having a giant ice dragon guarding the only entrance might be deterrent enough.

Mirzayael doesn't seem entirely content with the idea, but she relents with a sigh. "That will have to be sufficient for now. I will additionally start scouting parties of our own to ensure the immediate area around the exit is secure." She frowns in thought. "Perhaps we could even join Ollie on some of these hunting expeditions..."

I smile. I knew she'd come around.

My next large project is also a project the Dungeon Core has a stake in. I've been working with Zakaiya, one of Mirzayael's young guards, to combine my Map Interface with their physical maps to help flesh out our combined knowledge of the cave system. I have a good idea where the hot springs originate now, and there's also a high likelihood there will be a vein of mana ore at its source. The Dungeon Core is very eager to discover this, but equally reluctant to go chugging any more spring water. That would be the easiest way to access more mana in order to mentally explore the caves and flesh out the Map Interface, but I don't know if the same trick I played the first time will work on the Core again. Now that all the mana is used up, the Core is hyper fixated on the gross tasting sulfuric water that's stored in its

Inventory, desperate to expel it. Sometimes I think it has the memory of a goldfish.

Whatever remaining free time I have after warming stones for the dracid, speaking with Ollie, and trying to deduce alternate paths to the origin of the springs, I spend with Mirzayael continuing to explore the Catacombs. Nek and a couple of the younger guards accompany us most days, clearing out the passages of wild beasts as we go. Mirzayael had initially regarded the task as a waste of time, until Nek pointed out how much the surplus of food was benefiting morale in the Keep. Despite her frequent grumblings, exploring the abandoned city with her is my favorite pastime.

"This place is truly magnificent," I say, running a hand over a column of intricately carved stonework. Fantastical creatures and people are engraved in the surface, each of them no bigger than my finger. "I'm not sure I believe Fyreneth could erect such a place in a month. A year, perhaps. But one month?"

"It doesn't seem so unbelievable to me," Mirzayael says, wandering further into the room. The palace is full of many such ornate halls. "You burrowed a dragon-sized hole up through the earth in under an hour with nothing but your bare hands."

"I'd say the Dungeon Core did more work than my hands." I chuckle. "But that's different. The tunnel to the surface was simple and crude. This palace—these details—are on an entirely different level. It's so... *artistic.*"

"I do not see how that is so different in principle," Mirzayael says. "A matter of skill and practice, perhaps."

Is that true? Could I learn to create such wondrous marvels with enough practice? Maybe if I'd studied architecture in my previous life. I've never had much of an eye for creative things like that. I've always gravitated to the derivable, solvable, and practical.

"Here," I say, running my hand over the stone. From the Dungeon Core's passive range, I can sense the materials in the wall, and given all the practice, I can start to tell when the consistency changes. "There's another thin vein here. It's so fine." Almost like electrical wires in a house—but these are made of stone instead of metal. Why this ore? What was the purpose? Everything here is so intentional, I know it must mean something. But after digging into the wall a bit and feeding some to the Dungeon Core, the rock seems entirely unremarkable. It has no special thermal or conductive properties, and its density and mass are similar to the surrounding stone. So why was it placed here?

The mystery excites me. I *have* to find out.

Mirzayael shakes her head. "What's so important about these veins of ore you're tracking, anyway?"

"Honestly?" I say. "No idea. But you never know which resources might be important."

"*Surviving* is important," Mirzayael says.

"Well, maybe this could help with that," I reply.

Mirzayael raises a skeptical brow. "Is that what your motive for these outings has been? Finding resources to improve the Keep's quality of life?"

"It might also be *a little* bit of curious exploration," I admit with a smile. "However, building up the Keep isn't exactly what I have in mind. I've done what I can with what there is to work with, but we are rapidly approaching the limits of what the settlement can offer. How many years have your people been living there?"

Mirzayael's mouth becomes a thin line. "Nearly eight hundred."

"Exactly," I say. "If it had the potential to develop into something bigger, something more prosperous, it would have by now. But it's not placed properly for that. It's too cold. Too far from the thermal springs. Not enough space to properly cultivate crops and livestock.

All your energy is put back into surviving rather than growth." I sweep a hand around the room. "Meanwhile, not far from the Keep, there's an empty city with the infrastructure for all these things already built into the design, quietly waiting for its people to return."

"You want to move our people back into the Catacombs?" Mirzayael asks, surprised. Then she frowns, shaking her head. "Impossible."

"Why?" I challenge. "It's your rightful home. The home of your ancestors."

"It's filled with stingers and other wild animals," Mirzayael presses.

"Nek and your guards have made good headway in clearing them out."

"There is no warmth here," Mirzayael says. "No water. No food."

"I just need to flip the circuit breaker," I say. Mirzayael stares at me, uncomprehending. "Once I find the source of the mana ore, I should be able to bring this city back to life. Heat. Water. Light. Harvests. Imagine what it could be! And we're so close to getting there—I can feel it."

Finally, Mirzayael's mouth twitches with a small smile. "It's a noble vision."

I let out a breath, chuckling. "You must think I'm a fool."

"No," Mirzayael says, "I think you're a dreamer."

"Well, that's not so bad." I remove my hand from the wall, leaving the mysterious stone circuits behind. "The world could use more dreamers."

Mirzayael snorts. "I don't know. You're plenty to handle all on your own."

I continue to fill in my Map Interface as we explore. Funneling my mana into expanding the Dungeon Core's range at strategic points has helped uncover over half of the buried city. Unfortunately, the map doesn't provide much insight into what's inside each room—apart from the type and shape of rocks found there—so Mirzayael and I take notes with some slate and chalk anytime there's something of importance. We've explored most of the palace proper and plenty of the lower city, uncovering bathhouses, war rooms, training grounds, servants' quarters, pastures, and even various dilapidated hints at tools and establishments in a merchant district. In each of these places I try and fail to imagine how it might have looked, bustling with people, in its prime.

The largest section left unexplored is the south quarter of the city, and it's not for lack of trying.

I step into a room, holding up my Spark, and let out a groan as the far wall sparkles in the firelight. "It's here too."

Mirzayael follows me in. "I told you as much. That glacier has probably ground this portion of the city to dust by now."

She might be right, but it's still frustrating. No matter how far I explore along the south side of the Catacombs, I inevitably run into another wall of impenetrable ice. Not only is it stubbornly preventing me from fully mapping out the city, it's also closing me off from what I expect to be important parts of the castle, such as the throne room.

I head over to the wall and run my hand over the ice, its chill wicking up into my fingers. Goosebumps sprout along my arms from the cold; even the warm layers I now wear aren't enough to stave off the arctic bite. It's even worse on the surface, and Mirzayael's hunters have had to start layering up until they can hunt enough prey for thicker coats.

Unfortunately, unlike the thermal springs, this ice is just normal water: not a drop of magic to give. Which means making the Dungeon Core eat it will cost me rather than net me mana. And given the incredible scope of this glacier, chiseling all the ice out of the Fortress would be an incredible task whether magical or conventional means were used.

A frustrating enigma. But I'm sure I can solve it if I keep mulling things over.

Just as we've done the last few nights, we begin to head back to the Keep for supper. First, however, we detour toward Ollie's cavern. The main purpose is to close off the tunnel to the surface, but I've also been using the opportunity to tell Ollie a bedtime story.

I've since refined the path to the dragon's lair, both making the route shorter and smoother. It's about a twenty-minute walk from the Keep, and despite my insistence that Mirzayael can go ahead without me, she maintains that I must be accompanied 'for security purposes.' As we walk, we chat about my next planned expedition to search for the source of the thermal springs.

"If you want to cut through the glacier, you're going to need to get that Core under control," Mirzayael says. "Maybe another dip in the water will get it to fall in line."

"More likely to throw a tantrum, I think." I look thoughtfully down at the stone on my wrist. "Sometimes it feels like a child. Yet other times..."

I feel I should treat it with more wariness, and yet, I'm not even sure how I'd go about that.

"Other times?" Mirzayael prompts.

The cave rumbles, and we both stop.

"What was that?" I ask.

"It came from the dragon's lair, I think."

We both hesitate for a moment. I take a cautious step forward. The cave rumbles again, and this time it's accompanied by a distant roar. Mirzayael and I look at each other, then we leap into action, sprinting down the corridor.

Even missing one of her legs, Mirzayael is much faster than me. In a matter of seconds, she vanishes down the hallway, spear raised, her legs a blur of motion. I push harder, but mine aren't made for running. My wings want to catch the air, but without wind magic to bring them lift, the drag only slows me down. I try to fold them tighter against my back and press on, as fast as my awkward, taloned gait can take me.

Mirzayael's voice cries out ahead of me. "Watch out! Frost wolf. Defend yourself!"

That's all the warning I get as a great shadow comes racing down the hall in my direction. I skid to a stop, summoning fire in either hand and flaring them fast and bright.

The animal falters, ducking its head against my sudden blinding light, but it doesn't stop. Now bathed in my firelight, I get a good look at the predator before me.

It's certainly a wolf, that much is true. But it's as white as sleet, its eyes an unnerving bright blue, and its fur is clumped together in spikes like dozens of giant icicles. I have a feeling those sharp points are for more than just show.

Oh, and it's as tall as I am.

The frost wolf comes loping straight for me, lips peeled back to reveal its fangs, a growl rumbling from its chest. I don't hesitate a moment longer.

Throwing both palms forward, a fireball explodes from my hands.

CHAPTER NINETEEN
FROST WOLVES

Fire explodes down the hall as I loose a Blaze.

[Mana: 231/250] Echo reports, the numbers rapidly depleting. I dismiss the visual notification and focus on the fight. I pour more mana into the attack, ice evaporating from the walls of the tunnel as the wolf vanishes behind the torrent of my flames. Then a shadow appears in the flames, and I only have a fraction of a second to react as its jaws tear through the fire and come for my neck. I fall to the ground as the wolf flies over me. One of its claws catches my shoulder as it passes, and a burning pain lances through my arm.

[8 points of Slashing Damage sustained.]

I grimace as I roll away. I can hear the wolf's claws scraping across the stone, scrabbling to turn around and come at me again. My fire did nothing to stop it. The wolf was too fast, and my flames too diffused. Quick, no time to think. I need to fight back with something solid. Something—

Core! My mental shout is so loud and so sudden, I feel the Dungeon Core jump in surprise.

A wall! I need a wall, I say, picturing what I intend, willing the construct into existence. I open all my mana to the Core. *Help me!*

The Core lunges at my mana with the hunger of a ravenous wolf pouncing on a—well, pouncing on a harpy, I suppose.

It's jittery with excitement. Building? It LOVES to build. Why don't I let it build more? It has so much stone in its Inventory as it is and—

"Now!" I cry, scrambling back as the wolf comes at me a second time. "Do it now!"

Strength vanishes from my limbs in an instant as my mana is sucked away. I stumble, unprepared for the spiritual punch to my gut, and raise a hand in weak defense, summoning another flame to my fingers as the wolf closes in.

Here is a wall! the Dungeon Core happily announces. Isn't it awesome?

And the wall appears. One moment, the wolf is a handspan away from tearing me to shreds. The next, a wall of earth launches from the ground, catching the frost wolf from beneath and rocketing it toward the ceiling. The wall crashes into the stone over my head, then continues through, burrowing into the ceiling as the cave shakes around me.

The wolf is gone.

It didn't even have time to let out a yelp of surprise.

[147 points of Bludgeoning Damage dealt,] Echo happily reports. [Frost Wolf defeated.]

Good god.

The Core had formed that wall before I even had a chance to react. Once more, I am shaken by its power—its danger. I'm beginning to suspect I'm barely using the Dungeon Core to a fraction of its potential. Perhaps I should be thinking bigger.

Assuming I want to give it that much power. Assuming I can still maintain my control over it.

I shakily stand up, reorienting myself now that there's a giant wall bisecting the passage. Mirzayael and Ollie are on the other side—and based on the yells I'd heard before, I suspect they're trapped back there with more wolves.

"Good job," I tell the Core, and it preens at my praise. "But now I'll need you to take it down. We've got others to help."

The Core is a bit disappointed. It just made that wall! And now I want it to destroy it? It's hurt. Wounded!

"Those are synonyms." I put my hand on the wall. "Quickly now. You'll have a chance to make more walls. We just need to get through this one."

The Core deflates sadly, but the prospect of getting to build more walls is enough for it to go along with my request for now. The stone beneath my hand dissolves into sand, and the Dungeon Core affects a disgusted face. Digesting stone it's previously eaten does *not* taste as good as natural stone. Not by a long shot!

Ignoring the Core's commentary, I jump through the hole in the wall as sand still cascades around me. I shake the earth from my feathers as I dash forward, expanding my sense of surroundings through the Core's spatial awareness and Map Interface. It doesn't help me see Ollie or Mirzayael, but it helps me anticipate the turns in the corridor before I get to them. I can hear sounds ahead. Footsteps—

I turn the corner and nearly skewer myself on Mirzayael's spear. Both of us are running full-tilt toward one another, but Mirzayael reacts before I do. She jerks to the side, whipping her weapon out of its lethal trajectory, as we both skid to a stop.

"You're alive," she says, and I feel slightly insulted to find surprise in her tone. "The wolf?"

"Taken care of," I say. "You?"

"Of course, the same," she says. Then she flicks her spear back in the direction she'd come; back toward Ollie's cave. "Come quickly then; there are more back in Ollie's chamber, I believe."

She's already moving before I have a chance to ask for elaboration. I run after her, wishing desperately that these wings could be put to some use.

Get ready, I tell the Core. *If any more of those wolves are still standing, I'll need you to act quickly.*

I send it several rapid-fire mental pictures of what I mean: holes opening in the ground beneath the wolves' feet, stalagmites dropping on them from the ceiling, cannonballs of stone firing at the beasts from the walls. The Core eagerly agrees to my plans, excited by all the new applications for its stonework it can try out. Should I be concerned it has so little value for life that it doesn't even question crushing an animal into bonemeal? Or should I be more concerned I made those orders without hesitation?

Of course, the wolves are predators. They aren't sapient, and they won't hesitate to kill me. The self-defense on my part is justifiable.

A nuance the Dungeon Core is blissfully ignorant of. Would it even notice if it crushed one of my allies along with an enemy? I'll need to keep a tight leash, just in case.

We pass a dead frost wolf on the way, its white fur stained red as blood continues to pool around it. I don't let my gaze linger on the gore as we rush past. Another few twists and turns through the passage, and a bright light at the end of the tunnel marks the entrance to Ollie's chamber. Mirzayael leaps through, and I'm hot on her heels.

I skid out onto the top of the staircase in time to watch the seven-year-old-boy-turned-dragon gleefully toss one of the wolves in the air and catch it in his mouth, devouring the animal like a gummy fruit snack. Around him, the floor is littered with the body parts of what must have been half a dozen other wolves.

Then again, all those pieces could have come from just one creature.

Ollie licks his chops and turns to us, letting out a happy chirping noise as he catches sight of me. *"FYRE!"* He bounds over to the stairwell, resting his chin on our ledge. I hesitantly pat his nose, trying hard to ignore the liberal layer of blood covering his muzzle. Tufts of hair are plastered among the gore.

"DID YOU SEE WHAT I DID?" Ollie cries. *"I BEAT THEM UP GOOD!"*

I wince at the mental volume of his voice which I'm beginning to suspect he'll never get under control. "Yes, you did great. Did you notice if any other wolves made it through?"

"NO, I ATE ALL OF THEM!" he happily and incorrectly declares. *"THEY WERE REALLY CRUNCHY AND SALTY. JUST LIKE BARBEQUE POTATO CHIPS!"*

But at least two made it through to Mirzayael and I. How many more might be running loose through the tunnels? We need to get back to the Keep to make sure everyone is safe.

Mirzayael must have come to the same conclusion. "I cannot linger here. I have to ensure the city remains protected."

"Go," I tell her, and she rushes back into the cave system. I turn my attention back to Ollie. "Where did the wolves come from?"

"DOWN MY TUNNEL, I THINK," he says, nodding toward the path that leads to the surface. *"I WAS TAKING A NAP, AND WHEN I WOKE UP, ONE BIT MY TAIL. THAT'S SO MEAN!"*

Damn. If I'd gotten here sooner, I might have been able to stop them from entering—or maybe I would have run face-first into the entire pack. Mirzayael isn't going to like this.

"We might need to be more careful about when we leave the tunnel to the surface open," I say. "Not just sealed at night, but anytime you're not above ground. Mirzayael might be right—we shouldn't leave it unguarded."

"*I CAN GUARD IT!*" he objects. "*I'M REALLY GOOD AT GUARDING.*"

I smile, patting his nose. "I know you are. But it's better to be safe than sorry."

Ollie pouts as I head down the staircase into his cavern and make my way over to the giant passage that slopes up to the surface. The floor is absolutely filthy, and the cave has begun to smell musty and stale. Ollie certainly doesn't seem to mind the state of his cavern, but it could desperately use a good cleaning. In fact, a pile of... *things*... have begun to form in one corner of his cave. I'd call it the start of a hoard, but that would be generous. Even as I have the Dungeon Core summon a wall of stone to seal off the exit to Ollie's cave, I watch from the corner of my eye as he scratches at the remains of one of the wolves and pries something from the corpse. Once the desired artifact is finally free, he flings it over into his collection.

Where it *clangs* like something made of metal.

I tip my head. "What was that?"

Ollie's head dips, like a dog caught in the middle of vandalizing a trash can. "*WHAT? NOTHING!*"

I head over to his treasure trove, wrinkling my nose at the smell of rotten meat as I find a pile of antlers, bones, and colorful rocks swept into a haphazard pile. Clearly, Ollie's found a hobby to fill his time. But the item on top of the pile is different. It's a metal plate connected to a strap of leather. I pull the object out of Ollie's collection.

He nudges me lightly from behind, which is still enough to cause me to go stumbling forward.

"*THAT'S MINE!*" he objects. "*I EARNED IT.*"

"You did," I agree, turning the plate over in my hands. There's the symbol of a shield and eye hammered into the metal. An insignia? "And it is yours. Ollie, is it okay if I borrow this? I just want Mirzayael to see it. Then I'll bring it right back."

The boy is clearly not pleased with this proposition. "*PROMISE?*"

"I pinky promise," I say, holding up a clawed pinky.

Ollie uses the tip of his tail to grab my pinky—though it's so wide it actually wraps around my whole hand.

"*COME BACK SOON,*" Ollie says. "*WE STILL HAVE TO DO STORY TIME TONIGHT. YOU HAVE TO TELL ME IF ALICE GETS SMALL AGAIN!*"

"I will," I promise, making my way back up the stairs.

I don't have to go all the way to Fyreneth's Keep before I find Mirzayael, however. She's near the frost wolf she killed back in the tunnel, bent over the animal and pulling something from its hair.

The same plate of metal I found.

But this time I can see what the strap of leather was for: it's a collar.

"I guess I'm late to the party with my discovery," I say, holding up my own identical accessory. "Do you know what it means?"

"It means this wasn't some random pack of wild frost wolves," Mirzayael says.

"They're domesticated." Not exactly hard to gather from the use of a collar. "Who sent them?"

Mirzayael traces a finger over the shield and eye insignia, her face twisting with disgust. "The shield against the unfaithful," she says, voice dripping with bitterness. "Those who wield the gods' will. The only nation around for leagues, still stationed here just to make sure Fyreneth's followers don't rise again." Mirzayael sneers. "Our betrayers. The Kingdom of Jorria."

Chapter Twenty

THE GLACIER

"Bad news," Beryl says, glancing from the pot she's stirring to the Jorrian symbol we placed at her side. She tosses some herbs into the stew and a bubble pops, splashing drops of liquid across the metal plate. "Bad omen. Where did you find this?"

Mirzayael relays the details of the wolf attack, the two of us seated in Beryl's hut as she continues to work on her brew. Mirzayael's legs are all tucked up around her torso, and I'm briefly given the impression of a cat with its paws hidden away and folded beneath its chest.

Granted, a very large, spindly, seven-legged cat.

Beryl lets out a long sigh once Mirzayael has finished. "Well. It would happen sooner or later. Actually, I thought they'd find us decades ago. When your parents' scouting party left and never returned, I always suspected the Jorrians would arrive in their absence."

I give a start, looking at Mirzayael. "Your parents?"

Mirzayael pointedly does not return my look.

God, no wonder she'd been so insistent that the last scouting party wouldn't have abandoned the Fyrethians for greener pastures. No wonder she believes so fiercely that nothing save an ambush would have stopped them from returning.

"Regardless," Mirzayael says, addressing Beryl rather than me, "the Jorrians have found us, now."

And they were able to get inside because of me.

"Is it possible the attack wasn't deliberate?" I hesitantly ask, desperately hoping for the best. "They were a pack of wolves, perhaps trained to hunt animals. That doesn't necessarily imply Fyrethians were the target."

Mirzayael scoffs. "Foolish question. Of course they were targeting us."

"These people—the Jorrians—they betrayed Fyreneth almost a thousand years ago," I say. "It's a different generation of people who live there today. They don't bear the sins of their ancestors any more than you should be persecuted for yours. What if they can be reasoned with? If they do show up at our doorstep—be it in search of us or their wolves—shouldn't we at least attempt to speak with them?"

Mirzayael looks at me in disgust. "Never have I heard such naivety, *Outsider*. You do not know our history, our suffering, as we do. You don't understand what it means to be forsaken by the gods. What it means to be given a task *by* the gods. What weight this holds, and what consequences would meet anyone who would defy them."

I grimace. "You're right: I don't know your culture, histories, or religions. But we did have religion on my world. Many varying beliefs in gods. Sometimes, myth can be distorted by the passage of time. What if this acrimony is a misunderstanding, perhaps driven by centuries of superstition?"

Mirzayael looks like I've slapped her. "I never expected *you* of all people to spew such ignorance. Our history is not superstition. The extermination and persecution of our ancestors is very much real—"

"Of course," I hurriedly say. "That's not what I—"

"But you have the audacity to suggest we're merely naive zealots, too afraid of a myth to venture from our caves? That we choose to waste away here out of nothing more than ignorance?"

"No, not at all," I object, horrified at how quickly this conversation had taken a turn for the awful. Before I can try to rectify things, Beryl sets a mug down on the table, hard, causing both me and Mirzayael to jump.

"Hush," she says. "You're being too loud."

Mirzayael angrily snaps her mouth shut. I wisely do the same.

"For your shoulder," Beryl tells me, steam still rising from the mug. "To prevent infection and encourage healing. Drink the whole cup." She sets another one down in front of Mirzayael.

"I'm uninjured," she says tightly.

"Then it will help you stay that way."

I pull the mug over, muttering my thanks.

The silence in the room grows tight as Mirzayael stiffly looks down at her drink. I glance into my own mug, my reflection swimming distorted on the surface. The new me: not the reflection I'd grown used to over a previous lifetime.

"I'm sorry," I say to Mirzayael. "All that was wrong of me. It got me in trouble in my last life, too. Drove wedges between myself and others. To question things is baked into my nature. I doubt that will ever change about me, nor do I think it is something I should necessarily change. But sometimes I default to it, challenging ideas for the sake of objectiveness, without taking into account how very personal something might be."

I think of her parents. How their loss must have shaped her. How me challenging her perception of the Jorrians also challenged her view of her parents' deaths.

"So again, I am sorry," I say. "And also, I want to extend my thanks. You've taken me in and shown me immense hospitality. More than I deserve, perhaps. While adjusting to this world has been easier than I expected, the real challenge has been in shaking off ingrained assumptions from growing up in a world very different from this one. I don't know that I can make myself think differently overnight. But I can try to be more open-minded going forward."

Mirzayael presses her mouth into a line, but does not respond with any biting remarks. Instead, she returns to her drink, and I do the same.

To be honest, I'd already forgotten about my injury. I Check my HP out of habit: 97/100. I know I took more than three damage in that fight. The passive healing must be helping me out, which means this potion isn't strictly necessary. Still, I'm not about to argue with Beryl—especially not after I just picked a fight with Mirzayael, however unintentional that might have been. Best to keep the peace.

I take a sip, and the moment the salty, bitter concoction hits my tongue, my stomach is thrown into revolt, roiling threateningly. I steal a glance toward Mirzayael, and notice her face has gone stoically unreadable. Like she's spending every atom of willpower available on smoothing her face muscles into an impassive mask. I'd laugh if I wasn't worried I might hurl.

I open my mouth, stop breathing through my nose, and gulp down the mug in four painful chugs. Mirzayael's eight eyes blink at me in surprise.

[HP Restored.]

"Tomorrow I'm going back to the glacier," I gasp, coughing to cover up a gag. "It's time to carve a path through and see what's waiting on the other side."

"I thought you couldn't get the Dungeon Core to store enough mana needed to eat away the ice," Mirzayael says, her still-full mug clasped between her hands.

"Perhaps not," I say. "But I don't need to rely on it for everything. Besides, I've had the power needed to cut through ice this whole time at my fingertips." I raise a hand, summoning a Spark to my palm.

I might not be able to control the sociopolitical situation between the Fyrethians and Jorrians, but this is something I *can* control. Helping these people, bringing warmth to the residents, restoring their original city—these are things within my power. And if we really are about to be under siege, as Mirzayael is implying, then gaining access to every resource this cave system has available might become a dire and imminent need.

The hints of a smile threaten to overtake Mirzayael's face once more. "Good. I look forward to seeing what you uncover." She tips her head back and downs the brew, then chokes halfway through and spits a mouthful of the potion back into her cup. "Blazing Abyss, Beryl. What the fuck did you put in this?"

The dwarf cackles.

I check the Map Interface once more. At least from the perspective of a disembodied entity that can only see rocks, the entire castle is now mapped out. That is, all of it except for the south side, where the glacier has bisected a portion of the city, slowly cutting away whatever structures had been there previously.

"The glacier also intersects this corner of Ollie's cave," I say, dismissing the mental interface to focus on the wall of ice before me.

We're partway up one of the staircases, where half the wall appears to shift from stone to ice. "Since his cavern is slightly lower than the base level of the rest of the city, this provides the easiest access point to bore through the glacier." And given the spring that runs beneath Ollie's cave, and the city's pipes that likewise are buried in the nearby walls, now severed by the glacier, I know we're close to the spring's source.

His cavern is currently empty, save for Mirzayael, me, Nek, and a couple of her young guards who have come to watch. Just as well that the boy is out enjoying the sunlight. This operation might be delicate.

"And what makes you certain that reaching this lost portion of the city is so significant?" Mirzayael asks.

"I'm *not* certain," I admit. "Call it an engineer's intuition." Some of the circuit-like stone in this corner of the fortress have also been cut off. I have a hunch about what might power it, but first I need to complete the circuit. Which means melting the ice away, locating the severed section of the city, and rejoining it to the main body.

"Ready?" I ask the others, summoning a fireball to my hand. "It's about to get warm in here."

[Blaze spell activated.]

"Ready," Mirzayael says.

The others take a step back.

I mentally tap at the Dungeon Core as well, getting its attention. *I'll need your help, too,* I tell it. *I'd appreciate it if you could rough up the floor for me. Digest it, I mean.* I recall the way it had cubed the stone up into bits of sand, sending it this memory to emphasize what I mean. Cutting up the material seems to consume significantly less mana than eating entire blocks of it.

The Dungeon Core regards the ice with extreme suspicion, clearly still scarred from my last encounter with the thermal springs. I allow it to chip away at the ice, and it takes the tiniest sample available, like a kid suspiciously nibbling at a vegetable. After a moment, it reluctantly agrees this frozen water *might* taste better than the stuff before. Still not as good as other rocks, though.

"Great," I say, holding out my hands. "Then let's get started."

My fire flares, but instead of allowing it to grow, I mentally compress it down, focusing the energy into a smaller area while still pushing mana into the flames. The fire grows blindingly bright, a white sphere of shimmering heat that burns itself into my vision. I step toward the wall of ice, and the glacier melts away before me.

I aim my path on a very faint upward trajectory, so the melting ice runs back out the hole and down into the lowest point of Ollie's cave, draining into the thermal spring. The Dungeon Core starts chewing at the ice beneath my feet, roughing up the path enough to create friction.

After only a half hour of such work, my mana begins to dwindle. From the Map Interface, I can tell we're nowhere close to the end of the glacier.

I snuff out my fire, and the cave goes dark. Surrounded by ice, the world feels close and silent. Water drips from the ceiling, quietly adding to the faint breaths of the others who shuffled in behind me.

"Does anyone have a light?" I ask the others. Not that I need to see, as I can navigate by the Map Interface instead; it's more for the others' comfort than my own. "I need to conserve my mana."

"Here." Mirzayael steps forward, the tip of her spear glowing a soft blue. Our ice cave flickers uncertainly in the dim light. I close my eyes, handing a few points of mana over to the Core to expand our awareness into the surrounding ice.

The missing corner of the Catacombs is farther away than I expected. There must have been a crack in the rock that the glacier expanded into, slowly migrating the missing stone away from its source over the last several hundred years. It's far enough away I won't be able to melt through the ice and get the Dungeon Core to manipulate the giant slab of rock back in place with the scant amount of mana I currently have. In fact, it will likely take several days operating on a full mana tank just to make it to the other side. If I could get the Core to absorb more of the spring water, this could go much quicker. But in this moment, with what I currently have at my disposal, what are my options?

As I'm pondering this, I notice something else. Beneath the wall of ice that separates the two parts of the kingdom, there's a pocket of air, and then more stone, far beneath that. But the properties of this stone don't automatically populate into the Dungeon Core's Map Interface as soon as the Core senses it: that means we haven't encountered this type of rock, yet. This is something new.

"Interesting."

"What is it?" Mirzayael asks.

"There's something beneath us," I say. "Stone we haven't encountered before. And that's rare given how much we've explored. I think this is important."

"You can't melt a path straight down?" Nek asks.

"Not with my current mana," I say.

"Should we head back then?" Mirzayael asks. "We can return tomorrow when you've more magic at your disposal."

Which would mean another day burned and little to show for it. I'd rather not waste such time. If Mirzayael and Beryl are right—if the Jorrians really do pose a threat—then I have to do something to help ensure these people are protected. Because it's my fault they were exposed in the first place.

Additionally, there's a part of me that still feels guilty for the things I said to Mirzayael the other day. I want to make it up to her. I want to do better. I want to *be* better.

"Let me think," I say, crouching down to run a hand over the cool, wet floor of the glacier. I might not have enough mana to burn my way down there, or enough for the Core to eat its way down, but it costs me nothing to bring matter *out* of the Dungeon Core's Inventory. What's more, I can change the properties of whatever I summon, similar to how I was able to change the thermal capacity of the stone in the dracid chamber. But even then, what would that achieve?

I could fashion a tool of some sort. A stone drill, perhaps. Though without leverage or a way to power it, that seems impractical. What else could help me carve a path through this glacier? What will get me through the ice?

Ice.

"Aha."

It's been a long time since chemistry class, but I'm very used to salting my walk when it gets icy in the winter. Sodium chloride. I know there are elements that are more reactive to water than sodium, but off the top of my head I can't recall which those were—and without a periodic table, it probably wouldn't be wise to experiment. Besides, I'm limited to whatever elements the Dungeon Core has consumed, and it's certainly eaten up a good amount of salt compounds.

Can I separate out just the sodium? I wonder, sorting through the Core's chemical interface.

[Affirmative,] Echo says. [Although altering items within the Dungeon Core Catalog will incur a mana cost.]

I'd figured as much; it had been the same when I'd altered the thermal capacity of the stones in the dracid chamber. I pull up a mineral rich with sodium, and mentally picture sorting the stone's elements so all of the sodium has been separated to one side. *How much mana would this cost me?*

[1 mana,] Echo says.

I blink. That's practically nothing! Then again, this is only a few small grams of sodium. I guess it wouldn't hurt to start with just a handful and see how effective it is.

Alright, Core, I say, showing it what I intend and handing over a few points of mana. *Let's make some salt.*

The Dungeon Core finds this activity very interesting, and happily obliges. It strips out the sodium with an almost practiced ease, flicking the rest of the minerals back into its catalog. Then, before I have a chance to specify what to do next, it summons the sodium.

Right in the air in front of me.

I have a brief moment to note that, curiously, the element doesn't look like the handful of white crystals as I was expecting it to. Instead, it appears to be a tiny cube of metal.

It falls to the ground before me.

Immediately, the cube begins to hiss and spark, tiny flames spitting off of the sodium. I jump to my feet, vaguely recalling similar demonstrations in undergrad chemistry classes decades ago.

"Everyone back!" I say, backpedaling myself. "Watch o—"

The sodium explodes.

CHAPTER TWENTY-ONE

CHEMISTRY 101

Tiny flecks of molten sodium fling in every direction, and pinpricks of pain sear through my hands, raised in defense.

[4 points of Fire damage sustained. Damage reduced. You have resistance to Fire type damage.]

"Blazing Abyss!" Nek cries. Rei and Zakaiya, heeding my warning, have already bolted back down the tunnel, and all that's left of them is their retreating footsteps. "What was that?"

"An experiment," I sheepishly admit. "And frankly, a bad idea. I'm playing outside my wheelhouse here."

"That was fire magic?" Mirzayael asks, seemingly unperturbed by the explosion. She steps forward, peering down at the small singed crater, still hissing and popping as bits of metal burrow into the ice.

"Not exactly," I say. "Or I guess more accurately, the closest my world got to magic. The Dungeon Core did most of the work, though."

"I don't understand," she says.

"It was a chemical reaction," I explain. "Admittedly, stronger than I was expecting. My knowledge of this field of science is fairly stunted, however, so I probably should be wary of dabbling too much with this."

Aerodynamics is much safer. Stick an airfoil in a wind tunnel and the worst you have to worry about is a little turbulent flow.

"Can it be used as a weapon?" Mirzayael asks.

I think about all the ways chemistry and atomic physics has been applied toward warfare back on Earth. "Yeah, you could say that."

"Can you make more?" Mirzayael asks. "This could be a valuable asset."

"I could," I admit. "But it would be extremely volatile. It reacts with water, so storing it would be difficult. It would be best to only create some when we needed it. Have you something in mind?"

"Not... specifically," Mirzayael says, which makes me strongly suspect she does. "But I do want to see what your chemical reaction is capable of. Can it get through the ice?"

"Maybe," I admit. Given how little mana the last bit took to create, I could easily retrieve more from the Core's catalog. "However, I'd be concerned about all of us being too close when it ignites. We'd need a delayed delivery mechanism of some sort." I tap my chin, already excited by the idea of a new problem to solve, despite all reason cautioning otherwise.

Something that could slowly dissolve, gradually introducing the sodium to the ice? Not sure what that might be. A mechanical hinge of some sort, that could be used to drop the sodium from a distance? I suppose I could set up a pulley system with Mirzayael's silk. Or something timed rather than manual. Something that could be calculated...

"Ah!" I sort through the Core's catalog, finding the ore I was looking for. With a little prompting, the Dungeon Core withdraws a hunk of cloudstone we'd gathered.

It's so unintuitive to have to hold the rock to keep it from floating up and out of my grasp. Instead, I turn my hand upside down, balancing the floating rock beneath my palm. I push down like I'm dribbling a basketball, and the stone bounces against my hand.

"This should work," I say, taking hold of the cloudstone once more. I task the Core with shaping the stone into the form of a bowl while I mentally skim through the metrics that had been gathered on the rock when it was stored in the Core's catalog. Density, wind magic capacity, mass, and most importantly, buoyancy. That makes it pretty easy to calculate how much sodium would balance it. And from there, assuming this world's gravity is about the same as Earth—I mean, it *feels* about the same, though I should probably perform some experiments to calculate it more precisely—I can estimate the time it would take for a miniature cloudstone vessel full of sodium to sink and spill out over the ground.

As the cloudstone finishes forming itself into a bowl, I get the Core to start refining more sodium for me. This time I'm not surprised when the cube of metal appears before me, falling into my waiting bowl. Of course it doesn't look like table salt. Sodium is a type of metal in its purest form, isn't it? God, what chemists back on Earth wouldn't kill to have something like the Dungeon Core. Tragically, I lack the knowledge to utilize it to its fullest potential. Maybe I can try sketching out what I remember of the Periodic Table one of these days. What I'd give for a Chemistry 1 textbook!

After a minute of work, my airship of sodium is fully stocked. I carefully cup it between my hands, testing its weight and lowering my palms. It drifts gently down before settling in my hands once more. Good. We should be able to precisely time this.

"Alright, I'm ready," I announce to Mirzayael, who has been curiously peering over my shoulder as I work. Nek has also been hovering nearby, but with a much healthier amount of caution. "Once I release this, we should have thirty seconds before it reaches the ground. That should give us time to retreat back down the tunnel. After it detonates, we can come back down and check on the results."

"Thirty seconds isn't a lot of time," Nek comments.

"I could remove a few of the cubes," I suggest. "I'll need to recalculate how much time that would give us."

"No," Mirzayael says. "It's tight, not impossible. Besides, I am interested to see just what this magic is capable of at full strength."

"It's not magic," I remind her. And not nearly full strength, but I decide to keep that part to myself, lest she demand more fire power. It's a good thing the Core hasn't found any cesium. That would really be something.

"In that case," I say, "tell me when."

I position myself to run, holding the bowl out at arm's length.

Nek and Mirzayael retreat a few steps down the path.

"Ready..." Mirzayael says.

Nek turns tail and flees. "Now!"

I let go of the bowl, dashing after them. My heart hammers in my chest as my feet hit the ice, talons digging into the surface as I haphazardly slip and lunge down the hallway, laughter bubbling out of me.

How absurd this is! Dropping a slow-motion bomb and running away as quickly as I can. Like a kid lighting a bottle rocket and then diving behind a fence. How unscientific. How dangerous.

How fun!

It's the most that's gotten my heart going in years. I mentally count the seconds as I sprint through the tunnel, lungs burning, legs sore. Nek spares a horrified glance back at my giggling, which only makes me laugh harder. Light appears before us. We race down the slope and out onto the landing.

"Are you mad?" Nek asks, giving me a baffled look.

I shake my head, smiling and panting. "Ten," I say between breaths. "Nine. Eight. Seve—"

An explosion rocks the room as a loud *bang* echoes up the ice tunnel. Flecks of ice hiss down from the ceiling. For the next minute, secondary explosions crackle and snap from down the tunnel. Then, it all goes quiet.

Startling all of us, Mirzayael laughs. "Your count was off."

I grin. "I noticed."

Nek shakes his head, though I'm not sure which of us the gesture is aimed at.

I lead the way back up the tunnel, using my Spark to light the way. I quest carefully ahead, testing every step before I press forward, no matter how stable it may seem. I don't have enough mana to expand the Core's range, so I can only sense a few feet in any direction. Not nearly enough to trust the structural integrity of the ice beneath me. Even so, it holds all the way back to the end. There, however, the floor is missing.

I'm not sure if the sodium was enough to melt through the rest of it, or if it was merely enough to crack the ice and cause a section to fall away. Regardless, there is now a great hole in the ice chamber, and from it comes the breeze of a pressure differential—along with faint sounds.

Mirzayael stops just behind me. "You hear that?"

"Yes," I say, my stomach fluttering with excitement. "That rushing sound?"

"Running water," she says. "Not far down, I think."

It's the thermal spring, burbling somewhere in the chamber below. We're so close, I can taste it!

I hold my hand over the gap, but my firelight is swallowed by the dark.

"Step back," Mirzayael says. "This is where my abilities are needed."

Mirzayael quickly produces a length of silk, deftly knotting handholds into the rope. Eventually, she ties one end around her spear, wedges the weapon over the gap, then drops the rest of the thread into the chasm beneath us.

"Are you ready, Outsider?" she asks.

"I've never been more ready," I say, nervousness and excitement dancing through me as I peer into the dark. I won't be able to keep a light going while I climb down the rope. It will be in complete darkness.

Mirzayael smiles, exposing her needle-like teeth. "Good. Then follow me." She runs a hand along her silk, then skitters down the hole, vanishing into the abyss. The rope goes taut a moment later.

I cautiously sit at the edge of the pit, scooting up to the overhang and dangling my legs over the side. I have to lean forward to grab the rope, which is slightly nerve wracking, but at least the silk is less slippery than it appears, clinging to my hands with a comforting friction. I take a breath, glance back at Nek and the young scouts, who look as nervous as I feel, then push off and rappel down into the dark.

The rope swings slowly from side to side, and I occasionally have to kick off the ice as I descend. It's only around me for another few feet, however, and I can hear when I pass beneath the last of it. The distant sounds of running water shift from a muted closeness, to an echoing expanse. I can practically *feel* the open space around me.

My arms burn as I descend, hand over hand. I'd never had much upper body strength as a human—at least, not since I was a teen. This harpy body seems better suited to the physical task, but not by much. Soon the muscles in my arms and torso start to burn, and my fingers ache.

"Mirzayael," I call, my voice echoing into the black. "Watch out. I might slip."

Something touches my shoulder, and Mirzayael's voice speaks into my ear. "It won't be much of a fall."

I jump in surprise, my grip slipping from the rope. My feet hit the ground at the same moment, quickly crumpling beneath my weight. Mirzayael catches me, an arm slipping beneath my wings to stop me from falling the rest of the way to the floor. She pulls me back to my feet.

"Thank you," I say, regaining my balance. I blink rapidly against the black. "How can you see anything down here?"

"There's still a little light above us," she says. "My eyes are better adjusted to the dark. Come, let's get out of the way before Nek jumps down on top of us." Her hand tugs gently at my sleeve.

I carefully step over the uneven floor, following her pull, as I summon a new light to my hands. I squint against the brightness, but my Spark doesn't go far. Light shimmers off Mirzayael's carapace and dully lights the floor—stone again. But the chamber is clearly far too large for my flames to even begin to illuminate. The sound of running water is louder down here, somewhere gurgling off to our right, and it's accompanied by the smell of sulfur.

I grin. By my estimates, we're slightly upstream of the same river that runs through Ollie's cave. And that means...

Core, check out the stone beneath us, I say. *We couldn't sense what it was before, right?*

Sure enough, a simple scan of the rock comes back as Unidentified. Well then. Time to identify it.

The Core bounces around like a puppy the moment it can tell I'm going to give it the last dregs of my mana to analyze the stone. New ore! It can't wait. It's been so long since it's had anything new to eat!

You'd have more to try if you were willing to consume that spring water, I point out. *With that amount of mana we could have explored the entire cave system by now.*

The Core pointedly ignores this as it sets about tasting the stone, dissolving a few square inches beneath my feet.

The energy hits me like a shock of lightning, zapping straight from the Core's mind into my own. It's so intense, so concentrated, that it momentarily erodes all my other senses—sight, sound, sensation, gone in a flash.

[Bonus Mana: 1283] Echo reports.

"...er? Are you alright? What happened?"

I blink as my awareness returns, briefly disoriented. I'm on the ground, Mirzayael's hands tightly clutching my arm. The Dungeon Core, meanwhile, is ping-ponging around my head.

It found it! IT FOUND IT! It's been so long! It had almost forgotten what it tasted like. So perfect! So pure! So much *power.*

"Ow." I rub my forehead as the Core's thoughts reflect over the top of themselves like echoes in a cave. "Yes, I'm okay. I just wasn't prepared."

Mirzayael's grip relaxes. "Prepared for what?"

I Check the new stone that's appeared in the Dungeon Core's catalog.

[Mana Ore. A magical ore with absorptive properties which collects dense concentrations of mana from its surroundings over the course of decades or centuries.]

I can't help but grin, echoing the Core's elation. "We found it. The vein of mana ore."

Mirzayael helps me to my feet as I tap into the incredible mana reserves I now have, using it to feed the Core's range and expand our sense to fill the chamber around us. I can now "see" the lightning-bolt of ore zig-zagging through the surrounding stone, passing through the thermal river, and disappearing even deeper into the earth. If just this tiny scrape of rock gave me so much mana, I can't even begin to fathom what magic I'd be capable of if I allow the Core to consume the entire vein of ore.

In fact, I'm not sure that would be wise. But I don't need to absorb it all at once. Keeping such a vast amount of mana in reserve gives the Core an enormous area which it can sense and effect. As long as I have enough mana to maintain that sphere of influence, I should be able to harvest more of the mana ore remotely, no matter where I am in the Catacombs, anytime I might need it.

Because we're moving back into Fyreneth's Fortress.

Even without my light, I can sense the floor around me. Through the Map Interface, every nook, every pebble is apparent. The circuit lines in the Catacombs and the equivalent lines in the broken section of stone might as well be neon signs. With my mind buzzing with energy, half submerged in the Dungeon Core's consciousness, I can see it all so clearly, how it should fit together—where the mana ore also fit into all of this.

"Come," I tell Mirzayael, turning back around and leading her to the corner of the Catacombs that is exposed beneath the glacier. I can see the entire buried city this way. Every room and courtyard. Each collapsed wing and crumbling wall. I can fix it. I can restore it all.

"Where are we going?" Mirzayael asks, following me anyway. Now I'm the one guiding her through the dark.

"Just here," I say, raising my hand to the underside of the Catacombs. I brush my fingers over the rock, picturing what I want. My fingertips feel electric with possibilities. The Dungeon Core eagerly presses against my mind, waiting for my mana, waiting to turn my vision into reality.

"It's been long overdue," I tell her. "But it's high time the Fyrethians regained their home. Hold on." And I relinquish control.

The Core carves out more gouges in the ground and mana floods into me like a conduit. The stone rumbles beneath our feet. Ice cracks over our heads, showering us with flecks of snow. The earth comes alive.

I don't bother reconnecting the lost, broken sliver of the city. Instead I recreate it, exactly where the Catacombs are missing a piece. New earth appears in thin air, brought out from the Core's inventory, already exactly the right ore and shape it needs to be. More rises up from the ground to fill in the gaps, reaching around Mirzayael and I to flow into the wall like liquid. New tiny stone circuits replace the old, completing broken lines, fixing the damaged loops—and seeing it all come together, it's abruptly so obvious what they were for. Finally, after all the new stone has fixed itself in place, I make the last connection: the mana ore hooks directly into the circuits of the Catacombs, and with the will of the Dungeon Core, the city comes alive with magic.

Mana floods through the circuits. I feel the magical synapses firing, ancient and dormant spells being activated. The Dungeon Core's consciousness spreads through the Fortress, and I am pulled along with it, watching the runic lights in every room turn on, spells to move stale air begin to clear the palace, *life* breathed back into the dormant city.

Most of the pipes that were once used for plumbing are clogged, so we clean those out as well, widening the tunnels, pushing stones and earth through the pipes like giant earthen street sweeps. Once they're clear, the spells embedded in the tunnels activate and begin pulling water up from the springs. Some of it pours into the bathhouses, some of it runs beneath the streets to warm the city, while still more passes through filtering spells and becomes drinking water.

It's all so elaborate. Planned so meticulously, each spell a gear in a magical machine to an artificial paradise—this oasis in such a desolate terrain. My heart aches for what Fyreneth created. It went buried for so long without being able to act as the home for her people it was designed to be.

But no longer will they have to suffer quietly in their caves. Now they will be able to live and grow as they have always deserved to.

And I won't let *anyone* put a stop to that. Not the Jorrians, and certainly not the gods.

Chapter Twenty-Two

MOVE-IN DAY

The migration doesn't happen overnight. In fact, it takes a bit of convincing from Nek, Mirzayael, and the guards for people to even risk venturing their first trip out to the Catacombs. Centuries of fatigue carry a weighty momentum.

But the sight of the Catacombs—no, Fyreneth's Fortress—is impossible to dismiss. Even from just outside the Keep, its distant light fills the caverns with an ethereal glow.

The first time Beryl catches sight of the city, she stops mid-step, absorbing the details in silent awe.

"It's beautiful, isn't it?" I say. The lights in distant windows, spiraling up the full height of the great cavern, twinkle like stars in the night. It *looks* lived in. Bustling. Thriving.

"It is," Beryl agrees. "But it sounds like a graveyard."

She's right. When one would otherwise expect to hear the din of city life, the quiet that fills the cavern tinges the scene with an eerie undercurrent.

"That's the sound of potential," I say. "A city waiting to be filled. What do you say. Will you help us fill it?"

"I cannot make the people of the Keep do anything," Beryl says.

"But you're their leader," I start, however Beryl holds up a hand.

"I cannot make them do anything," she repeats. "But I will happily walk this path myself. I should like to see Fyreneth's vision with my own eyes. Should others follow in my footsteps, then so be it."

Glancing over Beryl's head, I meet Mirzayael's gaze with a grin. She offers a small smile in return.

"Come," I tell Beryl, helping to guide the ancient woman up the path. "There's so much I'd like to show you. There's an entire heated wing of the city—devoted to dracid, I think. Oh, I can't wait for Nek to show his wife and kids. And Ollie's cavern opens to the south side of the city; I'm thinking of building a footpath up to the palace for him. There are pavilions so large, it seems like they were *designed* for lounging dragons. And of course, the main palace is where you should live, as the leader. Although really, the entire town could probably fit in there."

"Hm." Beryl grunts. "Sounds a bit too roomy."

"Room to grow," I insist. "Give it a chance. I think it will surprise you."

Nek and his family are the first to follow. Though, bless him, I suspect he would have moved here if I'd asked even without Beryl's endorsement. The rest of Mirzayael's guards and scouts are the next to follow, as they've already helped clear the place out of most of the creatures that lived there. A few adventurous souls come to explore the city in the next few days, each huddling together in small groups, wide-eyed and whispering excitedly like a bunch of tourists. They return with more friends and family, the groups growing each time. A family of ten dracid is the first to officially make the move, carrying all their belongings into a heated section of the palace over the course of half a dozen trips. After that, the flood becomes inevitable.

"Food is the next issue to address," I say, brainstorming with Mirzayael, Beryl, and Nek over dinner in the palace's main kitchen. There's technically a dining hall designed for such a purpose, but given the communal nature of the Keep, when mealtime comes everyone gravitates toward the kitchen. Several giant stone cauldrons are set up along the walls, designed for a feast, it seems. The glowing red-hot runes beneath each pot provide a fireless, smokeless, source of heat for the simmering stews.

"Fuel needed for fire is solved," I say, nodding to the cauldrons. "And heat for the dracid. Clean water for the city. Plumbing for sewage. Shelter overhead. Fyreneth's Fortress meets all our basic needs, save for food."

"What are you talking about?" Nek says, setting his bowl of moss stew down. "We have plenty to eat! We just need to relocate the fungi farms over to the Fortress pastures."

To my merit, I don't grimace. "The mushrooms are certainly convenient to grow but they don't provide a lot of... variety." At least I've recently been refining table salt out of the minerals the Core has collected so far. That's helped. "Besides, as the community becomes more active—especially the dracid, who won't have to brumate nearly so long—we'll be needing more calories to make up the deficit."

"We can relocate the stinger corrals into the Fortress," Nek suggests. "There are enclosures in the lower levels of the city that appear to be designed for agriculture, and can be altered to accommodate stinger physiology."

"Perfect," I say. "Not to mention, we could even potentially find some different wild animals on the surface to bring back and breed as livestock. Mirzayael, you said before you were interested in organizing some hunting missions. Has that begun, yet?"

The circle goes quiet.

"It's on pause," she admits. "After the frost wolf attack, I suspected the Jorrians might follow; I have refrained from organizing any hunting trips since then out of caution."

"That was weeks ago." I shrug, trying to appear less concerned than I feel. "If the wolves were intended as scouts, and the Jorrians really do intend anything malicious, shouldn't they have followed up by now?"

The others exchange uneasy looks around the circle.

"Not on us to know the minds of zealots," Beryl says, stirring her spoon through her bowl. "The best we can do is assume malice and prepare for it."

I bite my tongue before I say anything I might regret. It seems such a pessimistic, isolated way to live. And given their history with the Jorrians, I can hardly blame them for clinging to that mindset. But I also don't want that fear to suffocate them and stifle their potential for growth.

"I doubt we will be caught unprepared," I say. "Ollie's promised to let us know if he sees anything. And we have your scouts, right?"

Mirzayael straightens, and I can see the pride in her posture. "Yes. Nothing else from the ice will catch us by surprise."

I nod in agreement, and leave it at that. Maybe the Jorrians will simply never try to make contact, and we won't have to know which way the cards will fall.

Even I'm not optimistic enough to believe that.

I don't bring the topic up again, but within the week, Mirzayael organizes her guards for an expedition out onto the ice. Gathering the handful of fraying fur-lined coats they have available, they strike out for the surface, accompanying Ollie for his daily expedition—and return that night with a slain arctic bear.

The mood skyrockets after that. Meat for meals, bones for tools, and a hide for better clothes all have young members of the colony clambering to sign up for Mirzayael's next hunting trip. Pleased to find new recruits, she takes the opportunity to begin training them in the way of the spear. She claims it's for hunting, but I suspect she has a different enemy in mind.

A family of dwarves has taken it upon themselves to develop the agriculture, transplanting and nurturing the mushroom fields, along with a variety of mosses and ferns. I'm desperately hoping Mirzayael's missions out on the ice will find some more variety of plants to bring back, too.

Ollie is delighted with Mirzayael's expeditions. He even offered to let her ride on his back, which she politely and firmly declined. Despite the communication barrier, however, he's still happy to fly ahead and signal to Mirzayael when he finds more animals for her to hunt. He's even joined in, a couple times, but the creatures he catches suspiciously never make it back to the Fortress. Quite the mystery.

I've thought about attending some of these outings as well. I can't say that riding along on Ollie doesn't appeal to me; the ability to fly, even by proxy, calls to me. But then I recall I'd have no way to stop my inevitable death if I slipped from his back, and that instinct is quickly quelled. Besides, I still have so much to do in Fyreneth's Fortress. Always more buildings to fix, logistics to plan, and small, daily problems to solve. Maybe one day I'll devise a harness. Until then, I can dream.

I'm in the midst of clearing a new pasture for agriculture, using the Dungeon Core to remove the dust so it can be filled with some of the Keep's soil, when Ollie's voice bursts into my mind.

I jump at the sudden noise; I'm not sure if I'll ever get used to it.

"*FYRE!*" he cries. "*FYRE THERE'S PEOPLE OUT HERE.*"

I pause what I'm doing and glance over at Mirzayael. Even when she's not around, she still has one of her guards following me—typically Nek. I should probably be offended that she still distrusts me, even after all this time, but at this point I suspect she's more worried about me hurting myself than me hurting someone else.

"*Can you tell who they are?*" At the same time, I turn to Mirzayael. "Do you have any hunting groups out?"

"No," she says. "Never without me. Why do you ask?"

"*I DON'T KNOW,*" Ollie admits. "*I DON'T RECOGNIZE THEM. I THINK THEY'RE STRANGERS.*"

Frost runs down my spine. "Ollie says there's people out on the ice," I relay. "Strangers."

"Jorrians," Mirzayael hisses, her hand tightening around her spear. "Quick, tell him to get back here. Do not engage. I need to assemble my guards. How far away are they?"

I repeat Mirzayael's message to Ollie. We're both already making for Ollie's lair. Mirzayael barks orders at any guard she passes, but I'm focused on what Ollie is saying.

"*UMMMM IT LOOKS LIKE A LONG WAY. AT LEAST AS FAR AWAY AS THE ONE HUNDRED ACRE WOODS,*" he says.

I blink. "*As far as what? One hundred acres?*"

"*IT'S THE PARK AT MY SCHOOL,*" Ollie says. "*IT'S CALLED THE ONE HUNDRED ACRE WOODS.*"

"*Like Winnie the Pooh?*" I ask, baffled.

"*I DON'T KNOW. IT'S PRETTY COOL! THERE'S ALL THESE TREES WITH LOW BRANCHES WE CAN CLIMB, AND SOMETIMES WE PLAY LIKE WE'RE LOST IN THE WILDERNESS AND HAVE TO EAT BERRIES TO—*"

"*Ollie, how far away*," I say, trying to wrangle him back on track. "*I don't know how big your One Hundred Acre Woods is.*"

"*ABOUT THE SAME SIZE AS THE PLAYGROUND, I THINK*" he says. "*MAYBE TWO PLAYGROUNDS. OR ACTUALLY MAYBE FIVE. NO WAIT, THREE.*"

I pass a hand over my face. "*Can you at least tell which way they are coming from?*"

"*OH YEAH, THAT ONE'S EASY,*" Ollie says. "*THEY'RE COMING FROM THE CLOUDS.*"

CHAPTER TWENTY-THREE

THE LOST COLONY

"The clouds?" I ask. *"What do you mean?"*

"THEY'RE FLYING," Ollie says. *"WITH WINGS!"*

I might have guessed that last part.

"THERE'S A WHOLE FLOCK OF THEM. THEY LOOK LIKE YOU," he adds.

"Harpies?" I ask, both mentally and aloud.

Mirzayael gives me a sharp look. "Harpies? Is he sure?"

"He says they've got wings and look like me," I report. "So... no, I'm not sure he's sure. Are there other flying species in this world?"

"Only beasts, not people," Mirzayael says. "Although..."

"...I'm not entirely sure he'd be able to distinguish the difference," I finish.

Mirzayael snorts. "I was going to say the same."

"What else can you tell us about them?" I ask Ollie.

"UMMMM THEY HAVE FEATHERS," he says. *"ARE YOU SURE I CAN'T GO TALK TO THEM? I CAN ASK THEM WHO THEY ARE."*

"*No!*" I object, a hundred disastrous scenarios running through my head. Not to mention, such an attempt would be difficult given his inability to speak. "*No. Don't approach them. Can you Check them instead?*"

I've interrogated him about his Echo before. As far as I can tell, they're the same artificial entity; or at least, copies of the same entity. It seems he largely uses his interface to chat with her, rather than analyze his environment. I can't imagine it's very good conversation.

"*OH! OH YEAH.*" He pauses a moment. "*SHE SAYS, 'HET-LANIR, LEVEL TWENTY-SEVEN HARPY WIND MAGE. SALVIA, LEVEL NINETEEN HARPY WARRIOR. DIZINIR, LEVEL TWENTY-TWO HARPY CLOUD ARTIFICER. MEY-NA—*"

"*Okay, that's good!*" I say, cutting him off before he could list off the entire flock. "*Great job, Ollie. Now come back underground, will you? I'll meet you in your cave.*" I turn to Mirzayael. "They really are harpies."

She taps at her lip in thought, frowning. "The Jorrian population is largely comprised of humans, felis, and dwarves. But this doesn't change our actions. We still need to arrange a party and head to the surface, in case we are their destination."

"Where else could they be going?" I ask. "I don't suppose there's anyone else you know of who might want to visit?"

"We don't get visitors," Mirzayael says shortly.

"But you don't think they're likely to be Jorrian," I point out.

Mirzayael grunts noncommittally. "I'll gather the guards."

As she splits off to inform the rest of her guards, I reach Ollie's cave and wait for him to return. Mirzayael's distrust is stubborn, but earned. An existence in hiding will do that to you. I suppose my lack of cynicism comes from my comparatively privileged upbringing. But not every new person needs to be met with suspicion. Not everyone that comes your way needs to have an ulterior motive. Not every stranger is a potential enemy.

In this instance, I desperately hope I'm right.

It takes some convincing to get Ollie to stay in his cavern while the rest of us make the trek to the surface.

"*BUT I SAW THEM FIRST!*" Ollie objects. "*I WANT TO COME!*"

"We'll send for you if it's safe," I assure him.

He sends me a mental impression of defiance.

I mentally return this with a stern glare.

Ollie huffs out a frosty breath, then curls up on his hoard of miscellaneous bones and shiny rocks to pout.

I pat his nose. "You can come save us if we get in trouble."

"*REALLY?*" he asks, perking back up.

"Promise," I say.

Dragon sufficiently tamed, I meet with Beryl, Mirzayael, and her scouts at the tunnel opening. I'm skeptical of Beryl's ability to climb the long, twisted path, but I know better than to voice my doubts of the elderly dwarf. Together, we make for the surface.

I use the Dungeon Core's interface to scope out our surroundings as we climb. The only living things it's able to "see" are relegated to the lichen, mushrooms, and various molds that are found growing in the cave system—all things it's inadvertently consumed at some point or another. It wouldn't be able to discern anyone heading our way. But

I focus on the pebbles along the path: the ice in the rocks. Nothing disturbed. As far as I can tell, no surprises await us in the caves.

As it turns out, that's because they're waiting for us on the surface.

A group of five harpies stands on the ice at a healthy distance, regarding us as we emerge from the tunnel. Beryl and Mirzayael step forward first, so I hang back with the scouts.

One of the harpies steps forward as well. His feathers are a muted green and blue. Two others have some green and blue markings, but the rest of the group comes in shades of white and brown. Both color patterns are a stark contrast to my fiery plumage of red, orange, and yellow. I Check the one in front.

[Hetlanir: Level 27 Harpy Wind Mage.]

One of the individuals Ollie had identified earlier.

"Hello," Hetlanir calls. "I apologize if our abrupt arrival has caused any alarm. We didn't want to draw closer when the dragon was about."

"The dragon is friendly," Beryl says.

Though Mirzayael faces away from me, I can perfectly picture her scowl at this: *Don't give away intel to a potential enemy*, I can hear her say.

"The question is," Mirzayael asks, "are you?"

Hetlanir quirks a smile. "The suspicion is understandable, so close to Jorria. We hail from the peaks south of here." He gestures to nothing but open planes of ice. If he's telling the truth, it must be *far* south of here. "We've been catching sightings of the dragon for a few weeks now. Fearing it might head our way, we've been keeping a careful eye, trying to determine where it might be nesting." He tips his head. "And that's when we caught sight of people out on the ice, hunting ice cats."

"Well, you've found us," Mirzayael says with a frown. "What do you want?"

Beryl smacks her staff against one of Mirzayael's legs, causing the woman to flinch. "Manners, Mir."

Mirzayael grits her teeth. "They could be Jorrian."

"Jorrian?" Hetlanir's feathers ruffle. "Absolutely not. We are of Fyreneth's flock."

Some of the young guards in our group rustle and murmur at his words.

"Forgive the reactions of my fellows," Beryl says. "They are not used to visitors. Especially ones claiming to be of Fyreneth's lineage. You see, we, too, are her followers."

"And not just her followers, but custodians of her domain," Nek adds. This earns him a glare from Mirzayael.

But his words stir a reaction in the harpies. "You mean you know the location of her Fortress?" a harpy pipes up. Echo identifies her as Dizinir. She appears about half my age and is covered in sky-blue and white feathers, a pair of bug-eyed flight-goggles pushed up onto her forehead. She steps forward eagerly. "You've seen it?"

"We live in it," Nek says, his hair puffing up with pride.

Again the harpies titter among themselves.

"It is unwise to disclose such information," Mirzayael murmurs to Nek.

"Why?" He splays his hands. "They're family."

"They're strangers," Mirzayael insists.

"Regardless, they know now," Beryl interrupts as a strong, frigid wing blows a gust of snow between us. She raises her voice to speak to Hetlanir. "There's no sense in getting frostbite while we continue to dance with words. Come. We may continue this discussion below ground, out of the weather. You have my word as a follower of Fyreneth, none of your people will come to harm while in our domain."

"Thank you. I believe you." Hetlanir dips his head, glancing toward me. "A phoenix walks among your ranks. That is an auspicious sign."

I fidget uncomfortably at being singled out. I object to being a sign of or for anything, however I deem it best not to say as much in present company. Anything that can help keep the peace shouldn't be taken for granted.

Mirzayael is still as tense as a coiled spring, but she obeys Beryl's command without objection, leading the way back down into the caves. Beryl waits for Hetlanir so they can walk abreast, while the scouts and harpies cluster into two distinct groups and awkwardly shuffle in behind. Nek, of course, is the first to mingle between the groups. He eagerly approaches the harpies.

"What do you know of Fyreneth?" he asks. "Are you from one of the colonies?"

"Colonies?" Dizinir tips her head in a rather bird-like manner. "I'm unsure about that, but we're the descendants of the few who fled her kingdom during its fall. It's said more joined us in later years; survivors who fled across the ice."

"It sounds much like our myths of lost colonies," Nek says, tail swishing excitedly. "Sometimes our people strike out in search of a more hospitable place to live, driven by rumors of Fyreneth's descendants who might have survived, like your own."

Dizinir's eyes go wide. "Maybe we are! Perhaps we are your colonies and you are our survivors. Wouldn't that be something?"

"Have you had any new members join your colony in the last few decades?" Mirzayael joins in, to my complete astonishment. "Arachnoids, perhaps?"

"No, sorry," Dizinir says. "The stories refer to people joining us centuries ago. Our caves have received no visitors in my lifetime."

"I see," Mirzayael says, lapsing back into silence.

Her parents, I think, giving her a pitying look. She is carefully watching the new harpies rather than me, however. I turn back to Dizinir. "You also live in caves below ground?"

"Oh, no, not at all," Dizinir says. "We live in the Ash Peak Mountains. There's a system of caves in the range, there; we make do." She giggles. "But can you imagine? Harpies living underground? How miserable would *that* be!" She stops just as quickly with an embarrassed look toward me. "I mean, not that there's anything wrong with living underground."

I chuckle to reassure her that I'm not offended. "I'm sure our residents would rather not be stuck underground given any alternatives. Is your whole colony harpies, then?"

"Oh, no, we're just the only ones mobile enough to make the trip," she says, glancing around the tunnel as we descend. "But this place is fantastic! The cuts are so smooth. We've a couple of ice mages back home, but no earth mages, which makes carving passageways like this difficult. You must have a whole team here."

I resist the urge to cover up the Dungeon Core, its ruby stone glittering on my wrist. "Yes. Something like that."

"What about that dragon, though?" Dizinir asks. It seems she's the only one interested in making small talk, aside from Hetlanir, who is speaking in soft tones with Beryl at the front of our brigade. "Your leader said it was friendly. How does one tame a dragon? In fact, we've not heard tales of one around these parts in over a century. Maybe you found it as an egg? Raised it from a hatchling? But it's so big! It can't have spent all that time underground. What did you use to train it? No, wait, I bet it's food-motivated."

"He's a rather new addition to the family, actually," I say. Though as much as I'm delighted to find another curious mind, getting into the details of my and Ollie's arrival can wait for another day. "But he's not a beast; he's intelligent, and although he can't speak with his dragon-sized vocal cords, he's perfectly capable of understanding you."

Dizinir's eyes widen. "Really? An intelligent dragon? Amazing! I'll definitely have to talk to him. I'm sure such a grand, ancient beast would have incredible wisdom to impart."

Mirzayael snorts.

"Ollie would love to chat with you, I'm sure," I say.

"Fantastic!" Dizinir says. "How do you communicate?"

"Ah, I formed a Pact with him," I say, again trying to figure out the most streamlined way to get through what otherwise might be a myriad of questions. It seems interplanetary travelers are not considered common knowledge on this world, as I had initially hoped.

"Fascinating!" Dizinir cries. "How did you know it was sentient?"

Maybe it's futile to avoid a myriad of questions with this individual after all.

"I have a spell that allows me to communicate telepathically," I say.

"You do?" Dizinir asks. "Mind magic is incredibly rare. I thought you were a phoenix harpy."

"I am," I say, now slightly confused myself. "I have a Fire affinity, but no Wind. What has that got to do with mind magic?"

Although Dizinir is the only one talking, the other harpies have drifted over as well, and now they appear very much interested in my answer. Not that that's a bad thing, but perhaps I should be more careful with what I reveal.

"You really don't know?" Dizinir asks, confused.

"Know about what?" I ask.

The harpies look at me in amazement, but it's Nek who responds. "Fyreneth had mind magic, too."

I inwardly groan. Of course she did.

"That's an… interesting coincidence," I say. "I'm new to the city, so I'm still learning the history."

"New?" Dizinir says. "Where did you come from?"

I'm saved from answering yet another difficult-to-answer question as we arrive at the base of the tunnel.

"*FYRE!*" Ollie bounds forward when we come into view. Hetlanir, to his merit, holds his ground, but all the other harpies scatter. "*LOOK, IT'S ALL THE BIRD PEOPLE I TOLD YOU ABOUT! ARE THEY FRIENDS? ARE THEY GOING TO STAY WITH US?*"

"They are friends," I tell Ollie. "I don't know if they're staying. For now, we're just talking." I turn to the others. "It's okay! I promise, he's friendly. Ollie, this is Dizinir. Dizinir, Ollie."

The harpy steps forward, peering up at Ollie in apparent fascination. "I prefer Dizzi, actually. How did you know my… ah, right, the mind magic. Well, that's certainly a demonstration. Hello, Ollie!"

Ollie leans down for a nose pat as I mentally slap my forehead. "Right. Sorry. I didn't mean to pry."

Dizzi chuckles. "If nothing else, I suppose your powers will easily confirm our honest intentions."

If only Echo worked that way.

"Too bad demonstrating trust won't be as easy to prove going the other way," Hetlanir remarks.

"Not all of us have telepathy," Mirzayael says. "I'd say it still needs to be earned both ways."

"If introducing you to the dragon doesn't show we mean you no harm, I'm not sure what will." I force a laugh, but the tension between the two parties—and especially between Mirzayael and the harpies—only seems to grow more taut. I let the laughter awkwardly peter out.

"How about a tour, then?" Nek suggests. "We could continue our conversation while Fyre shows what she's been doing to restore the Fortress."

"I wouldn't want to bore you all," I object.

Mirzayael also looks ready to cut in, but Beryl silences her with a look. "A tour will do fine. If our guests are interested?"

Hetlanir dips his head. "We would be honored."

"Then it's settled." Beryl hobbles forward, not waiting for the rest of us to catch up.

"What did you say your name was?" Dizzi asks as we take the shortest tunnel to the Fortress. "The felis mentioned it briefly."

"Ah, they call me Fyre," I say, cringing at how that must sound on top of everything else. "It's a nickname."

"Short for…"

"Nothing," I say quickly.

At least Dizzi can catch a hint. "So! Tell me about the Fortress."

"We've only just begun to move in," I say. "Large portions of it are still under construction. Mirzayael's team has been cleaning the last stinger nests out of all the nooks and crannies."

I look to Mirzayael, hoping she'll jump in, but she pointedly ignores the conversation.

"At any rate, it's proven a better home for the dracid especially," I continue. "We've been able to pump water from the hot springs through the palace, providing heating as well as fresh water—once it goes through some filtering spells."

"She's changed our lives," Nek insists. "Finally we can do more than just survive."

"It was the castle, not me," I object. "The spell circles that keep the place running were there far before I arrived. I don't know how half of them even work; I just hooked things back up to the power source."

"That sounds fascinating," Dizzi says. "I'm an artificer myself, so I'd love to take a look. The more complex a system of spells are, the more difficult it is to function. Being able to investigate something designed by Fyreneth—that would truly be a once-in-a-lifetime opportunity!"

I can't help but smile at that. The young harpy is already growing on me. Enthusiasm for learning something new, puzzling out a complex problem—that's something I can relate to.

"Insight on the magic would be welcome," I say. "I feel I've barely begun to learn anything on the subject."

"Well you must know more than nothing to be able to restart an ancient series of spell circles," Dizzi says. "Unless your feline friend over here is overstating your abilities."

"He has a tendency to do that," I say.

"Hey," Nek objects.

Gradually, the tunnel widens as we approach the landing that leads into the fortress. The tiered city opens up before us, abandoned streets and buildings now lit by a network of spells which simulate the time of day. The lights twinkle throughout the streets like a cloud of fireflies, gradually shifting from their daytime orange to their nighttime purple. As the levels of the city spiral upward, they transform into the ornate spires of the palace, appropriately placed at the top of the ensemble. The entire city from base to tip must be as tall as a skyscraper, and even though it now stands mostly empty and still, its magnitude is breathtaking.

"Welcome to Fyreneth's Fortress," Beryl says as the harpies look on, silent and awestruck. "Where would you like to start?"

Chapter Twenty-Four

CAMPUS TOUR

Nek is so excited to show off the Fortress that he speaks more than I do.

"And here is where we've relocated the dracid," he says as we pass a large hall from which a warm breeze wafts like the opening of a furnace. "Now that the cold no longer sends them into brumination, we've been more productive than ever."

"Nek?" Sora comes to the door. "There you are. I thought I heard your voice."

Nek sweeps his wife up in an enthusiastic hug, spinning her around as she laughs.

"What's this?" the dracid asks, turning to the group once he sets her down. "More outsiders? Harpies? Are they from your colony, Fyre?"

To this day, Beryl, Nek, and Mirzayael remain the only ones I've told about my true origins. Not that I particularly think it would be dangerous to reveal that I'm from another world—assuming anyone would even believe that—but given my reincarnation here, I'm still averse to throwing any more fuel on the fire of the theory that I'm Fyreneth reborn.

"No," I say. "In fact, it seems they may share more history with you."

As the Fyrethians excitedly introduce themselves to each other, Dizzi hangs back with me.

"So you're a new arrival here as well?" she asks.

"About a month," I say.

"You've managed to make quite the impression in that time," she notes.

I shrug. "I'm an engineer. I suppose trying to fix things is in my nature."

She quirks a smile. "It's satisfying, isn't it? Getting something working again."

"Sometimes it's the only time I feel like I'm doing something right," I admit.

Dizzi nods. "Is that what brought you here?"

"I'm not entirely sure what brought me here," I say, dancing between truths. "But I'm glad this is where I ended up."

"And you're from..."

Nervousness tingles through me. I don't even know enough about the rest of the world to throw out a random location. "A far away land to the north," I say, fully aware of how flimsy that sounds. "You wouldn't have heard of it."

"This seems like an awfully remote place to end up."

I meet her raised eyebrow with a coy smile. "I'm fully aware of what you're getting at, and I'm afraid this response will have to satisfy your curiosity for now. That's a story for another time and place."

Dizzi chuckles. "Fair enough, fair enough. I know better than to go gliding in a gale. So what *is* safer territory for our discussion?"

"I'd be more than happy to discuss what I've been working on in Fyreneth's Fortress," I say, relieved she isn't intent on pushing the subject. "And I would love to get your insight on a few spells still inactive in some of the rooms. Without much magical theory, I can't deduce what they're for or how to activate them." Echo helpfully labels each of these as "dormant spell circles."

"I'd love to be of assistance," Dizzi says. "Lead the way."

After the dracid and harpies are done with introductions, our tour of the palace continues. Some of the spells I'd mentioned to Dizzi are in towers stationed around the outer walls of the Fortress, which separate the lowest tiers of the city from the surrounding cavern. However, given the perilous climb and remote locations, Mirzayael wisely steers the group (and, specifically, Beryl,) to remain in the palace instead. Eventually we end up in Fyreneth's throne room—a location I've been studying extensively.

The room is framed with ornate pillars covered in marble and gold carvings of all sorts of species, including some I've never seen before. Many appear to depict Fyreneth in various scenes: speaking with people, giving or receiving gifts, raising the city itself. On the ceiling is a fiery mosaic of the harpy, her wings wreathed in flames and a black and red crown atop her head. And at the center of the room is her throne.

It's a peculiar thing. There are slats in the arms to accommodate her wings, and the headrest is capable of hinging forward and down. Having sat in it before to test a theory, I indeed found the strange back can fold down to cover the seated's face, blocking their vision. It doesn't seem particularly useful to address an assembly.

Apart from the strange shape, its composition is also peculiar. It's made of hundreds of different types of stone, only half of which are already in the Dungeon Core's catalog. Each ore is kept separate, however, and is even distinctly visible within the throne, striping the seat with all sorts of colors and textures. These lines of rock each diverge from the chair, shooting through the floor and into the palace like radiating lines of a sun. The entire setup of the room is as striking as it is strange—and perhaps it's just me, but it all gives me the faintest sense of foreboding as well.

"Amazing," Dizzi says, making a beeline for the throne. "I've never seen anything like it!"

Mirzayael and I follow after her—me out of curiosity and Mirzayael out of irritated suspicion, I suspect—while the rest admire the art in the columns and mosaics.

"What about it is drawing your attention?" I ask.

"The spell lines, of course." Dizzi traces one of the radiating threads of stone back to the throne. She crouches at its side. "It's so intricate. So delicate. I can't even wrap my head around the amount of crafts-manship it would take to form such fine lines—not to mention the whole network's purpose! I don't suppose you've been able to suss out its use?"

I tilt my head. "What do you mean by network?"

"The spell network." Dizzi points out miniscule patterns embed-ded into the arms of the throne that I'd mistook for decoration. "Don't you see? These runes here. They indicate that each of these lines are connected to a spell circle. Perhaps even a string of spell circles. Incredible. How could so many spells come together like this to form something coherent?"

"Of course." Now that she says it, it's so obvious I feel ridiculous for not having seen it myself. No wonder the throne arcs over the user's head. You're not meant to see visitors—you're meant to look inward.

"It's a user interface." A computer. A magical logic network, and each of these lines is a different thread on a circuit board leading to a different gate or function. Now I, too, am stunned by its scope. It would take incredible precision—or an incredible ability to multi-task—to link yourself into this network and parse out all the different lines?

Running my hand over the arm of the throne, I close my eyes and use the Dungeon Core's interface to scan the lines, searching for any compositions I recognize from the Core's catalog.

Aha! There. One of these is the same substance as the magical lines used to provide power throughout the fortress. And another one is connected to the lines that control the plumbing system. Does that mean each of these operates another function in the castle? But there must be a hundred more!

"Fyreneth truly must have been extraordinary to operate such a magical construct," Dizzi says.

"Or she had help," I say. If I let the Dungeon Core's presence move along one of these lines, tracing its entire extent throughout the fortress, would I be able to deduce what its purpose is for? Could I do that with all of them?

Abruptly, I realize the room has gone quiet.

"What is it?" I open my eyes. They're all staring at me.

Or, more accurately, my wrist.

The ruby-red stone that is the Dungeon Core is glowing faintly, as it frequently does when I tap into its abilities. I quickly stop and the light fades out.

"I didn't mean to interrupt the conversation," I say.

Dizzi clears her throat. "Where did you say you got that bracelet?"

I tuck my hand behind my back. "Sorry for the distraction. We should continue the tour, then, shouldn't we?"

Hetlanir is looking at the ceiling. "It looks rather like her crown, doesn't it?"

I glance up at the mosaic and wince. Her crown features a ruby-red stone, shining like a flame, fixed in place by wiry bands that wrap around Fyreneth's head like a thicket of vines.

Or veins. Not dissimilar to the rocky veins of ore that have wrapped around my wrist.

"I think perhaps that's enough of a tour for now," Beryl says, breaking the stretching silence. "Where should we go from here?"

There's a pause as my gaze dances around the room, attempting to avoid all the eyes that seem plastered to me. I meet Mirzayael's, silently pleading for some sort of rescue. Her mouth twitches in a hint of amusement.

Traitor.

"I think," Hetlanir finally says, "that I speak for all of us when I say we'd very much like to reunite our people, if you would have us."

Murmurs of agreement pass between the harpies. Nek is all smiles, already welcoming the new members into our fold. Dizzi is looking at me with calculated curiosity. Even Beryl seems pleased with this arrangement.

"Praise Fyreneth," someone says.

I want to sink into the ground.

The migration doesn't happen overnight. While the harpies are only half a day's flight from our caves, all of the non-harpies must walk, and the trek over the ice is a two-day affair, including one night camped out on the ice in subfreezing temperatures and cutting winds.

Despite all that, I was rather curious to see their cave system, but Beryl insisted I was of more use here, working on restoring the

Fortress, and I reluctantly had to admit she's right. I couldn't have flown back with the harpies even if I wanted to—though Sora has been working with some arachnoids to create a harness for me and Ollie, fashioned from the hide of animals that have been recently hunted. Maybe in another few weeks I'll get to stretch my wings.

Mirzayael tasks Nek and some of her guards to assist the newcomers with whatever is needed, but she too stays close to home. Despite Beryl's stamp of approval and a complete lack of suspicious behavior on the harpies' part, Mirzayael continues to treat them with distrust.

"What are you doing?" Mirzayael's voice cuts through the room.

I jump, hitting my head on the throne's visor, then scramble to climb out. "Sorry," I say, my wing snagging on the throne and causing me to tumble over one of the arms. "I was just examining the circuits..." I trail off once I realize Mirzayael wasn't actually talking to me.

I'd thought I was alone in the throne room—the only time I risk a visit is when there aren't other people here to compare me to the highly detailed art of Fyreneth that covers every inch of the hall—but Mirzayael appears to have snuck in while I was focused on the throne. Presently, she's just inside the entryway, spear held across the frame to block the entrance.

Dizzi peaks her head around the doorframe. "Am I not allowed in? I thought no room was off limits."

It's only been three days since the harpies first showed up at our doorstep; we're expecting the first group of transplants to arrive any day now. And with each that passes, Mirzayael seems to have another rule about what the newcomers are and are not allowed to do.

"You're allowed in the room." Reluctantly, Mirzayael removes her spear. "But no sneaking."

"I see," Dizzi says. "So if I come in *un*-sneakily, I should be in the clear, right?"

I snort as Dizzi spreads her azure wings and gives them a good flap, a gust of wind accompanying the move to help flip her over Mirzayael's head and into the hall. She lands with arms spread wide and wings pointed to the ceiling.

"Ta-da!"

Mirzayael is decisively unamused.

"Hey, Fyre!" Dizzi says, heading over to me. "What are you doing on the ground?"

"Examining the floor," I say. "Could use a good dusting."

"Harpy feathers are great for that." Dizzi shakes out a wing. "Just wait until molting season, and we'll have a duster for every household."

I pale. "Molting season?"

"So what are you investigating today?" Dizzi asks, taking a lap around the throne as I pick myself up. "Ooh! Figure out any more of the functions?"

"A couple." I gesture over to a workbench I've set up against the nearest wall. "Wrote some of them down. It's a lot to keep track of. One has to do with keeping the earth in the gardens properly fertilized, I think."

"Oh, fascinating! Let me see." Dizzi skips over to the work bench, another gust of wind helping her glide most of the way with her feet barely scraping the ground. A twinge of jealousy needles through me, but I brush the feeling aside.

"She's trouble," Mirzayael grunts, stopping at my side.

"She's spirited," I say. "A young scientist. I can't fault her for that."

Mirzayael scoffs in a way that indicates she can, and *will*, fault her for that.

"You know, as a scientist myself, I've observed something over the past couple of days," I say.

Mirzayael glances at me with a frown. "Something important?"

"Depends on your perspective." I wink. "Do with this information what you will. But I've noticed that the deep suspicion you had for me seems to have switched to them. Am I no longer considered an outsider?"

Mirzayael frowns. "Don't be absurd. You're still an outsider, Outsider. Now there's just more of you."

I smile, shaking my head.

"What?" she asks, bristling. "I can be suspicious of multiple people at once."

That does get a laugh out of me. "Clearly!"

Glowering at my amusement, Mirzayael wordlessly follows me over as I move to meet Dizzi at the workstation. "Say, do you think she was serious about the molting thing?" I ask.

Mirzayael raises an eyebrow. "Do I look like a harpy to you?"

At the workbench, Dizzi is rooting through my papers. "Really interesting stuff," she says. "If you're able to trace each of these lines to their source spell circles, I should be able to read a bit more into their intent. Say, what's the blocky page here for?"

I peer around her shoulder to get a better look. "Ah, yes, that's my amateur attempt at making a periodic table." Or reverse engineering one, really. There's a handful of elements and atomic weights I can remember off the top of my head: hydrogen, helium, lithium, beryllium, boron, carbon, nitrogen, oxygen—thank you Mrs Betcher in 10th grade chemistry class—but beyond that I've mostly lost the plot. I figure I can fill out what I know, and use the knowledge gleaned from Echo and the Dungeon Core to deduce many of the rest. Or at least, many of the more common ones. At any rate, it will be helpful for avoiding future sodium fiascos.

Or perhaps creating more effective ones.

"I've not heard of many of these terms," Dizzi says. "Are they alchemic?"

"Scientific," I say. "That's... the study of nature. A methodical approach to uncovering how the physical world operates."

Dizzi snorts. "I know what science is, Fyre, I'm not six years old."

Heat creeps up my cheeks. "Right—of course—sorry. I still sometimes struggle to distinguish what's common knowledge from what's extraordinary, here."

"Right," Dizzi says flatly. "Your homeland sure does seem to lack a foundation in magical theory. Pretty impressive, the scale of magic you're able to do, considering."

I glance at Mirzayael, and she returns the look with a miniscule shake of her head. Probably for the best. Even if I didn't share her distrust, getting Dizzi to believe I'm from another world is a rather large pill to swallow.

"So anyway," Dizzi says when I don't respond. "Tell me about this table of yours. What's it for?"

"Distinguishing the composition of materials I work with, mostly," I say. "Different elements will have different properties. It will help me catalog all kinds of ore within the cave system and what they can be used for."

"Sounds good for construction," she says.

"It is," I admit. And a lot more. "I dabbled in materials science a little in my past, but only when it came to composites for airplanes."

"Airplanes?" Dizzi asks, leaning forward. "What are those? Tell me!"

I can't help but smile at her enthusiasm. Finally, territory I feel comfortable in. "A contraption to help people fly who don't have wind magic. In fact, it works for anyone without any kind of magic—it operates entirely on an intricate understanding of physics and aerodynamics. The basic principle is working out the balancing act between weight and lift, and thrust with drag..."

Mirzayael lets out a heavy sigh as I dive into an overview of flight dynamics. It's an excited, rambling explanation she's been reluctantly subjected to before. But this time, I have a willing audience. Dizzi cranes her head over the papers as I sketch out the shape of an airfoil, marking the camber and chord as I explain the importance of each.

"So *that's* why the wind has to shift around the wing when we fly," Dizzi says, nodding along. "Manipulating the magic eventually becomes instinct, but I never really thought about the mechanics of it before."

"Yes, it's all about the center of pressure relative to the center of gravity," I say.

"Fascinating," Dizzi says. "You know, if you could make a circle to track each of those quantities, you might be able to create a self-correcting flight spell that the user wouldn't even have to adjust. It could compensate as needed to keep the mage airborne."

"You could do that?" I ask. First the Dungeon Core's meticulous cataloging system, then Fyreneth's circuit-like magic network, now programmable spell circles. Magic is sounding more and more like sufficiently advanced technology by the day.

"Of course! It should be easy." Dizzi pauses. "Okay, no, actually it would be really hard. But theoretically, it should be possible."

"I'd love to work through the idea with you," I say.

Dizzi beams. "I'd be honored! I mean, who'd pass up a chance to experiment with a new spell circle application?"

Mirzayael frowns. "Sounds dangerous."

"That was rhetorical," Dizzi says.

I glance between the two, chuckling. Somehow, I feel like Mirzayael will take even more time to warm up to Dizzi than she did to me. But it's a temporary inconvenience I'm more than willing to suffer through.

Perhaps my dreams of achieving flight are not so distant as I once thought.

Chapter Twenty-Five

MAGIC 101

Like frost from a long winter finally melting in the spring, life begins to bloom in Fyreneth's Fortress. Over the next week two groups arrive from the lost colony and begin to make homes within the palace. Suddenly, the vast cavern, previously silent save for the occasional drippings of condensation, is now filled with quiet murmurs of life: footsteps in the halls, chopping and bubbling in the kitchens, kids playing in the streets. By the time all of their people have relocated, our population will have nearly doubled. It's starting to feel like a real city.

Every one of the newcomers visits me within the first day or two of their arrival. It's uncomfortable. I've never been a socialite, and I certainly don't like the underlying motivation for why they want to meet me. But I try to be patient and kind and... me. Maybe being me is the only way I can convince them I'm just some engineer with a rudimentary understanding of magic, and not a mythical figure reborn.

"Excuse me."

I inwardly wince at the hesitant new voice and set down the airfoil I was working on. It's made of cloudstone, which completely screws up every aerodynamic instinct I have when working with the wing. Fascinating stuff.

"Hello," I say, turning to the newcomer. I don't recognize the dwarf standing in the doorway. Another new arrival come to introduce themselves and ask for blessings, no doubt. "Can I help you?"

"Sorry to bother you," the man says. "I was told I would find Captain Mirzayael here."

"In my workshop?" I ask, amused. Although calling it a workshop is a bit of a stretch. I've adapted a room adjacent to the throne room, possibly originally designed for meetings or banquets, and co-opted it as my own personal laboratory. Right now, that only entails various notes on stone compositions, Fyreneth's throne, spell circles, my incomplete periodic table, and a dozen conceptual drawings of airfoils and flying apparatuses which incorporate the cloudstone—but every scientist needs to start somewhere. "Why would she be in my workshop?"

"Ah, I was told she's usually where you are," the dwarf says.

"That's... not entirely wrong," I admit. She really does spend a lot of time with me, doesn't she? "Regardless, she's off doing guard business today. What was it you needed her for? I could pass on the message."

"The scouts spotted people out on the ice," he says, wiping all of my amusement away in an instant.

"People?" I ask. "From your colony?"

He shakes his head. "The last of our people are scheduled to start the migration tomorrow. These were different. The scouts saw them disappear in a flurry of snow, but they were heading in the direction of Jorria."

I frown. So far as I've gathered, there haven't been any clashes between the two groups in modern times, but even the Fyrethians from the lost colony harbor a deep-seated fear for them.

"Thanks for letting me know," I say. "Here, just a moment."

I retreat to my workbench, where I retrieve a small white spider made of silk. It almost looks like a stuffed animal, but it has a rune emblazoned in its back. Mirzayael had left it with me in case I needed to contact her.

"I'm not sure where she is, at the moment, but this should take you to her," I tell the man, holding out the tracking spider.

"Thank you." The dwarf accepts the spider with two hands, nodding his head respectfully as he steps back to leave, then hesitates at the threshold as if he wants to say something more.

"Is there anything else?" I prompt.

"Is it true you wield Fyreneth's crown?" he blurts out. "I've heard the others speaking of a magical stone..."

I hold in a sigh and gesture to my head instead. "As you can see, my head is bare."

"Right," the dwarf says, deflating a little. "But your name—"

"Was given to me by people who draw unwarranted parallels," I say. "Please, though, Fyre is the complete name, not short for anything."

"Of course," he says, though he doesn't sound convinced. "Thank you, Lord Fyre." The man bows and retreats back into the hall.

I let out a long sigh as I turn back to my workbench. It seems that my days of being able to wander about the Catacombs, exploring new wings and searching for hints of magic, have come to a close. With all the newcomers, Beryl has been hinting that she'd rather have me contribute to the city in a more sociopolitical manner. Would be that I could continue hiding myself away and experimenting on stone and spell circles in isolation. Well, mostly isolated. Mirzayael would be welcome company. But I suppose with great power, and all that...

Another knock comes at the door, and this time I do wince. What is it now?

"Heya!" Dizzi pokes her head in, and I relax. "Can I steal you for a minute? There's a spell circuit I found and I want to figure out what it does. I figure my options are either shoot some magic into it and see what happens, or use you to trace it to its source to potentially avoid blowing stuff up."

"My vote is for option number two," I say.

"Figured as much." She sighs. "Old people are predictably boring like that."

I quirk a smile. "Do you want my help or not?"

"Don't pretend like you're not already on board," Dizzi says. "Come on! It's down in the crypts."

I blink. "Crypts?"

Despite Dizzi's dubious naming convention, there are no bodies or graves to be found. Which is frankly a relief, because at this point, I'd have no excuse for not having mapped out every inch of the Fortress. With the mana ore readily available, the Dungeon Core is never low on mana, and neither am I. All I have to do is close my eyes and tap into the Map Interface, and I can see the entire buried castle—all of it at once. It's like the Dungeon Core's consciousness has expanded to inhabit the city itself. I still can't see the *people* in the castle, but everything made of stone shows up, and even some other substances the Core has previously consumed, such as moss and mushrooms. It makes me wonder if any like-object the Core consumes will become visible in our interface. If it ate a person, would I see people? That would be equally useful and disturbing. Not a theory I'm willing to put to the test, at any rate.

"These are storage rooms, Dizzi," I say as we walk through the network of cold, underground chambers. Though given how they're so remote from the main part of the castle, and how there's still so few of us that we're all localized in the palace, we haven't made use of this space yet. "Why did you think it was a crypt?"

"Um, because it has a distinctly creepy vibe about it, obviously," Dizzi says. "Like where *else* would you put your dead?" She pauses. "No seriously, where do you guys put with your dead? Back home we'd leave them outside on the Slumbering Mountain. The direwolves or ice cats took care of the rest."

The frivolity with which she says this shakes me. "That sounds so cold."

Dizzi shrugs. "The world is cold."

"Sorry," I say. "I didn't mean to judge. But, ah, I believe Mirzayael says there's a grove where they take the bodies. The plant-life consumes them. I've not seen it yet myself."

"Sounds nice," Dizzi says. "Not too different from what we do, but more peaceful. There's a nice symmetry to death sustaining life, don't you think?"

"I suppose, yes." In theory I'd agree with her; a body is merely a body, after all. But the bluntness of the conversation has thrown me off my stride. It seems her people might have lived an even harsher life than those of Fyreneth's Keep. And yet, there are people like Dizzi who are bursting with so much joy and enthusiasm.

"So, the spell circle," I prompt.

"Right!" Dizzi says, perking up. Not that she ever really seems to be *un*-perked. "It was in the back room over here. Part of the wall is collapsed, which is why I can't make all of it out. But I'm trying to figure out why it would be down here of all places."

"Why were *you* down here of all places?" I ask.

"Don't be ridiculous, Fyre," Dizzi says. "I've gone in every room of the palace I've been allowed access to."

I raise an eyebrow. "You're not allowed in some?"

"Ugh, I know, right?" she huffs. "Mirzayael said something about the north-east quadrant of the city being off limits because the terrain was 'unstable' and there were 'deadly wild beasts' or something. Totally unfair. I could just fly away if I got in trouble! That's what I've always done before."

"That might be slightly more difficult in a tunnel or small cavern," I point out.

"Ugh, now you sound like Lord Hetlanir." Dizzi ducks into a room, hunching her wings down as she passes under a low, slanted doorway. The roof itself is angled down, too. She's right that there was a collapse of some sort; I'll need to straighten that out with the Dungeon Core and make sure the structural integrity hasn't been compromised. I duck in after her, my silhouette briefly casting the room in darkness.

"Aw, crap, I should have brought a light," Dizzi says.

"Here." I summon a Spark in my palm.

"Oh! Right. Nifty, that." Dizzi shuffles back to give me more room, watching the fire with an impressed look. "Keep forgetting your thing is fire instead of air. Must be neat."

"Rather frustrating, actually," I say, holding the light up to the wall. Sure enough, there's a partial spell circle inscribed in the stone, half of it concealed by the tilted ceiling. "I'd much rather have air given the option."

"Why don't you learn it, then?" Dizzi asks.

I frown. "What do you mean? I thought I could only learn magic that was within my affinity."

"I'm talking about learning a new affinity," Dizzi says. "Just because you weren't born with a certain affinity doesn't mean it's impossible to develop later in life. In fact, in harpy communities it's pretty common practice to train young phoenix harpies to gain a wind affinity. But of course, you probably already know all this. Right?"

I glance away. "No. There weren't any other harpies in Fyreneth's Keep before you all arrived."

"Right," she says flatly. "And before you arrived here?"

I'm fully aware of how weak my backstory must seem. "I wasn't around harpies then, either."

"Uh huh." She raises an eyebrow. "Well, here's some Magic 101: there's technically no limit to the number of affinities you can have. But gaining new ones is tough. If you don't have an innate knack for it, you need to learn the hard way. Not all phoenix harpies are able to develop a wind affinity, even after years of trying."

"But how is it done?" I ask. "What are the mechanics behind it?"

"That's tough to say," she admits. "Some people say it's finding a way for the magic to touch your soul. Sometimes, that's a catastrophic event. I've heard some harpies who have been struck by lightning—and survived—came out the other side with an electric affinity."

"Trying to replicate that method sounds... inadvisable."

Dizzi giggles. "Yeah, I wouldn't recommend it. But it's one way your soul can come to 'know' the element, I suppose. The more practical way would be through study. Meditation. Trying to gain an understanding of the magic or element on a spiritual level." She wiggles her fingers at me. "Also not the most concrete method of study."

"Hm." I don't think anyone who's ever known me would describe me as a spiritual person. Trying to understand a property of nature on a metaphysical level feels counterintuitive. But if such a thing is possible, then there's no reason not to try. "How effective is this method?"

She shrugs. "It really depends on the individual. I've heard that it's easier to gain an affinity for people who already embody the spirit of the type of arcana they're trying to learn. You know: passionate individuals might be more prone to learning fire magic, whereas stubborn people might be predisposed to a field of earth magic, and so on. That said, some people can develop an affinity within a few days of dedicated study, whereas it might take years for others. With phoenix harpies, we work with the kids from a young age. That usually helps."

"I might be a little late to the party on that one," I joke. "And I'm unsure that my personality type aligns with wind. But I have a history of studying the subject. Maybe that will make up for lost ground."

"Can't hurt," Dizzi says. "Try meditation sometime. Somewhere you can feel the wind. I suppose that's easier on a mountain than down in these caves. Just... try to connect with it. See what happens."

"I'll give it a shot and report back on my findings."

Dizzi laughs. "I knew I liked you. Now, will you help me with this spell circle, or what?"

"Right." I step forward, spilling firelight over the markings in the wall. The wind magic experiment will have to wait until later. Still, an intriguing idea.

"This rune, here, refers to earth arcana," Dizzi says, pointing out the markings. "And this other one is indicative of a direction, I think. But that's all I can make out from the partial circle."

On the off-chance Echo can save both of us some time, I Check the spell circle.

[Check,] she says. [Partial spell circle.]

Well, it would have been nice.

"Let me try something," I say, placing my hand against the wall and mentally nudging the Dungeon Core to get its attention.

You awake?

The Dungeon Core has no idea what I'm talking about.

I was being figurative. I've got some rock for you to eat.

This causes it to perk up. I've been doing way too much exploring not *nearly* enough excavation. It's starving!

This will be a bit more delicate than a typical excavation, I think. See here? I need you to eat the ceiling away a bit without disturbing these markings. All while making sure that won't collapse the room on top of me. Also, if there appears to be different lines of ore in the rock, it might be more magic circuits, and I want to leave all of those undisturbed.

Rules! So many rules.

I did say it was going to be a delicate operation. I smile at the Core's sullenness. *Come on now, none of that. You'll just have to eat slowly. Try savoring it, maybe?*

Savoring? The Dungeon Core doesn't recognize this concept either.

I send a mental impression of what I mean. *Eat slowly, and enjoy it. Come on, give it a try and let's see if you learn something new.*

The Dungeon Core doesn't need much prompting to start eating away at the rock. I remind it to be mindful of causing a cave in, but the warning wasn't necessary. Slowly, bits of stone vanish away, nibbled off by an invisible mouse as the stone on my wrist glows with ruby light. Dizzl watches with rapt attention, saying nothing as bits of the spell circle are revealed. While the Core works, I close my eyes and mentally plunge into the Map Interface, borrowing the Core's sense to locate the spell circle in the wall and push my consciousness into the stone, feeling out the composition of its surroundings. Sure enough, there's a vein of rock connected to the spell circle, distinct from the rest of the wall. I push my mind along that path and follow it deeper into the earth.

"Ah," Dizzi says. Despite standing right next to me, her voice seems distant. "I think I'm starting to see. It has to do with moving the stone. But that's just a piece of it..."

I trace the path to another spell circle buried in another underground chamber. This one is truly sealed off from the outside world, its spell circle completely buried by rubble. But the spell circuit doesn't stop there. It splits off again to another spell circle, and that leads to another. I follow the daisy-chain of spells through the earth in an enormous loop which encircles the entire Fortress.

"It's meant to move the city," I say. Or, I try to say it. For a disorienting moment, I can no longer feel my body. I have no mouth. No ears or eyes. Everything I experience is through the Dungeon Core's interface. Claustrophobia abruptly crushes around me, and I reel, throwing my mind back toward my body.

"...yre? Fyre? Hey! Hello? You okay?"

I gasp in a deep breath, eyes fluttering open, and catch myself against the wall before I fall.

"Woah!" Dizzi grabs my arm about five seconds after it might have helped. "What happened? You got quiet. Real quiet. I wasn't even sure if you were breathing."

"I... maybe wasn't," I admit. "How long was I like that?"

"Not sure," Dizzi admits. "Thirty seconds to a minute, maybe. Not to sound like a mirror bird, but what happened?"

What indeed? That's the third time this has happened now. I need to be more careful about how I utilize the Dungeon Core. What happens if I can't reconnect with my body after one such instance? Or what if I leave it for too long?

"I disassociated, I think," I say. "It happens when I dive too deep into the Core's senses."

"Core? You mean Fyreneth's crown?" Dizzi pointedly asks.

I grimace. "I'd rather if people didn't call it that."

"Whatever helps you sleep at night." Dizzi frowns, but it's with concern rather than skepticism. "You sure you're alright?"

"Yes." I straighten myself up. "However, I don't think I will be trying that again for some time."

"No shit," Dizzi snorts. "You know, maybe you are the type to get struck by lightning to try to get an electric affinity after all."

I weakly smile. "I'll strive to not give that impression from now on. Besides, I think I gathered all the information I could through that method, anyway."

"Oh?" Dizzi glances at the spell circle, now fully unearthed. "What did you find?"

"There's a dozen other spell circles connected to this one," I tell her. "They create a giant circle that encompasses the entire city. And they're not the only circles set up that way: there's a series of them, each linked to one another, creating a sort of... massive, underground, magical palisade."

"Incredible." Dizzi runs her hand over the spell circle. "And unless I'm wrong, this spell circle is designed to move an enormous amount of stone. What were the other spell circles for?"

I shake my head. "I couldn't tell from the Core's interface. However, the way they were all joined created the web or net-like pattern. One which spanned the entire base of the city."

"Almost as if it cupped the city?" Dizzi asks. "As if it were designed to move the entire Fortress?"

The implications are groundbreaking—literally, perhaps. "You don't think this spell network is how the city came to be sunk beneath the ground in the first place?"

"It would be a series of extraordinary circumstances for that not to be the case," Dizzi says. "However, I'm even more interested in what the reverse implications might be. If the spell circles could be reactivated..."

A chill runs down my back. "Then Fyreneth's Fortress could be raised again."

Chapter Twenty-Six

CLOUDSTONE CAVERNS

"...but when spring arrived, something miraculous happened," I recite, scratching the scales on Ollie's head. He heaves a contented sigh, curling tighter around his pile of found treasures. The newcomers have only added fuel to that fire, as it's become a tradition for each new member of Fyreneth's Fortress to gift a small token to the dragon upon their arrival.

"Charlotte's children, hundreds of tiny spiderlings, emerged from their eggs and began to spin webs of their own. They floated away on a breeze, ready to spread messages of friendship and kindness across the land, just as their mother had."

"Hundreds?" Mirzayael interrupts. "That's an excessive amount of children."

"I thought arachnoids could have a clutch of a dozen kids?" Dizzi asks.

"Almost always in pairs," Mirzayael informs her. "But anything above six is rare."

"Charlotte was a spider, not an arachnoid," I clarify. "Like, the small bug variety which live in the crevices of your house."

"Well that makes no sense at all." Mirzayael crosses her arms. "Spiders are not intelligent. How did she write messages in her web?"

"Although that does explain why they left her out in the barn in the winter to die," Dizzi adds.

"It's a children's tale." I sigh. "It's not real. Now can I finish without any further interruptions?" It's like this every night.

Mirzayael grunts, indicating she wants me to continue even if she'd never actually personally request that I do so.

"Right," I say. "So, each year Charlotte's children would return, sharing stories with Wilbur, just like their mother had. They reminded everyone that true friendship knows no bounds—not time, or space, or even their differences could separate them. Charlotte's legacy of kindness and wisdom lived on."

"*THAT'S A GOOD STORY*," Ollie says. "*IT'S SAD.*"

"What part makes you sad?" I ask.

"*THE SPIDER DIED EVEN THOUGH SHE WAS JUST NICE TO EVERYONE. SHE SHOULD HAVE GOTTEN TO LIVE.*"

I pat his head. "Everyone dies someday, Ollie. Whether you're nice or not. But that doesn't have to be the end." For Ollie and I, that's doubly true. "Charlotte lived on in the memories of others. She made people happy even after she was gone. That's what it means to have a legacy."

"Or become a legend," Dizzi adds. "Sometimes your actions in life can transcend death."

"*OH, OKAY*," Ollie says, letting out a sleepy sigh. "*HEY FYRE?*"

"Yes?"

"*WANT TO COME FLYING WITH ME TOMORROW?*"

The abrupt change of topic catches me off guard. "I can't fly yet."

"YOU COULD SIT ON MY BACK. I'M VERY STRONG."

"I'm sure you are." I rub circles around his forehead, just between his horns. "Maybe when Sora finishes making me that harness. Until then, it will be a little dangerous without wind magic of my own."

Ollie grumbles in disappointment, but doesn't say anything as I continue to rub his head. His eyes flutter closed.

"You could tie yourself down in the meantime," Dizzi suggests. "Rope should be enough."

"Don't give him any ideas," I murmur.

She smiles, but lowers her voice. "You could also work on developing that wind magic. I heard there's some cloudstone around here?"

"A cave system off the main branch," Mirzayael says. "Why? What's that got to do with it?"

"Let's visit it tomorrow," Dizzi suggests. "Maybe that's the bit of inspiration Fyre needs to develop a wind affinity."

Mirzayael frowns, but I nod appreciatively to Dizzi. "Actually, I've been meaning to visit it at some point anyway. I need some more to work on my airfoil designs—the Dungeon Core can manufacture the stone itself, but it's empty of wind arcana, which rather defeats the point. Tomorrow seems as good a day as any."

"Is he asleep?" Mirzayael abruptly asks, nodding to Ollie. She gets like this around Dizzi—well, all the newcomers, really.

I give Ollie a gentle pat. "Getting there, I think."

"Do you really come down here to tell him stories every night?" Dizzi asks, more than happy to roll with Mirzayael's blunt change of topic.

"Yes," I say. "He's just a kid. He'd get lonely by himself. I wish I had more time to spend with him, actually. For now, opening up passages around Fyreneth's Fortress and fixing up pavilions for him to sit on at different levels is the most I can do."

"That's quite thoughtful," Dizzi says. "You must really care about him."

And it strikes me that I really do. I look at this giant beast curled around its hoard, but what I see is a little boy hugging a teddy bear. A snapshot of Caroline returns to me, looking up with a gap-toothed grin, eyes wide with delight as I gave her a moose stuffed animal she'd later name Maple. She'd lost both her top front teeth at the same time; "Just like me!" she'd said, showing Maple off to anyone who'd listen.

I swallow down a knot forming in my throat and gently take pull my hand away. "I care about him very much. We're all each other has got."

"*FYRE?*" Ollie says, his voice slow and tired.

I grimace. I'd thought he was too sleepy to be listening. "Yes, Ollie?"

"*WHEN CAN I GO HOME?*"

The question hits me like a slap. My chest aches, and an acute pity and sorrow wells up from deep within my heart.

"I'm not sure," I admit. Truth be told, I don't even know if it's possible. Surely if a soul can come to this world, then it must be reversable—not accounting for entropy, of course. Although, trying to find a way back to Earth isn't even something I've begun to investigate. In fact, I'd rather not go back at all. But Ollie... For him it would be worth looking into. Somehow.

"It might be a while, kiddo," I say.

"*I MISS MOM AND DAD.*"

The pressure becomes too great, and my heart breaks in two. I lean over and wrap an arm around his snout. "I know."

"Alright, everyone, listen up," Dizzi orders, and the kids snap to attention. "Lord Fyre needs our help. Who's in?"

"This really isn't necessary," I object, but the kids and young teens are all bouncing with eager energy. I glance over at Mirzayael, begging for rescue, but she just meets my gaze with an impassive "This is what you get" sort of look.

"Our mission is to retrieve some cloudstone," Dizzi continues. "Captain Mirzayael here is going to show us to the chamber, then I expect everyone to work together to obtain a proper sample. Understood?"

"Understood!" the kids cry.

"Captain Mirzayael." Dizzi salutes, though her mouth twitches as if she wants to laugh. "Please lead the way."

Mirzayael rolls her eyes, but jerks her head in the direction of the cave system we'll be entering. "Come on, then. And stay quiet. Noise attracts stingers. If they get to you before I get to them, you'll have thirty minutes to find an antidote."

The kids exchange a collection of excited and nervous glances, then follow after her. I hang back with Dizzi at the end of the troop.

"You know, when you asked if others could accompany us, this isn't what I had in mind," I say to her.

She chuckles. "It's all in good fun. The parents need the kids out of their hair for a bit while they get settled. And it's good for kids from the two colonies to mix together. Besides, they've all been dying to spend more time with you, and this seemed like a harmless adventure to take them on."

"I wish you wouldn't feed their superstition," I say.

"I'm not," she says. "What better way to show them who you really are than for them to spend some time getting to know you?"

"Hm." I hadn't considered that angle. Perhaps giving them the opportunity to see I'm just flesh and blood like the rest of them will help dispel some rumors. "That's actually a very thoughtful idea. Thank you, Dizzi."

"No problem, boss." She nudges me in the arm. "Say, Mirzayael didn't really mean that thing about the stingers, did she? Because it would look really bad if I came back with a dead kid."

"No, she's just trying to scare them." I cast a nervous glance toward Mirzayael's back as she stoically leads us into the cave system. "I'm pretty sure, anyway."

The trek takes us through a winding network of passages, in and out of caverns, up and down rocky slopes. We're a bit far from Fyreneth's Fortress, however Mirzayael still seems confident in the path we're taking. I haven't actually scoped out this section of the cave system yet, as I've mostly been focusing on completing the Core's map around the city itself, but every step we take in this new direction eats away more of the Fog of War on my mental display. If nothing else, I'll be able to backtrack our route perfectly.

"We've arrived," Mirzayael abruptly announces as we step into a cavern.

There are no spell circles or runes carved into the walls to light the space, so I summon a small blaze and toss it up toward the ceiling. Given how much mana the Dungeon Core has consumed from all the mana ore, I have more than enough to keep the ethereal fire burning for the duration of our stay.

The room warms with orange light as my magic rises toward the ceiling. It's a couple stories tall, with the standard array of stalactites and stalagmites, though an additional interesting feature adorns this room. A large pile of rocks and boulders are scattered over the ceiling, as if a bag of stones had been spilled across the surface... and then defied gravity to stay there.

"There we are." Dizzi nods. "That's cloudstone for you. Alright, soldiers, you know what to do!"

"Perhaps we should scout the area first," Mirzayael starts, but the kids are already rushing into the cavern in excitement. The harpy children jump into the air, gusts of wind accompanying their flight, while the handful of dwarf, dracid, felis, and arachnoid kids scatter, examining stones on the ground and veins in the walls.

"Don't worry," Dizzi says, flapping her wings and rising with the other harpies. "They'll be fine. I'll watch the ones up here if you watch the ones down there."

"Be careful," I say anyway. She waves as she circles up toward the ceiling, where she runs a hand through the collection of stones floating there. The rocks bounce and bobble like leaves on a wave, then slowly settle back down.

"You don't think they're really in danger, do you?" I ask Mirzayael.

"We haven't cleared every inch of the cave system," she says. "In fact, we've only had the resources to start hunting stingers in earnest since you arrived."

I pale. "Then the kids could get hurt?"

She shrugs. "It's possible."

"But we're nowhere near the city," I say, concern mounting. "If they get stung, what will we do about needing an antidote?"

Mirzayael pulls her pack around her shoulder and flips open the top. Inside are several jars. "I came prepared."

I sag in relief, then shake my head, chuckling. "If I didn't know you better, I'd think you were looking to give me a scare for the fun of it."

She quirks a smile, slinging her pack back in place. "Maybe you don't know me better, then."

We watch the kids explore the cavern for a few minutes in comfortable silence. The harpies have gotten distracted from their rock gathering mission as they kick a round stone around in some kind of gravity-defying game of football. Meanwhile, the kids on the ground have also gotten ahold of a few cloudstones with a lower mana density and are playing a bizarre looking game of "keep it up" with a couple small boulders.

"I'm starting to think this was more just a field trip for the kids than it was actually a scientific investigation for Dizzi and me," I say to Mirzayael.

"No idea what would have given you that impression," she replies.

I elbow her playfully. "So what do you think by now? Still convinced they're all untrustworthy outsiders?"

"Yes," she says. "Not enough time has passed yet for them to earn my trust."

"You could always try to *give* trust first," I say. "It goes a long way toward building bridges."

"Or set up pitfalls if built upon a faulty foundation."

"Don't be like that," I say. "You trust me, don't you?"

She gives me a sideways look. "You've earned it."

"That misses the point," I say, "but I'm flattered."

We stand quietly together for another minute as the kids laugh and race about.

"She's trying to impress you," Mirzayael abruptly speaks up.

"Dizzi?" I ask. "She's just a curious soul, like myself."

"But she wants you to like her," Mirzayael says.

I chuckle. "I don't think that's a crime."

"She's attempting to buy favors," Mirzayael grumbles.

"Or just forge a friendship," I point out. "Does that bother you?"

She hesitates. "I just don't want to see you get hurt."

"She won't hurt me, Mirzayael."

"If she ends up betraying us—"

"Why?" I ask, exasperated. "How? You have no reason to suspect her, except that you just suspect everyone. No one else in the city harbors this much wariness for outsiders. Where is this coming from?"

But I can practically see the woman close herself off. Her shoulders go stiff, her back rigid, and her face smooths into an impassive look. "It is safer to be wary. More difficult to be hurt if you're discriminate in who you let in. If you only rely on yourself, you'll never be disappointed."

"That sounds like a lonely way to live." Is that how she's lived? Pushing away anyone who ventured too close?

"It's practical," she says shortly.

Because your parents left you when you were a child? I think. *Was that the only way you were able to cope with their loss?* But I say none of this aloud. Her stance is too tight, her body wound up defensively. If I try to push the subject, she'll only withdraw more. Instead, I give her arm a gentle pat. She shoots me a questioning look, and I smile reassuringly. Wordlessly, she returns to watching the kids, but I can feel her relax, just a fraction.

After a few minutes longer, Dizzi comes spiraling back down. She lands with a gust that stirs up all the dust around us, then holds a stone out to me. "Here! I picked the best specimen I could find," she says with a wink.

I take the cloudstone. It wants to lift from my hand and float back into the air—such a strange, paradoxical sensation. "What makes it the best specimen?" I ask.

"Because I gave it to you, of course!" Dizzi laughs at her own joke, and I smile as well. Mirzayael's mood darkens like a smog, but I try to let Dizzi's enthusiasm shine through.

"You really think I can use this thing to gain a wind affinity?" I bounce the stone between my hands, watching it float in fascination.

"It can't hurt to experiment," Dizzi says.

I chuckle. "Now those are words to live by."

Chapter Twenty-Seven

THE FULL TRUTH

The halls of the palace are warm and humid, thick with the rich aroma of a dozen brewing cauldrons of stew. Beryl and Hetlanir are coordinating a feast for when the last of the newcomers arrive. Nek says the best way to forge bonds is over a hot meal, and I tend to think he's right.

Fyreneth's Fortress has been completely excavated at this point. We don't have nearly enough people to fill the city, so right now most of the families are staying in the palace or the abodes just beneath it. Mirzayael's scouts still patrol the streets to make sure stingers aren't making nests in any of the empty lodgings, but for the most part the streets are lit, warm, and safe. It's hard to imagine only a month and a half before, the people here were barely scraping by.

I roll my shoulders and stretch my neck, trying not to slouch as I chop up a board full of mushrooms. It's all-hands-on-deck for the feast, and there's a festive atmosphere in the air as everyone bustles about, discussing which rooms have been set aside and prepped for which newcomers and what sort of local cuisine each group prefers.

"So, Fyreneth's Crown," Dizzi says, appearing at my elbow.

"The Dungeon Core," I correct her.

"Sure, whatever you want to call it. So can it eat stuff other than rocks?"

I hold up a mushroom stalk and mentally nudge the Dungeon Core. It takes a moment to notice what I'm drawing its attention to, but as soon as it catches my intent, it happily snatches up the fungi like an eager dog. The stalk vanishes between my fingers in two invisible bites. It proclaims the mushroom is not as good as rocks, but definitely better than spring water.

"That's wild," Dizzi says, grinning madly. "Does it digest it? Is there waste?"

"Er, no." Thank god that isn't the case. "It gets stored in a sort of virtual Inventory. Anything that gets consumed by the Core can be recalled back into reality at a later point, given a small mana cost." In fact, using that ability, I've been working with a family of dwarves to establish some herbal gardens in a few of the rooms near the kitchen. "I can also alter the matter that's inside the Inventory."

"Fascinating," Dizzi says. "Can it eat people too, do you think?"

I grimace. "I've not yet tested that theory and have no intentions to. Though it seems it can only consume biomasses that have already perished, so at least there's that. Here." I push half of my mushrooms in her direction. "Be productive while you hound me."

"Aw, come on," she says. "You love the questions, admit it."

"I do love questions," I agree. "I don't particularly love being hounded."

She picks up a knife and tentatively slices a mushroom. Clearly this is not one of her practiced skills. "Do you want me to stop?"

I sigh. "No, you're right. I'd be a hypocrite to discourage such curiosity. Ask away, then."

Dizzi ruffles her feathers in excitement. "Excellent. In that case, tell me all about this Interface you've mentioned. How does it work? What's the Inventory look like? What are all of its capabilities?"

As I respond, some of the other kitchen workers come around and take our bowl of chopped vegetables, replacing it with more ingredients to prepare. Dizzi cuts awkwardly and slowly, leaving all the pieces in mismatched sizes, and often stops working altogether while she listens to something I say with laser focus.

"As an artificer, I've made a lot of magical objects in my day," Dizzi says, "but I've never heard of anything this complex. It sounds like it basically has a mind of its own."

"I believe it does," I admit. "It's certainly like no consciousness I've ever encountered. Vast and ancient, yet it harbors a childlike naïveté. Incapable of empathy, but curious and hungry."

"Not unlike Ollie," Dizzi teases.

I chuckle. "With the exception of empathy, a fairly apt comparison. Neither seem to be fully aware of the power they wield."

"Sounds dangerous."

"It could be," I agree. "If wielded by the wrong hands."

"And you think you're the right hands?" Dizzi asks.

I glance down at the Core, sitting dormant on my wrist. Do I? Is it arrogant to think I'm capable of directing such a dangerous force? Of wielding it responsibly? "I don't know if I'm the right one. But I think I'd rather it be with me than with someone who might have more ambition for power."

"Hm. That's a fair response, I think," Dizzi says. "How'd it come to end up in your hands, anyway?"

"It was just sitting there in the cave when I woke up," I say. "Literally stumbled upon it. I was able to forge a Pact with it, which gave me access to its Interface, and gave it access to my mana, and the rest is history."

"Woke up in a cave, huh?" Dizzi glances at me, eyebrow raised. "How'd you end up there?"

I stop chopping the vegetables. I hadn't even realized she'd guided me to admitting how I ended up here. "That was tricky."

"Sorry," she says, though the grin she flashes indicates she's not *that* sorry. "You kept being so dodgy, I knew I'd have to dig it out of you."

I wrinkle my nose. "I don't appreciate being manipulated. Did it occur to you there might be a reason I was keeping this information to myself?"

Dizzi's smile falters. "Actually, no. I, uh, was just thinking about how I was going to weasel the truth out of you. Sorry."

I frown. It's not that I don't trust her, like Mirzayael. But the rumors of my nature—however inaccurate—have already been incessant, and I'd very much prefer to not compound them.

Then again, Dizzi's probably already knows everything and is just looking to confirm rumors; Nek is a terrible gossip. Maybe sharing the full truth will help put a stop to the rebirth theories that the half-truth has perpetuated.

I sigh. "Tell me what you've already heard."

Dizzi jumps at the opportunity, leaning forward and blurting out everything in one breath. "That you're Fyreneth reborn and wield her lost weapon and appeared in the same location as her grave, wreathed in flames."

"Wreathed in flames?" I repeat, laughing. "Someone is taking liberties."

"What about the rest?" she asks, eyes wide and eager.

"I'm not Fyreneth," I say firmly. "But there may be some truth in the other parts. I don't have proof that this Dungeon Core is the crown Fyreneth once wielded, but given its capabilities, I think it's likely."

"And you really appeared over her grave?" she asks.

I hesitate. "On that, I'm unsure. There were signs a battle took place in that location. The bones of Fyreneth's enemies, according to your myths. But there was no indication of Fyreneth's remains being there."

"There wouldn't be, if she reincarnated," Dizzi says. "They say that can happen with phoenix harpies."

"Have you ever witnessed such a thing?" I ask.

Now it's Dizzi's turn to hesitate. "No. But it's a common belief."

"I'll believe it when I see it," I say dryly. "In your scientific opinion, do you believe there is evidence to support that phoenix harpies can reincarnate?"

Dizzi hesitates for a long moment, likely experiencing that unpleasant dissonance that transpires when reason disrupts desire. Then, she sags in disappointment.

"You really aren't her?" There's a hint of disappointment in her tone. She actually thought I was some mythical hero.

I offer a sympathetic smile. "No, I'm really not. Just a victim of extreme coincidence."

Dizzi doesn't appear entirely convinced. "Even if you're not Fyreneth, there's too much correlation between your story and hers for *all* of it to be a coincidence."

I splay my hands, helpless. "I'm not sure what to tell you."

Frowning, Dizzi goes back to her cutting board. "Okay then. Going with your version of events. Why do you use her name?"

"I don't," I object. "Well. Okay it is a shortened version of her name. But it's one that was picked for me. I guess you can say I was named after her."

Dizzi snorts. "If you're trying to avoid the association, you're doing a bad job."

"Tell me about it." I chuckle.

"Follow up question. How did you get into the cave?"

Now that's a tricky question to answer. But I've resolved to share the whole truth. Why not, after all? The only harm in revealing I'm from another world is not being believed.

"Well," I say slowly, "the long and short of it is that I died on another planet, my consciousness got caught up in some sort of extradimensional conflict, and then I woke up shivering in a cave—and in an entirely different body."

Dizzi stares at me. "You're not messing with me?"

"I am absolutely serious," I say firmly.

"Boiling abyss," she swears. She's silent for a moment. Then she slams her hands down on the counter. "You have to tell me everything. What's your world like? How advanced is its arcane body of knowledge? What caused your consciousness to switch worlds? Do you think you could get back? Could I visit?"

"It's complicated, it's nonexistent, I have no idea, I have no idea, and I have no idea."

"Those are incredibly disappointing responses," Dizzi says.

I laugh. "Sorry I'm not everything you were hoping for."

"Are you kidding me?" Dizzi cries. "This is way more interesting than a reincarnated old lady. Coming from another world creates countless new possibilities and implications! Okay, I have follow-up questions."

"I suspected you would." I tap her board. "Come on. Your hands aren't broken while you talk."

Dizzi groans, picking her knife back up. "I don't know how you can expect me to perform mundane chores while reeling from existential discoveries about the nature of reality."

"Imagine my surprise when I ended up here," I say with a chuckle.

"Yeah, so about that," Dizzi says. "A different body?"

"I'm rather new to being a harpy," I admit.

"Okay now *that* makes complete sense. That's the most sense you've made since I got here. You're the least harpy harpy I've ever met. You didn't even know about the different affinities. Wait." She stops. "What were you before?"

"A human," I say. Then it's my turn to pause. "You *do* have humans here, don't you?"

"Of course we do," she says. "I mean, theoretically. I've heard they don't do well in the cold. They say about half of the Jorrians are human, but I've never met one myself."

"Well, now you have."

"Huh." She stops chopping again. She is really bad at this. "So should I think of you as a human or a harpy?"

"Oh," I say. "Hm. I'm not entirely sure about that myself. Actually, no—harpy. I'm a harpy. The person I am now is not the person I was before. I like this version of me much more. And I want to embrace all of it."

"That's pretty cool," Dizzi says. "And surreal. Like, wow. I'm still trying to wrap my head around all this. Do you think there are more other-worlders like you?"

"I know so." I nod toward the window, which looks out onto one of the many pavilions I've fixed up for Ollie. He's not out on the platform right now, but one of his toys—a giant shield he found who knows where—is sitting discarded on the surface. "Ollie's from my world, too."

"What?" Dizzi squawks. "No way! The dragon?"

"Yes," I say, "though he was just a little boy back home. A human boy."

Dizzi shakes her head, smiling. "This keeps getting stranger."

"I haven't even begun to tell you about our technology yet, either."

That lights a hungry spark in her eyes. "You said your world was light on arcana theory. You've made up for it in other ways?"

"If by light, you mean nonexistent, then yes. On Earth, our research into fields of science was quite broad—"

"Your planet is named after dirt?"

"—and my specialty was aerodynamics." I choose to ignore the question, as I quite frankly don't have a satisfying answer. "You know the airplanes I mentioned before? They were needed because *no one* on my world could fly. I mostly worked on wing designs, though I dabbled in avionics for a while as well..."

As I talk about airfoils and ailerons, Dizzi wicks up my words like a dry sponge. It's delightful to have someone to talk to about these things. Of course, I've discussed these topics with Mirzayael before, too, but those conversations were met with confusion and incredulity rather than rabid enthusiasm. In fact, we're still talking by the time all the rest of the meats and vegetables are taken care of. And when we're ushered out of the kitchen as the finishing touches of the feast are being prepared, we've only just touched on astronautics.

The palace bustles with activity and warm voices as we head back to my workroom, discussing how my knowledge of physics might be better married with Dizzi's knowledge of artificing. Throw the Dungeon Core into the mix—a magical fabrication lab—and then you've really unlocked some interesting potential. All these together, and there's no reason Fyreneth's Fortress can't rise to its previous levels of prosperity. Exceed them, even.

Heads bent over the worktable, we begin to sketch out our wildest dreams.

Chapter Twenty-Eight

A Taste of Prosperity

The mess hall is a roar of voices. The entire population of the underground is packed into one extravagant and sprawling hall. I'd even opened up the back wall to allow Ollie access, though he can only poke his head and forepaws through the opening to share the meal. On Beryl's insistence, (and with the Dungeon Core's help,) the giant stone tables that had previously stretched the span of the room have been removed and replaced with cushions of moss and fur. Countless communal circles are situated around pots of stew, with both original residents and newcomers mixed into each other's ranks. Our ring, conspicuously placed at the head of the room, consists of me, Mirzayael, Beryl, Nek and his family, Dizzi, Hetlanir, and a dracid named Torim who is the harpy leader's second-in-command. I have Echo run a quick tally of the rest of the hall: there's over two thousand of us.

"I've never seen anything like this," Nek says, leaning against his wife's shoulder as he looks around the room in awe. "So many people. So much *food.*"

"And so warm," Sora says as she snuggles against his fur. Their son rolls his eyes, and their daughter makes a fake gagging sound. I chuckle at the kids' reactions; some things really do appear to be universal.

I can't feel the heat as keenly as a dracid can, but the sight of her awake, of the children running around and playing—that fills me with more warmth than the room ever could. I take a sip of the soup; it's hot and meaty, and its day-long stewing has filled the palace with a rich, mouth-watering aroma. I'm in agreement with Nek. Finally. *Finally* it feels like we're getting a taste of prosperity.

"Lord Fyre," an arachnoid says, approaching with a respectfully bowed head.

I twist my grimace into a smile. "Please, such formalities are not necessary."

"Of course." The young man straightens up, a look of reverence on his face that makes me want to squirm. "I wanted to offer you a gift, as a token of my family's appreciation."

"Oh, I couldn't," I weakly object. I already have a stack of such gifts in my room, and it's not getting any less awkward to accept them.

"It's not much," he says, holding out a bone-carved dagger. "But it would make me happy to offer it to you."

"Fyre is currently not accepting any offerings," Mirzayael abruptly cuts in. She sets down her bowl, but doesn't stand; the way seven of her legs are tucked up around her, with the eighth severed limb awkwardly set to one side, I suspect it's more effort to get around than she tries to make it seem. "You can keep your dagger."

I wince at Mirzayael's bluntness, especially as the newcomer's face falls.

"But you know," Dizzi jumps in, "Ollie would just love it. In fact, all further offerings can be redirected to the dragon."

The man's face lights back up at Dizzi's suggestion. "Thank you. It would be my honor to please your familiar." He bows to me again then shuffles away, cautiously approaching Ollie's perch.

"Oh, no," I say. "But he's just a little kid! He shouldn't be given a knife."

"He's a dragon the size of an ice floe," Mirzayael says. "A dagger won't even pose the threat of a splinter."

"Besides," Dizzi cheerfully adds, "he's already got tons of rusty swords and things in his collection. Have you dug through that pile yet? There's some gnarly stuff in there."

I grimace, resolving to investigate exactly that after the feast. Ollie looks up from his cauldron—the bones and stinger chitin that had been used to brew the broth for the rest of us—and tips his head as the arachnoid approaches. He raises the dagger above him, which Ollie gives a sniff. Then he nuzzles the man, and only the fact that the arachnoid has eight legs keeps him from being bowled over. Still, he laughs as Ollie excitedly nudges him over to the small hoard he's been accumulating over the course of the evening, and the man is all too happy to add his blade to the stash.

Mirzayael and Dizzi are both probably right that things like blunt swords and little daggers are no threat to Ollie, but it's hard not to worry. A parent's instinct, I suppose.

"They don't really think he's my familiar, do they?" I ask as I watch Ollie and the arachnoid.

Mirzayael snorts. "Of course they do. You're the only one who can understand him."

"Yeah, and you've got some kind of mental bond," Dizzi adds.

"That's just a telepathy spell," I object. "I could form one with anyone. It just takes a bit of mana, and he and the Dungeon Core are the only ones I've really needed to use it with."

Dizzi sighs wistfully. "That's so cool."

"Don't feed her ego," Mirzayael warns.

"Fyre?" Dizzi scoffs. "What ego? If anything, she could stand to take a little more pride in her achievements."

"You'd have me exasperate the Fyreneth rumors?" I counter. "Nothing good will come of that."

"Nonsense." This time, to my surprise, it's Beryl who speaks up. I hadn't even known she'd been listening. "They already see you as a leader, whether you want it or not."

"It's about deserving it," I object. "They only treat me with such respect because of another person's legacy that's been projected onto me. Every gift they offer makes me feel like more of a fraud."

Beryl barks out a laugh. "Is that so? None of their respect comes from you restoring Fyreneth's Fortress?"

"And giving us enough warmth to be able to live a full life," Sora says.

Nek hugs his wife. "And taming a dragon!"

"Forging a path to the surface so we can scout and hunt again," Mirzayael says.

"Not to mention, sharing your knowledge," Dizzi adds.

Hetlanir tips his head to me in respect. "You helped facilitate the reunion of our people."

Even Torim, who I've hardly exchanged three words with, joins in. "That arachnoid addressed you as Fyre, not Fyreneth. Perhaps trust others to be genuine when they express their gratitude."

I lean back, at a loss for words. Of course, bettering their lives of the Fyrethians has always been my goal. I wanted to give back in any way I could—show my appreciation for their kindness and hospitality. If I hadn't found Mirzayael, had she not taken me back to the Keep, I most certainly would have perished.

But the assistance I had to offer was such a piecemeal thing that I hadn't realized how much had been accomplished until they laid it all out like that.

"I'm not sure what to say," I admit, feeling a touch sentimental at their words. "Thank you. Your faith in me—the kindness you've all shown—it's more than I ever could have asked for." And some part of me believes more than I ever deserved.

Beryl nods stiffly. "If you're feeling charitable and want to show your appreciation, then the next time someone offers you a gift: take it."

A humbling lesson, to be sure. "I will."

"Good," she grumbles. "Now everyone get back to your bowls before the soup gets cold."

We don't need a second reminder. The meal passes in a blur of laughter, heavy food, and even, to my surprise, a cask of libations. Brewed by a family of dracid, the drink gets passed around, its flavor bosting an uncanny likeness to jet fuel. Even so, it produces a pleasant buzz, and even Mirzayael appears to lighten up a little. As the conversation turns idle and my mind drifts, I turn my attention inward.

I remove the piece of cloudstone Dizzi had given me from my personal Inventory. I don't often use my personal Inventory, since it only has one slot while the Dungeon Core has access to hundreds of thousands. But there's something more personal about putting a keepsake in my own Inventory, like carrying a lucky charm around in one's pocket.

I pass the lighter-than-air stone between my hands, idly playing with the rock. I desperately wish to unlock a wind affinity, but I'm skeptical this bit of stone can help me with that. I've tried meditating with it several times now, but so far, I haven't felt anything. I must be doing something wrong. Maybe the alcohol will help free me of any subconscious inhibitions I've been harboring.

Eyes closed, I take a deep breath in, and slowly let it out. I concentrate on the stone between my hands, trying to feel the mana trapped within its pores. The Dungeon Core interface immediately surfaces, ready to analyze the mass, density, and mana volume, but I brush it aside. I'm supposed to be resonating with it. *Feeling* the magic. Not mathematically picking it apart like a science experiment.

It feels like... a rock. I know there's wind mana trapped inside this cloudstone, because Dizzi and the Core's interface have both told me that's the case. But if it weren't for the fact that the rock was trying to float out of my hands, it would feel like any other hunk of stone. Cold. Solid. A bit dusty. I frown, squeezing it tighter.

"Drifting off to sleep already, Outsider? I didn't take you for such a lightweight."

I jump at Mirzayael's voice and crack open an eye. "Isn't it obvious? I'm trying to get in touch with my spiritual side."

A light laugh bubbles out of Mirzayael. "You have a spiritual side?"

"I'm beginning to think I don't." I pass the cloudstone from hand to hand, studying it. "Dizzi said affinities can be obtained through dedicated study, though so far I've yet to make a breakthrough. I'd desperately love to learn wind magic. My heart has been in the clouds ever since I was a child."

Mirzayael holds out a hand, and I pass the stone to her. "Well, that's a good start. Having passion helps. But it's not dedicated study, exactly. It's more like... finding the resonance."

"Have you learned any types of magic you weren't born with?" I ask.

She shakes her head. "I've never tried. In an ideal world, anyone can learn any type of magic, given unlimited time and resources. But down here, every choice mattered. At a young age, you had to pick what your place in society would be and then dedicate yourself to that. For me, that was becoming a guard of the Keep, as my parents were. I trained in combat, scouting, navigation. And yes, some basic fields of magic, primarily related to combat, communication, and survival. But as with any skill, learning magic takes time. More so if it's not something you already have an affinity for." She bounces the cloudstone between her hands, then passes it back to me. "I deemed it best to develop the strengths I already had."

"What are you saying?" I play the stone between my fingers. "That I should stay in my lane? That it might be futile to dream of flight?"

"I doubt anyone can stop you once you've set your mind to something," Mirzayael says, a faint smile pulling at her lips. "But perhaps gaining an affinity for wind arcana is not the only way to achieve what you want. You're intelligent, and already know quite a lot about the sky. I am sure you will figure it out one way or another."

I absently run my fingers through the feathers of one of my wings. "God, can you imagine? It would be amazing. You know, I wanted to be a pilot when I was a kid—someone who flies one of those airplanes I've mentioned. But I... well, it never panned out for me."

Mirzayael tipped her head. "Why not?"

I squeeze the cloudstone, then let go, catching the rock with the other hand hovering above. "No reason, really. A lack of nerve, perhaps. Engineering seemed... a more stable career path. Safer. Building them is no less important than flying them, after all."

"But it's not what you wanted," Mirzayael surmises.

"I suppose not," I admit. "I guess that's my life in a nutshell. Always picking the easier path over the one that excited me. Low risk, high stability."

"That *was* your life," Mirzayael says. "This person you've described—low risk, lack of nerve. They are not the same person I have observed exploring caverns, fighting wolves, and blowing holes in glaciers."

I laugh at that. "Maybe you're a bad influence on me."

Mirzayael sniffs. "I am not a bad influence on anyone. If anything, my upstanding nature provides a good example of what you should aspire to."

After all this time, I've started to pick up on Mirzayael's dry sense of humor. The fact that she's joking with me, even if it it's in her own subtle way, fills me with warm affection. She doesn't trust many, but knowing she's opened up a bit to me makes me feel more humbled than any offering ever could. "I think perhaps you're right about that."

"Of course," Mirzayael deadpans. "I always strive to be correct."

I chuckle, tossing the cloudstone toward the floor, then catch it as it rises back up. I thoughtfully examine the advice Mirzayael had just suggested. Alternatives to wind arcana. What alternatives do I have to work with? Sora and a family of arachnoids are in the middle of crafting a saddle for me to use with Ollie. But being able to fly independently is the real goal.

The cloudstone is an obvious solution, of course. Dizzi and I have already brainstormed dozens of lighter-than-air designs, though we've yet to fabricate any prototypes. Maybe even if I can't fly on my own, I could still use it to create a craft and take flight the old-fashioned human way.

I'm in the middle of tossing the rock back and forth between my hands, widening the gap each time, when a guard bursts into the hall. The commotion isn't immediately noticed by others until they come running up to our circle.

"Captain." The felis salutes Mirzayael with a sharp gesture, but the twitch in their tail betrays their nerves.

She looks up from her meal. A brief flicker of surprise quickly melts into an all-business frown. "Scout Rei. Report."

"There's a troop of people on the surface," they say. "Perhaps two dozen individuals. One of Lord Hetlanir's scouts confirmed they're not from the lost colony. They're carrying weapons and accompanied by direwolves." They swallow before continuing. "We... we think they're Jorrian."

Chapter Twenty-Nine

THE JORRIANS

Mirzayael leaves to gather her guards as I follow Beryl, Nek, and Hetlanir toward the tunnel leading to the surface. Dizzi and the other non-combatants stay behind, but no one objects to me accompanying the leaders. The faint buzz I'd been experiencing before is now drowned beneath a wave of concern. I can practically feel the tension in the air around us, stretched tighter with every passing moment.

"I will do the talking," Beryl says as she leads the way up the slope. "No one is to take any action without my say so."

"Lord Beryl, if a fight breaks out, you will be in danger," Hetlanir says. "They'll target you as our leader. I'd advise you to stay behind."

"Bah," Beryl grumbles. "Better that they target me than any of you young ones."

"*FYRE!*" Ollie cries, the cave shaking as he races up the slope behind us. "*WHAT'S GOING ON? CAN I COME?*"

"Go back to your cave, Ollie," I tell him. "It might not be safe."

"Perhaps that's all the more reason for him to come," Hetlanir says. "It might dissuade any inclinations to pick a fight."

"Or encourage it." Nek gives Ollie a worried look. "I can't imagine anyone wouldn't be nervous to stare such a creature down."

"*LAST TIME YOU SAID I COULD COME PROTECT YOU IF YOU WERE IN DANGER,*" Ollie says, displaying better memory than I gave him credit for.

"Only if I'm in danger," I agree. "Which we might not be."

"*REALLY?*" Ollie asks. "*THEN WHY IS MIRZAYAEL ALL DRESSED UP?*"

Ollie squishes himself up against the side of the cave to let Mirzayael and her guards catch up with the rest of us. Sure enough, she's now wearing armor. She and all of her guards carry spears.

"Ollie can come," she says shortly. "Hetlanir is right; we may need his power, even if it's just for show."

Worry clenches my jaw and pinches my brows. "I don't want Ollie to get hurt." The others don't see him as a child, like I do. Without his voice in their heads, they may *know* he's young, but that's easily overshadowed by how he appears: a dangerous and powerful creature.

"I will not let any Fyrethian come to harm." Mirzayael fixes me with a hard, confident look. "I have prepared for a conflict such as this my entire life."

"Assuming there will be a conflict," I say, a sinking feeling already forming in my gut. I think about her parents; about the thirst for revenge that must have been parching her throat for decades. "*Please,* Mir. Tell me you'll try the peaceful way first."

"If the peace is broken, it will not be our doing," she says, turning away to catch up with Beryl and the others.

I guess that's as good an assurance as I'll get.

Ollie excitedly follows us up the tunnel, though each step we ascend pushes my spirits deeper into the earth. Mirzayael gives orders to the other guards, assigning positions and telling them to be ready to act at her word. She assigns two guards to Beryl, and even orders the young arachnoid guard, Zakaiya, to protect me. I'd be flattered that she cares about protecting me as much as the Fyrethian leaders, but the thought pales beneath the current of fear that's rising within me. This is becoming very real, very quickly.

In another few minutes, we reach the surface. It's late afternoon out on the ice, and the winter sun scraping the horizon. In the distant north are the mountain peaks of the Jorrian capital. Typically shrouded by clouds and snow, today the plains between us remain clear. The mountains are stained red by the setting sun, affecting a grisly appearance of bloody fangs. And beneath them, rather closer than I was expecting, are the forms of an approaching group. Two flags are being carried on either side of the unit, and though they're too far to make out, I strongly suspect they bear the same shield and eye I'd seen before on the frost wolves' collars.

"Ollie, get behind us," I tell him. I'd rather him not be up here at all, but now that other adults have already given him permission, I know that's not an argument I will win. He's currently at my side, his tail swishing haphazardly over the snow, stirring up flurries and spraying us with ice.

"*BUT—*"

"*Now*, Ollie. I'm not asking."

The dragon dips his head, but slides around behind us. Good. He's safer further away from the front lines, and less likely to inadvertently start a geopolitical conflict.

Plus, his presence at our backs looks pretty damn intimidating. I hope Hetlanir and Mirzayael are right about this.

As the Jorrians approach, I see they've brought backup of their own. The party consists of twelve humans, six felis, and six dwarves. Two Jorrians bear the flags I'd seen before, nearly half of their ranks wield bow and arrows, and the rest carry swords and shields. Additionally, two humans ride atop a pair of intimidating white wolves the size of horses. The animals' lips are peeled back, revealing the pink of their gums. I'm suddenly glad Ollie is with us.

I Check everyone as soon as they're close enough to distinguish, starting with the wolves and their riders.

[Level 26 Greater Direwolf: Steed to Biorne Gylfis]

[Level 24 Greater Direwolf: Steed to Alis Gylfis]

[Biorne Gylfis: Level 34 Human Ice Paladin]

[Alis Gylfis: Level 29 Human Court Inquisitor]

The archers are all between level 18 and 27, with an occasional magic bent to their class name—most of them ice related. The average sword wielder is level 25.

Not the highest levels. But compared to our group, my concern is only growing. I'm still only level 21, Mirzayael is 29, Nek is 26, Hetlanir is 27, and Beryl is 46, though she's a healer, not a fighter. The rest of our young guards and scouts hover around level 20. At least we have Ollie at an astounding level 43. But even with his size and brute force, we're outnumbered. I don't like our odds if it comes to a fight.

I'll just have to do everything in my power to make sure it doesn't.

The Jorrians stop a respectful distance away—or maybe they just want to keep outside of Ollie's jaw-snapping range. For a moment, their troops shuffle in tense silence. A flurry of snow dances between us.

One of the riders, Biorne, urges his wolf forward. He's dressed in layers of thick fur, but the sunlight catches on bits of armor complementing his attire. His face is sun-tanned and weather-worn, hair shaggy but short. I also notice Mirzayael has wrapped her braids up in a tight bun; both practical hair styles that can't be taken advantage of in a fight.

"Hail," Biorne calls to us. His voice carries easily across the quiet plains. "My name is Biorne Gylfis, ambassador to my kingdom. I speak on the behalf of all of Jorria, ever faithful servants to Lorata. We have not seen signs of travelers so deep into the Wastes in many years. What cause draws you to such a desolate place?"

I can feel Mirzayael tense up beside me as Beryl steps forward.

"My name is Beryl, elder of my people. I speak on behalf of Fyreneth's Keep, our home, ever faithful servants to those in need. We have not been drawn anywhere, nor are we traveling. You stand on the doorstep of our domain. Should you be capable of keeping the peace, I would invite you inside."

A stir goes through the Jorrian soldiers, and likewise the Fyrethians shift uneasily at the open invitation.

This time it's the other wolf-rider who moves forward. "You are disciples of Fyreneth?" Alis asks. The woman appears much like the man, but older, her frown crinkled with crow's feet.

"We are her descendants," Beryl says.

Alis wrinkles her nose. "Then we have little to discuss."

"Wait," I instinctively object. Biorne speaks up at the same time, and I shut my mouth, abashed. It isn't my place to speak for the Fyrethians.

"Perhaps a mutual agreement can be discussed, first," Biorne says, looking sidelong at his relative. Alis's face is sour in apparent disagreement.

Beryl rumbles with a tired sigh. "I think avoiding bloodshed is something both our people would find preferable."

"A bold assumption," Alis sneers.

Biorne silences her with a sharp gesture. "I would like to think tensions between our people could be resolved peacefully. I am willing to explore such options. Tell me, Forsaken. What are your intentions?"

"Intentions?" Beryl repeats. "We merely intend to survive."

Alis looks displeased with this response, but Biorne tilts his head thoughtfully. "You have no intent to resurrect Fyreneth's Fortress?" he asks. "No plans to gather troops? To challenge Jorria?"

Resurrecting the Fortress is, in fact, something Dizzi and I have been looking into quite extensively, though our research is incomplete, and we've not yet brought our findings to the leaders. I wisely keep this bit of information to myself.

Mirzayael's lips curl in distaste. "Marching on the enemy rather sounds more like your territory than ours."

"Mir," Beryl snaps, silencing her.

She huffs, but clacks her teeth shut.

"No," Beryl says to Biorne. "We have no intention to do any such things. We are much too preoccupied with our own survival."

Biorne looks pointedly to Alis, who shakes her head. Even so, he turns back to the rest of us. "If you speak truly, then I would be more than happy to leave you to your own devices. Your ancestors were driven underground as penance for defying the gods. Should you remain there, I see no reason for conflict to escalate further. It is our duty to stop any uprisings. Perhaps I am more liberal in my interpretations of the creed than some of my peers," he says, and Alis scoffs. "But to me, the verdicts can be read to mean uprising as in emerging from your confinement, rather than simply growing in number or becoming organized, as *some* choose to interpret." Biorne offers a smile. "I hope we are in agreement?"

It's laughably offensive. We're supposed to accept that being forced to live in caves is not only a mercy, but a favor. If Biorne is more open-minded than the rest of his kingdom, I shudder to imagine what the rest think of Fyrethians.

Then again, best not to go poking sleeping bears. As problematic as his reasoning may be, at least he's willing to leave without a fight. If they leave us alone, perhaps we can bide our time and grow in power and ability until they no longer pose a threat.

Mirzayael lets out a low growl, luckily too quiet to drift across the ice, and I put a hand on her arm.

"We can't start a fight we can't win," I say to her quietly. "As Beryl said, we are preoccupied with survival enough as it is. Let's just focus on that."

"They deserve to face justice," Mirzayael hisses, thankfully keeping the words between us. "They deserve to be held accountable for their crimes."

"These individuals are not responsible for what happened to your ancestors," I say. "Though they do seem to hold... problematic views of their own. Please. Leave it for now. Vengeance can wait for another day. Jorria isn't going anywhere."

Mirzayael's grasp tightens on her spear, her knuckles going white. Then she growls out a breath with a shake of her head.

"We are in agreement," Beryl calls to Biorne, voice clipped. "You will return to your mountains, and we to our caves."

"Good. Good!" Biorne says, smiling. "I'm glad an agreement could be reached. I told my sister you all could be reasoned with. Even those who are Forsaken can be redeemed."

I can practically feel the hate radiating off Mirzayael in waves, and I don't blame her in the slightest. Biorne's words threaten to boil my blood, too, but fear for Ollie's wellbeing is stronger yet. I tighten my grip on her arm, and she grinds her teeth.

"Then unless there's anything else," Beryl says, thankfully inter- jecting before Mirzayael can reply with something that might undo the tentative peace that was just established, "we will be returning to our home."

Biorne dips his head. "It will be the same for us as well."

"*IS THAT IT?*" Ollie asks, his sudden voice causing me to startle. I guess I'm a little jumpy right now. "*THAT WAS BORING. ALL YOU GUYS DID WAS TALK.*" He cranes his head back and straightens his tail out behind him, stretching out his spine with a content sigh. "*CAN I GO FLY NOW?*"

"*Maybe later,*" I think, nervously glancing toward the Jorrians. The wolves growl, and some of the soldiers stir at Ollie's movement. "*After our guests have left.*"

"*UGH. BOOOOOOORING.*" He yawns, revealing his dagger-like fangs, then shakes out his wings to settle into a more comfortable position.

Several of the archers nock arrows.

"Wait!" I call, my heart jumping to my throat. "He's just tired. It's not a threat."

"It sure looks like a threat," Biorne remarks, cautiously eying Ollie as he reins in his uneasy wolf.

"He's restless," I say desperately. "Just needs to stretch his wings. He'll settle down after a flight—but we can wait until after you've returned to your kingdom. I promise he means no harm."

"Flight," Biorne repeats, a dark look passing over his face. "I'm afraid there's been a misunderstanding. The verdict that you all return underground includes your... *pets* as well."

His words summon a swell of protective anger within me, and my fingers itch with the urge to summon a fire. "Ollie is not a pet," I snap. Then I take a deep breath, reining my emotions back in as I force the heat out of my voice. I need to stay cool. We have to maintain the peace. "He's as intelligent as you or me."

"He is a dragon," Mirzayael adds. "You cannot expect him to stay underground."

"He poses a threat," Alis retorts. "He kills our livestock. Terrorizes our people. That beast is a menace."

I wince at the mention of livestock. I knew Ollie had been finding animals out on the ice to eat, but I'd been too preoccupied with my work on Fyreneth's Fortress to pay attention to his diet. Had he really hunted some of their animals? Or is that just being used as an excuse to ground him?

"He can move hunting grounds," I say. "We'll make sure to keep out of your kingdom's skies."

Biorne sadly shakes his head. "I don't think you understand. He cannot be allowed to roam the surface any more than the rest of you. The fact that he is a tamed beast makes no difference."

"That's not fair," I object. Fear and anger wrestle for dominance, and it feels like my flames have come to life in my veins. I'm starting to experience an acute understanding of what Mirzayael must be feeling. But I can't let my feelings control me. We can still work this out. The Jorrians must be able to see reason. They must!

"There isn't enough food for him in the caves," I explain. "What would he eat?"

Biorne offers a shrug and a grimace of mild sympathy. "Sacrifices must be made on all sides, I'm afraid. Perhaps that beast of yours could be better put to use as meat to feed your people."

I see red.

Beryl, Nek, and Mirzayael all speak up at once in an unintelligible objection.

"WHAT?" An uncertain, scared growl rumbles from Ollie's throat. *"WHAT DOES HE MEAN, FYRE? ARE THEY GOING TO HURT ME?"*

At the sound of the dragon's growl, one of the archers looses an arrow. It snaps toward Ollie before I even have a chance to react—where it skips off a plate on his chest and vanishes into a snow drift.

"*HEY!*" Ollie cries, his startled fear digging deep into my own psyche. "*THEY JUST THREW SOMETHING AT ME!*"

"Hold!" Biorne calls.

In a fraction of a breath, images of my daughter blink through my mind like pages of a flipbook. On the playground, crying as she looked up at me with skinned palms. In the back seat of the car, sniffing after a trip to the dentist. The soul-rending helplessness I felt when I watched the video of her falling to the floor of the basketball court, screaming as she clutched her dislocated knee. The bleary, pained look in her eyes after she got out of surgery and asked me why I hadn't been there.

The way she screamed at me when she found the papers, voice filled with more hurt than I'd ever heard from any injury.

The way her smiling face dimmed on my phone's screen as my most recent call went to voicemail. The three cardboard boxes in the corner of the motel room blurred into senseless smears of color.

Running through a hundred thousand scenarios of what I should have done differently. Cataloging all things I wouldn't do to take her pain away.

What I wouldn't trade for a second chance.

All this in under a heartbeat, and then my simmering anguish explodes from me, unable—unwilling—to contain it any longer.

"Don't you *dare* touch him!" I snarl. Fire sparks around my fists. I'm shaking with fury. A hair's breadth away from unleashing everything I have on these people. "You will *not* harm this child."

"Is that a threat?" Alis demands. She lifts a staff. "They mean to attack us!"

"You just attacked *us*!" Mirzayael cries, taking a step forward. "Hypocrites, the lot of you! Claiming to want peace when you really just want us dead."

"*WHY IS EVERYONE YELLING NOW?*" Ollie asks. His tail swishes back and forth in fright. "*WHAT'S HAPPENING?*"

For a moment, his words cut through my fury. We can't risk a fight while Ollie is here. I have to protect him. We have to delay this conflict—at least until he's safe.

"*Ollie, get back inside,*" I say, trying not to let my fear and anger and desperation bleed into him. "*Now!*"

Ollie lets out a frightened hiss, pressing himself flat against the ice, but he doesn't move toward the cave. "*I CAN'T. ECHO SAYS YOU'RE IN DANGER!*"

The non-sequitur knocks me off balance. Echo? What is he talking about?

"They're going to set their dragon on us!" Alis bellows. "Archers, at the ready."

"Guards," Mirzayael calls as well. "Arms up."

"Steady," Beryl warns, but the guards seem uncertain if they should listen to Beryl or Mirzayael.

No, no, this is all spiraling out of control too fast. There's no time to think. But there must be a way out. A solution—

"Biorne," I shout in panic. "Biorne, call them off!"

He looks at me with a pitying expression, and says nothing.

Alis sneers. "Archers—"

Mirzayael juts her spear forward. "Attack!"

Chapter Thirty

BATTLE

The fighting breaks out in an instant, and by the time I've even registered this fact, it's too late to stop.

Arrows fly toward us, and the guard Zakaiya steps forward, raising a hand. A web of light appears before us, and the arrows clatter harmlessly off the construct. Mirzayael charges forward the next instant, before the archers have a chance to draw another arrow, and her guards sprint after.

My heart shatters. Nothing I say now will matter, not in the heat of battle. I can't stop this; I can only try to protect as many people as possible. And that means I need to fight.

"WHAT'S GOING ON?" Ollie asks, alarmed. *"WHY'S EVERYONE FIGHTING? ARE THEY GOING TO BE OKAY? FYRE, I'M SCARED!"*

"Get back in the caverns!" I shout, aloud as well as mentally. I stand in front of Ollie, summoning fire to my hands as the troops clash.

[Blaze activated.]

My bonus mana ticks down, but given the amount the Dungeon Core has absorbed from the mana ore over the last few weeks, I've more than enough for a couple of fireballs.

On their wolves, Biorne and Alis retreated outside of Mirzayael's range when her fighters attacked, but now are coming back in a pincer formation. The direwolves will tear them to shreds. I split my Blaze in two, one in each hand, and condense the attack, fueling more and more mana into each white-hot furnace of flame. I wait until the wolves are running full-tilt toward the battle. Then, I loose my attack.

[Fireball spell obtained!]

The Fireballs sear toward the wolves, maneuvered by my will more than my throwing abilities. Biorne's wolf notices first and digs its claws into the ice, pivoting and leaping to the side. The fireball impacts harmlessly in front of him even as Biorne is thrown from his saddle and goes tumbling across the field.

Alis's wolf isn't so quick to react. It attempts to skid to a stop, and the fireball strikes the ground directly in front of its path, blasting ice into the face of the wolf—as well as Alis. The woman cries as the wolf snarls, shaking the ice and fire away and knocking Alis from its back.

"Alis!" Biorne cries.

He climbs to his feet, stepping in his sister's direction, but Mirzayael intercepts him first. Her spear comes down at his head, and he only barely draws his sword in time to parry. He knocks her attack back, then follows it up with a lunge of his own, stabbing for Mirzayael's abdomen.

My stomach lurches with each cut and parry, expecting her to slip, waiting for each of the sword's strikes to be the one that takes her down. I can't bear to watch—not that I have much time to.

Alis groans, rolling to her feet. She raises her staff to point at me, and I brace, raising my own flaming hands. What magic does she have? What's about to come my way? The uncertainty fills me with fear as much as determination.

[Check,] Echo says in response to my thoughts. [Icebeam.]

Well that doesn't sound good.

"*FYRE!*" Ollie cries. "*WATCH OUT!*"

His tail whips around me as Alis fires off her weapon. A blast of ice launches my way, crashing into Ollie's tail and exploding into a cascade of icicles. The spears of ice freeze to his scales.

"*OH!*" Ollie lifts his tail up to examine, sending a spray of ice flecks my way. I sag in relief as I get a better look: no blood. The dragon rumbles, and Ollie giggles in my head. "*THAT KIND OF TICKLES!*"

Alis gawks at the scene as the dragon swings the make-shift mace through the air. He slams it back down onto the ground, shattering the ice. Shaken from her surprise, Alis puts two fingers to her mouth and blows a series of sharp whistles. The wolves whip their heads in her direction. She points at Ollie.

"Strike!"

The direwolves round on the dragon.

"*AH!*" Ollie cries as they spring toward him. "*NO! STAY AWAY!*"

He swipes his tail at the wolves, and one of them catches it in its mouth. The creature bites down, and Ollie's scream tears through my mind. Aloud, the dragon roars, and maybe it's just because I know it's coming from a child's mind, but it sounds terrified.

"Stop!" I sling more Fireballs at the wolf in a panic, all of them dissipating as Ollie whips his tail back and forth in an attempt to dislodge the wolf. The second direwolf dodges around the first, lunging for Ollie's neck.

"NO!" I snap my arms open, and an enormous ball of fire swells in front of me, growing until it's even larger than myself. Before I have a chance to loose it, Ollie catches the wolf with a claw, batting it aside and sending it skipping across the field.

I turn my attack toward the first, which still has a hold on his tail. Ollie desperately tries to lash it from side to side and tear it from the wolf's mouth.

"*HELP!*" Ollie cries, panicked. "*IT HURTS!*"

Adrenaline his crackling through my body, and my fingers twitch, but I don't launch my attack—I'm just as likely to hit Ollie as the wolf. I throw it at Alis instead, a wave of heat simmering over the ice as it races her way. She's forced to retreat, which buys me a split second to think. My mind races as I try to analyze my options. The Dungeon Core. Can I use its powers to summon stone from its catalog, or eat away ice beneath the Jorrian's feet? No, it's too chaotic. Our lines are mixed. Like with Ollie, any of my attacks that could hit a Jorrian are just as likely to hit one of our own. Panic tears through me as Ollie's fear spills into my mind. I have to protect him. I have to do better this time. But what can I do? I have magic at my fingertips, and I've never felt so helpless.

A shimmer of light catches my eye. I turn in time to see Alis raising her staff, its tip glowing a cold white. She points it at Ollie, and my heart skips a beat. *Check!* I think at Echo, starting to summon a new flame.

[Check: Paralysis spell.]

Nek tackles Alis to the ground as her staff fires. The arc of light goes wide, flashing into the sky before flickering out.

Mirzayael is still locked in combat with Biorne. Hetlanir is guarding Beryl as several of the Jorrian soldiers target the old dwarf. Nek is trying to wrestle Alis's staff away from her.

I can't do any wide range attacks when the troops are mingled like this. I'll have to get close—intimate.

"Ollie, keep still!" I call, dashing toward the wolf still latched onto his tail.

"IT HURTS," Ollie cries. But to his merit, he stops thrashing.

I summon another Fireball as I bear down on the wolf, squeezing my hands toward each other and condensing a white-hot ball of flames between them. The wolf growls as it catches sight of me, releasing the tail to turn and snap at me at the last second. Without letting go of the Fireball, I slam the spell into the wolf's waiting jaws.

The fire explodes. An inferno roars around me, hot wind combing through my feathers and buffeting my face.

[73 Fire damage dealt.]

My hand feels hot—painfully hot, which is a first. The wolf shrieks, a bone-chilling sound I never would have expected from such an animal. As the flash of fire dissipates, the wolf staggers away, its fur burnt and its muzzle charred black. My stomach churns at the sight. I did that. I burned a living creature.

The unease vanishes beneath a wave of fury as I catch sight of Ollie's tail, red welling up from the deep puncture wounds in his scales and beginning to stain the snow.

"Ollie—" I start.

A massive white paw crashes into the injured wolf, skipping it across the ice. Ollie curls around me, keeping his trembling tail carefully still.

"IT HURT ME!" he cries, nuzzling his face toward me and nearly knocking me off my feet. *"I HATE THIS. I WANT IT ALL TO STOP."*

I rub my hand over his nose, wishing I could give him the hug and physical attention he's craving, wishing I had the time or abilities to tend to his wounds, but the fight is still raging on. For him to truly be safe, we need to end this.

Alis blows another sharp whistle, and one of her wolves comes loping back to her. Nek breaks away from Alis, glancing back at the direwolf heading his way. He won't be able to defend against both of them.

Mirzayael's guards are losing, too. They're outnumbered and out-trained. It seems the only advantage they have against the Jorrian soldiers is that their fighters don't seem accustomed to fighting people as biologically diverse as arachnoids and harpies. Even so, the Fyrethians are giving ground.

Mirzayael is the only one truly on the offensive. Biorne backs away with each of her strikes, bracing against her advance. Her face is twisted in a merciless grin, and she cries out in victory each time she lands a blow and cuts another line of blood from Biorne's clothes.

But I can see something she doesn't: With each advancing step, she's drawn further behind Jorrian lines.

"Mir!" I shout, breaking away from Ollie. "Retreat!"

Mirzayael doesn't react to my warning, but Biorne does. "Now!" he cries.

Alis steps away from Nek, the wolf springing forward to defend her, as she whips her staff around to point at Mirzayael. The Jorrian soldiers also break away from the scouts, opening a line of fire. Mirzayael whips her head around in time to catch the blast of Alis's attack.

"No!" I lunge forward, summoning and hurtling a dozen Fireballs at the Jorrians. The guards scatter in the confusion, falling back toward Ollie as my attacks blast several Jorrian soldiers from their feet.

Mirzayael collapses, too.

"*Mir!*" I scream. Now that our scouts are separated from the Jorrian soldiers, I summon an inferno, launching it at Alis. The woman raises her staff, countering with a blast of ice. The two attacks meet midair and explode in an eruption of steam. Fyrethians and Jorrians are sent fleeing from the super-heated air, retreating back to either side.

"We warned you," Alis hisses, stalking over to Mirzayael's crumpled body. "My naive brother gave you a chance to go back to your caves, and you threw that in our face. Our mercy ends here, starting with your leaders." Then she points her staff again.

I follow the direction of her attack a hair two late. I summon another fire blast, intending to counter it, but Alis's attack is lower than I was expecting, and my fire goes high. The spear of ice heads right for Beryl.

Hetlanir dives in front of the dwarf, grabbing her and twisting to the side. The ice strikes both of them, and the pair go down.

"No!" I cry, torn between Beryl, now vanished beneath a cloud of frost, and Mirzayael, who's being dragged away by the enemy. "Let her go!"

I surge forward, but the direwolf leaps between me and the Jorrians, snarling and baring its teeth. Ollie's head cranes over my shoulder, growling back at the beast with a sound of grating boulders.

"Hold, Alis," Biorne says, grabbing her staff.

She scoffs. "You can't be serious. Even after they've shown their true colors?"

"We are guardians, not executioners," Biorne says. "We will take this one back home, where she will stand trial for her people's transgressions against the gods."

I roil with outrage. Not executioners? A trial? It's a sham. They're hypocrites. Bullies. Oppressors, every one of them!

"I won't let you," I cry, reaching for the Dungeon Core. It sits up at what I have in mind. Ice—it doesn't particularly like ice. But the scale of what I want—now *that* sounds fun.

The ground rumbles. A crack snaps through the air like a gunshot. A fissure zags across the ground, starting from my left and shooting toward the Jorrians like an arrow. Some of the soldiers flee, but they're only running toward their deaths. A crevasse opens beneath the flee-ing soldiers, swallowing their screams. It wraps around behind the Jorrians and then continues off to my right, placing a sudden chasm between them and their home. If Mirzayael wasn't there, I would have opened the fissure beneath their feet instead.

For a moment, the realization breaks through my fury, like a bucket of water dousing my flames. I just killed people. People who had dreams. People who were in love. People who were daughters—people who had daughters. They might have been the enemy, but they didn't choose which nation they were born into, and now they're gone, and people I don't even know will experience heartbreak and mourn their loved-one's loss. Because of me. I caused that pain and suffering.

And I didn't even hesitate.

Biorne steps back from the ledge. "This power," he says, stunned.

"It's Fyreneth's," Alis says. "They still wield her weapon; only it could achieve something of this scale. In defiance of the gods! You see, brother, it is not enough to expect them to submit. They must be exterminated."

For once, Biorne doesn't voice any dissent.

Alis raises her staff, and I have fire in my hands before I even realized I'd summoned it. I throw the flames her way, and she counters them with more ice, sending up another cloud of steam. This time, however, a second attack shoots through the air before the steam's had a chance to dissipate. The spell bursts between our groups, filling the sky with a sudden fog. As the air thickens, I can hardly make out Ollie's tail a few feet away.

"Back!" Nek calls through the dim. "Retreat and regroup!"

Feeling Ollie's fear reverberate through my mind, I put a hand on his hide. "Watch out for an attack," I tell him. "Flee back into the tunnel the moment they try anything."

But Mirzayael is still with the Jorrians. What do I do? I can't attack blindly or I might hit her. But what if they kill her while I hesitate? I need to dissipate this fog.

The ground rumbles, and this time it's not my doing. I blast a burst of fire into the air, hoping to burn off the mist, but it stubbornly persists. It's absurd. I can't have all this power at my disposal and still be so useless! I should have prepared more coming into this encounter. I should have planned on them attacking. I should have—

The fog vanishes as quickly as it appeared, the spell sustaining it apparently expired. It falls away in time to reveal an ice bridge spanning the chasm, and the last of the Jorrians racing to the other side. Even as they step back onto solid ground, the bridge behind them crumbles away, falling into the chasm. I look wildly around for Mirzayael, but she's nowhere to be found. On the other side of the crack, a wave of ice rises from the ground and then rushes away from us, carrying the Jorrian soldiers along like driftwood caught on a crest.

And Mirzayael is with them.

I can barely make out her form, draped over one of the direwolves' backs. My heart briefly soars, realizing they wouldn't take her if she were dead.

But how long do they intend to keep her alive before they execute her?

And her life isn't the only one on the line. If they make it back to Jorria, they'll tell the others Fyreneth's weapon is active once more. They'll march on Fyreneth's Fortress. They'll kill everyone.

I can't let happen. I won't let them make it back to their kingdom.

"*WHAT DO WE DO?*" Ollie asks.

I open my mouth. He could catch up to them. With a dragon on our side, it shouldn't ever have been a real fight in the first place.

But he's not just a dragon. He's a child. A hurt, terrified little boy, thrown into impossible circumstances. It's not his responsibility to put his life on the line. That's what adults are for.

I close my mouth, tapping back into the Dungeon Core instead. It takes more coaxing to get the Core to close the gap. That isn't *nearly* as fun as making it in the first place! But eventually, grumpily, it complies. Thousands of mana is sucked away as the fissure snaps shut.

Several Fyrethians cry out, alarmed, as the glacier crashes back into itself, but I'm already on the move, running after the fleeing Jorrians.

My wings threaten to balloon out behind me as the wind snags at them, and again I desperately wish I could fly. It truly must be a cruel magic system to give me wings—to tempt me with the possibility of flight, the one thing I've craved my entire life—only for them to be useless. I need thrust. I need lift! I need—

The realization hits me like a punch to the gut. Thrust. I have thrust. And lift! It's been staring me in the face this whole time. Mirzayael had even said as much: she believed I would achieve flight, but didn't think wind arcana was the answer. I summon a Blaze to each hand as I run, and turn my palms toward the ice.

What a fool I am. All this time, so set in my ways, only viewing flight from the aerodynamic angle of my aerospace degree.

But rockets don't need wings to produce lift.

Fire erupts from each of my hands, searing through the ice beneath me. I pitch forward, blown off my feet and throw my arms in front of me; the reverse thrust stops me from careening into the ground. Before I've even recovered, I flex my talons, then summon a flame beneath each of them as well. With four sources of thrust I come to a stop, hovering precariously in the air. I steady myself, bracing my arms and legs. Then I test each hand and foot, gimballing their flames.

Wobbling, I spread my wings for stability, and summon another flame beneath each of them.

[New Spell Obtained,] Echo says. [Jet.]

Six searing jets of flame, one beneath each limb, and I finally feel in control. Steady. Powerful.

And I'm in the air. I'm flying. I'm really flying!

I laugh, but the sound isn't full of delight, as I might have expected this moment to be. It's a victorious laugh. A sad, ironic laugh.

Because I know I've won.

I flare my flames and pitch forward, rocketing toward the enemy.

My flight is still precarious. A missile aimed in one direction. It will take time to master this kind of flight, but I don't need agility or precision right now. I just need speed.

I close the gap frighteningly fast. The Jorrians look over their shoulders as I approach, and they cry out, their faces full of terror. The sight fills me with grim satisfaction. They'll regret attacking us. They'll regret hurting Mirzayael and Ollie. I descend on the Jorrians, prepared to do what I must.

[Role Requirement.]

Echo's voice makes me flinch. Role Requirement? What does she mean?

[Role Requirement,] Echo repeats. [Now leaving The Dark Lord's territory.]

[Sanity Level: 95%]

"Ah!" My flames falter as an unexpected static crackles through my mind. I drop several feet before catching myself. Snuffing out one of my flames, I press a hand to my forehead. "What is this?"

[Role Requirement. The Dark Lord must return to her kingdom.]

[Sanity Level: 91%]

The static sharpens into pain. A numbness follows, beginning to cloud my thoughts and blur my vision. I pinch the bridge of my nose, but it won't stop.

[Sanity level: 83%]

A lancing headache starts from my skull and shoots down my spine. My flames sputter and I fall again, but I still manage to catch myself before I hit the ice. The Jorrians are getting away. I can't let this stop me. I can't let them take Mirzayael! I push forward, desperately trying to follow, and the static erupts through my whole body like I've been struck by lightning.

[Role Requirement,] I hear distantly as I crash into the ice. [Return to designated territory immediately. Sanity Level: 76%]

I try to push myself up, fighting the pain of every movement. For a moment I forget what I'm even doing, staring dumbly at the snow beneath my hands, watching as snowflakes melt against my skin.

The Jorrians. I have to go after them. I look up and can make out a blur of dark colors against the white, steadily retreating.

[Sanity Level: 64%]

It's becoming hard to think. Difficult to concentrate on anything but the all-consuming static, the overwhelming mental pressure urging me to turn back, retreat to my fortress, where I instinctively know I'll be safe—where the pain will stop.

But even giving into that urge is starting to seem like a remote possibility.

[Sanity Level: 52%]

Darkness tunnels around my vision. I have to get back. I need to protect Fyreneth's people. My people.

[Sanity Level: 46%]

I'm crawling. Which direction, I don't know. I just know I have to move.

[Sanity Level: 39%]

A blur overhead. Screams.

So many screams.

The darkness closes in.

CHAPTER THIRTY-ONE

TETHERED

Against my better judgment, I crack my eyes open. The stone room is lit with a soft yellow light, but even that sends lances of pain shooting through my skull. I squeeze my eyes shut once more and groan.

I'm alive. But how? And where am I now? Did the Jorrians take me?

I try to lift a hand to my forehead but find it hampered by blankets. Definitely not Jorria, then.

I'm in a bed. And a rather cozy bed at that, considering sleeping on two wings is still a new and mildly uncomfortable experience.

The next time I open my eyes, the mosaic pattern in the ceiling detailing a flaming harpy standing atop a castle confirms what I already suspected: I'm back in Fyreneth's Fortress.

The question is: How?

The Role Requirement ringing in my ears is the last thing I remember. The all-consuming pain it caused. The strange, foreign instinct it instilled in me to return to my palace. My lips twitch in the faintest ghost of a smile. *My* palace. As if I own it.

But what this Role Requirement did to me is no laughing matter.

Echo, I think, still too tired to try to speak. *The Role Requirement. Tell me about it.*

[The user's Role is The Dark Lord,] Echo says. [To fulfill this Role, the user must protect their Kingdom.]

Kingdom? I ask. *You mean Fyreneth's Fortress?*

[Affirmative,] Echo says.

I let out a long sigh. But I *was* trying to protect us. I was trying to save Mirzayael.

[The user left the zone designated as The Dark Lord's territory. Leaving the designated zone unprotected violates the Role Requirement.]

This rule isn't actually about people, then. It's about staying within the boundaries. It's so arbitrary. Absurd. Like a children's game.

A game whose rules could get me and others killed.

Are there other aspects of the Role Requirement I should know about? I ask. I'm frustrated with myself to have taken this long to dig into it. There was always something more immediate, more pressing, to spend my time on. I can't make that mistake again.

[Protecting the kingdom is the sole objective of The Dark Lord's role requirement,] Echo says. [This includes ensuring the safety of the kingdom and the survival of its citizens. Leaving the kingdom unguarded is prohibited. Allowing the kingdom to be destroyed is prohibited. Allowing the inhabitants of the kingdom to be eliminated is prohibited.]

"Yeah, I got it," I mumble. I'm anchored to this place.

I feel like the implications of such a revelation should bother me more, but at the moment, I'm far too tired to unravel the existential consequences.

Besides, there's other things to be worrying about.

Like Mirzayael.

"Hello?" Nek's soft voice rumbles across the room. "Did I hear a sound? Are you awake?"

In a herculean effort, I manage to lift my head. The felis is hesitating in the doorframe, his tail swishing nervously.

"Nek." My voice comes out in a croak, so I clear it and try again. "Is Mirzayael alright?"

Instead of answering, Nek turns back to the hall. "She's awake."

A dracid hobbles in on a walking stick a moment later, flanked by Nek. I recognize the dracid as Hetlanir's second in command, and after I get Echo to Check him, I am reminded his name is Torim. I study both their faces carefully as Nek helps the dracid sink down onto the edge of my bed with a grimace. No one else comes in after them.

"Mirzayael—"

"The Captain is fine," Nek says, pulling up a chair and heaving a heavy sigh as he sits himself. "She's resting in her room."

Relief floods through me. "Thank goodness." Battling gravity, I force myself upright, pulling my wings free from the blankets to drape over either side of the bed. I wince as something pulls in my left wing.

"That one was broken when we picked you up," Torim says, nodding to my wing.

"We were going to ask Beryl to help, but you heal remarkably fast," Nek adds. "By the time we got you up here, we couldn't find the break anymore."

I Check myself over just to be sure.

[HP: 90/100]

I should be fully healed in the next few hours. "Beryl's alright, then?"

Nek grimaces, and Torim's face becomes grave. My heart skips a beat.

"She's alive," Nek says. "But injured and resting."

"Hetlanir was not so lucky," Torim adds before I have a chance to feel relieved. His face twists in pain. "Our leader gave his life for hers. He must have thought highly of her." He passes a hand over his face, composing himself. "I am here in his place."

"I'm so sorry," I say, recalling the moment they were struck by Alis's attack. It happened so quickly. It hadn't even seemed to be that big of an impact. My stomach turns in a sickly way, realizing I had witnessed his death.

"It could have been worse," Nek says. "Everyone else made it back alive, thanks to you. We wouldn't have scared the Jorrians off—or recovered Mirzayael—without you."

I knead my forehead between my fingers. "Thanks to me? I don't even remember what happened toward the end. How did you get Mirzayael? I remember falling to the ice, and then..."

Screams. A shadow.

"It was your dragon," Torim says. "We couldn't make out much from where we were, but after you went down, the dragon lost it."

"Ollie landed right on top of them," Nek continues. "I was terrified he was going to kill Mirzayael. But he grabbed her, and he grabbed you, and then came right back." Nek leans back in his chair. "He's a good kid."

My heart swells with pride. "He is." And yet, I shouldn't have put him in that position in the first place. The poor child. It must have been terrifying. "I'd like to go visit him soon. Just to make sure he's okay."

"Of course," Nek says. "He's down in his cave, sleeping it off like the rest of us."

"Rest is important," Torim agrees. "We'll need the energy."

"For what?" I ask.

Torim frowns. Nek looks away.

"The move will be a lot of work," Torim says. "People are already packing."

"What do you mean?" I ask. "Everyone has already moved into the Fortress. Are there more still to come from your colony?"

He shakes his head. "I'm not talking about moving here; I'm talking about moving out. We need to leave the caves."

"Ollie managed to take out some of the Jorrians," Nek says. "But not all of them. They will have made it back to their kingdom by now. With news of our resistance. With news of..." He trails off awkwardly, but Torim doesn't let the words go unspoken.

"With news of Fyreneth's weapon being wielded once more," he says. "With news of Fyreneth herself reborn."

My skin prickles where the Dungeon Core is secured to my arm. It's my fault. I'm the reason these people will be targeted.

"If the Jorrians come in numbers, we won't be able to beat them," Torim continues. "We must risk fleeing back to our caves on the other side of the arctic. It's dangerous, but our only hope for survival. If we leave soon, we may have enough of a head start to avoid any more battles with the Jorrians. One thing is certain: we cannot idle here as an army readies to march on us."

He's right about that. If we do nothing to prepare, they'll overwhelm us with sheer numbers. Mirzayael hardly has two dozen guards trained to fight, and even if we added all of Torim's scouts and every able-bodied adult in the mix, it would still pale in comparison to what Jorria could amass.

There's only one problem with the resettlement idea: I can't go with them.

I sigh, rubbing my eyes. How do I even begin to explain this dilemma? And should I? I have no right to ask these people to stay here and die for me. But if I tell them I can't come with, some would surely stay.

Nek and the dracid, likely. But if they stayed while the rest left, I'd be condemning them to death.

I don't know what to do. I need to spend some time thinking through all this. Not to mention, no decision-making process is robust without first gathering all relevant information. I need to speak with Ollie.

"I understand," I say, meeting the other two's grim looks. "Do what you have to do to keep everyone safe." I push the blankets aside, grimacing against my weariness and aching muscles. "Speaking of which, I need to go see Ollie."

Torim dips his head in acknowledgement, and Nek stands up, offering the dracid a hand to help him to his feet. Torim pauses, however.

"Fyre," he says. "I want you to know that your actions yesterday were honorable. You risked yourself for all of us. What you've done for the dracid here, what you've done for all of us, does not go unnoticed."

Nek nods his agreement. "You may not have been born here, but you are no outsider. You are one of us."

Their words warm me, even as they break my heart.

On Earth, I never really could figure out how to be part of a community. Friends drifted away. My wife and daughter left me—deservedly, I might add. I always kept my distance.

Yet somehow, here, it's come naturally. Finally, everything seemed to feel *right*. Without even realizing it, I began to call this place home. Not the city itself—not Fyreneth's Keep or the Fortress—but the people. They felt like home.

And now that they have to leave, I wish more than anything that I could go with them.

"Thank you." I force myself to smile. "That means more than I can say."

"We'll take our leave, now," Torim says. "There is much to prepare for."

"Let me know when you've returned from Ollie's cave," Nek adds. "When you're ready, I'll take you to see Mirzayael."

"Thank you," I repeat, slipping out of the bed. I wince as I straighten up, cracking my neck and stretching my wings and arms.

I've much to prepare for as well.

"Ollie," I call as I head down the passage, trailing my hand over the railing. Since achieving a nigh inexhaustible mana pool to tap into, I've made little alterations to the passages every time I've passed through them, smoothing out the floor or stairs, adding handrails, and adjusting the placement of torches and lighting runes that Mirzayael and the other scouts set up. Slowly but surely, I've been shaping the caverns into a home—one that might soon become abandoned.

"Ollie, are you there?" I echo the thoughts mentally as well. I feel his mind stir.

"FYRE?"

The boy sounds miserable, and when I step out of the passage and onto the landing at the top of Ollie's cavern, I see he looks it, too.

The dragon is curled atop his small, eclectic hoard, full of bones, rusted plate armor, glittery rocks, and even some broken weapons and pottery. I suspect Mirzayael's guards have been indulging him with findings from Fyreneth's Fortress, passing off whatever they deemed too broken to fix.

He lifts his head as I enter. *"FYRE! I'M GLAD YOU'RE OKAY."*

"Me too," I say, heading down the staircase to his floor. "Thank you for saving me. Nek told me what happened. You were very brave."

"*I WAS SO SCARED!*" Ollie says, his wings fluttering in agitation. "*I THOUGHT YOU WERE HURT! YOUR MIND WAS SCREAMING.*"

"I'm sorry," I say. "I didn't know that would happen."

"*ARE YOU OKAY NOW?*" he asks.

"Yes, I think so." Though really, I'm not so sure. Being magically bound by something like this is troubling. I don't like that this Role Requirement is infringing on my free will. "But enough about me. How are you doing? How's your tail?"

Ollie curls it around to show me. There's a jagged white scar on his tail where the direwolf had nearly ripped off a chunk of flesh. I gently run my hand over it.

"I'm sorry you got hurt."

"*IT'S OKAY,*" Ollie says. "*BERYL HEALED IT FOR ME. SHE SAID I WAS A MIGHTY DRAGON.*" He grins, showing all his pointy teeth. "*I AM MIGHTY!*"

I laugh. "You are!"

Just as quickly, his mood dips. "*BUT FYRE. I HURT SOME PEOPLE.*"

"I know," I say, patting his snout. "That's okay. You couldn't help it. And you saved Mirzayael's life."

"*OKAY,*" Ollie says, but I can sense through our mental bond that he's holding back something else.

"What is it?" I prompt.

Ollie wiggles uncomfortably. "*I DID SOMETHING REALLY BAD.*"

"It's okay to hurt people if you're protecting yourself," I say.

But he shakes his head. "*SOMETHING WORSE THAN HURT-ING.*"

"Killing?" I ask, as softly as I can. Nek said he'd landed on top of the Jorrians. It doesn't take an aerospace engineer to figure out how that might have turned out for the soldiers.

Ollie buries his face beneath his claws. "*YES. BUT EVEN WORSE.*"

I frown. What's worse than killing? "It's okay," I say, patting his nose. "You can tell me. I won't be mad. Promise."

His mental voice drops down to the dragon-equivalent of a whisper. "*I ate people.*"

A cold shiver washes through me. Whatever I had been expecting, it wasn't that.

I force myself to respond, hoping he didn't notice my momentary shock. "It's okay." I pet his nose, trying to coax him out from under his claws. "You didn't mean to, did you?"

"*NO!*" he wails. "*I WAS JUST TRYING TO PICK THEM UP AND GET THEM OUT OF THE WAY! BUT THEN I MIGHT HAVE BIT TOO HARD AND THEY GOT STUCK IN MY TEETH AND THEN I SWALLOWED SOME—*"

"Okay," I say, cutting him off as I attempt to not let my horror show. "Yes, I understand. It was an accident."

He nods emphatically. "*BUT FYRE. DOES THIS MAKE ME A CANIMAL?*"

I pause. "A what?"

"*A CANIMAL,*" he says miserably. "*AM I A CANIMAL NOW?*"

"I... don't know what that is," I say, wracking my brain.

His mental voice dips back down to a whisper. "*Someone who eats people.*"

"A cannibal," I say, chuckling at the absurdity of the conversation. "I mean, technically speaking, a cannibal is someone who eats a member of their own species, and since you're a dragon..." But I doubt Ollie is interested in the semantics of the issue.

It raises an uncomfortable question, however. Is he no longer a human? Am I? I've admittedly adapted to being a harpy relatively quickly, but my change is much less significant than what Ollie went through. Are you your mind, or are you your body?

Or some combination of the two?

"No, Ollie, you're not a cannibal," I say, giving his nose a hug. "And you didn't do anything wrong. Any people you hurt was on accident, and you did it to save my life. You're a big hero." And I'm certainly glad he's on our side.

When I lean back from the hug, I Check Ollie out of habit.

[Name: Ollie]

[Species: Frost Dragon]

[Class: Hunter]

[Level: 44]

[HP: 2500/2500]

[Mana: 850/850]

[Role: The Dragon]

Echo, what are the role requirements of Ollie's Role? I ask.

[User does not have access to that data.]

It was worth a shot.

"Ollie, can you check your stats for me?" I ask. "What does your Role mean?"

Ollie tips his head to the side for a moment. *"ECHO SAYS MY ROLE IS THE DRAGON. IT MEANS I'M A SERVANT TO THE DARK LORD AND AM SUPPOSED TO HELP HER DEFEND*

OUR KINGDOM. DEFENDING A KINGDOM SOUNDS FUN! WHO'S THE DARK LORD?"

"That would be me," I say, troubled by this reveal. So the roles don't have to bind you to a place, they can bind you to other people as well.

"WHAT'S IT MEAN?" Ollie asks.

It means I'm the bad guy. But I can't tell Ollie that. "It means I have to protect Fyreneth's Fortress."

"THAT'S COOL," he says. *"YOU'RE A PROTECTOR, JUST LIKE ME!"*

I smile sadly, wishing I had the bravery to tell him what it really means for the both of us. We'll be trapped here, alone, as the rest of the Fyrethians escape. And, alone, we'll have to survive the Jorrian's attack.

But I don't have the stomach to scare him like that. Not when I've just settled him down a bit. Instead, I give his nose a tight hug.

"I have to go talk to Mirzayael now," I tell him. "I'll come get you when it's time for dinner, and we can talk again then."

"OKAY," Ollie says, though he sounds a little sad that I'm leaving so soon. His mind is brimming with loneliness. *"FYRE? I'M NOT GONNA SEE MOM AND DAD AGAIN, AM I?"*

The knife in my heart twists another notch. "I don't know," I tell him honestly. I can't lie about this. "I'll do what I can to see if it's possible. But it might be a very long time."

"YEAH," Ollie says, and even though that brimming loneliness spills over into a throbbing pain, I can feel he's not surprised, either. *"THANK YOU, FYRE. I LOVE YOU."*

My throat tightens up and I blink rapidly, holding back the tears, as I lean forward to press my head against the boy's. "I love you, too, Ollie. I'm going to do everything I can to take care of you."

A caring warmth passes between our minds. *"I KNOW."*

Chapter Thirty-Two

SPIRITUAL SUCCESSOR

I stop outside Mirzayael's chambers. Her door is closed. It occurs to me now I've never actually been inside before. It's taken me this long to realize it's always her coming to visit me—in my lab, or the throne room, or Ollie's chamber, or anywhere else I might be investigating. I should have gone to her before now.

Gently, I push the doors open. The light from active wall runes are glowing from inside, so I poke my head in.

The chamber is decorated sparsely. That's not out of place for Fyrethians; most don't have a lot of personal belongings. But Mirzayael's is even more bare than others I've seen. Apart from a chest for clothes, a water basin, and a stand for her armor and spear, all that's left is a bed.

Designed to accommodate arachnoid physiology, it's more like a nest, or perhaps a kind of giant beanbag chair, made from moss, furs, and whatever else could be scrounged up. That's the next thing I should work on fixing: find a way to produce textiles.

Then again, there won't be a "next thing" to fix when everyone is gone.

"Are you just going to stand there all day, or are you going to come in?" Mirzayael asks from inside the cocoon of blankets.

"Sorry," I say, slipping through the door. My wing gets snagged on the handle on the way in, and I end up stumbling into her room. Still not used to those things, sometimes. "I didn't want to bother you if you were sleeping."

"Well, I'm not," she grumbles.

I smile. If she's feeling well enough to be cranky, then she must not be too badly injured. "Nek told me you've been seen by healers?"

"Haven't lost any more limbs, if that's what you're worried about." Mirzayael struggles to push herself upright within the folds of her nest, but I gesture for her to stop.

"Stay there. Just rest. I'll come to you."

"I'm not helpless." Yet, she sags back into the bed.

I gently sit down next to her. "I never said you were."

She blows air out her nose, looking up at the ceiling instead of at me. "I hate being useless."

"You're not—"

"I was!" Mirzayael spits, and I flinch back in spite of myself. "I was entirely useless against the Jorrians. All my life I've trained as a guard, as a scout, as a Captain, and when it came down to it, I fell to just one of their attacks, and was used against my allies." She turns her head to the side, away from me, but I can still make out the pain and disgust in her expression.

"It wasn't your fault," I say. "We weren't prepared. None of us were."

"I'm pathetic," Mirzayael says. "A disgrace."

"Hey. Enough of that." I give one of her legs a shake through the bedding. "You're allowed to feel hurt. You're allowed to feel helpless, and frustrated, and upset. But I won't sit by and listen to you talk down to yourself. You deserve so much more than that."

Mirzayael scoffs. "A guard who can't guard—a captain who can't lead—deserves nothing but demotion."

I roll my eyes. "Oh, please. Now you're just being dramatic."

"You're an outsider," she says. "What do you know of our values? What do you care if I am punished for my failings?"

I soften my expression. "I care quite a bit about you, Mirzayael."

Beneath the blankets, I feel her tense up. "What do you mean?"

I chuckle. "What do *you* mean, 'what do you mean?' We've spent every day together for the last two months. You've shown me around your home. Introduced me to your people. Taught me how to live here. Perhaps most importantly, you see me for me, not for some idol. Your honesty and kindness has meant quite a bit to me. The time I've spent here has been more meaningful than the years—decades—I spent in my previous life."

Mirzayael snorts, finally looking at me and searching my face. "Kind is not a word often used to describe me."

"Well, perhaps I can see through your tough front in a way that others can't," I say. "I know you're so blunt and abrasive only because you care very much about protecting those you care about. More so than your own image."

Mirzayael's face pinches in an unfamiliar expression. Annoyance? No... Guilt.

"You're being far too understanding with me," she says. "Especially after how I've treated you. I continued to distrust you after all the help you offered. Always suspicious of ulterior motives."

I attempt a smile, but it turns into a grimace. "I've never blamed you for that. In fact, I felt it was entirely deserved, considering my initial actions on this world unwittingly resulted in the loss of your leg." My gaze drifts down the covers, where I estimate her injured leg is tucked away. My heart aches at the thought. "I'm so sorry I hurt you. I should have apologized months ago. I just never knew how to broach the subject. I... I think I was afraid."

Mirzayael's expression goes stony. "Fearing me is understandable, given how I've treated you."

"What?" I say. "No! I was never afraid of you."

She gives me a skeptical look, and I laugh. "Well, not after the first day or so. But I wasn't afraid of you. I was afraid of saying something that might have pushed you away." I nervously fiddle with a corner of her blanket. "In my previous life, I always ended up alone. Everyone I cared about drifted away. It was my fault. I never knew how to show I cared, what to do or say. So I avoided it. I kept to myself and buried myself in my work—the only thing that I ever felt I understood. But since coming here, for the first time, I finally feel comfortable in my own skin. Like I'm free to be the me I always should have been. As if this mask I never knew I was wearing had been cast away. And as a result, everything has come so much easier. *Talking* to people is so much easier." I take a breath, letting out a nervous laugh as I realize I'm rambling. I raise my eyes to her once more. "Well, I've gotten better, at any rate. So, in conclusion, I'm sorry I hurt you. I'd do anything to take it back."

Mirzayael's face softened over the course of my speech, until by the end she was smiling faintly at my meandering apology. "You know, I don't give two shits about my injured leg." I start to object, but she cuts me off. "In fact, if I'd known your arrival would cost me a leg, I'd have cut one off years ago. More than that, I regret that I played into your fear of being alone." She grimaces. "I'm sorry that I've kept you at arm's length."

I smile sadly. "I never took that personally, for what it's worth. Everyone else seemed to receive the same treatment."

Mirzayael shifts uncomfortably. "The lost Fyrethians should have been welcomed with open arms, not treated with suspicion."

"Luckily for them, not everyone here shares your level of wariness," I tease. "I don't believe any of them feel alienated."

She passes a hand over her face. "Rationally, I know I shouldn't be so suspicious. It's just... hard to let others in. It exposes us to the possibility of betrayal. And there's always people like the Jorrians out there, waiting to take advantage. If you don't allow others to get close, you can avoid the pain when they disappoint you. Or leave."

I wonder if she's talking about the lost Fyrethians, or her parents. I wonder if she even knows.

Timidly, I put my hand over hers. "Well, my walls are down. My door is open, if you ever want to venture inside."

She looks at me with a mix of hope and hesitation. "But I thought you and Dizzi... never mind."

"Dizzi? What about her?" I ask, tipping my head. What has she got to do with any of this?

"Forget I said anything," Mirzayael hurriedly says. "I was being foolish."

It slowly dawns on me. "You're asking if she and I are... an item?" I laugh. "You *are* being foolish."

"I'm sorry," Mirzayael says, flustered. "You just seemed to get along so well."

"A common interest in inventing does not a relationship make." I shake my head, grinning. "Don't get me wrong, she's a very nice girl. But she's half my age. I'd be more prone to see her as a daughter. Or apprentice, perhaps." My chest faintly flutters. "Why do you bring this up now?"

"No reason," she says quickly. "It's irrelevant. At any rate, I should be getting up now. Make sure all the others from the confrontation are alright."

Quickly, the lighthearted mood evaporates. I don't even have to say anything; Mirzayael can read it on my face.

"What?" she asks. "What's wrong?"

I grimace. "Your guards are all alive, but Beryl was injured. And Hetlanir was killed."

Mirzayael's expression crumples with despair. "Hetlanir. I should have gotten to know him better. He seemed a good leader. He shouldn't have died because of my rashness."

I shake my head. "It wasn't your fault. I suspect the conflict would have happened no matter what any of us said or did. What Biorne wanted, to banish us back beneath the ice, wasn't just. But even if we had caved to his demands, Alis was looking for blood and an excuse to spill it. What happened happened, and now we need to move forward." I squeeze her hand. "With Hetlanir dead and Beryl injured, your people need a leader, Mirzayael. They need you."

She closes her eyes and shakes her head. "I am a guard, not a leader. I protect, I don't rule. You should be the successor. They already worship you anyway."

I snort. "You know I don't want to be worshiped. But my station is beside the point. The Fyrethians are planning to flee, and they'll need someone who knows this world to guide them." I hesitate before adding, "I can't go with you."

"What?" Mirzayael's gaze snaps toward me. "Flee? Where? Why can't you come?" She struggles to push herself upright. "What's happening?"

"There's something I never told you about the strange magic I have," I admit. "The visual magic that provides me with statistics of what I can see."

"You've mentioned it before." Mirzayael frowns. "What has that got to do with anything?"

I take a breath. "Ollie and I each have a unique stat that no one else in this world seems to have. A quality called a 'Role.' I never really understood what it meant before, so I didn't think much of it. That was a mistake. My Role is The Dark Lord."

Mirzayael searches my expression. "I don't understand. What does that mean?"

"I think it means I'm the villain," I admit, and now it's my turn to glance away. "The Role Requirement is that I must stay within my domain—Fyreneth's Fortress—and protect it. The name of the Role itself, The Dark Lord, is indicative of what part I have to play, whether I wish it or not. Clearly, I've been set up as the antagonist to overcome. I fear, when the Jorrians attack, the end will not be favorable for me."

Mirzayael blinks. "You think you're evil?"

I shrug helplessly. "According to the System, it seems."

"Fyre."

I look up in surprise. That's the first time she hasn't called me Outsider.

"That's the stupidest fucking thing I've ever heard."

I cough out a laugh. "I, uh. Sorry? What?"

"You heard me," she says. "That's idiotic. You think you're evil? Listen to yourself for half a second."

"Well, that's not exactly what I meant," I say. "I just mean that the System is trying to push me into such a role—"

"Absurd," Mirzayael cuts in. "You've done nothing but help people since you've gotten here. If you aren't Fyreneth's literal reincarnation, you're her spiritual successor, at the very least. And the fact that you'd even entertain otherwise makes you dumber than I gave you credit for."

I blink. "Is this supposed to be a pep talk?"

"So you're supposed to be a dark lord," Mirzayael says. "What makes you think that's a bad thing?"

"The... name?" I say, holding up my hands helplessly. "I'm not sure what else that could imply."

"Fyre, we live in a cave," Mirzayael says flatly. "It's dark. Literally. If you're a lord of this place, you'd be a dark lord."

"I don't think that's what—"

"We also live at the pole," Mirzayael continues to bull her way through the conversation. "Half the year we don't get much sunlight. Right now, it's literally dark for most of the day. Dark Lord. There you have it."

I can't help but laugh. Her explanations are absurd. Far too blunt and literal. And yet... do I have any evidence she's wrong? "This is certainly a unique way of looking at it."

"What does this System of yours say about your Role?" she demands. "Does it specify that the Dark Lord is evil?"

I ask Echo to repeat her definition of my Role Requirement. "No, actually. It's just that I have to defend my kingdom."

Mirzayael looks at me pointedly. "Yes, that sounds very evil."

I chuckle, but my laughter quickly dies out as I recall what spurred this conversation in the first place. "That's not all, I'm afraid. During the Jorrian fight, I discovered the limitations of this Role: I can't leave Fyreneth's Fortress."

Mirzayael raises her eyebrows. "That *is* annoying. I would not want to be restricted in such a way. Even if the restriction was mostly irrelevant. It sounds as though you will be fine as long as you stay within our realm?"

"That's the issue, unfortunately." I smile sadly. "Nek and the others have already started to organize an evacuation. The plan is to leave the Fortress and retreat back to the caves in the Ash Peak mountains. If they move quickly, they should be able to escape before the Jorrians arrive. However, I won't be able to come."

"What?" Mirzayael snaps. "Absolutely not. We are not abandoning our home."

"That's not up to me," I say. "And I have no right to try to dissuade—"

"Ridiculous." Mirzayael throws her bedding aside and stumbles her way to her feet, kicking off a blanket. "You have just as much of a say in the future of our people as anyone else."

"Careful!" As she trips out of her bed, I catch her arm. "You shouldn't be up yet. You need to be resting still."

"Rest is a luxury for when we're not preparing for a siege." Mirzayael uses my support to steady herself. "Now where is Beryl? We need to discuss war plans."

"She's also in bed recovering." I follow Mirzayael to her chest. "Like you should be. She was gravely injured."

"If she's well enough to flee across the arctic, she's well enough to talk." Mirzayael snaps open her trunk and tears out a cloak, throwing it around her shoulders. "Go gather the others. Nek, my guards—any of Hetlanir's scouts. We'll hold council in Beryl's chambers in ten minutes."

I wisely opt to make no more objections and hurry out of the room.

Chapter Thirty-Three

FYRENETH'S WILL

We gather around Beryl's bedside. There's no sign of injury. Her bloody clothes have been replaced, and all the cuts and bruises she sustained from the Jorrians healed. But she's never looked so old to me before, and she rests there with her eyes closed, breathing slowly, despite being awake.

Nek, Dizzi, Mirzayael, Torim and I are all seated by the bed. Mirzayael clears her throat.

"I'm sorry to disturb your recovery, Lord Beryl, but it has come to my attention that the decision has been made on behalf of the community to flee back toward the Ash Peak mountains, and this is an option I will not accept."

Good to see she's as diplomatic as ever.

The others exchange uncomfortable glances.

Beryl cracks her eyes open. "I did not agree to this course of action lightly." Her voice is quiet and gravelly. "But the safety of our people should always be our top priority."

"If we stay here, we'll be slain," Torim says. "Surely you see we can't fight them? Their kingdom outnumbers us ten to one."

"I see that your fear of conflict has clouded your reasoning," Mirzayael shoots back. "This is our home. If we lose it, what does that make us? What does that say of Fyreneth's legacy?"

"Homes can be replaced," Beryl sighs. "Lives cannot."

"I hate to say it, but they're right," Nek adds. "I don't want to leave, but I don't see an alternative. Protecting our families matters above all else."

"And how will they be protected out on the ice?" Mirzayael demands. "Fleeing for indefensible mountains almost twenty leagues away. Now that they're watching for us, we will all be picked off before we even arrive."

"Do you have any alternatives to suggest?" Dizzi asks. "'Cause look, I'd rather stay here, too. This place—these people—are all amazing. But if Jorria wages war, we can't hope to defeat them."

"Perhaps that's true," I cut in as Mirzayael's eyes begin to twitch. "Though we hold a defensible position here. We don't need to beat them with numbers if we can cause their troops to bottleneck and pick them off in more manageable numbers."

Torim grumbles. "If at all possible, a direct conflict should be avoided entirely. If we can escape without any further loss of life, that is the path we should pursue."

"Then what about Fyre and Ollie?" Mirzayael demands. "Don't they deserve to live as well?"

The others look at me, perplexed.

"What does she mean, Fyre?" Dizzi asks.

I grimace. "Regardless of what you all decide, I have to stay here. My Role—the magic I have access to—prevents me from leaving."

"Prevents you?" Dizzi cries. "What does that mean?"

"Exactly what it sounds like," Mirzayael snaps. "She can't leave."

"I'm... *obligated* to stay here and protect the Fortress," I say. "It seems it is my duty to fight for this place, whether or not anyone else remains. Ollie's magic also binds him to me, meaning he might not be able to venture far from the caves either. Honestly it's lucky he hasn't hit a range limit yet while he's been out hunting. Perhaps, due to his larger size..."

Mirzayael can probably tell I'm getting sidetracked by theories, as she cuts in once more. "Regardless, she can't leave, and that's all that matters."

"It sounds less like a type of magic and more like a type of curse," Torim says. "You do not know how to remove it? How was it placed on you originally?"

I shake my head. "As soon as I woke up here, it was already a part of me."

"It's not a curse," Nek says. "It's Fyreneth's will."

I open my mouth to object, but his words strangely make sense. It would have been her will to protect this place and her people, wouldn't it? She would have wanted her kingdom to endure even after her death. Maybe it's why I woke where she died, why I was reborn in her form. Some ghost of her lived on, etched into the stones of this place, and when I woke up here, it shaped me as well.

Certainly, the idea that I've inherited her last wishes is more palatable than being perceived as her reincarnation.

I give Nek a strange look. "Perhaps there is something to that idea."

"But why didn't you tell us before?" Dizzi demands. "We can't just leave you to die! Did you really think we'd be okay with that?"

"I didn't think it was my place to object to your plans," I say. "The safety of your own people comes first, and I didn't want to risk that."

Beryl lets out a labored sigh. "Fyre. You are as much part of our people as the returned Fyrethians."

"Moreso," Mirzayael says. "You've been with us longer and given us so much."

"We're not going to leave you here," Nek fiercely adds.

Torim clears his throat uncomfortably. "Are you suggesting we don't move forward with the migration? Even if Fyre occupies an important position of authority within the community, is it enough to risk the lives of the rest of us?"

"That's precisely what I didn't want," I start, but Beryl silences me with a sharp gesture.

"Until I finally keel over, I still intend to lead this community," she says. "But I can't make the right choices without being provided all available information. In the future, you will be forthcoming with me about any hesitations you might have or obstacles you might foresee. Is that understood?"

I dip my head in apology. "Of course. That makes complete sense."

"Then it's settled, is it?" Mirzayael asks. "We remain and fight for our home."

"I'm in," Dizzi says. "Whatever skills I can offer, I'd love to help. Especially artificing skills. I'm really good at that. Actually, that's about all I have to offer."

"I will also lend my aid however it's needed," Nek agrees.

Torim frowns as everyone turns to look at him expectantly. "Retaining our homeland would be preferable. But I want assurances I won't be leading my people into a deathtrap." He looks at me. "You mentioned we might have the advantage of being in a defensible position. Do you have any ideas to back up your claim?"

I hold up my wrist. "The Dungeon Core—Fyreneth's Crown—whatever you prefer to call it, is a powerful tool. I can already think of a dozen ways it could assist in a siege. So long as I remain within range of the mana ore and am able to pull more mana from its source, the Core will have access to some extremely powerful options. It could open chasms beneath the approaching armies. Collapse walls on top of them. Change the passages they walk through, leading them into a labyrinth of dead-ends. And that's just the mundane approaches involving moving rock about. Altering chemical and thermal properties could prove just as potent."

Torim looks a little startled by my suggestions. Even Nek's eyebrows are raised.

Dizzi just laughs. "I'm glad you're on our side."

"Indeed," Mirzayael says. "But we could speak strategy all day. First we need to establish if anyone else wishes to express doubt. If you believe we should still make a bid for the Ash Peaks, now is the time to say so."

Silence stretches between us. Even Torim merely shakes his head.

"Good," Beryl says after a moment. "Go tell the rest to stop packing. We have a siege to plan for."

As the others hurry about, scurrying off to track down the scouts and put a stop to the migration preparations, I pull Mirzayael aside.

"I was truthful when I said we will likely win the siege," I tell her. "Down here, we do have home-field advantage. However, I worry this plan is shortsighted."

"You mean mistaking winning the battle for winning the war," Mirzayael says.

I nod. "The mana ore down here is incredibly potent, but it's not an unlimited resource. If this becomes a war of attrition, we will eventually deplete the resource that is keeping us alive, and after that we'll be defenseless."

"Are you suggesting we should flee after all?" Mirzayael says.

"No. Not today." I chew on my lip, mind flipping through and discarding a dozen different ideas. "But mobility will be necessary eventually."

"What are you suggesting?" she asks.

"I've been mulling over an idea," I say. "More of a vision, really. I hadn't intended to implement it anytime soon. Building up the community's resources comes first. But given the Jorrian attack, I think the timeline needs to be expedited."

"What sort of vision?" she asks.

"Do you recall the runes Dizzi and I discovered beneath the kingdom? The ones designed to move stone?"

Mirzayael raises an eyebrow. "You wish to raise Fyreneth's Fortress in anticipation of the Jorrian's siege?"

"In a manner of speaking," I say. "However, it would not be exactly as Fyreneth originally intended. This version would be far more defensible."

"Explain," Mirzayael says.

So, I do. I lay out all my plans, ideas that have been gestating since Dizzi and I first learned the Fortress was designed to be unearthed. "We'll need to be conservative with our mana stores," I add at the end. "And I'll need to enhance the structural integrity of the Fortress, first. I'm worried moving so much earth might cause parts of it to come apart."

At first Mirzayael looks awed, then she laughs. "Your dreams really do know no bounds. But do you think we'll have time for such elaborate preparations?"

"I'm not sure," I admit. "If Beryl and the others sign off on the idea, Dizzi and I can get started on the work right away. But if we don't finish in time..." My stomach twists into a knot at the idea. We'll be thrown into battle. A real war. If I can't stop it, people will die. "We'll need to prepare for battle regardless. But I'll do everything in my power to keep this kingdom safe."

Mirzayael smiles at me fondly. "I know you will."

Chapter Thirty-Four

No Time

My mind moves through the stone, buoyed along by the Dungeon Core. The Core is delighted by all the work I've been giving it of late. We zip through veins of rock like electrons on a circuit, flashing through the network of spells strung together throughout the fortress by threads of mana-conducting stone. It's enormously complex—more than my mortal mind can comprehend at once. But for the Dungeon Core, picturing all these intricate and interconnected threads of rock is trivially simple. I wonder if it's some sort of magical AI, like Echo. Even the Dungeon Core doesn't seem to know what it is. Not that it ever really thinks about it.

We finish threading the last bits of mana ore into the throne room, where every spell circle in the palace eventually feeds back to. It's tricky to find a path that doesn't interfere with another spell circuit. Add too many spells, make the system too complicated, and one small, overlooked error could bring down the entire network. Which is why we have to be careful. Take our time with each new strand.

If only time was something we had in abundance.

A vast distance away, I can feel something faintly tugging on my arm. I want to resist the pull and take one more pass through the stone circuit the Dungeon Core and I just built, ensuring the stone was transformed into the right element properly, and along the correct pathing, but I know better than to leave my body for long. Reluctantly, I release the Core's interface and let the physical sensation guide me back.

"...Fyre? Hey, wake up!"

I crack an eye open, and Dizzi's face is before me.

"How long?" I ask.

"Seventy-two seconds," she says, letting go of my arm.

We'd decided not to let me immerse myself in the Dungeon Core's interface, separated from my body, for longer than I could reasonably hold my breath. Just in case, you know, my body stops remembering how to breathe while my mind is elsewhere. Perhaps overly cautious, but merited, given the potential worst-case scenario.

"Is the circuit done?" Dizzi asks.

"I'd like to triple check it, but yes, I believe it's ready to be wired into the network." I glance around the cavern and find the stone Dizzi's marked with a spell circle. I head over to it. "Is this complete?"

"Yep," Dizzi says, planting her hands on her hips as she looks over the chalk drawing. "Ready to go."

"Then let's." I put my hand on the stone and nudge the Dungeon Core into action. As it's done five times before now, it begins eating away at the chalk, carving the spell circle into the surface of the stone. At the same time, I give it the mental image it needs to shape the boulder into its appropriate form. A few seconds later, and the spell circle is now embedded in a giant, vertical slate of shale.

"My turn?" Dizzi asks.

"Go for it."

She puts her hand on the carved spell circle, and it lights up with her magic—a lime green color. The magic wraps around the fin of rock, reinforcing the material while maintaining its thin and lightweight nature. The light also spreads through the fin and vanishes into the nearby rock, following the circuit of stone I'd created back to the throne room. Using the Dungeon Core, I cast my mind toward the throne just to be sure.

"It's connected," I confirm.

"Whew." Dizzi lets go and wipes a sheen of sweat from her brow. "Six down, six to go."

"We should finish by the end of the day, if you've got the energy to keep going," I say.

Dizzi nods, expression determined. "Doesn't matter if I'm tired. We have to keep going. These control surfaces aren't going to build themselves."

I just hope they'll be enough—and that we're fast enough. Creating the dozens of house-sized stabilizers all across the fortress is only step one, but it's the step I need Dizzi for, given her understanding of spell circles and magical networks. And we have to finish all this before we can move to step two.

"We better head to the next location, then," I say. "No time to waste."

"Right." Dizzi grabs her water flask and takes a swig as we pack up and get ready to move.

She's taking all this magic work a lot harder than I am. Is it because so much of what I do is through the Dungeon Core's interface? None of it is really *my* magic. All I can do without the Core is summon fireballs. Perhaps it's taking on the arcane strain in my place. Interesting. Something to experiment with, perhaps—at a later date.

Just as we're preparing to leave, a kitten-sized white spider comes rushing down the hallway. It skids to a stop at my feet, looking up at me expectantly. Up close, it's clearly made of silk, like a crocheted toy. There's a piece of paper strapped to its back.

I lean down to retrieve the message, then unfurl it and read it aloud for Dizzi's benefit.

"Status report: Troops have been spotted at the foot of the Jorrian Mountains," I read. "They still appear to be gathering. We now estimate two days before the siege—less if they start marching today."

Dizzi grimaces. "Two days isn't a lot of time."

"We might have more," I say, considering what I'd do in their circumstances. "Given they're still gathering, and the limited daylight is nearly over, I suspect they'll at least wait until tomorrow, so they can be sure they're not marching into a trap. They've seen the canyons I can open. If they wait until the next daybreak, we'll have at least another 18 hours before they start moving. With only five hours of sun, they might camp on the ice overnight, and close the final distance over another day after that. That should give us three to four days, I think."

I flip the paper over and write out a quick 'received' message to send back to Mirzayael.

"I'm still not sure four days will be enough," Dizzi says.

"It will have to be." I send the spelled spider off, then turn for the next passage. "Let's make sure it is."

Stage two of the plan is tricky. In theory, it should be simple: transform all of the stone at the base of Fyreneth's Fortress with another. Like the dracid chamber which I altered to have better insulation, only on a city-wide scale. However, in practice, it isn't so simple.

"I can only select one type of stone at a time," I explain to Mirzayael and Dizzi over lunch, as I take a rare break to scarf down some stinger stew. "And the Fortress is made of hundreds of types of rock. I should be able to, say, select all the granite in the area at once and replace it, however I won't know the consequences of such wide-scale alterations until after the change has taken hold."

"You're worried it might cause structural failures," Mirzayael surmises.

I nod. "The Dungeon Core gives me incredible power over geology, however it provides me no insight into the implications of such changes. I desperately wish I could run some simulations before committing to each of these alterations. In the meantime, I'm going to have to limit myself: start small, altering just local areas, and gradually increase the range as I grow more confident in the structural stability. Dizzi and I have tested it out on a small scale and the theory is sound, but given the stakes, there's no room for error."

"How much have you already transformed?" Mirzayael asks.

"Uninhabited houses in the lower city, mostly," Dizzi says. "We figure no one will miss a couple of abandoned buildings if we break them."

"That's not much," Mirzayael says.

"I know." I run a hand over my head, ruffling the feathers there in place of hair. "We need to scale much faster."

"The troops have begun to move," Mirzayael reminds me. "It will be less than two days until they arrive."

"I know," I repeat, my stomach churning. "But this plan has to work. It has to."

"It's an ambitious plan," Mirzayael says. "But right now we need to survive today. I'll prepare my troops. And you need to make sure you save enough mana for yourself. Don't let the Dungeon Core consume everything and leave you defenseless."

"I won't," I assure her. But in the back of my head, I'm rationing how much mana I can afford to keep for myself. It's already going to be tight.

I try to take a sip of my soup, but there's a pit in my stomach. The lack of sleep over the last couple days probably hasn't helped, either. "I should get back to it."

Mirzayael nods, then pauses to regard me. Her brows knot in a concerned frown. "You're doing alright, aren't you?"

"Best I can manage, given the circumstances," I say.

"Make sure to get some rest before they arrive." Mirzayael glances at Dizzi. "*You* make sure she stops to rest."

"I'll take a nap once I'm done with the stone conversions," I promise. Of course, that doesn't mean I'll actually be able to fall asleep. I spent all of the previous night tossing and turning, anxieties and images of the coming battle waking me before I even fully fell unconscious.

"I'll do my best," Dizzi tells Mirzayael. "But ultimately, I don't think I'll really be able to stop her from working if she's set on it."

Mirzayael huffs. "Disappointingly true."

I stand, taking my bowl over to the basin for cleaning. "Let me know if anything changes."

"Of course." Mirzayael sets her half-eaten meal down as well. I guess I'm not the only one who lost her appetite. "Good luck."

We'll all need it.

\#

[Area selected. Mana cost: 2853]

My eyes are closed so I can focus on the Map Interface. *Initiate material replacement.*

[Initiating.]

Through the Dungeon Core, I can feel the stone change. Bits of the rock are replaced and instantly filled in with different ore the Dungeon Core had already consumed and stored in its inventory. The new rock tastes less dense. Crunchy and light. A hint of sourness. The Core finds it very tasty, but even it isn't tempted to consume rock it's already eaten once before. That's just weird.

[Transformation complete.]

I open my eyes. Visually, it doesn't appear any different. Running my hands over the stone, it doesn't feel different, either. But I know it is.

"Next?" Dizzi asks.

"Keep going," I say. Over 80% of the conversion is complete. Still, there's hours left of work to do.

"The next zone is this way," Dizzi says, consulting the grid she'd laid out as we walk.

It helps to have some of the work offloaded from my mind. I've enough to keep track of as it is. I shake my head, trying to dispel some of the heavy weariness that's gathered over the last few days. It's fine, though. I can push through. Soon enough, we'll all have much bigger things to worry about than a little sleep deprivation.

"Here we are," Dizzi says after a time, gesturing to the walls.

"How many more zones?"

Dizzi consults her notes. "Sixty-four down, eleven to go."

We're so close. I place my hands on the stone and close my eyes, summoning the Dungeon Core once more.

[Area selected. Mana Cost: 2931]

As I initiate the conversion process again, a familiar staccato of footsteps comes racing down the hall.

"Fyre!" Mirzayael cries, her voice distant. "Fyre!"

"Here!" I call back, removing my hand from the wall. She's coming herself, rather than sending one of her spell constructs as a messenger. I know what that must mean. My heart sinks.

[Conversion complete.]

Mirzayael skids around the corner, fear stark on her face. I've never seen it so plainly visible before. No attempts at disguising her anxiety. She looks at me, and I don't even need her to tell me.

"They're here." I didn't finish in time. Will I be able to do the rest from the throne room? It will cost more mana to reach deeper into the fortress and alter the stone remotely. Mana we desperately need for the coming fight.

I suppose we won't have a choice. We're out of time.

"Fyre?" Mirzayael says.

I exhale all my hesitations and worries out in a single breath. "Let's go. We've a battle to win."

CHAPTER THIRTY-FIVE

THE EVE OF BATTLE

The Jorrian troops send vibrations through the ice and down into the stone as thousands of armored boots stomp against the ground in time. Through the Dungeon Core, I count them by the number of footfalls. I determine they've also come with frost and dire wolves by the variance and weight in their gait. Their progress is slow and intentional as they approach the entrance to our kingdom.

Ollie and a few harpy scouts confirm what I sense before retreating underground. I seal the exit after them, shutting us all away beneath the ice.

"*WHAT DO WE DO?*" Ollie asks, resting his head on the floor through an open balcony designed for his access.

I send him a wave of confident reassurance. Or at least, I hope it comes across that way. "*Don't worry. You'll be safe down here.*"

Ollie rumbles with unease, and his low tone thrums through the rest of the war room, which is tense and quiet.

Torim remains glued to a basin of water. He spelled it with scrying magic, which allows him to look through it to any other bodies of water that are linked to its network. His scouts erected a sheet of ice on the surface the previous day, through which Torim has been carefully watching ever since.

Mirzayael surveys the table in the middle of the room, and I finish creating stone figures to add to the surface, each representing a troop of soldiers. Dizzi is fluttery and nervous, madly scribbling out calculations on a slate at the end of the table. Beryl is seated in a chair next to her, but her eyes are closed, and her breathing is labored. Despite her insistence at being present, I'm not sure we will be able to count on her leadership. Instead, when anyone asks questions, they always turn to Mirzayael or me.

"The remainder of the army should reach the entrance within the hour," Torim reports. "Though some troops appear to have stopped further back. I suspect that's due to what they know of Fyre's abilities from the fissure she opened on them before."

"We should have expected such wariness," Nek grumbles. "It was a good strategy."

A cold pit forms in my stomach; it had been such a good strategy, it's exactly what we plan to open with now. But the Jorrians are still too dispersed for our plan to be effective, and waiting too long makes me nervous.

"Should we strike anyway?" Nek wonders, no doubt having similar thoughts. "Better to take a smaller portion of their army than to wait for them to try something first."

"I'd rather open with a decisive blow," I reply hesitantly, unsure if it's even the right call. "It would be ideal if we could stop this battle before it begins." And perhaps stop any unnecessary bloodshed, too.

"Ideally," Mirzayael repeats, the word dripping with skepticism. "Things are never so easy. But if we open the ground now, enough of the army will survive that they can swarm into the open hole."

"That shouldn't be a problem, right?" Dizzi asks, absently looking up from her notes. A line of chalk is smudged across one cheek. "Fyre can just collapse all the tunnel networks before they get in."

"Except my scouts are still down there," Torim says. "They haven't finished setting up the scrying network."

"How close are they to finishing?" I ask.

Torim frowns. "An hour or two more, I think."

"That will take too long," Mirzayael decides. "Call them back now. Whatever current surveillance spells are active will have to be enough. As soon as your scouts are back within the Fortress, we'll make our move."

"Yes, Captain," Torim says, flicking a finger over the water. The image shimmers, and while it doesn't seem he can transmit sound through the spells, he catches the attention of a few dracid on the other side and gives them a series of hand signals. He repeats the process at least a dozen times.

"Everyone remember how to activate the spiders?" Mirzayael asks the rest of us as Torim works. She gestures to several dormant spell constructs she'd created over the last week, the white silk spiders lined up on the edge of the war table like a parade of stuffed animals.

"They're so cute!" Dizzi says, gently nudging one with a claw.

Mirzayael scowls, swatting her hand away. "They are not cute, they are tactical communication equipment."

"They're cute tactical communication equipment."

Dizzi acting silly seems to be how she deals with stress, while Mirza-yael only seems to get more blunt and impatient. It's not a good combo, each of them escalating the other's stress like a runaway chemical reaction.

"We know how to use them," I assure Mirzayael, attempting to offer her a reassuring smile. Her glare shifts to me, but when she meets my gaze, her expression softens.

"Something's happening," Torim interrupts. He's switched back to the outside view. "They're activating some type of magic."

Mirzayael and I hurry over to look. The troops have peeled away to allow a group of unarmored people through. They're all wearing thick, white robes, with the symbol of an eye stamped into the front. A few of them carry staffs; they're kneeling along the ground, bare hands pressed to the ice.

Check, I think, attempting to deduce the soldier's levels and magic specialties.

[A target must be within direct line of sight to be Checked,] Echo says.

It was worth a shot. Though even without Echo's help, it's not difficult to guess what branch of the army these individuals comprise.

"Mages," Mirzayael says as the ice lights up in an aurora of colors as their magic penetrates the ground.

"What are they doing?" Torim asks.

"Let's not wait and find out," I say. "Torim, what of your scouts?"

"Still in the tunnels, but they know what area to keep clear of," he says.

"And my guards are all within the Fortress's main cavern." Mirzayael nods to me. "When you're ready."

Nervousness flutters through me, and I take a steadying breath. I know what I have to do. I won't be taking these lives directly, face-to-face and by my own hand, but when the ground vanishes beneath the soldiers and they fall to their demise, their deaths will weigh on me nevertheless.

And yes, I now understand the animosity they harbor. I know all too well that they chose to come here with deadly force, intending to slay the Fyrethians—my friends and family. They are inviting the inevitable loss of life upon themselves.

But they are still *people*, people who once were innocent children untainted by the hate of a society they didn't choose to be born into. I mourn the circumstances which brought us here. I mourn what I must do. And even now, a part of me is trying to puzzle out a better solution. One where everyone can walk away from this alive.

I look at Ollie. At Dizzi, Nek, and Mirzayael. My actions led to the Jorrians being here today. I am responsible for this situation. I am responsible for the Fyrethian's lives. And despite all that, they believe in me. Not because of some myth, but because of what I've done to help. Because of how we've all come to depend so much on one another. They're putting their lives in my hands, and I'd do the same for them in a heartbeat.

Mirzayael is still watching me closely, expression faintly concerned. I offer her a weak smile, and let out my breath. "Okay. Here we go."

Between the mage's first move and my response, the battle officially has begun.

Closing my eyes, I dive into the Dungeon Core's interface. The perception of my surroundings balloons outward, spreading through the stone, city, and surrounding caves. By now, every inch of the Fortress falls within the Dungeon Core's range, all the Fog of War long since eaten away by my explorations. I press toward the surface, where stone gives way to ice.

It's not the Core's favorite material to consume, but I can't afford to let it be picky today. I mentally trace the area where I want the chasm carved. It's a radius around our cave system's entrance, which we left sealed but obvious, in order to ensure the Jorrians would congregate around it. Ideally, we would have waited until more of the Jorrian soldiers had pressed closer, but taking out the mages will have to be the next best thing.

In anticipation of this moment, Mirzayael and Torim's soldiers were informed of which area of the cave system to avoid, and that is the area I mentally highlight now—a giant cylinder of stone right beneath the mages and surrounding troops. It makes me nervous to be doing this when not all Fyrethians are back within the Fortress's safety, but I'll have to trust Torim when he says his scouts will be fine. Bribing the Dungeon Core with some extra mana to chew on, I point it toward the Jorrians and then loose the sentient stone to do what it does best.

Large swaths of rock vanish as the Core eats everything up, replacing tunnel systems and caves with nothing but emptiness. The small handful of things it couldn't consume in those tunnels—living bugs and mushrooms, mostly—fall into the open chasm. As it finishes with the stone, it moves to the ice, intending to eat that as well—but reels back as pain and distaste lance through us.

"Ah!" I flinch, the hurt echoing in my mind like the stab of a sudden headache.

[Authority to manipulate material denied,] Echo says. [Material is Attuned to a different mage.]

"What is it?" Mirzayael grabs my shoulder, and I wince as her fingers dig into me. She forcibly relaxes her grip. "Are you alright?"

"I can't remove the ice they're standing on," I say, opening an eye and massaging my still throbbing forehead. "It's Attuned. I'm not sure if they're Attuning it now, or if they brought their own pre-Attuned ice to feed into the ground. Either way, the Core won't be able to eat it. Or 'see' it, for that matter."

"What does that mean?" Dizzi asks, looking up from her calculations.

"It means it won't show up on the Dungeon Core's interface," I say. "If the Jorrians burrow through the ice and enter the cave system, both the people and their Attuned elements will be invisible on the Core's Map. The Jorrians might be able to use this to navigate without me noticing. We'll only know where they are if we see them in person."

"Clever," Dizzi remarks, her feathers ruffling nervously, reminding me that she's the youngest strategist in the room by a wide margin. "Too clever. They've come prepared for you."

"But not for me," Torim says. "This is precisely why we created the scrying network in the first place. Don't worry. We're still one step ahead."

"What about the scouts?" Nek asks. His hair is beginning to rise, meaning he's only slightly less nervous than Dizzi. "Will they make it back in time?"

I'm scared of closing off passages behind our scouts in case I unknowingly cut them off—or worse, hurt someone—but maybe gravity can buy us time. "The Jorrians may not know about the chasm that has just appeared beneath them," I say, thinking aloud. "If they're not actively reinforcing their ice, they could fall through. Either we can wait for their troops to overwhelm its structural integrity, or we can try to disrupt it ourselves."

"*OH!*" Ollie says. "*ME! CAN I GO BREAK THROUGH THE ICE? IMAGINE THEIR FACES.*" He giggles as his tail whips back and forth, and I mentally see an image of the dragon exploding up through the ground. "*SURPRISE! IT'S ME AGAIN!*"

It would certainly be surprising, I'll give him that. But I won't risk putting Ollie in danger if I can avoid it. I still have options with the Dungeon Core. I mentally scan through its various features. Which would be the most effective? If I pick wrong and do anything to clue the Jorrians in—

"They're moving," Torim says.

My attention snaps back to the scrying pool. Mirzayael swears. The mages have opened a hole in the ice and soldiers are beginning to rappel through. Then the scene shatters, and the water clears.

Torim grunts in disappointment. "They broke the scrying pane."

I tap into the Dungeon Core's Map and frantically pan through the cave system. The Jorrians themselves, or any ice structures they might be forming within the chasm, are invisible to me, but I grab a boulder from the wall where I suspect they're descending and yank it from its surface, launching it across the cavern. It passes through the air unhindered, crashing against the wall opposite. Then I grab both walls, and slam them together. Enormous chunks of mana disappear from the Dungeon Core's reserves. Far below, I feel impacts on the ground, but whether it's Jorrian or debris from the stone, I have no idea.

"I'm shooting blind," I say to the others. "I'm not sure where they are or which way they're going. Torim?"

He's flipping through the scrying panes he still has access to. "I'm looking. Most of the scouts are halfway back. I don't see any—no, wait. There." The image in his water settles. Jorrians appear at the end of the tunnel.

"Where?" I ask, trying to orient myself and identify how this maps to what I can see through the Dungeon Core. But as soon as the word leaves my mouth, the Jorrian seems to point right at us, and the image flickers out.

"Screw this," Mirzayael says, snatching up her spear. "I'm going to go escort those scouts myself."

"Mirzayael," I try to object. If she'd been the ones in those tunnels, she would have wanted me to leave her there, even if it meant locking her on the side with the Jorrians. She'd never abandon her own soldiers, though.

Mirzayael fixes me with a critical look. "How long do you need until the Fortress is ready?"

"I don't know," I admit. "Dizzi and I weren't able to finish the Fortress's preparations before the siege began."

"Is it close enough? It doesn't have to be perfect." She crosses to the table and taps several of her spell constructs on the back, their runes lighting up with the blue of her magic.

"Maybe." I frown, trying to guess if our progress is within my factor of safety. There are so many moving parts. Too many things to keep track of. Add the pressure of the battle on top of all that, and it's nearly overwhelming. I start to have Echo run some calculations.

"No," Dizzi cuts in before I get very far. She taps her slate. "I've been crunching the numbers. We can't raise the Fortress in its current structural state. I estimate we need to convert at least another seven percent."

"How long would that take?" Mirzayael asks.

Dizzi looks to me.

The Fortress is so close to being complete. At the rate I'd previously been going, it would take another four hours to finish converting the stone, readying it for the Fortress's ascension. But we don't have four hours. How long until the Jorrians make it to our doorstep?

"Seven percent?" I confirm with Dizzi. "Are you sure?"

"Completely," she says, squeezing her chalk. "I've mapped out the areas to convert that will provide the most structural stability and will require the lowest volume of conversion."

I'm nervous to accept her word without double checking the numbers myself—everyone's lives are at stake if we're wrong—but we don't have time, and more importantly, I need to have faith in her. We all have our own pieces to contribute if we want to win this battle. We have to trust each other to do our part.

"One hour," I tell Mirzayael. "I can be ready in an hour."

Mirzayael nods curtly. "Good. I can buy you that." Several of her silk spiders jump from the table and scurry away. "I'm sending the constructs ahead to help find and direct scouts back toward me. I'll have them return with information on when and which passages you can close. Ideally, we'll get everyone out before the Jorrians reach us, and you can seal the tunnels behind us. But if it comes to it, my guards have been waiting for a rematch."

"In the meantime, do whatever you can with whatever chance you get," she tells me. "Shuffle around the passages. Work with Torim to reposition the scrying panes. Attack if the opportunity arises." By the time she's done speaking, she's already heading for the door, signaling sharply for Nek to follow.

My stomach roils with worry. I don't want the sight of her walking away to be the last memory I have of her. I hate the idea of her heading out to battle while I remain in here. I won't be able to protect her from afar.

Swallowing down my anxieties, I call after her. "Be careful!"

She stops to look back at me with a smile. "Do not worry for my wellbeing. Things will unfold very differently this time. The Jorrians may rule the surface, but now they are in our domain."

Then, she's gone. Any more words I might have had for her die on my tongue. I hope she's right. She better be.

Just like with Dizzi, I need to believe her when she says she can do this. I have to trust that she will be okay. Faith isn't something that comes naturally to me. But for Mirzayael...

I choose to have faith in her, at least.

"We need to prepare for the next phase of battle," I say, turning to Dizzi. "Gather the harpies in the throne room as soon as possible."

"Ay, Captain." Dizzi salutes and flies off as well.

I turn to Torim next. "Alright. Where are your active scrying panes located? Show me on the map. I will try to keep them intact while making life difficult for the Jorrians..."

The next twenty minutes pass in a blur. With Dizzi's calculations, I begin remotely converting more of the Fortress's stone. Simultaneously, I work with Torim to fill a few caverns and reposition some of his scrying panes to assist with and prepare for Mirzayael's troops.

It's almost too much to juggle, and yet it feels like not nearly enough. We should have withdrawn Torim's scouts earlier. I should have stopped Mirzayael from entering the cavern to begin with. I should have...

No. I can't dwell on hypotheticals. That will only distract from the present. Perhaps in an ideal scenario I could have approached this all differently, but now, in the moment, I will simply do everything I can think to do with the resources available.

I'm so busy untangling these threads, that I only notice Ollie's discomfort when he verbally growls. I start, shifting my attention to him. He's agitated. Uncomfortable.

"*What's the matter?*" I ask him. He must be upset that I'm not letting him go with Mirzayael this time.

"*ECHO SAYS YOU'RE IN DANGER,*" Ollie says.

My stomach lurches. His Role Requirement. I didn't think it would activate if I stayed out of the battle myself. "*What is she saying?*"

"*SHE SAYS I HAVE TO PROTECT YOU.*" Inwardly, Ollie winces. Outwardly, he peels his lips back in a frankly terrifying expression. "*BUT YOU DON'T LOOK LIKE YOU'RE IN DANGER! I DON'T KNOW WHAT I'M SUPPOSED TO DO.*"

Are the Jorrians getting closer? Are they preparing something that will put me in harm's way? Is it simply just the fact that the siege has begun? Impossible to say. But if Echo is prompting him to do something, and punishing him if he does nothing, it will only be a matter of time before he won't be able to stop himself from trying to fulfill the requirement. We need to address that before it gets worse. My mind races for a solution.

"Would patrolling the Fortress help?" I ask. *"You can keep an eye out for any enemies that might have snuck into the main cavern."* Not that I think any could have made it this far in such little time, and I did try to seal all the countless cracks and tunnels leading into the Fortress's chamber, but it's theoretically feasible, and therefore it would be protecting me against an unlikely but possible threat.

Ollie tips his head, listening quietly for a moment. *"YEAH, ECHO SAYS THAT'S OKAY!"*

I sag in relief. Loopholes. If we survive today, I will have to dig deeper into these edge cases.

"SHE SAYS IT'S NOT AS EFFECTIVE AS FIGHTING BAD GUYS BUT IT WILL STOP THE SANITY STAT FROM GETTING WORSE," Ollie adds. *"WHAT DOES THE SANITY STAT DO?"*

Not a solution, but a stopgap, then. But if we can delay it long enough, then hopefully we'll all be out of danger and the role requirement will expire on its own.

"Doesn't matter," I say. *"Go ahead and start keeping an eye out for any Jorrians who might have snuck in. If you see anything, let me know, but do **not** engage."*

"YAY, SPYING!" Ollie dives off the balcony and out of sight.

I know this probably isn't the most optimal solution. But it's the best I can come up with on the fly that will keep Ollie safe, and that will have to be enough.

"Lord Fyre?" Torim beckons me back over to his scrying pane. "This passage is clear; we should be able to seal another group off here."

My heart flutters at the title. 'Lord' seems to be used for anyone of high esteem, but it's too close to The Dark Lord for my liking. Is this some sort of self-fulfilling prophecy? Was I destined to this Role, no matter what I did or how I approached it?

Mirzayael would smack me for thinking something like that. As she said, the Role is only about protecting my kingdom, and these people have done nothing wrong. They deserve protecting. If that makes me the bad guy, then I don't want to be on the side of good.

I follow Torim's directions and quickly have the Dungeon Core address the tunnel in question; the Core plays with the cave like a sandbox, disintegrating rock and summoning more elsewhere, plunging the path into deadly chaos.

"Done," I needlessly tell Torim as that pane's image goes dark. I check in on the Fortress's progress. Still a ways to go, but there are even more things I need to prepare for. "If you would excuse me, I need to go speak with the harpies now. I'll be out in the throne room if you need me."

Before I step out, I look at Beryl, who has remained quiet throughout all the previous battle preparations. I'd thought she'd fallen asleep, actually, but now I see her eyes are cracked open, carefully watching our war board.

"Lord Beryl?" I ask. "Do you have any suggestions?"

The dwarf grunts. "Nothing more than you all could suggest. The brain mush isn't as firm as it used to be, these days. And you seem to be well versed in strategy. I trust you young ones with whatever decisions you make. You're in command."

I swallow down the nerves that threaten to flutter from my stomach. "Thank you. I won't let you down."

In the throne room, Dizzi and most of the harpies have already gathered.

"What's going on?" one of the harpies asks. His name is Meritis, Echo tells me. He's covered in a delicate pattern of white and brown feathers, but it's his age that hits me. He can't barely be in his teenage years, and I'll be sending him into a warzone. "Will we not be needed in the fight?"

"You will be," I say. "It's highly likely this battle will be decided by air superiority."

"But we're underground," another objects. "We won't have much opportunity to gain any height on the Jorrians, except for in caverns. With respect, Lord Fyre," they hastily add.

"Pay no respects: speak to me bluntly," I say, heading over to the side of the room that had gradually been cannibalized by work benches and chemistry equipment. The harpies hurry after.

"We can't waste time on pleasantries in war, or afford to hold back an opinion that might save lives if spoken," I continue. "But to address your concern, we will be dealing with much more open air than that found in tunnels and caverns. You all have an air affinity, yes?"

"They do," Dizzi confirms.

"Good. Then these will be your weapons." I stop before a large stone basin I'd created with the Dungeon Core. It's nearly overflowing with hundreds of baseball-sized chalky grey orbs.

"Rocks?" Meritis asks.

"Bombs!" Dizzi cries with far too much enthusiasm.

She and I have been working on these for a while now. It took a lot of trial and error to stabilize the formula, but the end product of a chemistry-and-magic-fusion explosive device is something that fills me with equal parts pride and horror.

"These weapons are highly combustible and designed to explode on impact once the runes are activated with a spark of mana," I explain. "Even so, I feel I must caution you all to do everything in your power not to drop any unintentionally."

"But we're underground," a harpy objects. "We can't get enough space to use weapons like these."

"Leave that part to me," I say. "We're going to need every flight-capable individual we have access to, so as much as this hurts to hear, I'd like to ask all of you to abstain from the fight until we're ready to launch your platoon. Even if the battle makes it into the city, please do not engage. We may need every one of you."

At least that means I'll be keeping young harpies like Meritis as far removed from the battle as I can.

"Is it true, then?" he asks, hope and excitement flickering in his eyes. "Will you be raising the Fortress today?"

When Dizzi and I had finished decoding the chain of movement runes beneath the city, we'd taken our discovery to Beryl. The implication of the spell circle was clear enough, but Beryl had insisted I raise the possibility with the rest of the population as well.

"It's their home as much as mine," she'd said. "The choice should be everyone's."

We'd called a townhall after that to share the news and discuss what was to be done. Unsurprisingly, the decision had been unanimous.

"Yes," I tell the boy. "If the guards are able to buy me some time, we will restore her Fortress within the hour."

Despite my qualifier, the harpies excitedly murmur to one another.

"We won't let you down," Meritis says. And then he begins to cheer, and the others soon join in. "Praise Fyreneth! Long Live the Fortress!"

Praise Fyreneth, I think along with them. *I hope we're about to make you proud.*

Chapter Thirty-Six

THE DUNGEON CORE'S LAIR

As Dizzi begins organizing the harpies and laying out our plan, I turn to Fyreneth's throne.

Are you ready? I ask the Dungeon Core. *It's time to interface with the throne.* Since our Map Interface and range now encompasses the entire Fortress, we can remotely alter the state of anything in the entire city, no matter where we are. However, I can only activate spell circles that I'm in direct contact with. But that's where the Dungeon Core comes in. If I can hook it directly into the throne's spell network, then thanks to our Pact, I'll also be able to access the Fortress's spells from anywhere in the kingdom.

The Core buzzes with excitement. Oh? Is it time? Will it finally have a lair?

I tip my head at this. I'd forgotten that was something the Dungeon Core had asked about before. It had mentioned having a lair in the past, and wanting a new one; the brief impressions I'd received had been of a vast area it had influence over. A spiraling mountain of stone—or had that actually been a city?

"Huh." I guess in a way, I've been working toward exactly what the Core desired. "Yes, I suppose you will have a new lair."

Yay! The Core vibrates in my mind. When? Now? Can it have its lair now?

"In just a moment," I say, placing my hand on the stone. *Echo?* I think. *Add the Dungeon Core to my Inventory.*

[Dungeon Core added to Inventory. 1/1 slots occupied.]

The bracelet vanishes from my arm. And disturbingly, the Core and all of its interfaces vanish from my mind. I'd grown so used to its presence that it now feels as if there's a vast emptiness there. An unsettling quiet. My arm similarly feels strange and bare.

I hold out my hands. *Remove the Dungeon Core from my Inventory.*

[Dungeon Core removed.]

The bracelet blinks back into existence once more, falling into my outstretched hands.

Ahhh! The Dungeon Core cries, its mind swiveling around wildly. What was that?! It got all dark and nothing-y!

"Sorry," I say to the Core. "But if you're going to make this your lair, then you'll no longer be acting as my bracelet."

It did not like that place. Do not do that again!

"I won't," I tell it. "That was a one-time thing. Now..."

I set the spiraled bracelet atop the throne, where the backrest curves forward to cover the face of whoever might be seated there. I mentally nudge the Core, and it ingests my instructions and begins to work. The throne comes alive, crawling over and through the bracelet, weaving it into the circuit of spells that are imprinted into the stone. I step back, not touching the throne or the Core. Yet I can still feel them in my mind as if I'm tapped into the network directly. When the movement stops, the core is woven into the headrest of the throne. If one were to take a seat, it would be positioned over their head, much like a crown.

I grin. "It worked."

The Core is excited, too. Oh, oh! This is what it wanted! This was what it has been waiting for. Finally! So much space. So much room to stretch its influence. *Now* it feels at home.

The sentiment surprises me. Does it understand the concept of home? Am I adding a level of interpretation to its abstract thoughts? Or perhaps has it absorbed my own feelings for this place? Because it's right: we are home.

I smile fondly, patting the ruby stone now embedded in the throne, before taking a seat myself. I close my eyes. *Ready to protect our home?* I ask.

YES! The words startle me with the strength of their conviction. The Core will not let anything happen to its lair. It belongs to the Core! No one is allowed to take that from it!

I detect the undercurrent of a threat to the Core's thoughts. I might be worried if it wasn't on our side. That protective instinct is something we need right now.

Alright then, I think. *Let's finish the rest of the stone conversion. You know what to do after that?*

The Core does. It's not as excited about that part of the plan as I am, but it knows the plan comes with a *lot* of mana, so it's willing to indulge.

I chuckle, focusing our attention deep, deep beneath us. "Glad you're willing to cooperate." I locate the last few sections of rock Dizzi identified, and with the Core's help, begin the conversion.

I'm at it for less than ten minutes before a scream rips through my mind.

"AHHHHHHHHHHHHHHHH!"

I flinch back, slamming my head against the throne. I clamp my hands to my head with a hiss. The Dungeon Core also jumps in alarm, jittery and bouncing around my mind as it searches for the source of my panic.

"*Ollie?*" I call to him. "*Ollie, what's wrong?*"

But the screaming doesn't stop. I try to calm the Dungeon Core down, but it's hard to instill a sense of calm in the artifact while the unfiltered panic of a seven-year-old is ping-ponging around my head. I stumble off of the throne, looking wildly about.

"What's going on?" Dizzi asks. "Are you alright?"

"Somethings wrong with Ollie."

"What is it?" she asks. "Do you need to go to him?"

"Yes." It's taking all my restraint not to sprint from the room now. "Dizzi, the Core knows the plans for the Fortress. It's ready to execute them as soon as I'm finished with the conversions. But it will need one of us to guide it along the right path. The spells in the throne can be operated independently from the Core's influence. If I don't make it back, you have the controls."

Dizzi looks horrified. "What? Fyre—"

"I believe in you," I say, already hurrying toward the door. "You'll do fine!"

Dizzi's terrified expression is the last I see of her as I dash from the room.

"*Ollie?*" I call, rushing down the stone halls of the Fortress. "*Talk to me. What's happening?*"

"*FYRE?*" Ollie finally replies, panicked and pained. "*FYRE, HELP ME!*"

"*I'm trying to!*" I hurry down through the main palace, and out onto the city streets. I look around the cavern wildly, but there are no dragons flying about. "*Ollie, where are you?*" I turn to the cavern's only exit: the passage at the Fortress's main gates where Mirzayael and her scouts had entered the tunnels. My heart squeezes painfully tight.

His words pour through my mind in a panicked stream of consciousness. *"I'M SORRY I WENT IN THE TUNNELS BECAUSE ECHO SAID I COULD HELP YOU BETTER BUT THEN I GOT LOST AND THEN THE BAD GUYS ATTACKED ME PLEASE HELP FYRE HELP QUICK IT HURTS!"*

I summon fire to my hands and point them toward the ground. I haven't had time to practice flying since the Jorrian confrontation. It had been the heat of the moment then—something I wasn't even sure I could do until I tried. But Ollie needs me now just as much as Mirzayael did then. And this time, I won't fail.

[Jet activated.]

My stomach drops through my feet as I rocket into the air. I gasp in a startled, exhilarating breath as I launch myself over the city streets and toward the cave system opening, closing the distance in a matter of seconds. Butterflies light up my chest as I stabilize my flight just in time to land, stumbling before the cave opening. I'm shaking from adrenaline, and can feel my heart thumping fast and loud in my chest.

I can fly. Despite the severity of the situation, the thought still summons a thrill in me. I finally achieved my dream—all it took was death and rebirth, first.

Distantly, a roar rumbles through the cave. I sprint into the tunnel, following the sound.

Don't be rash, my subconscious whispers in my ear. *Stay level headed. Don't run into a situation unprepared. Get eyes on the scene before engaging.*

But Ollie's in danger, and he's hurt. I can't afford to be methodical.

Even so, I can still go about this with as much situational awareness as I can muster.

As I run, I dip my mind into the Dungeon Core's interface, relieved I can still sense it as keenly from this distance. I knew that should be the case, given the Core's range is the size of the city itself, but it's still a relief to find the theory verified. Using the Core's interface, I focus on the stone passageways outside the Fortress. In a few tunnels, I can feel where the pebbles are being disturbed—people are running through the caves there. But are they friend or foe? Without more information, I can't risk attacking them, so instead, I avoid them.

Further ahead, massive boulders are rolling around. Cracks splaying through the wall. A battle scene taking place at an oversized scale.

Ollie.

My legs and lungs burn as I run. My brain is spinning a mile a minute. I'm searching all the nearby caves, watching the stones for any sign that someone might be approaching, while at the same time directing the Dungeon Core to continue its work on the Fortress. My mind is split so many different ways, but I can't stop now. Everyone is counting on me.

When I reach the room that contains the oversized fight, I have to stop myself from skidding out the end of the tunnel and into the chamber ahead. Instead, I press myself to the wall and peek around the corner.

"FYRE!"

"I'm here!" I tell him. *"Just give me one—"*

A beam of ice blasts through the tunnel, narrowly missing me only because I'd kept close to the wall. I activate a Blaze and keep the fire close to my palm: dim but dense with mana. I run my hand over the ice, burning through a narrow gap that lets me out into the cavern beyond.

It takes me a moment to compute what I'm seeing.

A giant writhing mass of white takes up half the chamber, like living coils of rope in unending motion. Ollie is in there somewhere—I catch glimpses of his claws scratching desperately at his assailant, of his maw biting in panicked snaps. At first, I think the thing that's attacking him is another ice dragon. Until Ollie catches one of the coils in his jaws, which shatters beneath his teeth in a rain of ice.

It's all ice. A glacier turned colossal snake.

But how? Is it alive? A spell? Either way, one thing is for certain: if I try to get between the two, I'll be pulverized in an instant. As much as I want to jump into the midst of things and save Ollie this second, I'll mean nothing to him dead. I need to find a solution to this remotely.

I could throw a Fireball at it or stab it with stone—those would be the most intuitive approaches to take. However, they're moving too fast, throwing each other from floor to wall and rolling so rapidly, I would almost certainly hit Ollie. What are my other options, then?

I try to get the Dungeon Core to eat away at the icy creature attacking Ollie, first.

[Authority denied,] Echo reports. [The element is Attuned to a different mage.]

Magic, then. And if someone is controlling it, they must not be far.

I cautiously and quickly scan my surroundings: from the Dungeon Core's interface, I can tell there's three more tunnels which open onto this cavern, all of them above me. Is there anyone up there? I squeeze my eyes shut, focusing on every pebble, every slight vibration that shakes through the cave. Ollie and the ice serpent slam into a wall, sending shockwaves through the earth, disrupting stone in each of the tunnels I'm monitoring.

Damn, I can't tell. And I don't have time to waste trying to suss it out. I'll need to go see for myself.

"*I'm here, Ollie,*" I tell him again as I step out into the chamber. "*I'm going to help you, don't worry. Just hang on a little longer!*"

Ollie tries to struggle away from the ice serpent, looking around for me, but the creature takes the opportunity to bite into his neck, and Ollie roars, launching a beam of ice through the room and crashing into the ceiling.

"*HURRY, FYRE,*" Ollie says, yanking his neck free. Streaks of red fleck away as he does so. "*HURRY!*"

My stomach lurches at the sight, fear quickly turning to anger. I'll find whoever did this to him, and I'll make them pay.

I look to the first tunnel opening, two stories above me, and summon a Jet beneath either hand. Spreading my wings, I summon two more jets beneath each of them, then I launch myself into the air.

Just as before I'm filled with terror and an excited thrill, but each of them pale in comparison to the smoldering anger I'm nurturing for Ollie's assailants. I blast into the opening of the first tunnel, cutting off the fire and stumbling to the floor: empty. I launch a Fireball down the passage anyway. The flame blasts down the hall until it crashes into a wall, snuffing the light out. No one. Alright then. I reignite my flames, and jump back into the air once more.

[Jet spell Level up!] Echo announces. [Jet Level 2: mana consumption reduced by 10%. Flight dynamics precision and control increased by 10%.]

I don't have much time to celebrate or dig into exactly which variables Echo is referring to there as I rocket toward the next tunnel. Once again, I blast through the entrance with a burst of fire, which I quickly extinguish as I land. Another Fireball shows the same thing as the last: the tunnel is empty.

Is it possible they're remote? Manipulating the spell from a distance, through some type of interface like Torim's water scrying or the Pact I have with the Dungeon Core? That would be bad. They could be anywhere. Still, I again jump out of the tunnel exit, activating another Jet before gravity can take hold, and fire myself toward the last tunnel.

As I burst into the entryway, two figures let out a cry, falling back. I stumble to a halt as I turn my spell off, both of us equally surprised to abruptly be face-to-face with the enemy. I recover first.

"If you are the mages wielding the ice magic below, I must ask you to immediately desist," I say. "Failure to do so will be met with a swift show of force." While I speak, I give both of them a Check, mind racing as I take in every detail available. The man's holding a white staff. The woman, a sword. Both are garbed in white furs and armor, marked with the Jorria shield and eye.

[Check: Ingrid, Level 28 Felis Kni—]

Before Echo can even finish her summary, the man jerks his staff toward me. The tip glows white with energy. I mentally jump for the Dungeon Core, and it immediately reads my intent. The Core gleefully complies, snapping the walls shut around the Jorrians.

In an instant, they're gone. Two lives snuffed from existence. Two lives taken by my hand.

[EXP threshold met,] Echo happily announces. [Level up!]

[Name: Fyre]

[Species: Harpy]

[Subspecies: Phoenix]

[Class: Psion]

[Level: 22]

[HP: 100/100]

[Mana: 300/300]

[Bonus Mana: 243,927,469]

[Role: The Dark Lord]

A refreshing warmth washes over me with Echo's announcement, but I don't have time to dwell on the new stats—or the line I just crossed. I race back to the cavern, activating my Jets as I slow my descent toward Ollie.

"Are you alright?" I call to him verbally as well as mentally.

"*OWWWWW,*" Ollie moans as he disentangles himself from the ice serpent, now unmoving. He wriggles out of a loop of ice, shattering one of the snake's coils as he spills out onto the cave floor.

I land before him, sagging in relief. "Thank god." I'd gotten the right people.

Ollie's head nuzzles into me, nearly knocking me off my feet. "*I WAS SO SCARED! IT CAME OUT OF NOWHERE AND AT-TACKED ME. IT HURTS, FYRE.*"

"I know. I'm sorry. I know." I wrap my arms around his muzzle in a hug. "Now let's get back to the palace and get you healed up."

"*BUT WHAT ABOUT YOU?*" he asks. "*I HAVE TO PROTECT YOU, AND IT'S NOT SAFE YET!*"

"Don't worry about me," I assure him. "I'll be fine. Now come on, let's—"

Ollie's head jerks from my arms with a roar, and his tail whips around me. I hear a *thunk* and a *crack*. When I turn to see what had just happened, I'm met with the sight of the corpse of a Jorrian sliding down the wall.

"*OH NO!*" Ollie said. "*I SMACKED HIM TOO HARD!*" He drips his head sadly to me. "*IT WAS AN ACCIDENT, I PROMISE! HE WAS JUST SNEAKING UP ON YOU AND I WANTED TO PUSH HIM AWAY.*"

"No," I say, heart hammering in my chest. That was close. Way too close. "That's okay, Ollie. You didn't do anything wrong."

"*ISN'T HURTING PEOPLE WRONG?*" he asks.

I think of the two Jorrians in the tunnel above us. "Not if it's done to protect someone who can't protect themself."

"*DO I STILL HAVE TO GO BACK?*" he asks. "*IT WAS REALLY UNCOMFORTABLE BACK AT THE PALACE.*"

And it will only get worse.

I glance back at the broken fragments of the ice snake. It's not far from the entrance to our kingdom. If Ollie hadn't been here, it might have made it into the city before anyone had a chance to warn us or stop it. The open passage back to Fyreneth's Fortress concerns me, but I'm hesitant to seal the entrance with Fyrethians still in the tunnels. With Mirzayael still out there.

I turn back to Ollie, eying the ridges on the back of his neck. They wouldn't make for a terribly stable seat, but I have my Jets that can act as stabilizers. If his Role is going to push him into this conflict regardless, I would feel better about it if I was with him to help. The Dungeon Core is still converting the stone in the background. I can be more useful here than in the palace. Two heads are better than one, after all.

"Actually," I say, patting Ollie's neck. "I have a better idea."

Chapter Thirty-Seven

FIRE AND ICE

I duck down beneath Ollie's spine ridges as a spray of ice and stone showers us. My legs are squeezed tight around his neck, and my hands have a death-grip on his scales—even my wings are wrapped around more of his spines in a desperate bid for extra purchase. My veins are full of adrenaline, and I can feel every beat of my heart pulse throughout my body. I've never been so afraid, and so alive.

"OH, THERE, FYRE! I FOUND MORE OF THEM."

There are shouts ahead of us, and I peek my head above Ollie's neck to get a look. A group of Jorrians is backpedaling down the tunnel, unexpectedly face-to-face with a dragon. The warriors drop back as mages move to the front, hands and staffs raised.

I collapse the roof on top of them. When I open the tunnel back up again, there's nothing to indicate the mages had ever been there. It turns out, using the Dungeon Core's abilities to combat the Jorrians have proved far more useful in person than when I was remote: I can see exactly what areas of rock I want to affect, and I can ensure no Fyrethians are caught in the attack.

Ollie surges forward, launching an ice beam into the remaining soldiers, then crashes into them immediately after, shattering the wall of ice and all the people that had been inside.

[Level Up!]

Level 24, now. I guess the levels come a lot faster when you're in a war.

"Keep going, Ollie," I say. "We need to make sure this passage is clear."

We've diverted down several side tunnels over the last half hour, rooting out small and lost groups of Jorrians, but have now looped back around to the main passage that leads to Fyreneth's Fortress. Only when I've confirmed a side passage is empty do I seal it off, wary of stranding Mirzayael and her guards. It's slow going, but we're making progress.

Ollie's ear twitches. *"THERE'S ANOTHER GROUP AHEAD IN A CAVE. MY ICE BEAM CAN REACH. SHOULD I BLAST THEM?"* His teeth part, and a white light shines from his maw.

"No! Not until we can see them," I say. Clearly, verifying before engaging is a practice I still need to instill in Ollie. "But you can charge into the room if you want. Give them a good surprise." Mostly because it's completely impossible for Ollie to sneak up on anyone, anyway.

"YAY!" Ollie lopes ahead, keeping his wings flat within the confines of the tunnel. The ground shakes with each of his massive leaps. *"I LOVE SURPRISING PEOPLE. THEIR FACES ARE SO FUNNY!"*

Rocks and ice scatter before him, announcing our presence seconds before we burst into the cavern. There are cries of alarm—and also cries of relief. I scan the scene as Ollie drops to the floor and lets out a roar, spreading his wings in an impressive, terrifying display. I can feel his giddy excitement across our link, and I use it to direct his attention to the people before us.

Two dozen Jorrians are locked in combat with a group of Fyrethian guards, the latter outnumbered two to one. Both sides have stuttered with Ollie's appearance—a hesitation I fully intend to take advantage of.

"*Ollie,*" I start, already imagining what I have in mind.

He understands my plan without me even having to verbalize it. "*GOT IT.*" He opens his mouth and mentally cries, "*ICE BEAM!*"

I'm not sure what yelling the words for only me to hear accomplishes, but if it helps lessen the horror of all this, then I won't be the one to stop him.

The Ice Beam crashes into a ledge of stone above the Jorrians' heads. They scatter, fleeing the falling rocks and ice, allowing the Fyrethians to retreat toward me and Ollie. I take this opportunity to move the stone beneath both parties' feet, shepherding the Fyrethians faster toward us as I push the Jorrians away. I glance over both groups to make sure they've been appropriately segregated: no Fyrethian left behind.

Then I give Ollie a nod. "Do it."

He blasts the Jorrians with another ice beam, this time straight on. The people vanish beneath a white light and wall of ice.

"*OH!*" Ollie exclaims. "*ECHO SAYS I LEVELED UP! YAY! I'M 44 NOW. THAT'S A LOT HIGHER THAN MOST OF THESE PEOPLE, I THINK. OH HEY, I HEALED! I'M NO LONGER BLEEDING. THIS IS AWESOME!*"

Which is just what I was hoping for. Not that I want to traumatize the kid with so much death, but at least his Ice Beam is a bit more distant—and he gets stronger the more he uses it. If I truly want to protect this child, then I need to help make him as indestructible as possible.

"Fyre!" Nek races toward us. "Thank you! We were trying to hold them off, but more just kept coming."

"It's not a problem," I say. "At least they're dealt with now."

Nek shakes his head. "Some got around us and made a break for it. I'm not sure if they knew where they were going, but they were running in the direction of the Fortress."

Damn. If we didn't encounter them on the way here, then they either hid and slipped past us, took a side tunnel somewhere into the labyrinth, or had already made it through before we arrived. Either way, there are enemies unaccounted for between us and our home.

I quickly check the progress of the stone conversion: 2% left. Only another fifteen minutes to go. In that case, it's time for everyone to head back.

"Understood," I say to Nek. "Ollie and I will go looking for them. Any word from Mirzayael?"

Nek shakes his head. "The Captain and I got separated during an assault, and given the tunnels, she could be anywhere by now. The caves also make it hard to track the whereabouts of the other Jorrians; all I can say is that there are scores more behind us than ahead. A lot have been wielding ice abilities."

It seems many of the soldiers have forgotten the purpose of this rescue mission and are now taking the offensive. I don't blame them, but I worry about any getting left behind.

"Ignore the Jorrians behind us," I tell him. "Fall back to the main tunnel and hold off the advancing troops from there. We have ten minutes until we're ready for the Fortress's ascension, and we'll need everyone back within our walls before we can initiate it. Pass the message on to anyone else you come across!"

"Yes, Lord Fyre." Nek turns back to his soldiers. "You heard her. Regroup. Fall back. Hold the line!"

A chorus of affirmation meets his calls, and I mentally nudge Ollie that it's time to go. He turns and springs down the cave like an excited, two-story tall puppy.

Lord Fyre. The label is still so strange to hear. I've always seen myself as an engineer, a scientist, a bookworm. Leader of people? Not so much.

It's unfamiliar, but not unwelcome. No matter how undeserving I feel of the position I've fallen into, I intend to rise to their expectations. No, not just intend—I'm sure I can.

"Take this side passage," I tell Ollie mentally so I don't have to shout over the wind of his movement. I bring up the Dungeon Core's Map of the surrounding caves, and find one wide enough for Ollie. Based on the vibrations in the rock, I can detect a couple people this way. More still are in passages too small for a dragon, but there's nothing I can do about that.

"OKAY!" Ollie pivots, nearly flinging me from his neck as Newton's First Law makes itself known. I cling to his hide for dear life as Ollie mentally giggles, plunging into the cave.

Everywhere we go, there are signs of a fight. Broken arrows on the ground, scorch marks on the walls. Bodies—but none of them Fyrethian, yet. Mirzayael was right that Fyrethians had the advantage down here. I suspect she's engaging in guerilla warfare. Good. Whatever keeps the most Fyrethians alive. I press Ollie forward.

It's another two passages before we find any Jorrians. They hear us coming first and one of them raises a defensive wall of ice. I blast it apart with a Fireball, and then Ollie is upon them. His tail swats the soldiers aside like flies.

Between Ollie's overwhelming power, the Dungeon Core's control over the caves, and my strategic direction, we make for a terrifying force. Three more scouting parties are wiped out just as quickly, and

I gain yet another level. Good progress, but in the midst of the fights, I realize I've missed something bigger. Based on all the vibrations, something is happening at the front gates of Fyreneth's Fortress. I hurriedly turn Ollie in that direction, hoping I'm not too late.

By the time we find the main battle, both of us are healed, topped off on mana, and flooded with adrenaline. We don't even hesitate as we crash into the chamber.

In the large cavern just outside the Fortress's main gates, a desperate battle is taking place. Arrows, spears, and bolts of ice fly through the air. Swords and axes catch the firelight. Dozens of Jorrians and Fyrethians are locked in combat—Mirzayael among them. There are familiar faces on the Jorrian side, too: Biorne and Alis, the human leaders who had come to "treat" with us before.

Fire stirs in my gut as I lock onto Alis. She's the one who killed Hetlanir. Abducted Mirzayael. All the Jorrians need to go, but the animosity I feel toward her is personal.

Our presence in the chamber does not go unnoticed. Cheers rise at Ollie's entrance, while many of the Jorrians turn to us in surprise and fear. They're not unprepared for our arrival, however. Six direwolves peel off from the fight, all making for Ollie.

I feel a stab of fear through our mental link as Ollie falters, memories of the last fight flicking through his mind and into mine.

"Don't worry," I tell him verbally and mentally, just so I know he hears me over the dim of the battle. "It will be different this time. I'm here."

At my order, the Dungeon Core opens a hole in the ground. Two of the wolves tumble through with a surprised yelp as the rest leap over or skid to a stop. I snap the ground shut, and two of the wolves are gone. The rest are too close to Ollie to risk opening another crevice, but I still send spears of stone stabbing up from the floor like pixelated stalagmites. One stabs through a wolf's leg, though the others manage to dodge. Howls of pain fill the cavern, adding an eerie, beastly sound to the cacophony. Ollie leans forward and snaps the wolf up in his jaws, abruptly cutting off its cries.

"Good," I say, whipping my head around to try to keep track of the last three. "Now stay still while I—"

"*NO*," Ollie says, his earlier fear chased away by confidence. "*I'VE GOT THIS.*"

His tail whips out to one side as he launches an Ice Beam toward the other. The wolves dodge his attacks, scrambling back, but now clearly on the defensive. Not giving them an opportunity to counter attack, Ollie lunges forward, snapping at the nearest one.

He's right. He *does* have this. And maybe he needs it after his last encounter with the wolves.

"*Good job,*" I tell him, desperately clinging to his spines as his head whips back and forth. "*But I think I'll only get in your way if I stay on your back.*"

He hesitates. "*ARE YOU SURE?*" I can feel he's worried about me; I'm so small and fragile.

I smile at that. "*I'm the adult here. I'll be fine!*" Then I create another crack in the stone, forcing the wolves back. Ollie drops his head and pauses just long enough for me to jump from his neck. I hit the ground hard, even as the Dungeon Core tries to soften the blow, but I'm on my feet in an instant. And with an activation of my Jet, the next instant I'm in the air.

I leave Ollie to finish off the wolves as I rocket toward the fight, my attention everywhere at once. The stone conversion: 99%. More pounding footsteps throughout the caves; are they friend or foe? Mirzayael—where's Mirzayael—

I catch sight of her with a group of her guards fending off an onslaught of attacks from Biorne and Alis.

Alis catches sight of my approach first, turning and pointing her staff in my direction. I flare my wings, pulling up short and hovering mid-air so I can aim the fires beneath each of my palms in her direction. I summon a Blaze, as intense and as narrow and as fast as I can shape it, and send the beam of fire blasting down on top of her.

Her spell activates at the same time, and our magics clash in the air between us, red and blue bursting in a small explosion. I don't wait for the light to dim or the air to clear. I fire a second shot, and this time it doesn't meet resistance.

Biorne cries out, and I flare my Jets, darting to where I'd last seen Mirzayael. Not a moment too soon, too, as a wall of ice rolls through the space I'd been just before. From the cries of soldiers beneath me, people on both sides are caught in the ice.

I land next to Mirzayael, stumbling as I cut out my flames and regain my balance. "Are you alright?"

In answer, Mirzayael launches her spear over my head, then snaps her hand back. The magical line of silk attached to the weapon caused the spear to come spinning back to her. She catches it deftly, then launches it at another target.

"Now is not the time for small talk," Mirzayael says.

I smile. She's fine.

"Small talk, no, but strategy, yes." I lob a Fireball in the direction I'd last seen Biorne and Alis. The magical smoke from our colliding attacks still lingers in the air, and has settled down into the fight. I keep a careful eye on it while taking stock of the current scene. We're outnumbered.

"How many more guards do we have?" I ask. "Do you know where everyone else is?"

"All of Torim's scouts have been recovered," Mirzayael says shortly, still spinning, stabbing, and dodging in some macabre ballet. "Six units stationed behind in the tunnels to slow the advance of the enemy. The rest are here."

"We need to recall them," I tell Mirzayael. "I'm minutes away from being ready to launch, but everyone has to be back inside the Fortress walls, first. I told Nek's group to retreat, but I don't know if he's been able to pass it on to others."

"I'll send the message," Mirzayael says, pausing only to pluck a construct from her back. The messenger spider glows blue as she activates its runes, then it jumps to the floor and vanishes in the chaos of the fight. Mirzayael activates and deploys the rest she has with her.

"Will those be enough?" I ask, wondering if the fragile little things will even be able to make it through the battlefield.

Before Mirzayael can answer, another wave of ice surges our way. I blast through it with a Fireball big enough to melt through the ice, and my mana plummets. Luckily, I still have hundreds of thousands of Bonus Mana at my disposal, but I'll need it for later. More accurately, the Dungeon Core needs it.

As the steam still wafts from the hole I left in the ice, two forms stalk through the mist. Biorne and Alis step through. Biorne's white armor shimmers in the light of my flames while Alis brushes soot off her shoulders. Her hair is singed, but she looks far more angry than injured.

"So," Biorne says, his gaze landing heavily on me. "You've decided to join the fight after all."

I flex my fingers, running various scenarios through my mind. "I wish I didn't have to."

He frowns. "This is the path your people chose. It did not have to end in violence."

Mirzayael scoffs, and I can relate to the sentiment.

"You're always free to turn back," I say. "Retreat now before you endure more bloodshed."

Alis sneers. "We're not the ones who need to worry about enduring more bloodshed. You will soon be overwhelmed by our troops."

If we only intended to fight hand-to-hand, she'd be right. "I take that as a no, then?"

"Forsaken," Biorne says, "know that it is with a heavy heart that I enforce your sentencing on this day."

I snort, glancing at Mirzayael.

She rolls her eyes. "What an incredible load of crap."

"Precisely what I was thinking," I say.

We launch our attack.

CHAPTER THIRTY-EIGHT

REMATCH

Mirzayael stabs forward as I step back, diving into the Dungeon Core's interface to access the throne room's spell circuit. It takes me three seconds to find what I need.

I grab the spell lines powering the lights in this chamber, and I snuff them out.

The room plunges into darkness.

Well, near darkness. The Fortress itself is still lit, and the distant light from all its streets and halls reaches us like the glow of a cityscape. Even so, it's extremely dark, and the sudden absence of a well-lit space takes time to adjust to. Some adjust faster than others.

Mirzayael, like all arachnoids, has low-light vision. Felis, like Nek, also have this. So do dracid and dwarves. Harpies don't, but I'm the only harpy in this fight. And unless the human Jorrians are signifi-cantly different from humans on Earth, I'm willing to bet they don't have low-light vision either.

A startled cry is raised when the lights go out, quickly followed by cries of pain and death. I peer keenly into the darkness, waiting for flickers of movement to resolve into recognizable shapes. The moment

I can start to tell what I'm seeing, the same is likely true for the humans.

While I wait these handful of long, excruciating seconds, a mental ping zaps through my mind. I double check with the Dungeon Core to be sure.

The Fortress is ready to activate.

Snapping back to the battle, I realize I can see far too much of my surroundings. I slowly begin to raise the lights, knowing an abrupt flash would hurt my allies more than my enemies.

The surprise darkness had the effect I'd intended. The Jorrian troops fell back, pressed together in tight-knit groups as they attempted to fend off their unseen foes. More dead and wounded lay scattered across the floor, though not all of them are Jorrian. I wince at the loss, but there's nothing I can do about it now. We need to press the advantage while we have it.

Mirzayael has Alis on the defensive, wielding her own staff against her. I grin at the loop of silk wrapped around the Jorrian's weapon; she must have snagged it while the lights were out. I wish I'd been able to see it. Now that there's enough light to see by, Biorne attempts to join the fight and shield his sister, but I don't give him the opportunity.

I launch a Fireball at Biorne, and it crashes into his shield. The fire splashes harmlessly away to either side, but I've got his attention. He roots himself in place, raising his shield as I hit him with another attack. Wordlessly, Mirzayael drives Alis away, separating the two Jorrians.

"That was a clever attempt," Biorne shouts around his shield. He steps toward me, and I'm forced to retreat a step back, carefully rationing my mana. "But it won't be enough. There are hundreds more soldiers behind us. It's only a matter of time before this battle is over."

As he says the last word, his shield glows white, and a wall of ice rolls from the weapon and toward me. I sidestep the attack, calling on the Dungeon Core. Spears of stone stab up from the floor, shattering the ice. At the same time I send more to stab at Biorne from behind, but he rolls out of the way, and closer to the battle—close to other Fyrethians. I stop the Core from pursuing him further.

"That's one opinion," I reply. "I have evidence to suggest otherwise."

"You don't understand," Biorne snarls, slamming his shield into the ground. As it impacts, several daggers of ice launch from the blue stone embedded in its center. I meet them with a flash of fire, the attacks turning to steam between us. "There doesn't need to be this bloodshed. If you would just return underground, if you would hide yourselves away, my people would not see you as a threat. But if you continue to make yourselves known, if you continue to fight, we'll have no choice but to attack. And if you continue to fight back, we will be forced to wipe you out."

Anger and indignation flare within me at his words. I launch a Fireball in kind, which roars around him as he braces against my wrath. "Subjugate yourselves, or die? What choice is that? What people could possibly rationalize this stance to themselves? What god would endorse such hate?"

"It's not hate—it's protection!" Biorne says. "Lorata's will is sacred. She would not have ordered such drastic measures if the fate of the world didn't hang in the balance. You Forsaken, you made your choice to stand against her. To stand against all of us."

"What choice?" I demand. "Being born into the Forsaken's ranks is enough to condemn us?"

"The choice to continue perpetuating Fyreneth's blasphemy," Biorne says. "If you refuse to acknowledge the error of your ways and repent for it, you will be exterminated. We will not stop until the threat of every last one of you is neutralized."

"Oh really?" I say. "Then I guess we'll just have to neutralize you first."

A stir is going through the troops at the back of the cavern, voices raised. Biorne risks a glance in the direction, then grins.

"Make your threats all you like, but the outcome is already decided." Biorne jerks his head toward the back of the chamber. "Our reinforcements have arrived."

I launch a Fireball at Biorne while he's talking, hoping the distraction would provide an opening, but he merely deflects the attacks. Using the Dungeon Core to draw a chasm between us, I momentarily retreat, allowing myself to glance at the disruption Biorne had indicated.

He's right. More Jorrian troops are pouring into the cavern, and they clearly outnumber us. But what I also notice are the troops fleeing before the Jorrians: Nek and dozens of Fyrethian guards, all retreating toward the Fortress.

I have to make myself hide my grin, even as Biorne gloats in victory. I don't need to stall any longer.

"Fall back!" I shout. "Retreat to the Fortress! Clear a path, and get inside the walls!"

"You see?" Biorne shouts. "I warned you that it would come to—"

A blood-curdling scream shakes Biorne out of speech. Nearby, Mirzayael has Alis pinned to the ground with her own staff. In her other hand she holds her spear, which has been stabbed through the human's abdomen.

"No!" Biorne cries, his voice cracking with terror. "Alis!"

Biorne lunges for Mirzayael, screaming in rage. Mirzayael looks up as a shadow falls over them both.

One moment, Biorne is raising his shield, its surface glowing and pointed toward Mirzayael.

The next moment, he's inside Ollie's mouth.

The moment after that, he's gone.

"*OOPS,*" Ollie says, tip-toeing over the battle ground in a futile attempt to avoid stepping on bodies. "*I FORGOT I WASN'T SUP-POSED TO EAT PEOPLE.*"

"I think this one can be considered an exception," I say, hurrying over to Mirzayael's side. "He wasn't much of a person, anyway."

Mirzayael pulls her weapon from Alis's body. "Their leaders are defeated," she says, panting from the fight. "We have secured our vengeance." She turns to face the new Jorrian troops who have arrived.

"No," I say, grabbing her arm and pulling her back. "The Fortress is ready. We need to get inside the walls."

Surprise flickers in her eyes. "Now?"

I nod.

"*Ollie, I need your help,*" I call to him telepathically, given the din of battle.

His head swings in my direction, and I feel a burst of happiness and pride from him at me asking for his help. "*WHAT IS IT?*"

"*I need you to make sure all the Fyrethians make it through the gates,*" I tell him. "*Some might be hurt or get caught behind enemy lines. Only you can help get them out of there.*"

This is met with a swell of protectiveness. "*I WON'T LEAVE ANYONE BEHIND,*" Ollie promises.

"*Thank you,*" I tell him, mentally sharing my own pride I feel for him. "*I believe you.*"

Without their Commanders, the Jorrians are hesitating, some continuing the attack, while others set up lines as if in preparation for a longer siege.

"We can begin at any moment," I tell Mirzayael. "As long as you can confirm all the guards have made it back."

"One moment. Nek!" she calls.

Nek turns and catches sight of us as his group continues to flee the approaching Jorrians. Ollie stomps a foot and roars at them, which is extremely successful in stopping the troops from pursuing.

Nek is gasping for breath when he reaches us. Blood has matted the fur on his left arm, and a white, silken spider is sitting on his shoulder.

"Captain. We received your message," he says between breaths. "That's all of us."

"Well done, Lieutenant." She jerks her head toward the city gates. "Get inside. I'll help the stragglers."

"But," he gasps.

"Now!"

Nek gives the two of us a worried look, but it's clear he's in no shape to continue fighting. With clear reluctance, he says, "Yes, Captain," and limps for the gates.

Mirzayael turns to me. "You should get inside, too. I'll remain out here until everyone is in. Is there anything else you need?"

I tap on the Dungeon Core's consciousness. *Ready?*

The Dungeon Core radiates excitement. Its elation is so intense, it almost borders on hysteria. It is ready. It is very ready! Is it time to get all that mana now? Oh, how it has been waiting for all that mana! It has become so vast and powerful. And now it has a proper lair! With mana ore! And once it has all that mana—

"I would appreciate it if you could guard my body," I reply to Mirzayael, unnecessarily raising my voice over the Core's mental frenzy. "I might be distracted while I'm running things."

That wheedles a frown of concern out of her. "Be careful."

"I will," I promise. "It's just a precaution while my attention is elsewhere. I doubt there will be any—"

I never get to finish that thought. While I was talking with Mirza-yael, I had just turned over access of all our mana stores to the Dungeon Core, which it greedily accepted.

My plan had been to wait until everyone was safely inside the walls of Fyreneth's Fortress. In the meantime, I intended to set off the initiation sequence for the Fortress's awakening. And the Dungeon Core did just that.

What I hadn't anticipated was that I'd get pulled along with it.

The moment it taps into our mana stores, I'm caught in a flood of magic. It's not like being swept downstream in a river. This is something much more primordial. Something cosmological. Like a steep depression in spacetime, and I'm slipping inevitably down its gravity well.

The Dungeon Core's influence suffuses the kingdom, seeping into every stone and circuit, every pebble and wall. It *becomes* the Fortress.

As the Dungeon Core's power becomes more concentrated, my mind is whisked away into the stone. I'm only distantly aware as my body collapses to the ground.

Then, slowly, the Fortress comes alive.

Chapter Thirty-Nine

FLIGHT

As the remnant's influence spread through the fortress, following the instructions of its organic companion, memories tickled at its mind. It had once been interfaced with the fortress in such a way before. Some time in the past. It didn't know how long ago, because it didn't have any concept of time. Except for when the other voice intervened, with counters and numbers and all sorts of nonsensical information. That voice grated at the remnant. It was unnatural. The remnant only knew how to eat natural things.

The first thing it did, as part of its instructions, was to consume the stone above the castle. It had been very excited for this part of the plan. Eating was its favorite thing to do.

The caves rumbled as the stone was consumed, giant chunks of rock vanishing as if bitten off by a vast, invisible beast. Pebbles and dust, knocked loose from the disruption, rained down toward the city. The remnant ate those, too, greedily snatching them up before they could reach the ground. The ground was off limits. But there were no rules about not eating anything that fell, before it hit the ground.

On the surface, giant fissures cracked through the snow. Some of the Jorrian mages attempted to seal these cracks with beams of ice, but the effort was futile. This was no counter attack. Nothing was about to break through the top of the glacier. Rather, the shell of ice that had formed over the underground cave system was now losing its support, the rock beneath it rapidly vanishing into nothing. It only took another few seconds for gravity to have its way.

The Jorrian troops unlucky enough to be standing over the kingdom when the ice began to crack attempted, too late, to scramble back to more stable ground. In a near perfect circle roughly one kilometer across, the ice cratered, then collapsed down into the void.

The remnant snapped up the ice that fell. And as living organic matter became nonliving organic matter, that was consumed as well. There were bits of untasty ice, ice that the annoying mind voice told the remnant it couldn't eat, and these bits of ice fell to the streets unhindered. But they represented a small minority of material that was off limits to the remnant. It devoured all other matter, which vanished into its bottomless, never-satiated stomach.

Below, in the city, bewildered Fyrethians blinked up at the sky. It was late morning, but the sky still glowed purple, the sun only a sliver beneath the horizon at this extreme latitude. Stars sprinkled the heavens—real ones, not specks of bioluminescence in a cave.

The remnant took a moment to happily digest its meal. That was good. Nothing could ever compare to the crunch of rock between its teeth—the salty sour taste of limestone, the satisfying effervescence of baryonic matter dissolving on its tongue.

Not that it understood concepts like "baryonic." Or "satisfied," for that matter. No, it always craved more.

The remnant's attention moved beneath the Fortress next. Some of this work had already been done in the prior weeks, large swaths of stone carved away to create underground caverns beneath the castle. Giant pillars still attached the fortress to the surrounding rock, far too few and too thin to be able to support the weight of the kingdom. That wasn't their intended purpose, however. Quite the opposite, in fact.

One by one, each of these stone tethers was cut. The remnant swirled its awareness around the castle, checking every interface point it had been instructed to consume, but soon the excruciating slow movement of the fortress itself proved evident that its mission had been successful. The castle was completely excavated from the surrounding stone. And now, buoyed by the cloudstone which made its foundation—which it had slowly been transformed into over the last several days—it was beginning to float skyward.

The movement was imperceptible at first. Momentum kept it from drifting much in any direction, and the remnant's organic companion had been extremely meticulous about ensuring the ratio of cloudstone to conventional stone was measured such that the forces of both nearly canceled each other out entirely. Nearly, because it still needed to float. The goal was to do so at a controlled rate.

Fyreneth's Fortress rose into the air inch by inch. Above ground, the Jorrians were still reeling from the sudden crater which had swallowed a quarter of its forces. Below ground, people had begun to notice something was happening. A giant crack had appeared in the floor just before the walls of Fyreneth's Fortress, and a grating tremor was passing through the ground. The floor of the cavern had sunk—or perhaps the gates of the Fortress were rising. Either way, the gap was widening.

A few of the Jorrian soldiers who had breached the gate hesitated at this revelation. Some of them jumped back toward the cavern floor. Others were forced into the pit. A dragon swept its tail across the stone, scattering the troops and sending many screaming into the abyss. It circled protectively around a dozen soldiers, all of which climbed up its back or clung desperately to its spines. Then it stepped up through the gates, bringing the stranded soldiers with it. The portcullis closed behind it.

As the mammoth structure rose, several magical networks activated. Giant stone rudders that had been erected around the base of the castle flexed their joints and adjusted their angles. Control surfaces began feeding metrics back through spell circuits. The individual who was seated on the throne struggled to process all the information coming their way, shunting most of the information off for later analysis. At the moment there was only one command that needed to be executed: Rise.

And the fortress did. Glacially overcoming its inertia, the rate of ascent began to increase. It was no longer measured in inches, but feet. Soon, it would be yards.

The highest tower of the keep breached the surface of the tundra. Now the Jorrians had some idea of what was transpiring. Shock and fear turned to desperation and outrage. The mad scramble to regroup turned into a mad scramble to assert new lines and prepare for battle. For this battle was only beginning.

A tower on the west wall clipped a portion of the cave as it rose past. The structure crumbled, shaving off a sliver of the Fortress and sending boulders cascading back down into the caverns below. The remnant winced as it felt a chunk of itself cut away, then took the opportunity to eat the bits of stone that were now separated from the Fortress, and therefore no longer classified as being part of the city. It could fix that later, if it was asked to. It would rather not give up any of the matter it had consumed, if given a choice, but the mana it received in compensation was usually worth it. Mana tasted different from stone. It was sweet and clear and fluid, unlike the crunchy tang of solid rock. But its stream was drying up. It had done what it had been tasked to do. It rather would have liked to stay like this—actually, it rather would have extended its influence even more, spreading even further, taking more delicious matter into its domain. But now that it was separated from the ground, that would be more difficult.

Difficult, though not impossible.

For now, it would retire. Draw back in on itself and hibernate after a meal well earned, waiting until the next opportunity to pull more matter into its gluttonous core, ever gnawing at itself, never sated, like the quiet inevitability of a black hole.

I awaken to a pounding headache. A hand squeezes my arm a moment later.

"Are you alright?" Mirzayael. She sounds worried.

"I think so." I crack my eyes open, and the lighting is strange, though I can't pinpoint why. I'm outside on one of the streets. "What happened?"

"I was hoping you could answer that for me." She turns her face upward. "We're flying."

Oh. Right.

I sit up quickly, pushing past the spike of pain and swirl of dizziness this sends through my skull. I was going to prepare the castle for activation, but it looks like we're already way past that.

The Dungeon Core beams proudly in my mind. Look! Didn't it do its job so well? It ate up all the stone and ice overhead, and all the tether rocks underneath, and it only broke a *little* bit of the castle!

I do look, and now I understand why the lighting seems strange. We're no longer in a cave, lit only by scattered pinpricks of light.

Overhead is the open sky, a dark purple-blue, though even that seems full of light compared to the caverns.

Yet the cave walls still surround us. We haven't cleared the surface.

Using Mirzayael's arm, I pull myself to my feet. "Sorry for the scare. I only meant to start the sequence with the mana flow necessary for the launch, but I wasn't anticipating the Core's influence to be so... overwhelming. How long was I out?"

"A few minutes," Mirzayael says. "Ollie went to the palace to get help, I think. He seemed distressed."

"Help's not necessary." I mentally reach out to him to let him know I'm alright.

"*OH, THANK GOODNESS!*" Ollie cries in my mind, and I can't help but wince. "*IT'S REALLY SCARY WHEN YOU DO THAT.*"

"*I'll try not to make a habit of it,*" I tell him. "*Can you get back here and pick me up?*" I could probably fly myself up there, but given my still-pounding headache and slight dizziness, relying on Ollie is probably for the best.

As I'm speaking to him, motion flickers in the corner of my eye. I turn my head in time to see a ball of ice flying our way. I open my mouth, but Mirzayael reacts first.

"Incoming!" she cries, yanking me behind her. "Take cover!"

Guards scatter at the cry, diving behind buildings and trying to scramble out of its path. The ice explodes as it strikes a building one street over, sending shrapnel of ice and stone in every direction. Only a gust of cold wind reaches us.

"Thank you," I say, nerves electrified with a punch of adrenaline. If I wasn't awake and alert before, I am now. I extract myself from Mirzayael's protective grasp. "I need to get to the throne room and make sure the aerial units are ready. We need to counterattack as soon as possible. Buy us time to make it into the sky and out of their range.

If you have any ground units with ranged attacks, we'll need them stationed on the walls, too."

"Understood," Mirzayael says, yet she stays by my side.

I shake my head. "You don't have to babysit me. Ollie's on his way to pick me up." Even as I explain, the dragon wheels overhead, looking for a place to land that won't involve squishing any buildings—or people. I squeeze Mirzayael's arm. "Thank you."

Her expression softens with the faintest smile. "I'd tell you to be careful, but that didn't seem to help much last time."

I breathe out a laugh. "I should be safe in the throne room at least. It's the aerial units I'm worried about. Stay safe out here."

"I'll speak with you after the battle," she assures me.

I hesitate. There's something I've been wanting to speak with Mirzayael about for a while. It had slipped my mind prior to the battle, in the face of so many other things that needed to be done. But after experiencing the uncertainty and anxiety of not knowing her fate while she fought the Jorrians, I want to discuss it now more than ever.

"Actually, it would be better if we could stay in contact to co-ordinate our plans," I say. Nervous, I look up at her. "I know how you object to psionics, but if I established a mental connection with you—"

"Do it," she says.

"It's permanent," I tell her. "It probably bears some thought before committing to such a bond."

"We do not have time to analyze the long-term ramifications," Mirzayael says. "I am agreeing to this. That is enough."

My heart swells with her words. It might not have sounded like much, but for Mirzayael, she might as well have sworn her life to me. I squeeze her hand and activate Psionic Link.

[Spell Activated,] Echo says.

I reach my mind out for her and find it. Sturdy, warm, reliable. I can feel her mind turn toward me in surprise. Hesitantly, she extends a mental hand. I take it, and pull her close.

[New link established.]

Mirzayael glances around nervously. "Well?"

"I'm here," I tell her gently. She still jumps at my voice.

"Hello?" she mentally replies. *"How does this work?"*

"You're already doing it."

Her mouth twitches in a nervous smile.

Ollie finally lands behind us, tiptoeing around the buildings. *"THAT WAS HARDER THAN IT LOOKED."*

I let go of Mirzayael's hand and grab one of Ollie's spines, swinging up onto his back. "Good luck."

Mirzayael's face settles back into its natural, concentrated frown. "You as well." Then she adds mentally, tentatively, *"Thank you."*

I smile as Ollie takes us into the sky. The real sky, not just another large cavern. Already gusts of wind and snow are blowing over the Fortress. I make a mental note to reinforce the internal warming spells at a later date, counting on the fact that there will be a later date for all of us.

Ollie brings me to the palace in a matter of seconds, though in that time he's forced to dodge around another chunk of ice that's been catapulted toward us. More projectiles are being launched our way, now. If we don't fight back soon, they'll do serious damage before we're fully airborne. And if they damage enough of the equipment at the base of the castle—not to mention, if they chip enough of the cloudstone away, the only thing keeping this castle aloft—we'll be in serious trouble. Not that they should be aware of any of that, but the moment we clear the surface, the most critical portions of the castle will be the easiest target for them to hit.

I jump off of Ollie's back as soon as he lands on the platform, and I have to flare and gyrate my wings to keep myself upright as I half stumble, half run into the throne room. Dizzi is sitting in the chair, eyes obscured by the stone "crown" with the Dungeon Core glowing in its center.

I put a hand on her shoulder, and she squawks in alarm, hitting her head against the stone.

"Easy!" I tell her. "It's just me."

Dizzi scrambles out of the throne, relief clear on her face. "Thank the stars. I thought I was going to crash the whole thing. I don't know how you're able to keep so many commands straight at once."

I pat the Dungeon Core's jewel. "I've got some help with multi-task processing."

Dizzi gestures to the throne. "Well, it's all yours."

I mentally dip into the spell network through the Dungeon Core's interface and take control of the flight spells she'd been activating. Between her and the Dungeon Core, the Fortress is largely on track, but the wind is blowing it toward the east wall. I tweak a couple of the control surfaces, then set it to a magical sort of autopilot. "Well done, Dizzi. I have it now."

She raises an eyebrow. "Without sitting down first?"

"I don't need to sit on the throne to access its spells anymore. I can do that remotely, thanks to the Core. What I'm really here for is to make sure the harpies are ready." I glance around the room, but it's only Dizzi and I. "Where are they?"

"They're outside," Dizzi says. "Almost everyone went out to watch. Did you see the cave roof open above us? That was something else."

I frown. "Noncombatants should seek shelter indoors. It's about to become even more dangerous for everyone." I turn for a balcony myself. "I need a better view of what we're facing. Go track down the harpies and tell them we're ready to begin. Mirzayael is in the lower city; they can check in with her or me for further direction, whichever of us is closest."

"*Mirzayael*," I think, and I can feel her mind startle. I guess she's still getting used to the link, not that I can blame her. "*Some of the aerial units should be heading your way, soon.*"

"*Understood,*" she replies. I smile faintly; even her thoughts are blunt and spartan.

"What happens if we run out of munitions?" Dizzi asks, following me out.

"I can make more," I say, though I'm not sure when I'll have the time. "We just need enough to hold the Jorrians at bay until we're clear of their range. It should be smooth sailing after that."

"It's the before part I'm worried about," Dizzi says.

Same here.

But it's too late for doubts now.

Dizzi steps up onto a balcony, spreading her wings, then hesitates as she looks back at me. "Any specific message I should deliver?"

A steady, cold breeze ruffles my feathers. The Fortress groans and creaks like an ancient ship. I listen for the battle over the city's ambient sounds, but the troops must be too distant, still blocked by the walls of the cave we're rising through, and I'm instead left with an unsettling quiet. It doesn't feel like we're in the midst of a fight for our lives. That only makes it seem all the more tense.

"Launch at your command," I tell Dizzi and Mirzayael.

Dizzi salutes, then jumps from the palace walls and circles out of sight.

We've been on defense this whole time. We've been looked down upon, suppressed, and dismissed as an easily squashable foe.

It's time to change all that.

Chapter Forty

Aerodynamics 101

Using the throne's spell network, I don't need the Dungeon Core's interface in order to "see" across my kingdom. I can intuit the exact inflections of my rudders. I know how much lift the cloudstone is providing. I can tell the precise heading, pitch, and altitude of the Fortress at any given moment.

Okay, so it's not "seeing," exactly, but neither is using the Dungeon Core. I've got dragons and spider people to help me with that, anyway.

Unfortunately, the Fortress is currently situated such that I'm faced away from the side the Jorrians will be on.

"*I'm relocating,*" I tell Ollie. "*Mirzayael is on the East side. Can you find a pavilion on the West face to watch from?*" That will help me cover all angles.

"*WHICH SIDE IS WEST?*" he asks.

I point.

"*OKAY!*" Ollie jumps off his balcony and glides down to a lower level of the palace, passing out of sight. At the same time, I activate a Jet and rise into the air.

It's the first time I've seen the Fortress from this vantage point. Looking down on it from above, its scale and beauty is even more remarkable. The roofs of the buildings are all tinted red, yellow, and orange; colors I hadn't been able to make out in the dark of the cave. The streets circle up toward the palace in a gentle slope, like a spiraling flame. This was a kingdom designed for peace, not war.

I alight on a balcony opposite the side I'd started on. It doesn't look much different, since we're still rising through the tunnel of stone. But it won't be long now.

"*Ninety-two seconds until we clear the surface,*" I tell Mirzayael.

Then I tell Ollie, "*Only about another minute until we're at the surface.*"

"*Copy,*" Mirzayael says.

"*OKAY!*" Ollie replies.

I wish I had a way to speak to both of them at once so I didn't have to relay every message twice.

[Connections for Psionic Link available,] Echo says.

I tip my head. *What do you mean?*

[Established Links: User to Mirzayael. User to Ollie. User to Dungeon Core. Links within the network may be connected to one another.]

You're saying I could be communicating with all parties at once? I ask. *Could they speak to one another as well?*

[Affirmative.]

That opens up a world of possibilities! We could have used a communication network like this while we were trying to clear the caves. Too late for that now, but not too late for the final leg of our fight.

Alright, I tell Echo. *Let's make a group call.* I mentally wrap my arms around each of the minds I'm connected to and imagine pulling them in close.

[Connection established,] Echo reports.

"*Is this working?*" I ask, casting my mind out to everyone.

"*IS WHAT WORKING?*" Ollie asks.

"*Blazing Abyss.*" I feel Mirzayael tense. "*What was that?*"

"*WHO'S THERE?*" Ollie cries. "*FYRE, THERE'S SOMEONE ELSE IN MY HEAD! BESIDES YOU! AND ECHO!*"

"*Is... is that Ollie?*" Mirzayael asks, stunned.

"*OH MY GOSH THEY KNOW MY NAME!*"

"*Sorry,*" I say, trying to wrangle the conversation in. "*I should have asked first. I thought it would be advantageous to connect my communication lines together for the battle. Ollie, this is Mirzayael. Mirzayael, Ollie.*"

"*OH! IT'S THE SPIDER LADY. HI SPIDER LADY!*"

"*Incredible,*" Mirzayael says. "*He does sound like a child.*" She pauses. "*And he's as loud as one.*"

The first towers breach the surface, distant sunlight spilling over their spires. At the same time, a volley of ice appears overhead, great boulders of white crashing down toward the city.

"*Incoming!*" I cry.

The Dungeon Core notices my attention shift; it can feel the ice volleys now that they're in its range. Oh! Should it eat those? It wouldn't mind doing that, if I gave it a lot of mana. Please give it some m—

"Do it!" I shove my mana at the Dungeon Core.

"*WHO IS THAT?*" Ollie asks. "*WHY ARE THEY SO HUNGRY?*"

"*Holy shit,*" Mirzayael murmurs, clearly putting together the source of the new voice quicker than Ollie.

Ollie gasps. "*YOU SAID A BAD WORD!*"

Maybe I shouldn't have tied the Dungeon Core into this.

"The skies are momentarily clear," I report to Mirzayael.

"Deploying aerial units," she replies. A moment later, a dozen harpies whip past me, rocketing into the open air. At that point, my perch finally breaks the surface, and I get my first look at what we're dealing with.

The Jorrian troops have retreated from the edge of the cliff and set up a new line. There's a mix of conventional soldiers and mages, along with some giant devices that look like oversized drills. I smile tightly at that. They came prepared for an underground fight.

Unfortunate for them.

A set of make-shift catapults, made entirely of ice, are being loaded for a second volley, and several of the mages are raising hands to point toward us. The harpies move in at that point, dropping our munitions.

The melon-sized balls drop toward the earth, drifting apart as they're caught in the wind and blown off track. Even so, when they impact the ground, the effect is instantaneous.

The sodium spheres disintegrate on impact, scattering their contents in a three-meter radius, which in turn creates secondary explosions as the rain of metal pellets hit the ice.

I'd worked on the sodium bombs with Dizzi's help, and after I initially explained the principle behind the reaction, she took the idea and ran with it. Even as I watch, I see the harpies drop several artificed bombs Dizzi had designed. Some explode into fireballs on impact, others launch dozens of blades of ice, and still more are concussive blasts of air, launching troops into one another and blowing out the eardrums of anyone in range.

I watch this in silence for several minutes. The already decimated troops are dropping like flies. The harpies take out most of their front line and war machines. The Jorrians nearest the Fortress begin to scatter. But eventually, the harpies' attacks peter out.

Dizzi flies into sight at that point, rapidly wheeling down to land on my balcony. "There you are!" she says. "We're out of bombs. Will that be enough?"

I consult the Fortress's spell network. "The base should be clearing the surface as we speak. We'll soon be out of their range. But we still need to protect the base until then."

"*Fyre, the harpies say they have no more munitions,*" Mirzayael also alerts me. "*I think the Jorrians have realized it, too.*"

"*Copy,*" I mentally reply. Then I address everyone at once, speaking both physically and mentally. "Ollie, Mir, report on enemy movement. Dizzi, get some eyes on our base. I need visual confirmation of our altitude and that the last of the Fortress has cleared the earth."

"On it." Dizzi dives back off her perch.

"*THEY'RE DEFINITELY DOING SOMETHING,*" Ollie tells me. "*THERE'S A WHOLE GROUP OF THEM OVER HERE. I THINK—OH!*"

A distant rumble rocks the Fortress. From the disruption in spell circuit lines—and the Dungeon Core's sudden alarm—I can pinpoint the impact to the area beneath the north-west wall.

Mirzayael's voice appears in my mind. "*They're launching grappling hooks. Looks like they're made of ice. Two fell short, one stuck at the base. I don't think it's strong enough to stop the Fortress's ascent—*" I know that to be the case. "*—but it might tear a chunk of stone away when it goes taut.*"

And if it's cloudstone it's got a hold of, that could be a problem. Not in isolation—I built a factor of safety into the design—but the cumulative effort of enough of those hooks could easily jeopardize our flight or cripple the navigation system.

"We need to get the harpies to the south-west gates," I tell her. *"See if they can dislodge the grapple with minimal damage."*

But they won't be able to stop more from being launched. And they'll be exposed to attack themselves. We need to cover them. And for that, we need to get back on the offensive.

"Should I deploy them now?" Mirzayael asks.

"Give me one moment," I tell her.

I tap into the Dungeon Core, telling it my idea. It gets excited. *Very* excited.

"That feeling makes me nervous," Mirzayael says. *"Do I want to know?"*

"I'm clearing a path for the aerial units," I tell her. *"Have them at the ready."*

The Core and I begin rerouting the plumbing system in the Fortress. It's widest at the top and narrowest at the base, and I add some compression chambers in for good measure. In a matter of seconds, the system is complete, and a giant hole opens in the floor of the throne room.

Dizzi isn't back yet, which is a shame; I need visual confirmation to know if my aim is correct. It's a pity I can't see through her or Ollie's eyes. That would make all this...

The thought gives me pause. *Could* I see through their eyes? The Psionic Link spell was just supposed to link our minds, but what's the difference between visual interpretations and thoughts? It's all the same process: neural tissue, a firing of synapses. If one can be interpreted and transmitted, why not another? Mentally, I prod at Ollie's Psionic Link, wondering if I can alter it. Previously, I'd unlocked new fire spells by applying known spells in new ways. If I could just come up with a new application of the Psionic Link, if I could just envision what it's supposed to do...

In my mind, something shifts.

[New Spell Obtained,] Echo reports. [Psionic Senses.]

"OOOH," Ollie says, shivering. *"WHAT WAS THAT?"*

And then I'm inside his head.

Dragon vision is weird, for lack of a better term. At least the eyes are forward-facing like humans—and harpies, and most apex predators—so I don't have to experience a complete reorientation of my vision. Even so, the field is wider, sharper, and the colors are... *more.* I'm not sure how to explain it. Is this infrared?

I instinctively try to turn my head and find I can't. Right. I'm only seeing what Ollie's seeing; I'm just along for the ride.

But this gives me exactly what I need.

"Ollie, can you fly around the Fortress and look for a hole in its base?" I ask him. *"I need to know if it's aimed correctly at the Jorrians. But stay high!"* I hurriedly add. *"Don't get in their range."*

"LET ME GO LOOK," Ollie says, jumping from his perch and flapping into the air. I can feel the force of the wind gusting over us. It's exhilarating.

Ollie circles high above the battlefield. A handful of Jorrians launch arrows his way, but he doesn't even register the ineffective attacks. As he swoops overhead, some of the troops scatter, and I feel his amusement as he notices this. But his gaze shifts back to the Fortress a moment later, and then he pitches down into a glide, rapidly gaining velocity as he loops down and around the Fortress.

"OH! THERE IS ONE. I SEE IT!"

And I see it too. Based on the position and angle, I estimate my plan will be at least 40% effective. *"Okay,"* I tell Mirzayael. *"Launch on my signal."*

I turn back to the Dungeon Core. *You've been looking to get rid of this stuff for a while, right?*

The Core wails pathetically. Yes! It's terrible. Such a waste of space. It wants it out. Now!

"Request granted," I say, and then we dump the entire volume of previously consumed spring water down into the pipes.

I wish I was in the throne room to witness the bizarre display that must be taking place. The Core is manifesting the water directly above the hole we created, shooting it down through the narrowing pipes and compression chambers—and out onto the ice at the base of the Fortress.

"*Now!*" I tell Mirzayael. Moments later, harpies shoot through the air, diving for the side of the Fortress.

It's a lot more water than I expected it to be. Even as it geysers out the base of the Fortress, compressed like a pressurized hose as it blasts into the troops, I find I'm nowhere near close to disposing of all of it. No wonder the Core had acted so bloated after our first reluctant bath in the thermal springs.

I watch through Ollie's wide eyes as the water gushes over the Jorrian troops, knocking dozens off their feet and disrupting their attempts to launch more grappling hooks our way. An unintentional side effect of the water is that more of the ice begins to crack and melt, the thinnest and most precarious sheets falling into the sinkhole and sweeping many Jorrians with them.

"*Great Abyss,*" Mirzayael murmurs in my mind.

"That's the last of it," I say a minute later as the final dregs of spring water are fully evacuated from the Core's Inventory. I close the hole in the throne room and begin fixing the plumbing system the Core and I had disturbed. The Core gives a sigh of content.

Dizzi returns then. "Did you see that?" she excitedly asks, landing next to me. "That was wicked!"

"Altitude?" I ask.

"Fifty feet to go," Dizzi reports. "Then we'll be out of their range."

Still another fifty feet to defend from any last attacks, and I'm out of pressurized water.

"*THAT WAS COOL!*" Ollie tells me. "*I THINK WE'RE WINNING. CAN I DO ANYTHING?*"

"*Watch for more grapples,*" I say, at the same time Mirzayael says, "*Boulders.*"

I pause. "*Boulders?*"

"*Like your bombs,*" Mirzayael explains. "*Ollie could grab rocks from the caves or broken pieces of the Fortress and drop them on the enemy troops. It would be extremely effective.*"

And he'd be causing even more death and devastation—not that he particularly seems to mind. He isn't just a child, after all. He's a child dragon, and it seems at least some of those instincts have transferred to Ollie. As I learned in the caves, holding him back is only to his detriment. He's not helpless, so I need to stop treating him that way.

Besides, we need him.

"*Boulders,*" I tell Ollie, and through his body I can feel his tail excitedly lashing from side to side. "*Aim for any more grappling hooks, or any other large machines you see out there.*"

"*YAY!*"

He dives back out over the city, glancing down in time to catch sight of the harpies as they dislodge the first grapple. They let out a cheer, rising into the air behind him.

But as Ollie circles lower, heading for the ground, he comes within range of the Jorrians. A barrage of projectiles is flung his way, and I tense, helpless to respond, but the dragon rolls to the side at the same moment the harpies fly in, knocking the attacks back with gusts of concentrated wind. I relax. I need to trust my people, too.

"WOW!" Ollie cries as he catches sight of the cavern beneath us. *"THAT IS A BIG HOLE. IT WOULD MAKE A GREAT CAVE TO HIDE THINGS IN. FYRE, I NEED A BIGGER CAVE FOR ALL MY STUFF!"*

Excitement bubbles over into a roar, which is frankly terrifying and sends still more Jorrians fleeing into the tundra. But instead of dropping on the troops, Ollie drops into the cavern below, now hollowed out like a cored pineapple. Ollie rakes his claws along the rocks, carving enormous grooves in the surface as if it were made of balsa wood. Grabbing a boulder the size of a small car, he flies back out of the caves and implements Mirzayael's plan.

As she predicted, it's extremely effective.

The harpies flank Ollie as he flies, deflecting any projectiles that come his way. The dragon doesn't even notice them; he's too busy having fun rolling boulders through the troops, which scatter or are flattened like bowling pins struck by a wrecking ball. Ollie does this a handful of times, from a height the Jorrians can do nothing about, then gets bored and starts launching Ice Beams through their ranks. What little that remained of the army breaks rank and flees across the ice. No more catapults or grapples come our way after that.

Two minutes later, my spell network and Dizzi's harpies confirm that we're out of the Jorrian's range and rapidly rising.

A tension unwinds from my shoulders. We really did it. We survived. We're free.

I send the message to Mirzayael, who relays it to her troops. The harpies return to the city, landing on streets and rooftops and balconies. With the abrupt absence of bombs and siege weapons, everything is strangely quiet. In fact, looking out across the field, I'd estimate only a tenth of the Jorrian troops remain standing. I wonder if I should feel victorious or grim. For the moment, I only feel relief.

"*What now?*" Mirzayael asks after a span of silence.

I adjust the control surfaces at the bottom of the Fortress. We're mostly at the whims of the wind, though like a sailboat, I can still partially direct our path. Checking our projected speed and trajectory, I turn us north.

"*Now,*" I tell her, "*we head for warmer lands.*"

Chapter Forty-One

FYRE'S FLOATING FORTRESS

Pink and yellow sunlight spills over the palace as we drift silently over the arctic. All the guards, all the harpies, all the Fyrethians, from the original and lost colony alike, step outside to squint against the sun. For many of them, it's the first time they've ever seen it.

Ollie is with me, curled up on the balcony outside the throne room. His tail is hanging over the edge of the banister, flicking idly as he watches the clouds change shade with the sunrise. "*PRETTY,*" he says.

"I'm not sure I'll ever get used to that," Mirzayael mumbles, glancing at Ollie.

"I can separate the lines of communication now that the battle is over," I assure her.

"No, it's alright," Mirzayael says. "I like being able to speak with him. And I'm sure he'll enjoy the extra company."

Dizzi is perched on the edge of the balcony, her legs dangling over the edge in what would be an extremely risky posture if not for the fact, I have to remind myself, she can fly.

And I can fly, too. It's a strange thought. Strange, but comforting, and not just because we're currently floating a thousand feet above the ground.

"I'll need to introduce more safety measures," I think aloud, glancing down over the streets below. "Increase the walls around the base of the Fortress to ensure none of the non-flying occupants are at risk."

"You're thinking about that at a time like this?" Dizzi asks, amused. "We won! Let yourself relax a little. The fighting's over."

"Perhaps," Mirzayael says.

Dizzi tips her head at Mirzayael, then her gaze goes over her shoulder into the throne room. I also turn to look, and find Nek and Torim helping to limp Beryl across the room. I stand up and hurry to her side.

"What are you doing up here?" I ask. "You should be resting."

"Bah." The dwarf waves me off, continuing to make her way across the floor. I walk awkwardly beside her and the two guards as they glacially progress to the balcony with all the others. "I rested through the battle. I won't rest through this, too."

Beryl finally makes it onto the balcony, whereupon a gust of wind nearly knocks her over. It also nearly blows me over, catching my wings like kites, though Dizzi with her wind magic appears entirely unaffected. Ollie extends a wing over us to act as a windbreak, and I smile my thanks. A way to stabilize the air within a certain radius of the Fortress is another project I'll need to add to my list.

"It's cold out here," I uselessly warn Beryl.

"It was underground, too," she says, scrunching her face against the light. "Ahhh. But there's a new kind of warmth to this."

"It's rather pleasant," Mirzayael admits, turning her face toward the sun.

"And the air tastes so fresh," Nek agrees. "Like cool water."

I smile at all their reactions. I'm happy I could give this to them. But as I look down over the kingdom, I catch sight of the mountains rising in the not-so-distant distance, and my smile fades.

After a moment of silence, Beryl grunts, nodding toward the same valley tucked into the mountains that I'm watching. "Is that Jorria?"

"It is," Mirzayael confirms.

I grimace. "It looks like our current trajectory will be taking us over their land." It's not optimal, but until I develop a more controlled approach to the castle's steering mechanisms, we're largely at the whims of the winds.

"We need to discuss what we'll do when we arrive," Torim says.

"Diplomacy?" I ask. "We can't land the Fortress. Not without crushing all the artificed flying equipment we built along the bottom and destroying much of the cloudstone in the process. I suppose just the harpies could descend."

"Who they'd immediately slaughter," Torim says.

Mirzayael nods. "There's too few of them. It's not worth the risk."

"Then what is there to discuss?" I ask.

Torim and Mirzayael exchange a look.

"Now's our chance to strike back," Torim says. "End the threat for good."

"It may be our only opportunity to deal a crippling blow," Mirzayael adds.

"It's the right move," Nek hesitantly agrees "If we don't end things now, they will only keep coming for us."

My stomach turns at the thought. "Killing soldiers who have attacked our home is one thing. Attacking their home—causing civilian casualties—*child casualties*—is something different."

"They were willing to kill our civilians," Torim says.

A growl thrums from Nek. "And our children."

I think of my role, The Dark Lord. While Mirzayael's words had been comforting—perhaps Dark was a reference to caves or the planet's pole—that same argument no longer holds water now that we're in the air and mobile. So is it truly a reflection of the villainous role I'm supposed to play? Would this course of action play right into... whoever's hands I'm dancing in?

Once more, I ask Echo about the meaning of my role.

[The Dark Lord must protect her Kingdom,] Echo repeats.

Protect. That doesn't mean I have to be the aggressor. No matter what role I've been given.

"We can't do this," I say to Mirzayael, pleading with her rather than Torim or Nek. "It's not right."

"They'll come after us if we don't wipe them out," Torim says.

"Which would make us no better than them," I counter. "Wouldn't that only serve to reinforce their narrative? That we're the villains?"

"I don't care what they think of us," Nek says. "I only care that my family is safe."

"And they will be," I assure him. I turn back to Mirzayael, who's said nothing. I can feel her hesitance through our psionic connection. I can feel her uncertainty.

"They pose no threat anymore," I continue. "We destroyed their army. How would they come for us? With what soldiers? We're *flying.*"

"If they gained harpies..." Torim suggests, but even he seems to be unsure.

"If they come for us, we'll be ready for them," I say firmly. "We've only begun fortifying the Fortress. There is much more that can be done to secure our kingdom. *But,*" I add, "I don't believe it will come to that."

"Why not?" Mirzayael finally asks.

"Because there's no reason for us to stay and give them the opportunity," I say, and at that I can't help but grin. In a bout of bravery, I take Mirzayael's hand, and splay my other toward the horizon. "We have the whole world to explore! We can go anywhere. As far away from Jorria as we like."

"Somewhere warm?" Nek suggests.

"*LIKE A DESERT ISLAND!*" Ollie says. "*WITH BURIED TREASURE.*"

"Would it be safe?" Torim asks, skeptical.

"I'll make sure of it," I promise. "I'll stand between the Fortress and anyone who wants to wish us ill, no matter who they are—even if it's Lorata herself."

The others murmur nervously at that declaration, and Mirzayael pats my arm. I smile guiltily. Maybe it's a little early to be inviting the wrath of gods.

"*Well?*" I mentally prompt Mirzayael. "*Are you in?*"

"*Travel the world with you?*" A faint smile twitches at her lips. "*Sounds dreadful.*"

I chuckle, looking at the others. They still seem unsure, but I believe they're speaking out of fear, not bloodlust. They just need a little nudge. I turn to Beryl next.

The old woman raises an eyebrow. "Why are you looking at me? I desire no say in this."

"You're their leader," I say. "Your voice matters."

She grunts. "Beginning to think I might be too old for all this leader stuff."

"If not you, then who?" I ask.

Everyone looks at me skeptically.

"Oh, come on, Fyre," Dizzi says, hopping down from her perch. "It's gotta be you. We all know it."

I look around the group. There's no doubt in anyone's eyes. I can feel pride radiating from Mirzayael, and fondness from Ollie.

I suppose I'd always known it would come to this. And in my heart, I'd already accepted it.

"Okay," I say, and the group collectively sighs with relief. "I will accept my position as a leader within this kingdom. But I can't do it alone—I *won't* do it alone. It's not my place to rule without guidance from the people who came before me." I bow my head respectfully to Beryl. "I would sincerely appreciate your guidance."

"You're suggesting co-rulers?" Beryl asks.

I nod. "I would be more comfortable with that."

Beryl scratches her chin. "Bah. Alright. Two leaders, then."

"Thank you," I say, relieved. "I'm glad to hear I'll have your wisdom to lean on. Which brings me to my initial point. Regarding the Jorrians, I alone shouldn't be the one making this decision for the Fyrethians. What do you believe we should do?"

Beryl hobbles over to the edge of the balcony, peering out over the top. Jorria is steadily drifting closer. So close we can see bonfires lit among the kingdom's watch towers—perhaps a warning to their people.

"It would be a satisfying retribution to return onto them the pain we've endured for so long," she says. "We've suffered in silence for hundreds of years. They deserve any amount of vengeance we rain down upon them."

My heart sinks. My first act as a lord of this kingdom can't be to undermine the will of its people. But it's that, or commit war crimes. What sort of choice is this?

Beryl turns back to me. "My old bones have had much too long to soak up all that bitterness and spite. Time for some fresh blood to take the reins. Time for some fresh ideas. As my first official act as co-ruler of Fyreneth's Fortress, I abdicate the throne." She begins to hobble back past us inside, waving a hand at Mirzayael. "You can have it."

"What?" Mirzayael and I say at once.

Beryl doesn't respond, and she doesn't turn back. We all stare at her as she disappears into the palace.

"What does that mean?" Mirzayael asks, uncharacteristically flustered. "What did she mean by that?"

"I think she means I could use someone experienced by my side," I say, recovering from the initial surprise. "Someone who knows the people and what they want. Someone who's been protecting them long before I arrived."

Mirzayael looks around at the others, helpless.

"You fight well," Torim says. "You make a good commander."

"And a good guard," Nek says. "A good friend."

Mirzayael scoffs at that, meaning she's overcome the initial shock.

"You've got my vote," Dizzi agrees with a shrug.

I look to Mirzayael. "Well?"

I can feel her answer in my mind before she speaks it. "I accept."

"Wooo!" Dizzi pumps her arms in the air. "New Queens! Cool. Just please no one give me any responsibilities while that baton's being passed around."

"Deal." I laugh. "Though you'll need to become our royal artificer in exchange."

Dizzi looks dismayed. "I said no responsibilities!"

"And Torim. Nek," I add. "Mirzayael and I will need a council to help advise us on decisions made for the good of the kingdom. As Fyreneth's Fortress grows, we'll need all the help we can get."

"Growth?" Mirzayael asks. "So soon?"

"It's happened once already," I say, nodding to Torim. "We should be ready for anything. And it's in Fyreneth's spirit. Anyone should be welcome here; it should be a safe haven for whoever needs a home. Once we decide where to take up permanent residence, that is."

"That may be counting our eggs before they hatch," Mirzayael says, glancing over the balcony. Jorria begins to pass beneath us. Everyone else goes silent, watching the city pass below.

A horn blares in distant warning. But no one comes for us. There are no grapples or arrows. What must the people down there think, watching us drift silently overhead? They fear us, I'm sure. But maybe they will witness this act of mercy and think differently of us. Maybe they will recognize the opportunity we were given, the opportunity we didn't take, and begin to consider how different things could be.

The city moves behind us, and then only icy mountain peaks are ahead. No one says a word, but it feels as though we collectively breathe a sigh of relief.

Nek leaves to go find his wife and kids. Torim also excuses himself to oversee the healing of the injured. Dizzi launches into the sky, and Ollie is quick to chase her. The two loop through the air, vanishing into clouds and stirring up spiraling vortices in their wake. Already, everything has begun to feel lighter.

But there's still small doubts that gnaw at me. Mirzayael must catch some of my thoughts, because she bumps my shoulder. "What's on your mind?"

It's not the worst thing to have her in my head, privy to my emotions. It forces me to voice my fear aloud. "Do you think I'm too soft?"

Mirzayael flicks at a feather on my wing. "You're very soft."

I snort. "You know what I mean. I didn't finish them off. I couldn't. Is that weakness?"

Mirzayael raises an eyebrow. "Do you feel weak?"

I am flying a city-sized fortress. I wield a sentient weapon which is capable of eating mountains like they're rock candy. I have a dragon the size of a house to protect me. I am the newly appointed leader of a long-forgotten people who defied the gods themselves.

Weak is not a descriptor I would use for any of that.

"I feel tired more than anything," I admit.

Mirzayael chuckles. "All things considered, I think that is allowed. Come." She laces her fingers through mine as she gently pulls me inside the palace. "The kingdom won't fall apart without you awake to run it."

"Theoretically," I say. "But thank you. You're right. For now, rest is the best course of action. Then, tomorrow..."

Mirzayael tips her head when I don't continue. "What about tomorrow?"

I close my eyes, feeling the warmth of the sun on my wings.

Tomorrow, I'll need to start work on fortifying the castle. I'll need to investigate how our crops are doing at altitude. I'll need to calculate how much mana is left in the mana ore we brought with us, and how long the cloudstone can keep the Fortress aloft. I'll need to seek a new home for my people. Keep an eye out for this Lorata deity who condemned Fyreneth's people hundreds of years ago. Find a way to keep everyone safe.

And I will. I'll do whatever it takes to protect them—and that's not just the Role Requirement talking. These people are my people now. They need me, as much as I need them. No matter where we end up, no matter who comes next to try to tear us down, I'll be there to keep them all safe.

"Tomorrow," I say, determination burning within me. "Tomorrow is the first day of Fyreneth's Kingdom reborn."

Acknowledgements

First off, I want to thank my editor, Justine Manzano, for tolerating my adoration of em-dashes and polishing my story into something resembling a real book. I also appreciate the amazing cover art that Vexdye designed for me. I'm pretty sure it's a big part of the reason the book has gained as many readers as it has, haha.

Huge thanks goes out to my critique partners and beta readers for reading the early drafts of this story and helping to brainstorm ways to course-correct when I went wrong. I literally rewrote the end of the book because of your feedback, and it saved the story. Your insight is as valuable to me as your friendships.

And last but certainly not least, thank you, thank you, thank you to all of my readers from Royal Road, Scribble Hub, and Patreon. I couldn't have done this without all of your support and motivation.

NYTE IN SHINING ARMOR

NPSeeds SAGA

KIA LEEP

Nyte in Shining Armor Ch 1

Sneak Peek

A wave crashes over my head as I open my mouth to yell for my brother. It hits me like a punch to the jaw, and I'm sent reeling, spinning beneath the waves, bubbles crackling in my ears as I flail for the surface. I come up and gasp in a lungful of air, then hack and cough as saltwater splashes down my lungs.

"Álvaro!" I scream. "Álvaro!"

Behind the roar of the ocean, I can hear an answering call. "Nye! Nye, I'm here! Help!"

I lunge in the direction of his voice, even as the waves continue to throw me back and forth like flotsam. Panic is all that's keeping me going, thrashing against the cold and the burn of saltwater in my throat. I take a breath and hold it, ducking under the surface as another wave collapses on top of me. I breach, panting from the exertion, but still manage to summon the energy to call for my brother again.

"Here!" he responds, his voice hoarse and weary. "Here, Nye!"

Finally, the waves part long enough for me to catch sight of him. Water has plastered his hair against his skin, his head barely kept above the surface. He looks exhausted and terrified.

That makes two of us.

By some stroke of luck, the waters let me close the gap before the next wave crashes over us. I grab the front of his shirt to try to hoist his head up higher, treading water with one hand, and he latches onto that arm like a lifeline. I have to kick extra hard to keep us from both going under.

Weariness pulls at me like an anchor.

"I'm sorry!" Álvaro cries. "I'm sorry! I didn't mean to go so far. The rip tide—"

"Doesn't matter," I pant, whipping my head around. Which way is the shore? "Let go of my arm. Help me tread. We need to get back to land."

"I know," Álvaro sobs, like he's nine instead of nineteen, but he lets go. "I know. I'm sorry. I don't want to die."

"We're not going to die." I'm relieved to have found him, but the absence of that anxiety just makes room for the exhaustion to hit even harder. My bones feel like they're made of lead. "Can you see the shore?"

"No," Álvaro says, looking around frantically, eyes wide. "We're lost. Oh god, how did we get so far out?"

I don't waste my breath responding. We need to figure out which direction is our best bet and start moving. We can't survive out here much longer, even if our family knows to look for us. I glance to the sky, searching for birds, but only the storm rages overhead. Where had it come from? It had all happened so fast.

"Nye, watch—"

It's the only warning I receive before the wave crashes into me. My brother's shirt is ripped from my grasp as I slam into the water. I try to gasp in a breath, but I inhale a lungful of water instead. My body convulses, every muscle acting instinctively to expel the lungful of water. The same instinct forces me to draw in another breath, hoping for clear air. But I'm still underwater.

My mouth and nose and eyes burn from the salt. I writhe against the pain and wrongness, fingers clawing at the ocean, my throat, mind screaming for air. I kick my legs, desperate to reach the surface, but I no longer have any sense of up or down. I struggle and gasp and flail senselessly, terror overcoming every other thought and feeling.

I'm only semi aware that I'm fading as the darkness closes in.

The darkness changes. It becomes more disorienting, less physical, and I still think I'm drowning for a long time as I struggle and fail to understand where I am or how much time has passed. The very idea slips away from me as I try to grasp it, and the disorientation sends my mind spinning. Yet, I'm thinking more clearly now than when I was before.

Álvaro? I call. But I can't make a sound. My call echoes out into the void. I try to move, but I can't feel my body. Nor can I feel the ocean. I can't feel anything anymore. Álvaro? I call again, trying not to panic.

Hello? There's another voice nearby, though it isn't my brother's. What's happening?

I don't know, but that doesn't frighten me as much as not knowing if my brother's okay. I push past the strange new voice and keep calling for my brother. Álvaro? Álvaro?

There are more voices now. More... presences. I can't make sense of it. They're all afraid or confused. Some are clustered together, as if that could stave off the surrounding abyss.

But it's not exactly an abyss. There's another consciousness here, which I'd missed at first, because it seems to be everywhere. It's wrapped around us like a net. Abruptly, it tightens, snapping around us with malice so intense, it seems to be a physical pressure.

Some of the voices scream and struggle. The darkness is eating us. Biting into our very essence, stripping bits of us away. Like the others, I'm scared, and I try to escape, but it only hones my panic down to one idea: My brother. I need to find my little brother.

Nye?

Hope washes over me as I hear—feel—the voice. It's Álvaro! He's close. Like we're swimming through the ocean all over again, I struggle against the force of nature that's trying to drag me down, colliding into the mind of my brother. I want to hug him. I want to tell him it will be okay. But I can't do either.

I'm here, I say instead.

There's movement all around us. The... thing that has us trapped has turned its attention elsewhere, but that doesn't take the acidic pain away that's slowly dissolving my sense of self. I can almost see something. A distant spark of light. Muted voices. Sea salt. Flashes of emotions pulse through us: anger, indignation, hunger, triumph. And smaller flickers too: fear, concern, regret. I don't understand. Who's feeling these things? Why are we being made to feel them?

Some of the sounds finally resolve into words. "...I don't plan to die today."

They fill me with renewed defiance. We'll make it out of here, I tell Álvaro. I promise. Even if I don't know how, I'll find a way to do it.

There's movement. A struggle. It's all the rest of us can do but endure as we're whipped back and forth, more fragmented bits of reality reaching us.

Then, a flash of light. The minds around me vanish in an instant, including my brother's. No, I cry, reaching into the nothingness, desperately grabbing for someone who's no longer there. No!

I don't have much time to be scared for my brother, for the next moment, pain lances through every atom of my being. I scream, writhing against the malice which seems to have stabbed through my very soul, and I feel myself crumbling around it. Being consumed by it. This time, I'm fully aware when I realize I'm dying.

And then it's gone, and I'm gone, and I fall back into reality.

When I awake, everything is dark, and when I try to gasp in a breath, I discover it's because I'm lying face-down. I groan, spitting grit and sand, as I roll over onto my back and stare up at a beautiful night sky. A warm breeze passes over me, and stars twinkle overhead.

Had that all been a dream? Some horribly realistic nightmare? I can almost still feel that hatred eating into me, and I shiver at the thought. It had to have been a dream. There's no other explanation.

Then I remember what had happened before. The riptide. The storm. Álvaro.

"Álvaro!" I sit up with a jolt. That had been real. What happened? Have we washed up on shore? But as I look around and start to process my surroundings, my mind only spins with more confusion.

Despite the low light, I don't have much issue being able to see what's around me, but that does little to settle my disorientation. I'm at the bottom of a hill, I think—no, a crater. The base I'm sitting in seems to be rock and clay, but all around me the walls are made of sand. Like some sort of impact blew a hole in a playground. How did I survive whatever left this crater? In fact, as I continue to look around in bewilderment, I realize I'm not alone.

[New user recognized. Populating stats.]

I flinch at the voice, so close it feels right in my ear. Nearby, a man groans, shakily crawling to his hands and knees. He looks around frantically, and his gaze quickly lands on me.

"What was that?" he asks, his voice shaking. "Was that you?"

"What?" is all I can manage to croak out, thoroughly baffled.

The thing is... I'm not entirely sure the person I'm talking to is human. His skin is gray, and his ears are pointed, and through his grimace of fear, I can make out two fangs where his canines should be.

[Compilation complete. Role assigned. Displaying stats.]

[Name: Nye]

[Species: Dhampyr]

[Class: Guardian]

[Level: 14]

[HP: 125/125]

[Mana: 40/40]

[Role: The Knight]

I whip my head from side to side as the voice speaks, determining it's not coming from the man across from me; at the same time, the words appear in my vision.

The man yelps, swatting at the air in front of him. "What the hell is this? Dhampyr? Level? What's happening?"

Took the words right out of my mouth.

"I don't know," I admit. "But it looks like it's happening to both of us." Now that I'm speaking in complete sentences, my voice sounds strange to me. I clear my throat as I push myself to my feet, mumbling a few trial words to myself. I'm pretty used to pitching my voice slightly lower on a daily basis, but when I try to do that now, my words sound too deep. Weird. Maybe I'm coming down with a cold.

I start to dust off my pants, then stop. I'm wearing clothes, but they're not mine. Black boots, trousers, a shirt and a scratchy cloak—but it's the bits of leather strapped to my arms and legs and across my chest that have me tilting my head in curiosity. They look like pieces of armor, I think. The man across from me is wearing something similar. There's a dual crescent moon-like symbol etched over the chest plate that I don't recognize.

"No," the man is mumbling to himself, still on the ground. "No, no, no. This can't be happening. This isn't real." He moans, clutching his head.

I raise a skeptical eyebrow at him. I mean, yeah, this is all very strange and confusing, but that seems a bit dramatic. I decide to address the most pressing issue first.

"Álvaro!" I call, turning in a slow circle to survey our crater. "Are you there?"

Other figures are scattered over the nearby ground, besides the man experiencing a mental breakdown. I step toward the nearest one, but it doesn't respond. In fact, it doesn't move at all. I frown, wondering if I'd mistaken a boulder or bush for a person in the low light.

[Check,] the voice appears again. [Human remains. Skeletal.]

A chill runs down my spine. "What?!"

[Check,] the vaguely robotic, vaguely feminine voice repeats. [Human remains. Skeletal.]

I probably should have clarified I meant, 'What the hell?'

I take a step back from the bodies. Because as I glance around the crater, I can now tell that's what the rest of them are, too. "Who are you?" I say aloud. "Why am I here?"

[This unit has been designated Echo,] the voice in my head says. [The user's second request is unidentified.]

I guess it's not big on the existential type questions. "What are you?" I ask instead.

[This unit acts as an audiovisual interface between User and System,] Echo says.

"System?"

[The variegated arcane network which governs select neuromagical advancement.]

Yeah, that all makes complete sense. I turn back to the man who is still whimpering on the ground and wonder what his deal is. Once more, Echo is happy to oblige.

[Name: Hans]

[Species: Dhampyr]

[Class: Brawler]

[Level: 19]

[HP: 135/135]

[Mana: 50/50]

[Role: Beast Tamer]

Some notable similarities and differences. We both have around the same numeric stats, but different classes and roles. The same species, though. Wait. What does that mean about me?

I look down at my hands. Even in the reduced light, I can tell there's something wrong with my skin. No longer brown, all the pigment's been leached away to a dark gray, like I'm a living black and white photograph. I touch my ears, and find them slightly pointed at the tips. Running my tongue over my teeth, a prickly nervous sensation runs through my body when I discover the small fangs in place of my canines, just like Hans.

I nervously run my hands down my arms. Things just went from disorienting to unsettling. Why isn't this my body? I guess that explains the change in voice. And I don't hate it, exactly. This body is muscled, lean, and a couple inches taller than what I'm used to—which is to say, still on the short side. But I feel strong.

I feel like I should be freaking out more about all this. Maybe not Hans-level of freaking out, but something weird is happening, and I'm completely in the dark.

Right, dark. I glance at the stars overhead. Maybe this new body is why I can see in the dark, too.

"Hey," I say, heading over to Hans. "Pull it together, alright? We need to figure out what's going on here."

He's still mumbling to himself, so I lean down and put a hand on his shoulder in what I hope is a comforting gesture. It isn't until I'm close that I can make out what he's saying.

"I died, and it's going to kill me again. I died, and it's going to kill me again. I died, and it's going to kill me again."

I pull my hand back reflexively, his words giving me the willies. "We're not dead," I tell him. I mean, at least I don't think we are. I don't feel dead. But how had I gotten from the ocean to here? I thought I remembered drowning, the water in my lungs, but... I mean, if I died, I wouldn't be here, right? And where's Álvaro?

I shake my head, trying to dislodge the string of uncomfortable questions. No point in dwelling on them. I don't have the answers, anyway. I try to refocus on more immediate concerns.

"What do you think is going to kill you?" I ask.

That stops him, and he cocks his head. "Can't you hear it? The whispers."

"Echo?" I wonder. She's definitely strange, but her helpful (if not blunt) commentary doesn't strike me as murderous.

Hans shakes his head. "No, no. The whispers, underground. They're hurt. Mad. They're coming."

Another shiver goes through me. I can't help it, this guy just knows exactly what to say to give me the creeps. "Then maybe we should get out of here," I suggest.

Hans looks up at me in despair. "It's too late. They're already here!"

"What's here?" I ask, nervously glancing around the crater. The skeletons haven't gotten up and wandered away, so that's good, I guess.

He frowns, in concentration or worry, I can't tell. Then he looks up at me with wide, earnest eyes. "The cactus."

I can't help it. A laugh bubbles out of me. "Cactus? A cactus is coming for you?"

Seeing I clearly am not taking him seriously, his gaze drops back to the ground and he starts mumbling to himself again, scratching his fingers through his hair. "I don't understand. I don't understand what you want!"

I'm beginning to think this guy might be one crayon short of a full box.

"Okay, well, while you worry about the murder cactus, I'm going to climb out of here and figure out where we are," I say.

Hans begins rocking back and forth. "Requirement? What requirement? I can't do it. I can't!"

"Right," I say, drawing out the word. "Well good luck with—"

And that's when the murder cactus bursts from the ground.

Nyte in Shining Armor Ch 2

Sneak Peek

Sand and chips of dried clay explode upward as the monster erupts from the earth. Long, spindly vines of cacti crawl from the opening like feelers on an insect.

Okay, so, looks like Hans might not have been totally off his rocker after all. If I could hear the approach of a giant, underground, sentient cactus monster whispering murderous threats as it sped our way, maybe I would have been freaking out, too.

A spine-studded vine stabs in my direction, and I stumble back, narrowly avoiding being turned into a human pincushion. Er. Dhampyr pincushion? I'm not given a moment to consider this as more feelers race over the ground, all of them coming for me and Hans.

I take one look at the swarm of crawling cacti, then turn tail and run.

So, not the most heroic move. It's definitely not my intent to leave Hans to a spindly death. But there's nothing I can do against this creature barehanded; which means the first step is to arm myself.

As I dash out of the cactus monster's range, I run past one of the bodies that litter the field. Most have hints of some kind of armor on them, and some of them... there! I dive for the hilt of a sword and yank the weapon from the sand as I spin to face the cactus.

I test the weight of the blade as vines race toward me, grimacing as I note the rust and nicks along the edge of my sword. Hopefully that won't stop it from cutting through some plants. I've never used a sword before, but how hard can it be to swing a sharp implement around?

I quickly find out. One of the feelers spears toward my feet, and I sidestep the vine, chopping the sword into the ground. Sand sprays into the air as a result, some of it ending up in my eyes and lungs, which causes me to start hacking uncontrollably.

[6 points of Slashing damage dealt,] Echo reports.

Great start, I sarcastically think to myself. But at least I managed to cut through the cactus. And the damage report is interesting. It's like a game or something—only this feels all too real.

The severed limb sits inert next to me, leaking a clear juice into the sand. I might have actually overdone it with the chopping. Looks like these things don't need that much force to cut through them. All the better for me.

Spitting grit and blinking the sand out of my eyes, I quickly locate Hans—an endeavor made easy from all his screaming. One of the vines is wrapped around his leg, and it's dragging him back toward its main stalk. I don't know what it intends to do with the man once he gets there, but I think 'nothing good' is a fairly safe assumption. I charge in his direction.

More vines come for me as I run, and I hack them apart without breaking stride. Notifications pop up as I do, Echo reporting, [4 points of Slashing damage dealt. 6 points of Slashing damage dealt. 3 points of Slashing damage dealt,] as I cut each of them to pieces. It's kind of fun, actually. I love how powerful I feel with each swing of the sword. I love how I feel like I'm doing something. Protecting someone. Maybe it's just the adrenaline talking, but I could get used to a high like this.

I skid up next to Hans, slashing through the thick vine that's wrapped around his leg. The cactus monster squeals in protest, its injured limb whipping away, as I grab Hans and haul him to his feet.

"Come on," I tell him. "We need to get out of here."

He tries to take a step after me, but his leg crumples. "I can't," he gasps. "It hurts!"

I glance skeptically down at his leg, and find the severed vine is still wrapped around him. I grab the loose end and pull, which causes Hans to scream and a strange smell to hit my nose. It's sweet with a coppery tang, and instantly makes my mouth water. My stomach turns a moment later when I notice the rivulets of blood running down Hans's leg and I realize where the smell is coming from.

Dozens of finger-long cactus spines are embedded in Hans's calf, which is why the severed vine still hasn't fallen away. I swear, one-handedly swinging my sword to cut through more incoming attacks, then hoist Hans's arm over my shoulder and begin dragging him away. He cries out as I do, but he'll just have to bear it, or we'll both end up shish-kabobbed.

When we're finally far enough away from the main stalk, I unceremoniously drop Hans to the side, then turn back to face the cactus. Maybe if I can keep chopping off every vine it sends my way, it won't have any left to attack me with. Even as I think that, a dozen more stalks erupt from the ground and begin crawling over the sand.

I sigh. "You gotta be kidding me."

Our one saving grace is that the plant isn't only targeting Hans and I. It's also grabbing the skeletons half buried in the sand, attempting to drag their crumbling remains back toward its center. That might mean it's a scavenger of some kind. If it's just as interested in the bodies as us, then we have an opportunity to escape and leave it to the bones.

"Think you can make it to the top of the slope?" I ask Hans, still keeping an eye on the cactus monster. "If we can make it up there, it might not follow."

He only groans in response. Was the injury worse than it looked? I spare a glance down at him, wondering what's wrong.

[Check,] Echo says, answering my unasked question. [HP: 113/135. Status Effect: Sanity Loss.]

"Sanity Loss?" I repeat, alarmed. Sure enough, the man is groaning, rocking slightly back and forth as he clutches his head. "Why? What's causing that?"

[Failure to adhere to the user's Role Requirement may result in a decreased Sanity stat.]

"What the hell?" Whatever happens, I need to make sure I don't end up the same as him. But first thing's first. I have to take care of this—

Stabbing pain spikes through my ankle as I'm yanked from my feet.

[7 points of Piercing damage sustained.]

The sword is flung from my hand as I strike the ground. I lunge for it, but another tug on my leg pulls me away, and I grab only a fistful of sand. I scream through clenched teeth as excruciating pain radiates up my leg with each tug, and I roll over onto my back and kick at the vine with my free foot. A bloody spine protrudes from my ankle, and my stomach lurches at the sight. Focusing instead on the vine, I grind the heel of my boot into the plant, and succeed in breaking open its flesh. More watery liquid spills out, and with a final slam of my boot, I break all the way through. I hiss in pain as I drag my injured leg back toward me, struggling to claw my way through the sand and away from the monster. I leave drops of blood in my wake, and the smell once again prickles my nose in a way I can only describe as delicious.

This is so messed up.

I groan as I try to peel the vine away, each tiny shift sending fresh lances of pain up my leg. I can't get anywhere with this thing sticking out of me. Shit, no wonder Hans was screaming. But as damn painful as it is, at least it didn't hit any vital organs, and I'm in no danger of bleeding out.

"Do it fast," I growl to myself, grinding my teeth as sand crunches between them. "Like a bandaid. Quick—"

I yank the spine out of my leg and scream again, throwing the spine uselessly back toward the monster.

"Screw you," I seethe as blood oozes from my wound. I clamp my hands around it, but the pain has already lessened, and when I roll my ankle, it aches, but there's no new lances of pain. "Screw you, you stupid meat-eating... plant." Okay, not my best insult. But it's a little hard to come up with something snappy when you're in pain and fighting for your life. "Now you've done it."

I struggle to my feet, testing my weight on my injured leg, and find it can support me just fine. I thought it was worse than this, honestly. Maybe it wasn't as deep as I thought?

[Health Regeneration Rate: 1 HP per minute.]

Woah. I'll heal automatically? Nice! It's still aching pretty bad, but at this rate I'll be healed up in another couple minutes—assuming I can survive them. That cactus monster needs to be taken down. Now, it's personal.

More of the cacti feelers are crawling in my direction, so I limp quickly away, looking for my sword. I catch sight of it half covered in sand a dozen feet away, though a new twisting vine is between me and it. No matter. It's not the only discarded weapon in the crater.

Quickly checking Hans is still out of vine range first, I jog-limp away to the next nearest body. The skeleton's clothes are full of holes, and its armor and bones fall to pieces when I try to tug part of it out of the sand. If there's a sword strapped to its waist, it's buried, and I don't have time to go digging.

A glint of metal catches my eye, and I limp-run over to it next. The corner of something pointy is sticking out of the sand. I grab the edge and pull. The item shifts, but it's heavier than I expected. I take hold of the metal with both hands, then haul it up with everything I've got.

I go staggering back as the shield comes free from the sand. It's enormous—as big as me—and patterned with a wicked design of fangs and claws. Red stones glint within the dark metal like eyes, and an impression of teeth are engraved at its center. Honestly, pretty damn cool looking. But it's not a sword, and while a shield certainly doesn't hurt, this one is definitely of the two-handed variety.

At the very least, maybe I can set it up in front of Hans to buy us some time. I dash back over to Hans, finding the shield lighter than expected—or maybe I'm just stronger than I'm used to—and the ache in my leg lessening with every passing moment. One of the cactus's feelers is creeping toward Hans even as I arrive, and I slam the shield down on its limb, severing the vine as I lodge the shield in place. So not totally useless as a weapon. Neat.

"Okay," I say, gripping the edge of the shield as I look around for the next nearest available weapon. "If I were a sword, where would I..."

Something moves at the edge of my mind. I flinch, looking wildly around for the source of the deeply unsettling sensation I just experienced. What was that? Was it really in my head? Maybe I caught something in the corner of my eye—

The sensation happens again, and this time, it's accompanied by more concrete thoughts. A mind yawning into my own, stretching out like a cat waking up from a nap.

Blood. It tastes blood.

A faint light appears within the rubies on the surface of the shield. Spiraling out from the stones, red lines glimmer to life along its surface, tracing the carvings of teeth and claws etched into its face. My bloody fingerprints, which cover the shield where I'd been holding onto it, abruptly vanish as if absorbed into the metal itself.

[Bond established,] Echo says.

I snatch my hand away, taking an alarmed step back. What the hell? I mean, I know the demonic design probably should have clued me in to its suspicious nature, but how was I supposed to know it was literally possessed?

Even though I'm no longer touching it, I can still feel it in my mind. It's looking about curiously, taking in our surroundings. It notices me, and more specifically, it notices the open wound on my ankle.

Blood. It needs more!

"Uhhhh, yeah, no thanks," I say, backing further away. Unfortunately, that leaves Hans right next to it. The shield notices him, too.

God dammit.

I dart back in, grabbing Hans and hoisting him up by his shoulders, then give the creepy shield a kick for good measure, intending to launch it away from the both of us.

As it turns out, this was kind of a dumb move.

Nyte in Shining Armor Ch 3

Sneak Peek

As I kick the shield, I realize a moment too late I've done so with my injured foot. The worst consequence to this should have been that it just kinda hurt and was a little stupid and unnecessary. Instead, it's much worse.

The glowing red lights engraved in the shield whip out when I kick it, like text lifting from a page, and wrap around my foot. Alarmed, I try to yank my leg back, but only balancing on one leg while holding up another person is not the most stable stance.

I am successful in yanking my leg back. I'm not successful in yanking my leg away.

The shield comes with my boot, the weight of both tip over me, and then all three of us crash back into the sand in a painful, tangled heap.

I struggle to throw everything off of me. "Let go!" I cry, attempting to flail my leg.

The shield seems completely unperturbed by any of this, mentally prodding at the wound in my leg. Ah, there is the blood source!

"Oh, no you don't," I say, grabbing the shield and trying to yank it off of me. "No, no, no, no, no!"

The red bands of light shift, using the opportunity to let go of my boot and lash around my forearm instead.

"Crap!" I try to push the shield away with my free hand, but the magic has strapped my arm down against the inner surface of shield. It's really stuck now.

The shield finds my behavior very perplexing. Why am I acting this way? Don't I want to fight? Don't I want to win?

I manage to roll to the side, extracting myself from Hans, who at this point is still mumbling to himself and seems completely unaware of anything going on around him.

Must be nice.

But at least now that my foot is free, I'm able to stumble to my feet. I spend a moment dumbly flailing my arm around, which only succeeds in banging the bottom of the shield against my own shin several times, but the demon shield isn't going anywhere.

Well, this is just great.

"What do you want with me?" I demand, holding the shield as far away from my body as I can manage. Which is to say, half an arm's length.

The shield thought this was obvious: Blood!

"Okay, well, besides that," I say. "Because I'm not giving you any of my blood. I need that for not dying!"

It wouldn't need very much blood, the shield clarifies. It could do so much, with only a few ounces. Besides, I'm leaking it anyway. Wouldn't it be better for the shield to have my blood than for it to go to waste in the sand?

"That is the creepiest argument I've ever heard," I say. "Besides, I don't need your help. I was doing great earlier with just that rusty old sword, and I'm pretty sure that's going to be more useful to me than you."

Affront bursts through my mind like a physical blow, and I stumble back from its suddenness. A rusty sword? Absurd! How dare I compare the two! Don't I know what I'm dealing with? How powerful it is? Such disrespect is entirely undeserved!

I blink. Wow. I think I hurt its feelings.

The shield is still fuming at my insult when the next cactus vine whips my way. I spin the shield around, and the feeler skips off its face, deflected into the nearby sand. I pounce on the vine before it has another chance to attack, severing the end as I plant the shield in the ground.

The shield swells with pride. A pathetic attempt to damage it. As if it could be scratched so easily!

"I don't think it was aiming for you," I say.

Relegating myself to the fact that I'm stuck with this thing for now, I head back over to Hans. It's becoming a real pain trying to keep this man alive.

"Hey," I tell him. "I've got one less arm to use now, which makes getting you out of here kind of difficult. Could really use your help in the fight." Hans continues to rock back and forth. "Or, you know, just don't leave yourself open to attack." He mumbles to himself. "Like, even running away would help."

I sigh, stabbing the shield down on top of another feeler creeping our way. This just couldn't be easy.

It could be, the shield says, invading my mind once again. I am using the shield in such a rudimentary way. But it's so much more. It holds amazing powers beyond my comprehension! If only...

"Yeah, yeah, if only I give you some of my blood," I say, finishing the thought. "Didn't you already get a taste?"

It did. But that was only enough to establish the bond. To do anything offensive, it needs more.

"Offense?" I ask, knocking another vine away as I retreat a step.

Yes, the shield eagerly agrees. An attack! That's the only way I stand a chance of defeating this beast. A conventional weapon will not be nearly enough. And with just a bit of my blood, the shield could be so much stronger!

As much as I hate to admit it, the shield has a point. With Hans out of commission and lacking much of anything to fight with myself—even if I did grab another rusted sword—the likelihood of getting close enough to the cactus's central stem to deal a fatal blow seems low. I either need to find a way to get us all out of here, or I need a better way to fight.

"What kind of attack are we talking here?" I ask the shield.

The shield grins into my mind. It knew I would come around!

At the same time, Echo pipes up. [Check: The Crimson Aegis.]

[Currently available abilities:]

[Repel: Absorb and redirect kinetic attacks. Activation cost: 10 mana.]

[Devour: Apply a corrosive effect to the outer face of the Aegis. Activation cost: 1 mana per second.]

[Endure: Enhance the strength and shock absorption of the Aegis. Activation cost: 1 mana per ten seconds.]

I'm liking the sound of activation costs using mana instead of blood. "How much mana do I have?"

[Mana: 40/40]

"Sweet." I've got some options then. "You can activate these abilities if I spend my mana?" I ask the shield.

It grumpily admits this is the case. But using blood would be much more effective. And it has even stronger abilities I could unlock if I gave it just a few ounces...

"I'll take your word for it." Things are looking up, actually. The shield—the Crimson Aegis, apparently—might have, uh, particular tastes, but it seems it doesn't actually need blood. And having a sapient magical weapon on my side while attempting to fight off a man-eating plant can only count in my favor.

I've got 40 mana to work with, so I shouldn't start with the ability that drains 1 mana per second. It's probably the strongest, given the cost, but until I know what I'm dealing with, I'll need to be conservative with my mana.

"Let's try Repel, then," I say. It'll use a quarter of my mana, but being able to redirect attacks against the murder cactus will help me more than just making the shield better at being a shield. "Er, how do I make it work?" I mentally prod the shield.

Echo answers instead. [Mana transfer available via Pact formation. Initiate Pact?]

"Suuuure," I say, hoping this isn't a big mistake.

[Pact initiated.] And then Echo says, [Additional capabilities unlocked.]

A couple things happen simultaneously. First, I realize I can see through the shield. Not like it's transparent, exactly, but it's as if the stones on the front of the shield are actual eyes that I can use as my own. Doubled over the top of my normal vision, it's almost like a set of bifocals.

And second, the shield gets loud. If the Crimson Aegis had been a distant yet irritating whisper in my mind before, now it's a booming gale.

Finally! It has waited too long to taste power again. Even this is merely a fraction of its potential, but it cannot wait to exercise its will again! It will be good to crush its enemies and drain them of their blood.

"Uhhhh, or we could not," I say, abruptly having deep regrets.

But before I can ask Echo if any of this is reversible, she says, [Repel activated. Mana: 30/40.]

The light inside the rubies overflow, engulfing the Crimson Aegis in a faint red glow.

"Okay then." I blink rapidly, trying to adjust to the double vision. It's a little disorienting, but at least I can now see where I'm heading and what's coming at me. All I have to do is point the shield properly and make sure it takes some hits. That shouldn't be too hard, right?

I step forward, raising the Crimson Aegis before me, and right now, illuminated with its red magic, it's certainly living up to its name. As I move toward the cactus monster, it sends several vines my way. I duck beneath the shield, planting it in the sand so I don't experience any more ankle-stabbing surprises, and then flinch as several impacts smack into the shield, rattling me.

[Kinetic energy stored,] Echo reports.

"Hell, yeah," I say. "Let's see how it likes a taste of its own medicine."

A ripple passes through the shield's red glow, then it pulses outward like a forcefield, blowing back toward the cactus.

And it does... nothing. A handful of sand stirs at the attack. The cactus monster sways minutely, as if caught by an unexpected but light gust of wind.

[0 points of Bludgeoning damage dealt.]

"Are you kidding me?" I cry. "That was pathetic!"

The Crimson Aegis balks at my words. Its powers are anything but pathetic! It's not the shield's fault I don't know how to use its abilities properly. If I'd just waited for more strikes to hit, its counterattack would have continued to grow in strength!

"Oh." I guess that makes sense. "Okay then, let's give it another shot."

The shield simmers down as I ready a second Repel, its affront switching to eager anticipation as it looks forward to landing a critical blow. Man, it sure changes tune quick.

[Repel activated.]

[Mana: 20/40]

Once more the red hue covers the shield, and again I maneuver around the crater, raising the shield to block any incoming attacks, bracing against each glancing blow. I have to fight my instincts and stay standing there to take it each time. Cutting through the vines with the sword had been much easier, but I hadn't been able to deal any serious damage that way. Hopefully, if the shield can sustain enough hits, I can end this fight in one shot.

I'm not sure my arms are up to the challenge, though. Each new strike rattles the Crimson Aegis, and in turn me, the vibrations jarring through my hands and arms no matter how much I try to brace against them.

But there was that Endure spell, too. It said it would increase the durability of the shield and act as a shock absorber.

"Would that interfere with Repel's effect?" I ask Echo.

[Negative,] she reports. [The spells' effects may be stacked without impacting the efficiency of either.]

"That's what I'm talking about." The Endure spell costs 1 mana every ten seconds, though, which means I can't take forever on this. Hopefully, though, with a few more hits on Repel, I'll be ready.

I activate Endure as well, and a second effect appears over the shield; still red, like the rest of the magic, a staticky effect appears along the engraved lines in the shield, tracing all the fangs and claws and the hint at a monstrous face that are embossed in the surface. When I block the next vine strike, I don't even feel it. On the inner surface of the shield, however, magic ripples in the spot where the vine struck, like a stone cast into a pond.

Alright, I might be warming up to this murder shield. I dart around the field, circling closer to the cactus monster and drawing more of its attention. It begins coming at me from both sides now, and I have to spin back and forth to keep deflecting the attacks.

There's no way I could have moved like this before. Picking up the shield isn't effortless—it definitely still feels heavy—but I'm barely breaking a sweat. And yeah, I do spend a lot of time at the gym, but this shield has got to weigh at least two hundred pounds, and I'm swinging it around like it's made of cardboard. What am I now? A dhampyr? What does that even mean?

[Check,] Echo says. [Damphyr: one of the many native sapient species of the planet Lusio. Nocturnal and carnivorous in nature, dhampyrs require a diet of fresh meat and blood to survive.]

Dhampyr... like vampire? You gotta be kidding me. That explains why my blood smells so uncomfortably attractive.

It just figures I'd get saddled with a shield that's got the same craving.

"This is stupid," I grumble.

But something else Echo said also sticks out to me. The planet Lusio. Then this really isn't Earth anymore. I mean, the monsters and magic probably should have given that away, but...

How the hell did I end up here? Why in a different body? And why does the magic act like some kind of video game mechanics?

What in the world is going on?

Numbers blink in the corner of my vision: [Mana: 8/40]

Getting low. Another minute before I'm totally out, I think. Which means I need to end this now.

"Ready, shield?" I say, absorbing another couple of hits. "Looks like it's now or never."

The Aegis surges to the forefront of my mind, eager to let loose its power. That makes two of us. I dash forward, getting as close to the main body of the creature as I dare. More feelers are coming at me from every direction, now; there's too many to block them all. Instead, I slam the shield into the ground, point it at the monster, and release Repel.

The magic bursts from Aegis in a red shockwave. The vines nearest to us snap back so suddenly that they break into pieces and fly away. The main stalk bows beneath the pressure of the attack, and sand blasts into its flesh, peppering the surface and drawing out more of its watery fluid. A wind whirls around us, kicking up sand and forcing me to duck my head into my arm. Then the wind dies, and the crater is still.

[213 points of Bludgeoning damage dealt]

I peek an eye open, blinking away the grit and sand. "Did we win?"

Pain explodes through my side. I stagger and go down as something drives me into the ground, agony burning through my stomach and back.

[29 points of Piercing damage sustained.]

[Status Effect: Blood Loss]

I scream, twisting to get a look even as the movement wrenches new lances of pain from me. A fist-sized vine is stabbed through my side. Aw, damn. That doesn't look good. And I doubt I'm going to be given enough time for my healing to kick in.

In a herculean effort, I swing my arm around my body, dropping the shield on the vine. It severs the limb a foot from my body, but this end is still stuck in my abdomen. Crap. Crap crap crap.

Grimacing against every twinge and stab that's radiating through my side, I drop my head to the sand, turning it to the cactus monster.

"How?" I ask through clenched teeth. I thought we landed a direct hit.

[Check,] Echo says. [Carrion Cactus: Mutated by the naturally occurring arcana spawned from the Lifespring Oasis, carrion cacti are harmless when dormant, but voracious and single-minded when starved and in need of food.]

Great. Glad I'm getting this information now. But that doesn't tell me anything about how it withstood my attack.

[HP: 492/725]

Oh. That's how.

I'm so screwed.

If you've enjoyed this excerpt of *Nyte in Shining Armor* so far, you can check out the book on Amazon today!

BOOKS IN THE NPSEEDS UNIVERSE

Glass Kanin

A Little Salty

Friendly Fyre

Nyte in Shining Armor

About the Author

Kia is the author of their debut serialized series *Glass Kanin*, and specializes in writing comedic, quirky, queer fantasy. When not roller skating or sending people to the Moon, they can be found at home with a cup of tea working on any of their dozens of in-progress books.

You can find more about their projects on their website: www.KiaLeep.com

www.ingramcontent.com/pod-product-compliance
Lightning Source LLC
Chambersburg PA
CBHW031153310726
48969CB00001B/68